On Rainy Lake

and Other Stories

Jim Bates

ON RAINY LAKE

First edition. November 9, 2024

Written by Jim Bates

Table of Contents

Dedication

For Justin

Moonshine

I'll never forget Stephanie Halverson. We met one night in late spring at the Black Rooster, the only bar in the small town of Orchard Lake. It was the kind of place people like me, a local guy with not much else to do, hung out trading stories, complaining about our jobs, and getting drunk. I was twenty-five and maybe should have known better but didn't, being drawn to her long dark hair, tight black jeans, and red cowboy shirt unbuttoned just far enough to send my imagination into overdrive. Hell, why beat around the bush? I was just a horny guy looking to get lucky and I did. Stephanie (Steph) went back with me that night to the little one-room apartment I lived in and for all I knew the next morning that was going to be that. But it wasn't. She stayed, and it started me off the wrong road, one to this day I'm still not sorry I took.

Steph had just turned twenty-one and lived with her older brother and some of his friends northwest of town in an old trailer parked in the back of her grandparent's farm. She introduced me to him that first week we started hanging around together. Calling it dating would be too generous for what we were doing at the time. His name was Darren.

"Hey Ron," he greeted me the first time Steph and I walked into the trailer. "What's goin' on?" Except for the work boots, blue jeans, and tee-shirt, he looked like he could be selling insurance in the office next to the hardware store I lived above. He was unremarkable looking, to say the least.

"Not much," I said, smiling, enjoying the aroma of pot in the air. "It's all good."

Darren nodded and responded with, "That's good to hear."

He was about my age and had an average build, a clean-shaven oval face, lively brown eyes, short brown hair, and a prominent nose. Even more prominent, though, when he turned his head slightly, was the strawberry birthmark on the left side of his face that stretched from his cheek down his jaw to his neck. I thought at the time it made him look unique and soon found out he was, both in looks and how he lived his life.

Steph and I had walked into a big living room that made up most of the trailer. There was a radio on in the background tuned to a classic rock station and a poster of Einstein tacked to the wall. Off to the right was a kitchen area and he was sitting there at a round, yellow Formica table rolling a joint.

I hesitated just a tick before stepping across the worn but clean linoleum floor to shake his hand, just to be polite. The inside living conditions were pretty basic: a couple of couches, overstuffed chairs, a big screen television, and the table he was sitting at; nothing fancy but it was all tidy and neat looking, I had to give Steph and her brother that. The main thing that would set it apart from your average family-owned trailer home was the cloud of pot in the air.

Darren looked at me and then at Steph and then said, "So this's the guy?" He stayed sitting as he leaned forward and shook my hand hard, looking me right in the eyes while he did it. What he saw in me he didn't give away. I was tall and thin with long hair and a scraggly beard. I was dressed in faded jeans, a blue flannel shirt, and work boots. In retrospect, I probably didn't look like much to him.

"Yeah. This's him," Steph said, putting her arm around my waist and squeezing me. "He's my new guy."

New guy? What was she talking about? I had thought up until this point we were just fooling around and having a good time. I looked at her and she smiled a big, happy smile. It occurred to me right then that maybe I was something more to her than I thought I was. I have to say that it was a nice feeling, one I couldn't recall anyone ever having toward me before. I immediately warmed to it and nervously cracked a smile back at her. Then I gave her a cautious squeeze in return.

She giggled, stood on her tiptoes, and kissed me on the cheek. "My guy," she said. "Right?"

I grinned at her like a love-starved sheepdog. "You bet," I said. At that exact moment, I started to feel like maybe something good was happening in my life.

But it was Darren. There was something about the guy. He had an energy emanating from him that I felt right away when we shook hands, like an electrical kind of buzz. He held my gaze and his eyes bored into me seeming to go deeper into my soul than I'd ever been before, which, believe me, up until then hadn't been very far. It came to me at that moment that this was a deadly series dude who was wasting no time in letting me know he was in charge. I knew right then he was not to be messed with and given the right circumstances could also be dangerous.

He released my hand after giving it one final squeeze, which this time hurt, and said, "Well, sit down then."

I grabbed a wooden chair and did as told, suddenly a little uncertain as to what was going on. Steph ambled off to a couch in front of the picture window and sat down. She picked up a well-worn magazine and started paging through it. I looked at her once and she grinned at me and then went back to what she was doing, leaving me and her brother to ourselves. Darren looked me over, rolling the joint (still unlit) between his fingers and I can only imagine what was going through his mind. I was nothing more than a regular guy who had grown up in the same small town I still lived and worked in, not ten miles from where the trailer was located. A big deal I wasn't. His expression gave away nothing, but at least he hadn't kicked me out or beat me up for hanging around his sister. Maybe that said something.

Finally, he said, "Steph says you're a mechanic."

"Yeah. I work at Swant's Service."

He asked me what I did there and I told him about my job at the little gas station and auto repair place in Orchard Lake where I'd worked for the last eight years, ever since my junior year in high school. It was a block from the Black Rooster and two blocks from my little apartment. Like I said, it was a small town.

He asked me about cars and I told them I was pretty good with them and that they'd been a hobby of mine ever since I'd helped my dad tear apart one of the pieces of junk he was always messing around with in the front yard of our rented house two blocks off the main highway that ran through town. Even though he left my mom, my little sister, and me for good when I was fourteen, at least he left me knowing how to take apart the engine of a 1979 Buick Skylark and put it back together. That was something.

The more I talked with Darren, the more my initial discomfort faded. He seemed, if not friendly, as least interested in what I had to say (not many people were), so I relaxed a little and, embellishing my skills somewhat, told him I could fix just about anything mechanical and automotive related, which was seventy-five percent true.

"In fact, I've got a '57 Chevy that I've been working on for a few years. You know, restoring." I paused, enjoying the image of that shiny, two-tone teal and white beauty in my brain. Well, what I hoped it'd eventually look like anyway. Right now it was slightly rusted with an ugly tan and brown paint job. It also needed a new carburetor. And a new transmission. And...well, it needed a lot. I shook my head dejectedly. "It takes time," I told him. "And money," I added to which Darren nodded and replied, "Yeah, I get that."

We'd been talking for maybe fifteen minutes, just him getting to know me more than anything else when there was a pause in the conversation. Darren looked over at his sister and gave her a slight nod. Like I said, I'd only known Steph for a week, but I guess her word was good enough for her brother. He seemed satisfied with what he'd heard from me so far.

He flicked a stick match and lit his joint, took a deep hit, and then offered it to me. I took a hit and motioned it to Steph who declined, so I gave it back to Darren who gave his sister a 'what's up with you look,' that she responded to by grinning coyly at him. *What the hell was going on between these two?*

Darren took another hit and then suddenly stood up. "Let's go," he told me, sticking the joint in the corner of his mouth. "I've got something to show you."

I got to my feet to follow him and immediately had to steady myself against the table, feeling the sudden, fast effect of the weed. *Man,* I thought to myself. Then I couldn't think anymore. My mind seemed to go numb, and I took a moment to collect myself. It didn't help. The world started to spin a little and I almost had to sit down. Thankfully, Steph rushed to me and helped me maintain my equilibrium. It was the strongest pot I'd ever smoked in my life.

"Careful," she told me, holding my arm tight and guiding me across the floor. "I should have warned you about Darren's weed. It's pretty strong stuff."

She could say that again. But I wasn't thinking about Darren and his pot at that particular moment. The fact that Steph was so close to me...Man, she sure smelled good. Sweet and fresh. And the way she squeezed my arm. Well, what can I say? It was nice. It was all nice. Maybe it was the weed affecting my emotions, then again maybe not, but it occurred to me that maybe there was something more to us being together than I thought. I found myself suddenly hoping so.

With Steph gripping my arm to steady me, we went out the front door and followed Darren around the back of the trailer. It was a sunny day in early June with a clear blue sky and a light breeze. The sunlight kind of burned my eyes and I immediately wished I had my shades with me. From somewhere Steph had found a beat-up straw hat that she put on my head. "There you go. Now you're a real cowboy."

I adjusted the hat and glanced at my reflection in a window on the trailer as we walked by. *Not bad*, I thought to myself. I kept it on. If Steph liked it, who was I to argue?

Nearby, a tall cottonwood tree was tossing off white seedlings like a springtime snowstorm - an image that wasn't normally associated with my thought process, and right away I knew that the pot had hit me hard.

As we walked I tried to get myself together. I didn't want to seem like a drug-addled loser in front of Darren. Or Steph, for that matter. But, the day was beautiful, that was for sure, especially with the scent of freshly mown hay in the air, and, stoned or not, it reminded me how glad I was to live in rural Minnesota and not in a big city.

The land we were on was in the western part of the county. Steph's grandparents lived in a farmhouse about a hundred yards from us. She told me once they were both in their eighties and, as she put it, "Kind of old. They can't do much for themselves anymore. Me and Darren help them out." When I asked her about her parents all she told me was, "Don't ask." So I didn't and never brought them up to her again. Neither did she.

Being outside in the fresh air and sunshine was helping to clear my brain somewhat. I looked over at her grandparent's house, a nicely kept-up white, two-story frame home with a porch on the front. It had a few tall shade trees in the front and back and a little vegetable garden off to one side. "Nice place over there," I said.

"Yeah, with our parents gone, Grandpa Harold and Grandma Rosie are all we have left," she told me. "I keep the place clean and Darren pays their bills. We do what we can. They're good folks."

Her grandparent's land was out where old three and four-generation farms were being sold off for new housing developments and huge homes we called McMansions. But there were still holdouts, people wanting to hold onto their land and keep their old way of life going as well as they could and it was apparent that Steph's grandparents were among them. My guess was they had at least 180 acres. Their property and the land around it was a mix of rolling hills and fields of corn and soybean with woodlots with the occasional pond tossed in for good measure. It was pretty in a pastoral kind of way. *Was that the pot talking again?* I guess that's why rich people moved out here to the country - to live the rural life while working at high-paying jobs forty miles away in Minneapolis and commuting back and forth. It made the area a mix of young, freshly scrubbed newcomers and old, manure shoveling farm families. I didn't mind one way or the other, my interests leaning more toward just hanging out and having a good time. Politically or culturally aware? Well, it was not my strong suit, to be honest. Though I'd have to say, if pushed, my allegiances would always fall with the rural way of life. I was never comfortable the few times I went into Minneapolis or any other big city for that matter. Too many people and too much noise. Too much of everything.

Steph and Darren's trailer was about two hundred feet off the county road and had a gravel driveway leading to it from the county road. There was an old barn fifty feet beyond the trailer. Darren stood at its side entrance, a sliding wooden door, and waited for Steph and me to get to him. "Let's move it along," he glanced at the hat Steph had given me and frowned a little, but said nothing. She only squeezed my arm a little harder and giggled, joking with her brother.

Darren ignored her and slid the door open. "Come on inside," he said. "Take a look at what we've got in here."

Darren led the way and Steph and I followed him inside.

I'll tell you what I expected: What I expected was to see a falling apart building smelling of rotting manure, filled with old bales of straw, pigeons flying around, daylight coming through the ceiling, and mice running all over the place on a spongy wooden floor littered with loose hay and pieces of broken farm equipment. In short - a junk-filled mess. What I saw was not even remotely close.

"I've fixed it up some," Darren said, grinning in response to my slack-jawed silence.

I'd never been in a hospital before, but it's what the inside of the barn looked like I imagined an operating room would be like. It was a big, clean, open space, remodeled and brightly lit by huge fluorescent lamps hanging by chains from the ceiling. Its walls were newly framed and sheet rocked and painted a shiny, glossy white. The floor was spotless and looked to be made of poured concrete.

I'd never seen a room as clean in my life. While the outside was beaten up weathered grey siding that looked as old as it probably was, the inside was completely different. It was clean and it smelled brand new, not at all like the rotten-smelling mess I'd been expecting. Not by a long shot. And the amazing thing was this: in the center of the space were a bunch of big, shining, sealed, stainless steel containers with dials on them and copper tubing connecting them, like a bottling plant or something. But I was just pissing in the wind. I hadn't the faintest idea what they were or what they were being used for.

"What do you think?" Darren asked, watching me, obviously enjoying my amazement,

"What is all of this?" I asked after I regained my composure.

Darren grinned. "Take a guess."

I didn't know what to say but I took a stab anyway. "Are you brewing beer?" I'd seen stories in the news of people starting their own micro-breweries. It was a shot in the dark, but the only thing I could think of. Turns out I was wrong, but not too far off.

"Close," he said, grinning. "Guess again."

Steph came up behind me, put her arms around my middle, and squeezed. "Think of the olden days in Kentucky," she breathed in my ear and I had to struggle to maintain what little composure I had. Then it hit me. It was something I vaguely remembered hearing about once in high school, maybe in history class.

"Is it a still?" I asked cautiously, not wanting to seem like an idiot in front of Darren and especially not in front of Steph.

Darren laughed and slapped me on the shoulder. "Good man," he said. "That's exactly what it is."

I don't know why, but I felt good that I had guessed right. Like I had won a quiz or something.

"Wow!" It was all I could think of to say.

Next to me Steph giggled and rubbed my back. "Good guess, lover."

I grinned at her.

Darren made it a point of ignoring us. "Let me tell you what we've got going on here."

He started with the four shining, six-foot-high, stainless steel sealed drums, all grouped near to each other. "That's where the mash is cooked," he told me. "We use corn. Organic corn, in fact, from a few of my farmer friends around here. The rest we bring in from small, independent, organic farmers in the southern part of the state. There's nothing better for what I'm making and it's part of what makes my stuff so great." I found out later that he employed about ten farmers to grow the corn for him.

Then he showed me the next step in the process. Each drum was connected by copper tubing to one big, eight-foot-tall container. "We call this the Thump Keg. This is where the alcohol vapor travels to after it's boiled."

He talked like he was giving some people from the local Chamber of Commerce a tour and it was plain to see he was proud of his operation. He caressed the Thump Keg almost seductively. "If any mash from the still comes in with the vapor, it falls out here." He smiled at me. "My stuff's real pure," he said with obvious pride. "We compost the mash along with whatever solid stuff is left behind." He gave Steph a sly look before turning back to me. "I'll show you how we use it later."

He moved over a few feet. "Then the vapor is reheated and goes here." He pointed to a third and just as shiny container twice the size of a fifty-gallon drum, "This is called the Worm Box and it's where the alcohol distills out." He must have seen my blank look. Science and stuff like that was never my strong suit. "It's where the whiskey is formed," he told me.

Got it. A nice, simple explanation. I could understand that.

On the side of the Worm Box near the bottom was a tap. He stepped to a nearby row of shelves, grabbed a glass jar, like the kind my grandma used can tomatoes, and drew off some liquid from the tap. He swirled it around and held it up to the light. It was so pure and colorless that I could barely see it.

He turned to me. "This is my stuff," he said. "It's 97 % pure grain alcohol. Maybe you've heard of Everclear. It's 95% pure and everyone thinks it's the most pure alcohol you can buy. And it is. Legally buy, I mean. But mine's way better than that. Plus, I put some stuff in so it tastes good, not like you're drinking rubbing alcohol." I watched him slowly swirl it around in the jar. It was mesmerizing. "Want to try some?" he asked.

My hangover from the night before was almost gone. The effect of the pot was easing too, but must have still been present a little because I suddenly felt quite confident. "Sure," I told him, thinking I'd have a little just to be polite.

He handed me the glass and watched as I took in a mouthful and swallowed, just as he was reaching out his hand and telling me to "Take it easy."

Oh, man. Whatever I thought it'd taste like, I was wrong. Darren's "stuff" as he called it, hit me like that mule kick you sometimes hear about except a hundred times stronger. Make that a thousand times. I felt weak in the knees and I'm sure I staggered a few steps. I caught myself on a nearby table and was looking at him, unable to speak, when he raised a finger like, 'Just a second' and then the moonshine hit me. The heat in my throat went all the way down through my esophagus into my gut, burning like what I imagined lava from a volcano would feel like if you were fool enough to swallow it. I'm not kidding you, it was scorching. But after a few moments that sensation went away and was replaced by a warm, mellow feeling radiating from my stomach and flowing outward throughout my entire body, from the ends of my fingers down to the tips of my toes and then back up my spine all the way to my brain. It was a nice warm feeling like I'd just been wrapped up in a soft quilt sewn by my dear departed aunt. I kid you not when I say that, other than fooling around with Steph, it was the best feeling I'd ever felt before in my entire life.

Darren took me by the arm and guided me to a couch set against the side of the barn where he sat me down. Steph, who had wandered off, ran back and sat next to me.

"Darren, what the hell?" she yelled at her brother. "Didn't you warn him?" She rubbed my shoulder blades. "You could have killed him." I was perspiring, sweat running down the sides of my face. I leaned back against Steph as she dried my face. Somewhere along the way, Darren must have taken the jar from me. My straw cowboy hat had fallen off, too.

"Don't get mad, Steph," Darren said. "I just wanted to test him." He grinned at both her and me and moved so he was standing in front of us. He shifted the whiskey to his left hand and stuck out his right. "Shake, Ron," he said to me. "You did good. You did just fine."

I reached up and shook his hand after missing it the first time or two and then let go rest my head against the back of the couch.

Darren smiled and looked at the jar with fondness. He was obviously proud of what he had been able to concoct in an old barn out in the rural farmland of western Hennepin County. Then he quickly lifted the moonshine to his mouth and drained the colorless liquid, savoring the flavor and smacking his lips. There was absolutely zero effect on him other than pure joy and serious pleasure. It was apparent you had to get used to drinking Darren's "stuff."

I took a look at the still and the operation he had going and had the immediate thought that it would probably be a long time, if ever before I ever did get used to Darren's whiskey. Turns out I was right.

Darren interrupted thoughts of my future ability to drink 195-proof alcohol, when he asked, "You want to see what else we got going out here?"

What else? You mean there was more? I looked at Steph and she smiled and nodded her head, encouraging me. Then she kissed me quickly on the cheek, letting me know she was having a good time, and (I hoped), happy that Darren and I were getting along. I figured, why not? If Steph was happy, I was happy, even if I was a little high and probably drunk as well.

"Sure," I said, having no idea what could possibly top Darren's kick-ass moonshine whiskey.

"Ok, then." He gave me a friendly pat on the back, started walking across the floor of the barn, and said over his shoulder, "Steph bring him out to the greenhouse."

She stood me up and got me steady on my feet. I'm not sure what kind of scent she was wearing, maybe it was just her own natural, sweet aroma, but, man...being so close to her and not being able to do anything about it was starting to get to me.

"Steph! Ron! Come on," Darren called to us impatiently, interrupting my rapidly escalating fantasies. He stood at the sliding door and I swear he was tapping the toe of his boot. Steph hurried me along the best she could. I only stumbled a couple of times. In the next minute, we had left the pleasant coolness of the barn and stepped into the bright sunlight again. I covered my eyes with my hand and Steph plopped the cowboy hat back on my head. I never even noticed her pick it up.

We went around the barn to a glass-sided greenhouse about the size of a two-car garage. Darren took me inside and before I had a chance to collect my thoughts and to forget about the whiskey still we'd just left, he laid another surprise on me. The greenhouse with filled with plants. And not just your regular garden variety pansies and petunias either. It was packed with marijuana. Big, healthy-looking specimens, evenly spaced out in pots set on waist-high wooden frame tables covered by chicken wire (to let the water drain through, I found out later.) There had to have been over two hundred plants in there.

Darren smiled at my surprise. "What'd you think I had in here? He asked, "Friggin' daisies?

Well, actually, I sort of did, but I didn't tell him that. All I could say was, "Wow. This is awesome!"

I looked around, like I had done in the barn, and took in the scene, stunned beyond all belief. Darren not only had a moonshine still producing kiss-ass whiskey, but he also had another operation that was producing what I figured had to be kick-ass marijuana (if what I had smoked less than half an hour earlier was any indication, and it turned out it was.)

He had big blower fans strategically positioned along the sides keeping the air circulating, and some kind of a stainless steel tube and frame system with hoses attached to it running the length of the greenhouse above the plants which turned out to be an automatic watering system. It was a complicated yet simple setup and it was working. The plants were lush and green and healthy looking, even to my untrained eye.

It finally dawned on me that my new friend (because that's what he eventually became) was in the drug business.

I looked at him again and tried to improve on my previous comment. "Wow and wow!" I said and he just laughed.

We took a few minutes wandering around inside looking at the plants. I told him time and time again how impressed I was.

"It's not that big a deal," he said when we finally made our way back to the door. "I always liked science as a kid, but I never wanted to work for anyone. Too much of a hassle taking orders from other people and whatnot."

I understood him completely but, of course, like most people, I'd never done anything about it. What impressed me about Darren was that he had. "I started doing this," he pointed around the greenhouse and back to the barn, "Just for fun. Then I started taking it further and selling it. Turns out I can make money at it." He paused, giving me a direct and knowing look. "Good money." When I nodded my acknowledgment, he added. "Seriously good money."

"Do you sell the pot, too?" I thought to ask.

"Some of it," he said. "I use the leftover mash for compost for the plants. I found out I could use the flowers in the whiskey, so that's mainly what I use them for. You know. Just to give it some extra kick," he added, laughing.

Steph laughed, too. "It's part of what makes Darren's stuff special and taste so good." She grinned and pulled my hat down over my eyes, goofing around. "Just like you are to me."

Darren glanced at his sister. She shrugged her shoulders and laughed at him. I could see she enjoyed messing around with her older brother. It was nice to see. Kind of like a little family and it made me want to be included and become part of it.

We left the greenhouse and Darren led the way to a shaded grove of cottonwoods where a ring of field stone had been placed to form a fire pit. The grass had been recently cut and some Adirondack chairs painted bright green and blue were arranged nicely around it. We stood for a minute gazing out over a nearby field of soybeans that were dark green and healthy looking. Steph was holding my arm and playing around with the hair poking out from under my cowboy hat. I liked how affectionate she was toward me. She stopped long enough to say, "Our grandparents rent the land out to a local farmer." She pointed. "Those are his soybeans."

On the far side of the field was a stand of hardwood trees that looked like maples and oaks. I heard some crows cawing and looked up and watched as they flew over us. For some reason, it made me feel good to see them. In the distance way off to the right, I heard a tractor, probably the farmer who rented the land. He was probably working in one of the fields. It was the only evidence that anyone was around other than us. With the light breeze and blue sky and puffy clouds, looking out at the land was unexpectedly peaceful and relaxing, like I was on vacation somewhere or something. Or what I imagined a vacation would be like, since I'd never been anywhere before in my life except to go to Minneapolis a handful of times and St. Cloud once or twice, and that was just to get car parts. In my mind that didn't count. No wonder they built their fire pit where they did. The view was great and the setting was fantastic. I thought to myself, *I could get real comfortable here.*

I was glad when Darren suggested that we all sit down. Steph and I sat next to each other, not talking, happy to just hold each other's hand. We both watched a pair of mourning doves poking around in the gravel on the driveway about fifty feet away. They were cooing contentedly. It was pretty sweet and Steph and I grinned at each other.

Darren took a few minutes looking out over the countryside, seeming to take some measure of satisfaction as well as some inspiration from the rolling fields and land. Then he looked at me and turned serious. "OK. So you work at Swant's and you're good with cars. That's what Steph says and, after talking with you, I believe her."

I looked at Steph who was watching our conversation closely. She rubbed my arm. "I told him that you could fix anything."

Nice to be appreciated, I thought to myself. No one had ever told me that before.

I turned to Darren. "Sure," I told him, thinking of how this would put me in good with Steph. "I'm a pretty good mechanic. What do you have in mind?"

"So you're good with cars," he reiterated. "How about driving?" he asked. "Are you good with that? We're expanding our operation and what I need is a good, reliable driver. Someone to deliver my moonshine."

A chance to work for Darren? A chance to get to be closer to Steph? I didn't have to think. "Yeah, I'm a good driver," I told him.

"He's really good," Steph chimed in. "He's good with his hands...got a nice, soft touch."

I felt my ears go red. Steph stood up, came over, and gave me a quick kiss. Then she sat on the arm of my chair, nice and close.

Darren ignored her and looked at me."Good. Then that's what I have you do. I'll have you drive for me. I'll supply the car, you do the driving. We'll give you a try. If it works out, you've got yourself a job."

It dawned on me that this whole meeting with Darren had been sort of a job interview which apparently I'd passed. The image came into my mind of old black and white movies I'd seen with battered cars being chased by the cops down the back roads of Kentucky or Tennessee with guns blazing and bullets flying. Maybe it was the alcohol in me, or maybe the pot, probably both, but all of a sudden I had a romantic vision of Steph by my side as we outran the law, running moonshine whiskey and making a name for ourselves as outlaws and folk heroes.

Then I had a more sobering thought as I went back to the 'guns blazing' part of my fantasy. *Wait a minute. This whiskey-running thing could be dangerous.*

Darren must have seen my expression because he coughed out a laugh and said, "Don't worry Ronny, my friend. It's all perfectly safe."

I blinked my eyes and got them back in focus. Steph had stood up and moved behind me and was rubbing my shoulders, her long skilled fingers playing with muscles under my skin I didn't even know I had. I have to say, it was feeling awfully good. I had a sudden vision of her and me going back to my little apartment and fooling around a little. Or out to the back forty nearby if it came to that. It occurred to me, then, that working for her brother would really put me in good with my new girlfriend.

I looked at Darren. There was something about him that I liked. He had confidence. He was sure of himself and had enough initiative and know-how to build up what looked to be a nice little business. What the heck? He seemed to know what he was doing, way more than me anyway, that was for sure. I was glad to get a chance to be a part of it.

I put out my hand. "You got a deal, " I told him and we shook on it.

Steph pumped her fist enthusiastically and yelled, "Yes!" Then she hugged me tight, knocking my cowboy hat off again. Then she kissed me hard.

"Good, man," Darren said, ignoring his sister as he stood up. "Come on. Let me show you what I've got for you to drive."

With Steph smiling and kissing my cheek, nuzzling my neck, and holding my hand we followed Darren. It felt good to feel so...well, it felt good to feel like she cared so much about me.

We walked to our right off the lawn through an area of tall grass and weeds to an old building further out past the greenhouse. Darren took a moment to unlock a padlock and then pushed open the door. It was nothing more than a dilapidated shed. He motioned to me and we went inside. This time what I'd imagined was correct. It was just a busted-up storage shed but without the hay. An old, decrepit outbuilding with a dirt floor that smelled of grease and oil. In a good way, it reminded me of the service station where I worked, and I felt right at home. It was my kind of place. Except for what else was in it.

There was a vehicle inside covered with a big, old sheet. Darren motioned for me to help him pull it off and I did, dust flying. Underneath was the car he told me I'd be driving and let me tell you, that first time I first saw it I wasn't impressed at all. It was a piece of shit looking '82 four-door, two-tone grey Ford Crown Victoria. I took a minute walking around it, looking it over as best I could in the dim light. The paint was faded and covered in rust and looked like it wouldn't start without a jump let alone run at all. But, as they say, looks can be deceiving.

After checking it out for a minute, I looked at Darren and said, "Really? This's it?" I didn't try very hard to hide my skepticism.

Darren grinned, took a set of keys out of his pocket, and tossed them to me. "Yep. Start her up. See what you think."

I climbed in, pumped the gas, and turned the key, not expecting the rust bucket to even turn over. I was wrong. Way wrong. The Ford not only started the first time, it literally roared. I pictured flames coming out of the twin tailpipes. I pumped the accelerator a few times getting the feel of it. The engine vibrated through the steering column and steering wheel into my hands, all the way up to my shoulders and down to my butt. It felt like a stock car that could be racing at the Daytona 500. It felt good. Real good. I couldn't wait to drive it.

Darren tapped on the glass and motioned for me to roll down the window which I did.

"Sounds great," was all I could think of saying because it did.

Darren smiled and patted the roof. "Yeah, I paid a guy up in St. Cloud ten grand to overhaul it," he said, raising his voice to be heard over the loud, rumbling idle of the suped-up engine. Then he poked me in the shoulder. "If I'd known you were such a great mechanic..." he looked at Steph, standing, as always, nearby. "I'd have hired you."

I juiced the accelerator. The mechanic must have bored out the cylinders. Probably added a bigger carburetor, too, and supercharged it. The engine sounded like it had been modified to be twice as powerful as the 400 hp I guessed it was rated as.

I looked at him and smiled. "Don't worry about it." Then I juiced the accelerator again, visions of racing cops down dusty back roads under a nighttime full moon filling my brain.

Darren must have read my mind. "Don't get any ideas. I want you to drive this car like you're an old grandpa. I had the guy in St. Cloud give it more punch, just in case.

I nodded, getting his point. At least, at the time, I thought I did.

He motioned for me to turn the car off which I reluctantly did. I got out and helped him cover the Ford with the sheet and we all went back to the fire pit where we spent the rest of the afternoon smoking his weed and drinking his whiskey. Well, sipping the whiskey on my part. At one point three guys joined us. Darren introduced me to them as his crew of helpers, Lonny, Garcia, and Big Frank, all in their mid-twenties, and all of them, like Darren and me, fairly quiet.

Steph told me later that Darren liked to keep things simple. He was in charge of the whole operation and he didn't want any hassle from his employees. "He pays well, but he won't take any shit," she told me. From what little I knew of her brother I had no reason to doubt her.

Later on, I think I remember the sun setting and the stars coming out. I think I remember wandering with Steph out to the shed where the Ford was kept. And I think I remember...ah, forget it. I don't remember anything after that.

The way it worked was this: Darren had expanded his business to include moonshine-buying customers throughout the seven counties immediately west, north, and south of Minneapolis. They'd call him on a secure number, place an order, and then do something completely unexpected in this day and age of electronic banking. They'd send him a check for the whiskey through the mail! When I asked him about it, Darren told me it was the safest way.

"That way, I control everything," he said. "Makes the transaction simple to do and easy for me to keep track of. Plus, there is absolutely no risk."

Made sense to me, but then again I was just the driver. Darren was the brains of the operation. He made the deposit and once the check cleared the bank one of the crew would box up the order, pack it in the trunk of the Ford and I'd drive off and make the delivery.

Sounds simple, right? Well, it was. All I had to do was drive, watch the speed limit, meet the customer, and drop off the order. That's what Darren called it, an order. Then I'd head home. Easy.

Mostly Luke's customers were well-to-do young professionals who lived in big McMansions plopped down on what were once fields of corn or soybeans, or pasture land that had been used for cattle and horses. Generally, they were nice enough and treated me well, and if their fancy houses and three acres of lawns didn't seem to fit into the old rural Minnesota way of life I was used to, who was I to argue? I'd just drive up at a prearranged time, ring the doorbell, listen to the chimes echo throughout the house, and wait for either Zack or Ryan or Emily or Kara to answer. They usually had me bring the delivery in, so I got to see the inside of their home: their huge living room carpeted nine times out of ten in white or some shade of beige, their marble fireplace, the fancy tables with the inevitable vases of colorful flowers on them and on and on and on. I made a mental note after my first transgression to always remove my boots at the entryway when I came inside.

I'd take the delivery to whatever room they wanted it, unpack the bottles (usually twelve, sometimes twenty-four), take the box or boxes with me when I left, and hit the road. More often than not I was given, if not a twenty-dollar tip, maybe a fifty. And once or twice, a hundred. I got the impression these folks had money to burn and enjoyed showing off their wealth. I was happy to oblige them.

I found out from Steph that our customers liked to have what they called Moonshine Party's. I could only imagine what they were like. Having been exposed to Darren's whiskey that first time had taught me a very valuable lesson. Go slow. Go real slow. And for god's sake sip it, man, sip it! My one experience was good enough. If you drank it too fast it'd wreck you, if not kill you. In fact, in the lessons learned department, I pretty much quit drinking Darren's stuff or any other alcohol after that first day I'd met him. A beer or two on occasion yeah, maybe. And, of course, the weed. I did like Darren's pot, but the point I'm trying to make is that for once I felt I had a future that I hadn't had before and I was going to do my best to embrace it and not screw it up.

Steph trimmed my hair for me and I made it a point to keep it washed regularly. She even convinced me to shave the scruffy hair off my face. I bought some new flannel shirts (with Steph's help, of course), and even some new work boots. I felt good, even a little confident in myself, like I was cleaning up my act. I had direction in my life and, at twenty-five years old, didn't ever foresee it ending.

And, I have to say, driving those country roads was fun. Most of my deliveries were after six in the evening when my shift at the service station was over. I'd drive my Chevy out to the trailer, shoot the breeze with Darren and his crew, and then take off in the Ford. I made deliveries almost every night and I got so I loved it. The Ford handled like a dream and was great to drive, but it was more than that. I found myself enjoying being out in the country. I liked the rolling hills, and the farm fields lush with tall corn and low-growing soybeans. There was a certain rich, earthy aroma in the air that made me feel good, alive. Usually, I got to see a fiery orange sunset which to me was one of the most beautiful sights in the world.

Sometimes, if I was out way past sunset, I'd even pull over and stop on some out-of-the-way dirt road, turn off the engine, get out of the car, and just stand there looking up at the Milky Way and the stars. Now and then I'd even see a comet streak across the sky, and, if they were out (which they usually were) I'd listen to what seemed like a hundred frogs all making a racket in nearby swamps.

Being out in the peaceful countryside during those times was pretty special and something I'd never really done before. I couldn't believe I was taking the time to do it, but I was. And, (I hope this doesn't sound too weird), I have to say that I liked the feeling of serenity it gave me.

The country I drove through was populated with way more old farms and farmhouses than I thought I was going to see. I got the feeling that rural life was alive and well in this part of the state despite the new subdivisions and those big, modern McMansion monstrosities I delivered to. I even started imagining that maybe one day I could buy an old farm, move in with Steph, fix it up, and have a place of our own to call home. In short, over those months I drove for Darren I felt I was changing. I wasn't the skinny, grease ball mechanic whose only other skill was hanging out at the Black Rooster drinking beer and getting drunk. I'd never had any kind of dreams for the future before, but now with Steph, I did. It was something I wasn't used to, but was growing to like it. Maybe I was maturing or something.

Speaking of Steph, sometimes she'd ride with me. She'd usually sit close, nearly in my lap, and put her left arm across the seat behind me. She'd snuggle up with her head on my shoulder and her right arm around my waist. Sometimes we'd talk, and sometimes we'd just be quiet and enjoy each other's company, just like we were a serious couple, which we definitely became over that summer.

"Steph, I've got a question for you," I remember asking her on one of our drives together. "Do you like it out here? In the country, I mean."

It was in early August and we were driving north on a smooth, blacktopped county road through land where there were green fields of nearly seven-foot high corn rolling off to our right and left, and scattered wood lots and old farmhouses mixed in with the occasional single-wide or double-wide trailer. A fiery orange sun was low on the horizon, another picturesque sunset. No McMansions in sight. I had slowed down so we could take a look at a quiet little pond with cattails lining the edge. We watched a muskrat and some ducks swimming around before I accelerated slowly back up to forty-five miles an hour.

She kissed me on the cheek and went back to laying her head on my shoulder. "Sure, Ronny," she murmured. "As long as I'm with you."

Man, had I lucked out.

I'm not much of a thinker but, in addition to falling head over heels in love with Steph, I had time while I was driving to think about the other changes I was going through. My dad had worked for Cramer Electric in Orchard Lake as an electrician before he left Mom, me, and my little sister, never to be seen or heard from again. Mom had worked the next town over at Winslow's dry-cleaning, but I guess after Dad left she pretty much lost interest in most everything. She started drinking more than usual and a few years later died late one night in a head-on crash on Highway 12, a few miles outside of town. I was eighteen. My sister was two years younger than me and she went to live with our aunt in Minneapolis.

We split a little insurance money from Mom, which I stuck in a drawer and tried to save but eventually blew on the Chevy. I stayed in town. I had started working at the service station when I was seventeen, so I got my apartment that summer Mom died and had been getting on with my life ever since, essentially going nowhere and not doing much of anything.

Meeting Steph and now working for Darren had been an unexpected change in my directionless existence. For the first time in my life, I felt I had a purpose. I wanted to stay with Steph and I wanted to keep working for Darren. Steph and I were good together and Darren was someone who, the more I got to know, the more I admired. He was smart, he was savvy, and he had a thriving business. What more could I ask for? I felt that I was on a roll for the first time in my life.

By the end of the summer, I had a plan worked out. Darren paid well, so I had opened a bank account and was saving five hundred dollars a week. I figured if I could keep driving for him for a few more years, I'd have enough money in the bank for a good down payment on an old farm on the land I regularly drove through in one of the counties north and west of us. It was exciting for me to dream about. Things were looking good.

On top of that, Steph helped me clean my apartment so it didn't smell weird anymore, a complaint she'd had ever since that first night together. I remember the day well.

"Cleans up pretty good," she told me, standing in the middle of the room and looking around. It was early September. I had just used glass cleaner for the first time in my life along with a fistful of paper towels and cleaned the only window in the place, the front one, which now was wide open letting in fresh air. Then we sprayed the cleaner on any other surface we could think of, using almost half a roll of paper towels to wipe everything down. It was pretty disgusting, I have to admit, we got everything clean. To complete the transformation, I installed a new set of bright, white curtains Steph had brought over. When I finished we both admired them as they billowed out in the breeze. For the first time since I'd moved in seven years earlier, the place smelled and looked the way a home you cared about was supposed to be – clean, sparkling, and fresh.

We were both happy with the result and Steph moved next to me to give me a big hug. "I just might keep you around."

Well, how could I argue with that? I was happy and had a future that was looking as bright as the window we'd just cleaned. Brighter, even.

Darren had been selling his moonshine in small quantities for about a year before I started driving for him. He'd had no problems with customers or run-ins with the law that entire time. He was in the process of increasing his production and expanding his business when he hired me. Things went along smoothly with me driving throughout the summer and into the fall without a hitch. Then we had our first issue, and the weird thing was it had nothing to do with me, or, in fact, even one of our customers. It had to do, instead, with one of our customer's friends.

The story I heard was that about thirty miles west of us in the next country over there had been a moonshine party in conjunction with a Halloween celebration. It was for adults only. You can probably imagine the rest. Apparently, one of the guests had been drunk out of his mind and tried to drive home dressed as Darth Vader. After he'd driven only a mile or so he'd passed out and crashed into a tree. Soon after the crash, a guy out for a late-night jog found the wreck and called 911. An ambulance came and Darth Vader was taken to the hospital in St. Cloud. He was cut up and had a slight concussion, but other than that he was alright.

While the police questioned him I guess he let slip about the party he'd been to. Word had it he was blubbering and crying and everything. I knew from experience that Darren's stuff could affect you in unexpected ways, so when I heard how the guy had broken down under questioning by a county deputy while he was probably still drunk and lying in an unfamiliar hospital bed - well, the fact that he then ratted out his friend who had given the party didn't surprise me at all.

The long and the short of it was that the next day two deputies went unannounced to the party house, had the unsuspecting owner let them in, and proceeded to easily find Darren's whiskey in the liquor cabinet in the downstairs amusement room. As you can imagine, that didn't sit too well with the deputies. Word back to Darren from the customer was, 'They sounded like somebody pissed in their own personal punch bowl.' The deputies confiscated the moonshine and a judge eventually fined the customer some serious money, more than usual given the circumstances, because our customer wouldn't say who he bought the moonshine from - which earned him a free case of whiskey from Darren, which the customer regretfully declined, saying, "Sorry, man, I'm going to have to lay low for a while."

It was good advice and we should have followed it. Unfortunately, we didn't.

Darren was confident he wouldn't get caught. "I'm not going to be pushed around by any jerk cops, you can trust me on that," is what he told us at a meeting in the trailer a few days later and he was filling us in on what had happened. "I've got a business to run." So we went back to the way things were: Darren and the crew making the stuff and me driving the deliveries.

The problem was that now the cops in our county and the next couple of counties over were aware that something fishy was going on. In retrospect, Darren should have just shut things down for a while, but he didn't.

"I've got good money coming in so why stop?" was his reasoning. "We'll just be extra careful," he said and gave us all a look like he meant us. We got it.

So we soldiered on.

Darren had me oversee a modification on the Ford. In place of using the trunk, we put a false bottom in the backseat and that's where we put the case (or cases) of whiskey, hiding them just to be on the safe side in case I was stopped for some reason and the trunk was searched.

I was also told to drive extra cautiously, which did.

Within a few weeks, things were back to normal and the moonshine-making operation was again running smoothly. Word got out about the cops being on the lookout for us so we lost a few customers but we gained a few also - people who most certainly were drawn to the potential danger of buying from us. We didn't care. Money was money. So all was well.

Darren calmed down and was in a good mood. He even started working on a new formula to increase the whiskey's potency (as if that was necessary!) Steph, who never worried about much of anything anyway, was extra happy and started making plans to paint my little apartment sage green or something like that.

I was happy, too. I enjoyed working for Darren. He was as good a boss as I could ever imagine. I had a full-time girlfriend who I thought of as the love of my life. I was saving money for our future together. I couldn't have asked for anything more. Then we had an early snowstorm and everything changed in an instant.

It was the week before Thanksgiving and up until then, the weather had been fairly sunny and mild, around forty degrees or so during the daytime. Then for two days the temperature fell to single digits at night and rose to only the low twenties during the day. A leaden sky settled in with a thick blanket of gray clouds hanging low over the entire area. By this time of year, the fields had been harvested and the leaves had fallen from all the trees so the land looked dull, bleak, and brown, a stark contrast to the verdant, rich greens of summer and the brilliant oranges and reds and yellows of fall. Now, with the gray skies and cold weather, everything looked just empty and frozen and dead.

Steph, me, Darren, and the rest of the crew switched to wearing heavy jackets and gloves and knit hats with earflaps and waited for the inevitable first blast of winter. Snow. It began early that Saturday morning. The wind came up strong from the northwest, gusting across the land, and blowing the snow hard, causing white-out conditions on the roads making driving challenging. It continued throughout the day. When I got to Darren's that night he met me with a caution. "I just heard on the news that at least a foot has fallen and the roads west of here are pretty icy." He tossed me the keys. "Be careful out there."

"Will do," I told him.

I hiked through knee-high snow drifts to the shed and got the Ford running. One of the boys had plowed the driveway so it wasn't too hard to get out to the country road. I turned left and headed out on my deliveries.

This was the first major snowfall of the season and it took some getting used to driving in it. The Ford fishtailed a little when I accelerated so I backed off on the gas and settled into around forty miles an hour, ten mph or so less than I'd normally drive.

In a snowstorm like we were having the windshield got covered up fast. I had my defroster on high and used my wipers to keep it as clear as I could but even with that, I couldn't get it all. Some streaks of ice formed and wouldn't come off. After a few minutes, it accumulated and built up a thick layer, causing the wipers to be ineffective and making the visibility pretty bad. I had to stop about every fifteen minutes or so to scrape it off with my ice scraper. Plus, at this time of year, it was dark out and the few cars on the road had their headlights on. They seemed extra bright coming right at me reflecting off both the ice on the windshield and the snow blowing across the highway. Not the best night to be out and about, that was for sure, but I was confident I could handle the Ford in the rapidly diminishing driving conditions.

But however confident I was, I could tell right away that even though the roads had been plowed at least once earlier that day, the wind had continued to howl and the snow had continued to fall, covering the surface right back up. That made those little traveled back country roads icy and slippery, causing the big Ford to fishtail and slide if I pushed the speed too much. So I kept my cool and drove as carefully as I could, stopping to scrape the ice off as was necessary, which slowed down the delivery run big time, but I decided it was better to take it easy and be as safe as possible rather than risk an accident. During that night I drove nearly a hundred miles in just over three hours, making three deliveries. Other than a few slips on ice on some of the remote backroads, there were no problems.

After my third delivery, I glanced at my watch. It was nearly 9 pm. I had one more stop to make before heading back to Darren's where I'd pick up Steph and we'd go back to my place to ride out the remainder of the storm. My final stop was a couple who had been customers for just a few months. I'd only been to their house twice before but couldn't exactly picture in my mind how to get there, especially with the snowstorm making visibility so poor. I peered through the windshield, trying to keep the powerful Ford in the center of the highway while looking for any landmarks that would jog my memory. I couldn't see much. My headlights cut into the night illuminating the falling snow and nothing else. I could barely make out the road in front of me let alone anything on the side. I felt like I was driving through a swirling tunnel of white. On top of that, the wind was relentless, buffeting my car and causing it to shimmy now and then, which scared me a little. I had to use both hands to keep the big Ford on the road. I hadn't seen another car in over half an hour.

The house I was looking for was on a small lake in an out-of-the-way area of the county. I turned off Highway 18 onto Country Road 35 and slowed down, mindful of the steep ditches on both sides and the ghostly shapes of trees faintly visible past them. The snow, which had been falling heavily for the last few hours, abated a bit, allowing me to see a little more clearly, but I'm being generous. The next day the news guys would refer to what I was driving in as one of the biggest blizzards in the state in ten years and I wouldn't disagree with them. It was bad. But the weird thing was that despite my worry about the ice on the roads and the white-out conditions, all things considered, this first snowfall of the season was quite pretty. It made me think of a snow globe I once had as a young kid which was one of my favorite all-time toys.

To be honest, I think my mind wandered. Maybe I was imagining Steph and me living out in the country during a snowy night like tonight, curled up in front of a fireplace with crackling burning, sipping hot cocoa, snug, and warm and cuddly, handmade quilts wrapped around us for extra warmth. Or something like that. Anyway, the snow suddenly picked up and started blowing again in gusting blasts. I couldn't see more than twenty feet in any direction so I slowed down even more, just to be on the safe side. There were no tracks in the snow to follow. I felt I was the only person in the world.

I was in the middle of the road heading up a steep hill coming to the top of the rise. My eyes were flipping back and forth between watching the speedometer and the sides of the road all the while trying to keep the car from slipping off into the ditch. I was slowing down even more when the next thing I knew I was met head-on by a vehicle coming up over the rise from the opposite direction. It was an oversized pickup truck with huge, wide tires, and it materialized out of the storm riding up high on heavy-duty springs barreling hell-bent right at me. Its high-beam headlights hit me square in the eyes, blinding me. I jerked the wheel to the right to avoid a collision, blinking fast to clear my vision. The truck blew right past me, snow swirling around it, buffeting my car and obliterating the road in its after-wash.

I didn't panic. I'd grown up driving these kinds of roads and in these kinds of conditions. I quickly got control of the car, held the steering wheel firmly, took my foot off the gas, and pointed the big Ford straight ahead down the road on the other side of the rise all the while slowing my speed, waiting for the snow to swirl past me so I could see again.

My first mistake was assuming the road was going to go straight down the opposite side of the rise. It didn't. It dipped downhill and curved to the left and by the time I figured out what was going on, it was too late.

My other mistake was forgetting about the icy road surface. I spun the steering wheel to the left but my wheels skidded on some compacted ice and I felt the sickening sensation of losing control of my car as three thousand pounds of steel seemed to slide in agonizingly slow motion off to the right side of the road. Then, bang, it crashed into a snow bank left behind by a snowplow. The big car shuttered once and then came to rest. The only good thing was that the snow bank kept me from sliding further off the road and all the way down into the ditch. But it was of little consolation because even though I was still partially on the road, I was stuck, that was for sure. Stuck big time.

I cursed to myself, turned the engine off, got out, hurried around to the back of the car, and checked my predicament. I was in trouble. The huge county snowplows had been down the road earlier and I had slid into what they had plowed up and left behind - a slushy, messy pile of snow, packed and frozen as solid as concrete. My car was jammed into it and was now tilted with the back end angled down toward the ditch. The situation didn't look good but I had a glimmer of hope. While three wheels were stuck in the snow, the near left one was still on the pavement. Even with the wind blowing and the snow flying, my spirits lifted. Momentarily thinking I might get free, I jumped back into the Ford, got it running, and rocked it back and forth, shifting the automatic transmission between drive and reverse. The tires spun and spun and spun some more. I mentally crossed my fingers.

Then, just when I was thinking I was making some headway and might be able to get the car free and up on the road again, the back end gave way to gravity and slid further down into the ditch, leaving the front end pointed up at an awkward angle. Me and my Ford were stuck and stuck good.

I slammed my hand on the steering wheel, turned the engine off, and got out. The snow had picked up in intensity and I had to wipe it out of my eyes. The temperature outside was getting colder too. All in all, it was not the best night to be standing out in the country somewhere wondering what to do.

Both sides of the road sloped down at least ten feet. There was a forest on the side the Ford was on and I didn't see any lights from any house or farms of any kind coming through the trees. On the other side was some thick underbrush and more trees. I looked and looked and then saw something through them I hadn't noticed before. It was a lake. Since it was early in the season the water hadn't frozen over yet. It was a big black hole in the night. It looked dark and cold, and totally uninviting. But I could see lights coming from the houses on the shoreline, the nearest a hundred yards away. They looked warm and cozy, just like I imagined Steph and I being in our own place one day.

I was enjoying this brief mental interlude, picturing the two of us in a snug little place of our own, when my thoughts were interrupted. From the distance somewhere behind me I thought I heard a siren. I listened carefully, the sound being carried away at times by the wind. But after a minute or two I could tell it was for sure a siren and it was coming toward me. *Damn*! *It must be the cops*. Just as I was beginning to wonder what was going on (and expecting the worst) I saw coming up the road from the direction I'd been headed, through all of that blowing snow, the last thing I expected to see on a night like tonight. It was a guy and his dog.

He huffed up to my side and silently raised his hand in greeting. He was bundled up in a heavy jacket with a fur-lined hood pulled tight around his face. He took a moment to catch his breath. Then he told me he'd been out walking his dog. He'd seen my near miss with the truck and subsequent spin out and crash on the side of the road. He was worried someone was hurt so he'd called 911.

"Are you Ok?" he finally asked, his breathing getting toward normal. He was old, maybe seventy. The part of his face I could see was windblown and ice and snow were frozen into his mustache and beard. In spite of all that, he was able to smile a friendly, concerned smile which I appreciated. He seemed like a nice guy.

"Yeah, I'm all right," I told him. "It's my car I'm worried about."

We both looked over at the Ford. Then we looked at each other, neither of us having to say what we both thought. *That car's going to need a tow.*

The guy went to check my car more closely while I stayed back with his dog and fooled around with him, happy that I was going to get some help and get pulled out of the ditch. Then the reality of my situation hit me. *Shit! The moonshine!*

Just then the guy looked in the back of the Ford and yelled back to me. "Man, what you got in here? It smells like someone tipped over a bathtub of rubbing alcohol."

In the background, the sirens got louder. Whether it was cops or an ambulance or both, the end result was going to be the same and it wasn't going to be good. When they got to me hard questions would be asked about the moonshine. Questions I didn't feel like answering.

I took a look at the woods nearby and momentarily thought about making a run for it. I could see myself jumping into nearly twenty inches of snow leaving a nice trail for the cops to follow. Who was I kidding? They'd catch me in no time. I looked around trying to figure out some other way to escape, but it was pointless. The Ford was stuck, I was out in the country in a blizzard and I had nowhere to go. I was as stuck as my car was.

I walked a little ways away from the guy and his dog and turned my back to the wind. I took out my phone and hit speed dial.

Darren answered, "What?"

"We've got a problem," I told him.

"Tell me."

And I did, not realizing it was the last conversation I'd ever have with him. If I'd known, I'd have thanked him for being a friend and for all the other things he'd done for me, Not to get too sappy about it, but I can't help it. He was a good guy who believed in me, gave me a job, and didn't mind me being with his sister. Plus, I liked being around him.

But I didn't say any of that. All I said after telling him what had happened was, "Goodbye." And when I was hanging up the only thing he said to me was this: "Be safe." And that was that.

Then I went back to the Ford, stood around in the snow, shot the breeze with the old guy who introduced himself to me as Arnie Sample, and waited for the sirens to get to us. I even played around with Arnie's dog some more, a friendly border collie named Skittles if I remember correctly. In thinking back to that night, I can only say this. I was certainly pretty naive. I didn't have a clue how much my life was about to change.

It was the cops who arrived first and when they did they took one look in the back of the Ford and they knew right away they had the guy who'd been running moonshine throughout the western metropolitan counties. It didn't take a lot of detective work. The whiskey had broken up in its hiding place under the back seat and leaked out all over the inside of the car. It was even dripping out under the bottom of the backdoor into the snow. You could smell it from ten feet away even with the wind.

They found the false bottom under the seat in about thirty seconds and two minutes later I was in the back of the cop car heading for the county jail in Buffalo, about ten miles from where I'd been standing and twenty miles from Steph and Darren's place. One of the cops called on the way in and told the ambulance not to bother. I hunched up in the corner of the backseat. At least I was warm.

I was booked and held on bail that I couldn't pay, so I remained in jail until my trial right around Christmas time. The judge wasn't happy with anyone breaking both state and federal laws by making moonshine, so I got two years in prison in Stillwater. Happy holidays to me.

What happened to Darren, Steph, and the crew? They got away. How did they do that, you might ask? Easy. I didn't rat them out.

"No, it's just me and no one else," I told the judge and anyone else who would listen to me. Even my public defender. "I'm just an independent guy living an independent life doing my own independent thing," I said over and over again, trying to create a believable image of myself.

"And I'm not telling you where I make it either," I emphasized whenever anyone asked, which they did a lot, believe me. Which I'm sure didn't help my case but I didn't care. I thought of Darren as my friend, and Steph...well, let's just say I thought of her as lots more than just a friend. I wanted to protect them both.

The cops were smart. I'm positive they didn't believe a country bumpkin like myself could pull off an extensive whiskey-making operation and they were right. But one thing going for me was that I think they thought I was a little nuts, so maybe that gave them enough reason, if not to believe me a hundred percent, at least give them enough wiggle room to pretend that they had the right guy. So that was good. And in the end, no matter what the cops thought, at least dealing with me took their attention away from Steph and Darren, and that's all I wanted them to do.

The only wrinkle in my plan to keep Darren and Steph safe was the Ford. If I was afraid it would be traced back to Darren, it showed how I had underestimated him. It turned out the plates were stolen. The VIN had been acid removed (probably by that guy in St. Cloud who'd done the overhaul.) And the car for obvious reasons was not registered.

So my friends were safe. I played along with what Darren had done with the car except I made them think it was me that did it, which just made the case against me far worse. But that was all right. By the time the trial was over, try as they might they couldn't shake my story that it was just me running the moonshine business, even though I'm sure the judge and everyone else didn't believe me. There was nothing they could do except make me pay which is what they did. In addition to prison, they confiscated all the money I had in the bank. I guess it went into some general fund for county improvements or something. Like I said, the judge was mad at me. Anyway, by the time it was all over I was left with nothing except my old Chevy. Apparently, no one thought it was worth much and they were probably right.

I did my time in Stillwater Prison which is east of Minneapolis and St. Paul on the St. Croix River, the border between Minnesota and Wisconsin. All the time I was incarcerated I never once heard from Darren or Steph. Which bummed me out initially, but I figured, what the hell, they probably had their reasons.

When my eighteen months were over (reduced by six months because of time off for good behavior, which made me feel sort of proud) did I expect to see them when I was released? I didn't know, but I'll tell you this, I secretly hoped I would. It was the images I concocted in my mind of Steph and me living a peaceful life somewhere on a little farm in the country that helped keep me going while I was whiling away my time in Stillwater trying to stay safe and sane and working in the laundry. Just like my mom used to do, except not in prison, of course.

Steph was primarily in my mind all those months, but it was also thinking about my friendship with Darren that helped too.

I spent many idle hours laying in my prison bunk remembered nights at his place after my deliveries, sitting out back at the fire pit behind the barn, me and him and Steph, talking, smoking his weed, watching the moon and the stars, and hanging out. We all even played three-handed cribbage occasionally. He was as close a friend as I'd ever had in my life, and I'm not ashamed to say that I missed him.

So when I was finally released and stepped out into a warm spring morning a year and a half after my spin out in a snowstorm on a back country road in a rural part of the county and didn't see either Steph or Darren, to be perfectly honest I was a little disappointed.

I stood in the bright sun while holding a plastic bag containing my few belongings. I killed some time, looking around the big parking lot for maybe half an hour, watching cars and trucks come and go, sometimes even taking a recently released inmate with them. But no one came for me.

Finally, I gave up and walked the two miles from the prison into the river town of Stillwater. I'd earned a couple of hundred bucks working in the laundry so I used some of it to take a series of buses back to Orchard Lake, getting in late that afternoon.

While in prison I had kept in touch with both the service station and the hardware store. Charlie Swant gave me my old job back at the station, telling me he always thought I was a pretty good mechanic, which was nice to hear.

Jerry Sorenson, the owner of the hardware store and my landlord, let me rent my old apartment. I was touched that he'd kept it for me. "I liked the way you fixed it up, Ron. You're welcome to it if you want."

I took him up on his offer. I only had to move a bunch of stuff out he'd been storing there. I aired it out, too. The place stunk kind of mildewy.

Charlie Swant had always liked my Chevy. He'd offered to buy it from me after I was sentenced and I thought it was a good idea. I figured my treasured car wouldn't do me any good while I was in prison so I told him he had a deal. I sold it to him just before I was transferred to Stillwater. He told me he'd hold the money until I was released so the state wouldn't take it which he did, and he gave it to me after I got back to town. It was nice to have some cash. I reopened my old bank account and put the money in it.

So within a few days, I had a job, a place to live, and some money in the bank. I was starting to build my life back again.

About a week after I returned, I was working an afternoon shift at the station when Charlie took me aside and put a friendly arm around my shoulder. He was nearly sixty years old and always treated me like the son he never had. "Good to have you back, Ron. You doing Ok?"

It felt great to be free of prison and be able to do whatever I wanted to do, I can tell you that. "Yeah, it is," I told him and I meant it.

He smiled at me and nodded. "That's good."

We were both quiet then, neither of us much for making idle conversation. But he had something on his mind and after a minute he looked at me kind of funny. "What?" I asked him.

"After I got your car, I put it away in storage for a year. Last winter I took it out and got it running, got it painted, and all of that. Looks real nice."

Yeah, put another knife in my heart, is what I was thinking. "I'm glad," I told him, not actually meaning it. I really had loved that car.

Sensing my mood, he quickly hurried on. "Anyway, I forgot that I found this under the carpet mat on the floor in the back." He shoved a small, pink envelope into my hands. It was addressed to me with a heart drawn around my name. "I guess it's for you." He must have noticed something in my expression, so he added, "Take a few minutes if you want. Then get back to that oil change." He shook his head and gave me what looked like a sad expression. Then left me alone, thinking it had to be bad news.

If he only knew.

It was Steph's handwriting. I kid you not when I tell you that my heart leaped and started pounding in my chest like one of those kettle drums I saw a guy play once on television. Then my hands started shaking. I was so excited I didn't know what to do. Finally, I went out back of the station for some privacy. It was warm in the springtime sun. Across the street, Orchard Lake was blue and fresh looking and its surface sparkled like diamonds in the bright sunlight. There were a few boats on it with people fishing. It was a beautiful day, the kind of day that would be perfect for good news. But if was bad news? Oh, man...if it was, I didn't think I'd be able to take it.

I sniffed the envelope, thinking it might have a scent like Steph's, but it didn't. It smelled like my old Chevy and a gas station, but hell, it'd been a year and a half so what'd I expect?

As I held the envelope images of Steph suddenly came flooding back. The good times we'd had like riding in the Ford out in the country and making deliveries, hanging out in the county parks and making out and fooling around, stopping on dusty back roads near old farmhouses and imagining buying one and fixing it up for ourselves. All the plans I'd made and that we'd talked about and that she'd been on board with. So many of them. I'd never been closer to anyone in my entire life and I doubted I ever would be again. If there was such a thing as *The love of your life,* she was it for me.

But, be that as it may, I had reluctantly talked myself into believing she was gone forever. I'd borrowed Charlie's station's service truck the day after I'd come back to Orchard Lake and driven it out to their trailer just to see what there was to see. I didn't have to go any further than to pull off to the side of the road at the entrance to the weed-choked driveway. The trailer was dilapidated and uncared for, with rust stains running down the siding under the windows. Grass and brush and weeds had grown up all around the property and the place had the feeling of total abandonment. It was easy to see it had been vacant for a long time. After a few minutes, I turned around and drove back to the station feeling more alone than I had felt when I'd been in prison. It was a bad feeling. I was convinced that she and Darren were long gone and I'd never see them again.

Now there was this note. I took a deep breath to calm myself, opened the envelope, and unfolded a small piece of pink paper. It read, "Go out to the shed and look under the floorboard on the northwest corner. Love, Steph."

Love, Steph?

Well, well, well...maybe all was not lost.

I'm not sure how I got any more work done the rest of that afternoon. My heart was racing so badly that I thought it was going to have a heart attack. What had she left for me? My mind flew but I couldn't think of anything. What I wanted was to see her and hold her and be with her but of course that was out of the question. No one in town had heard from her or Darren since I'd been tried and sentenced. They had completely vanished. What would I find in that shed?

I had to wait until after my shift was over to find out. When it was I borrowed the service truck again and drove out to the farm.

Their grandparent's house was still there. The lawn looked freshly cut and the premises were well cared for. This time I stopped in and said a quick "Hi" to them. They were nice people and never had any idea what Darren had been up to on their property.

"Have you seen Steph and Darren?" I asked.

They hadn't, only telling me that Darren sent them money every month with no return address.

"So we can stay here on the farm," their grandmother told me.

"Until the day we die," the granddad added.

They both laughed at their little joke. Like I said, I always thought there were nice folks.

After I said goodbye, I went to the shed like I'd been instructed. The door was closed and the padlock was hanging so it looked like it was locked but it wasn't. I removed it and pulled on the door. It creaked on its hinges and I had to pull hard, but I finally got it open. The inside probably hadn't seen the light of day since Steph and Darren had left but there was still that faint grease and oil aroma I'd smelled the first time I'd been there to see the Ford. It smelled just as good.

With the door open, I looked inside. Yikes! I had a start I'll tell you, because what I was looking at was a dirty sheet with the shape of a car under it just like back that first time with the Ford. I took a moment to collect myself. What the hell was going on? Was I dreaming or something? Or was someone playing a sick joke on me? If they were it was too strange to be even remotely funny.

I hesitated for just a moment before my curiosity got the better of me. I reached out, my hand trembling. I half expected to see the old Ford underneath except I knew that wasn't possible. It probably had been junked long ago by the county. I pulled the sheet off and as it fell to the ground and revealed what was underneath I gasped, not believing what I saw. It was something I never in a million years expected to see. It was a bright and shiny, teal and white, 1957 Chevy! I was stunned beyond all belief and nearly fainted. But I didn't and, instead, reached out with a shaking hand and touched the hood just to make sure it was real. It was.

I was speechless with wonder. It looked so cool! Just like it was brand new. My eyes quickly scanned over the surface, taking in its glossy beauty, the depth of the paint, the shimmery glow, and the smooth feel of the refurbished steel. To say that it was incredible would not begin to do justice to what I saw before me. It was the best-looking restored automobile I'd ever seen, and I'd seen a lot of them. It was perfect.

Then I noticed an envelope addressed to me under a wiper on the windshield. I opened it and it read, "This is for all the hassle. I'm not sure how well it will run after two years, but if anyone can fix it, you can. Thanks for not ratting us out. Darren."

Well, I never.

I went around to the side and opened the door and sat down in the driver's seat. Darren must have put some peppermint inside to keep the mice away. It smelled good and looked even better. The interior was completely redone: the seats were teal and white like the outside, and the dash panel was shining teal and chrome. He'd left the key on the floor and even though I knew it wouldn't start I had the feeling that all the electrical lights and wipers would work as well as the radio. (When I got it running, they did.) It even had a new, white steering wheel.

I took a deep breath and let it out. The car was just like I imagined my old Chevy would have looked like if I'd been able to restore it like I wanted. But this was even better because it was from Darren. Right away I thought of that guy up in St. Cloud who had done the work on the Ford. A smile spread over my face. Darren had taken it upon himself to do something nice for me. He hadn't forgotten about me. To say I was touched by his generosity would be putting it mildly.

Something made me turn and look in the back seat, and when I did I couldn't believe what I saw. It was my old straw cowboy hat. Steph must have saved it from my apartment and put it there to surprise me. Boy did she ever. It was a touching gesture and made me feel as good as the car did, even better in some ways. Well, in most ways, actually. Neither Steph nor Darren had forgotten about me. I reached back to pick the hat up and put it on and when I did I smiled at the memories that came flooding back to me. Memories of Steph, Darren, and me together. I sat there in the front seat reliving the best times I'd ever had in my life. I sat there for a long time.

Finally, I forced myself back into the real world. Steph's note had told me be go back in the corner of the shed so that's what I did next. I got out of the Chevy and found the loose floorboard and pried it up. Jammed under the floor joists was a plastic bag wrapped up and bound with duct tape and twine. I took it out and used my pocket knife to cut it open. It took a minute to realize what I held in my hands. It was a thick bundle of money. I quickly fanned it out and couldn't believe what I saw. It was a stack of one-hundred-dollar bills. It took me maybe five minutes to count all up and when I had finished it came to just over twenty thousand dollars. Twenty thousand dollars!

Along with the money there was another note from Steph. "We moved the operation to Iowa. Here's the address. I'm so sorry about everything. Hope to see you soon."

No, 'Love, Steph,' this time but I didn't care. She hadn't forgotten about me. I knew right then and there what I had to do.

It took me less than a month to get my new Chevy running again, which was easier than I thought it'd be after sitting in the shed for a year and a half. Once I put on a new set of white sidewall tires, cleaned out the carburetor, put in new plugs, and tuned her up she was ready to go.

On the day I was set to leave I checked to make sure the twenty thousand dollars Darren had given me was safely hidden on the floor under my car seat. It was. Then I shook hands and said a final goodbye to Charlie and my landlord. "I've got a job lined up," I told them both. "Got a chance to make some serious money."

I'd told them all of that probably ten times before, but they were gracious enough to pretend I hadn't. They both told me to take care of myself and I told them I would.

Then I got in my Chevy, put on my straw cowboy hat, and started her up. The engine rumbled through the glass-packed mufflers and twin tailpipes and sounded like it would kick a little ass if I needed it to. I sat for a minute imagining for about the thousandth time since I'd read Steph's note what might lay ahead for me. I was headed to Iowa, the land of corn fields and rolling hills and old farmhouses. I was going to find Steph and get back with her and with Darren and the crew. My dream was alive again. I'd work for Darren, save up my money, and Steph and I would find a place of our own to fix up and live in, an old farmhouse somewhere out in the country. Life would be good.

Darren was the best friend I'd ever had. Steph was the best girlfriend I'd ever had. In fact, I was convinced she was my true love. The love of my life. I didn't want to lose her again. We were meant to be together, of that I was sure.

I juiced the accelerator and listened to the motor purr. I'd done a good job getting her running. I had the sudden thought that maybe I'd use the Chevy for the moonshine deliveries in Iowa. But then again, maybe Darren would want me to use some old beater of a car like we'd done with the Ford. It'd be less suspicious. Anyway, whatever he wanted, that's what I'd do.

I looked out the windshield, resting my hands on the steering wheel. I could see my future playing out before me and I liked what I was seeing. I was sure I was ready for it, especially with Steph by my side. Then, out of the blue, I suddenly made a decision I'd been thinking about ever since my first day in prison if not way before then. It was something I'd been imagining off and on for what seemed like forever, and right then and there at that moment, I decided I was going to do it. That decision was this: when I found

Steph, I was going to ask her to marry me. Then we'd be together for the rest of our lives. Then life would be perfect.

I put a big grin on my face, adjusted my cowboy hat, put my car into drive, and turned onto the highway. In a few minutes, I was out of town. It felt good to have a plan and to be on my way. I brought the Chevy up to speed, hardly paying any attention to the corn fields streaming by on either side as I took a county road out toward the interstate. I rolled the window down and cracked the side vent to get a breeze on my face. The sun was shining and the air felt fresh and clean. I was on my way to Iowa. Hopefully, a year from now I'd have enough money saved to put a down payment on a place with Steph. All I had to do was drive those back country roads and make deliveries of moonshine, just like I'd done here in Minnesota. I could do that in Iowa. Easy.

I pushed the Chevy faster, eager to get back with my friends as soon as I could. Then I had a sudden, sobering thought. I remembered my last delivery for Darren and the snow storm, the blizzard and the wind and the truck's headlights and my spin out and getting stuck and getting caught by the cops and finally being thrown into prison. There'd be snow in Iowa in the winter too, just like in Minnesota. The driving conditions would be just as slippery and just as treacherous. I made a pact with myself that this time I'll be extra careful on those Iowa back roads. No more accidents for me. No sir. And no more jail time either. Lesson learned. This time I'll keep my eyes on the road and treat that moonshine whiskey with the respect it deserved. And this time, for sure, I'll watch out for the ice.

The Fruitaholic

"I'd like to introduce you to Jesse. This is his first meeting." Noah gives me an encouraging smile. Then he moves off to the side and stands against the wall.

I get up slowly, feeling the muscles in my thighs stretch and my knees crack. At the sound, I self-consciously laugh out loud. "Sorry about that," I say, trying to make a joke. I look to my left where maybe a dozen people are seated in folding chairs in the small room. For some reason, I notice three of them: a guy about sixty with long, stringy hair and a full grey beard, a thin, prim-looking woman about forty in black, horned-rimmed glasses, wearing a green dress and a string of pearls around her neck, and a young kid with a buzz cut and facial piercings who looks to be maybe sixteen. Those three and everyone else just stare back at me. I'm one hundred percent on display and out of my element. Plus, I feel like I'm some kind of a nutcase for being here. Maybe I am. But one thing is for certain. No one laughs at my feeble joke.

I feel a hot blush rise from under my shirt up my neck and all the way to my ears. *Tough crowd*, I think to myself as I take three steps to the front of the room and turn to face them.

"Hey," I say, stammering a little. Like most everyone in the world, speaking in front of people gives me the willies. I look over at Noah Langston, my sponsor. He gives me an encouraging smile, nodding at me to go ahead. I cough to clear my throat and start again. "Hi, everyone. My name's Jesse," I say, happy my voice sounds more confident than I feel. "I'm a Fruitaholic."

"Hi, Jesse." The voices of all these unknown strangers drone back at me, filling me with trepidation. I'm suddenly petrified and not sure I'm ready to do this.

I fight back an urge to run and glance again at Noah. I'm sure he can read my mind so he gives me another smile and a thumbs up with both hands. Two thumbs up. I appreciate his vote of confidence. He's serious about me taking this first step on what I hope is the beginning of the road to recovery. I take a deep breath and begin, looking down at my feet, somehow taking comfort in seeing my worn, black, tennis shoes.

"Hi. Like I said, I'm Jesse and I'm here to tell you my story."

I glance up and make eye contact with a picture on the back wall that looks like a demented clown from a Stephen King novel. Thinking to myself, *That's exactly how I feel*, I begin talking. "I'm forty-seven years old and have been married twenty-five years to a wonderful woman named Iris. I have three great kids. My son's name is Joe, and my two daughters are Karin and Cate, all three of whom live in the Minneapolis and St. Paul area, and all three of whom are healthy, well-adjusted people. I work at the same job I've had for twenty-three years as a senior technician for Lakeside Industries where me and the team I'm on maintain all the computer systems for the company. We make boots and moccasins. You may have heard of us. Anyway, Iris and I have lived in Orchard Lake out west of here near Lake Minnetonka since we got married. Like I said, that was twenty-five years ago."

I pause and let my eyes rove away from the clown picture on the back wall to the opposite side of the room. I zero in on a photograph of downtown Minneapolis at night, the lights beautifully illuminating the city skyline which for some reason fills me with a sense of comfort. I am unable (or unwilling) to make eye contact with the people in the room. For now, all I can do is push back my fear and keep talking. I take a deep breath, let it out, and continue.

"So on paper, my life looks good, right? Well, it's not. Several years ago, um, eleven years, eight months, and five days, to be exact. I remember the day like it was yesterday. I began my love affair with fruit. It happened innocently enough at a neighborhood picnic, and it involved a huge bowl of red seedless grapes.

"I was talking to a neighbor when I casually reached into the bowl, picked out a grape, popped it in my mouth, and ate it. No big deal, right? Then I grabbed another grape, popped it in, and ate it. Then another one, then another, and another, and then more and more. Then I started grabbing grapes with both hands and stuffing them into my mouth, and then...well, I couldn't stop. In a matter of minutes, I'd consumed every single grape.

"I remember holding the bowl in my lap, seeing it empty except for some water and a few leftover stems floating in the bottom, and thinking to myself, *What the hell just happened here?* Before I could come up with an answer, I remember Iris standing next to me saying, 'Jesse, let me take that, and then let's get you home. You don't look too good.' She pried the bowl from my grasp, put her arm around my shoulder, and led me away. She told me later that the neighbors were pretty freaked out.

"I'd never eaten so much fruit at one time before in my whole life and I'll tell you one thing right now, I didn't sleep too well that night."

I quit talking as I finally got the nerve to look around the room. Most people were watching me intently, encouraging me, and nodding back. All except for one guy around thirty with a goatee and black-framed glasses who had fallen asleep. It seemed almost everyone in the room could relate to what I'd done in some way, shape, or form. It gave me the courage to go on.

"I guess that bowl of grapes was the beginning. I can't for the life of me figure out what caused me to do such a thing and my shrink couldn't figure it out either. I started seeing him a few months after my first overdose of those grapes when it became plain that I couldn't control my desire for fruit on my own. It was

Iris's idea. 'You need help, Jesse,' is what she told me, and I have to say that I agreed with her."

By the way, my shrink's name is Dr. Rosenblum, but I'm not supposed to use names in the group. That's what Noah told me anyway, so I didn't during my talk and, to be honest, I'm kind of surprised I remembered not to blurt it out, but I did. Remember, that is.

"You're definitely addicted, Jesse," Dr. Rosenblum told me after we'd talked awhile during our first session. "I've never had a case like this before, but you are clearly on your way to becoming an addict. A Fruitaholic."

I look up and glance out over the crowd again. Their encouraging looks help me to go on. "I have to say, the first time my shrink uttered those words, 'Fruitaholic,' I laughed out loud. I still do, on occasion, but the sad fact of the matter is this. He was right. I am a Fruitaholic. I'm addicted to fruit and that addiction has almost ruined my life."

Again, sage nods from everyone. Even Mr. Goatee, who had woken up, joins in.

I suddenly realized I had said all I had to say. I look at Noah and he smiles an encouraging smile and gives me one thumbs up and motions me from the front. I go to my chair and sit down, wiping the sweat from my brow. I hadn't realized I'd been perspiring so much. I take a deep breath and exhale. I am emotionally exhausted. Completely drained. Noah conducts the rest of the meeting, but I don't remember a thing he says.

When it's over, I stand up and make small talk with a thin, energetic, man named Randy who's in his forties. He has a nicely trimmed mustache and more energy than any three people I know. The guy jumps around so much as he tells me about his job in finance, shifting from one foot to the next, that I get dizzy. When he mentions that he runs marathons as a hobby I have no doubt he's probably won a few. I sit down and recover my equilibrium after he hops off to talk with Mr. Goatee. Noah strolls up to me and says, "Ready to go, Jessie?"

Was I ever. I nod that I am, realizing that I'm falling into the nodding habit of the other fruitaholics. Maybe I really did belong. Maybe...but I am too tired to contemplate the possible ramifications.

"Can we go get some coffee or something?" I ask. "I'm kind of wiped out."

Noah, bless him, takes me by the arm. "Let's go downstairs to the coffee shop. My treat."

I gladly follow him out of the meeting room and down the stairs. I can't believe how fried I suddenly am.

Leon Silverman is a meth-head who cleaned up his act fifteen years ago and decided 'Give back to the community,' as he purportedly once said, just prior to the beginning of a series of relapses that are still going on to this day. I met him once and he's a nice guy, just a little hyper for my taste, but still a pretty decent person. Thankfully, the coffee shop he opened is still going strong. It's in a two-story, white frame house built in the twenties in the Linden Hills neighborhood of southwest Minneapolis. It's called Jumping Jack Java (a nod to his favorite band The Rolling Stones) and the first floor is a hip, trendy, place with slanted wooden floors and mismatched, but comfortable, furniture.

It's usually packed with Gen Y'ers plugged into their electronic world, but it's also home to all sorts of other folks. You're likely to see young mothers with their kids parked next to them in strollers, businessmen conducting meetings or working on their laptops, people visiting with friends, folks sitting alone and reading, and sometimes even the occasional baby boomer hippie, nursing a cold cup of coffee, staring into space before putting pen to paper, jotting down a line or two of poetry. And, now that I think about it, just about every other kind of person and generational nametag in between. In addition to great coffee, it's a pretty good place to settle in for an hour or two of people-watching. But that's not why I am now sitting at a table with Noah nursing a mug of French Roast.

The upper floor is composed of small meeting rooms and that's where the Minnesota Chapter of Fruitaholics Anonymous meets every Tuesday night from seven to eight. After the meeting was over Noah suggested we go downstairs, get a cup of coffee, and talk, that's where we headed. Noah was sipping a mocha and munching on a chocolate chip cookie, while I chose plain oatmeal (no raisins, for obvious reasons) to go with the French Roast.

"So how do you think it went?" he asked blowing on his steaming mug, taking his time between sips, his dark eyes watching my every move.

I like Noah a lot. He's in his mid-fifties, has a bushy brown beard, and keeps his head shaved and oiled. He looks kind of like Alan Ginsburg. In contrast, I'm pretty normal-looking. I'm just under six feet, have a bit of a paunch, thinning hair, and am clean-shaven. All in all, pretty unremarkable. He's a retired airplane pilot, happily married, and enjoys swing dancing with Lois, his wife of over thirty years. He's tall and thin, favors plaid shirts and black jeans, and wears wire-rim glasses, keeping with the Ginsburg look. I like blue jeans, the aforementioned tennis shoes, and tee shirts. The flannel shirt thing with him I kind of dig and have started wearing them myself. He looks intellectual and he's quite smart but doesn't make a big deal out of it.

In short, he's a good guy and easy to talk with, and we hit it off right away. He's also kind, thoughtful, and caring, traits I'm not possessed with in massive amounts. Well, hardly any amount to be honest, but Noah is working with me on that.

"If you're willing to try to help yourself," he's told me time and time again, "and meet me halfway, I'll do everything I can to help you."

I guess you can't ask for anything more than that.

"I don't know," I say in answer to his question about how the meeting went. "Fine, I guess."

I really don't have a clue, to be honest. I was so nervous while I standing in front of the group that I mostly just spewed out a bunch of stream-of-consciousness stuff. If I had my talk on tape I'd probably puke listening to it. "What do you think?" I ask, stalling for time. In the back of my mind, I'm wondering if maybe he's gearing up to tell me he can't do anything for me. After a performance like mine, I wouldn't blame him.

But Noah isn't like that at all. As my sponsor, he is sincerely committed to helping me come to grips with my addiction and to finding ways to help me cope with it. He takes a sip of coffee before answering. "It was Ok," he says, a little hesitantly for my money. Then he takes another sip and sets his mug down before thoughtfully continuing. "You gave them a nice overview of yourself and your family and job and life. That was good." I smiled at him, thinking that he was going to compliment me further. But I was going to be disappointed because he didn't. "My biggest concern," he said, "is that I don't think you're taking your addiction very seriously." He looked at me hard. "Or the meeting either, for that matter."

Ouch. So, compliment then. Well, at least he was being honest.

I laughed out loud. Maybe, in retrospect, it was a sign that he was correct in his observation about me not taking the meeting seriously. "What do you mean?" I ask, trying not to sound defensive. "I did the best I could."

Noah took a quick sip of coffee and then set the mug aside. "Well, for starters, you made a few jokes about being addicted throughout your talk. Now, don't get me wrong, having a sense of humor about it is good. Really good, in fact. But in the beginning, like where you are now with getting sober and staying sober, well, your joking came across as disingenuous. In other words, like you aren't taking your addiction sincerely and using jokes and humor to hide the truth."

"The truth?" I stare right at him, trying to be assertive and probably failing, because deep down I know he's right. "What do you mean by the truth?"

"It's plain and simple," Noah says, taking another sip of coffee, giving me time to think about what he's saying. "I don't think you think you have a problem."

Well there you go, I think to myself. The cat's finally out of the bag. Forget about being defensive. I'm opening my mouth to defend myself when Noah cuts me short. "When was the last time you had some fruit?" he asks pointedly, his eyes probing mine.

I wilt under his intense gaze, "Three days ago," I confess. "Last Saturday night. I ate a bowl of strawberries."

"Was that all?"

"And an apple or two." I pause and then add. "Well, seven."

"And..."

"And nine bananas," I whisper. "I drove to an all-night convenience store and bought every single one of them that they had." Noah looks at me sadly, slowly shaking his head. He opens his mouth to speak, but I quickly jump in and interrupt before he can say something like, 'See what I mean?' Instead, I blurt out, "But that's all I ate! "I swear!" For some reason I cross my heart, something I hadn't done since I was maybe eight or nine years old. I can hear the pleading tone in my voice, a tone I'm not proud of.

Noah shrugs, reaches across the table, and touches my arm in a show of solidarity. "I get it, Jesse. I really do. Staying sober isn't easy. It requires, first and foremost, commitment on your part." He sighs and sits back and thoughtfully munches on his cookie. Then he quickly sits up straight and slaps the table with both hands, startling me. "So we have a lot of work to do. It's going to require time and commitment." He looks at me, challenging me, and asks, "Are you up for it?"

I think back to last Saturday night and my bout with the strawberries and the apples and the bananas. A bout I had lost. I'd ended up passed out on the floor with strawberry juice all over my face. The cramps in my stomach the next morning were unbearable. I had made a fool of myself in front of Iris, yet again. The entire episode had been another embarrassment in an increasingly long line of embarrassments.

I make my decision. "I am," I say, crossing my heart. Again! "I swear to you, man, I really am."

"OK," he says, grinning at me and rubbing his hands together. "Let's get started."

***

Most people would think being addicted to fruit was not all that big a deal. Hell, fruit is supposed to be good for you, right? Well, in one sense it is of course, especially when combined with grains and proteins. It makes for a healthy diet and everyone knows that. But the issue is not really fruit in its most elementary sense as a basic food group. The real issue for someone like me and my fellow Fruitaholics is the addictive behavior associated with our desire for fruit; when that desire (like the innocent enjoyment of a ripe pear or a sweet, juicy, peach) becomes such a powerful force that it literally takes over your life; when your thoughts every moment day and night are consumed with fruit and 'When will I get some?' (Hopefully, soon) and, 'How long can I go without succumbing to my desire for it?' (Hopefully, more than a few minutes.)

Noah put it well when we were talking later that night when he said, "It's not fruit in and of itself that's the issue. It's thinking about it all the time that's the real problem. The desire gets in your head and overwhelms you. All you think about is, 'Where's my next fix coming from?'" He used his fingers to finger quote *fix*. He looks at me, his gaze deep and intense. "And do you know why?" he asks.

When he's talking to me like this, it's like a teacher-student thing. I kind of like it. His confidence is reassuring, but I still don't have a clue as to where he's headed. "Not really," I say.

"Come on, Jesse. You're a smart guy. Think about it."

I appreciate his vote of confidence regarding my intelligence, something I would rate as a C+ at best. But I take a stab at answering him anyway. "Because that's all I do," I tell him. "I don't do any work. I don't have meaningful conversations with people. I'm distant from those I love and who love me, and not a lot of fun to be around. In a nutshell, I'm trapped by my thoughts of fruit, constantly thinking about when the next time will be that I'll be able to get some." I'd read enough self-help pamphlets and addiction-related books to take an educated guess as to what Noah was getting at.

"Exactly," he says. In my mind, I go *Bingo!* Noah continues. "It takes over your whole life. All you do is think about where your next *fix* (finger quotes, again) is coming from; whether you're awake and thinking about fruit or sleeping and dreaming about it. You understand what I'm telling you, right?"

I nod my head. "Yeah, I get that."

"Really?" he asks skeptically. "I'm not sure you do." I can feel perspiration suddenly forming under my armpits. At the rate this evening is going, what with all the sweating at the meeting and now this with Noah, I'm on my way to becoming severely dehydrated. I take another sip of coffee and think about what he's said. I hate to be challenged, especially when I'm trying to dodge the truth. He shakes his head sadly, "Apparently you don't get it enough to be serious enough to do anything about it. Remember what you told me about what happened at work a year or two ago?"

Oh. So that's what he was getting. That incident at Lakeside. The memory comes roaring back with a vengeance.

In the early days of my addiction, I had been able to keep my cravings for fruit under control, especially at my place of employment, sneaking an apple here, a slice of watermelon there, and not making a big deal out of it around the people I worked with. But that all went out with the bathwater a year and a half ago after I had a rather troubling experience with blueberry pie at a company dinner.

I had been approached by my boss, Ellen Downs, who told me she wanted me to give a presentation about the new data processing system we were going to be installing at Lakeside Industries the following year. All of the salespeople would be linked to it and it would help manage inventory more accurately and...blah, blah, blah.

"Just give the audience a basic overview, Jesse, and try not to bore everyone to death. I'll give you ten minutes."

I assumed she was joking about the boring *people-to-death* comment (although with her it was always hard to tell), so I laughed a little and watched her reaction carefully. When she didn't respond and stared back at me with a severe expression, I hastened to reassure her, and said with more bluster than was probably necessary, "Bore people to death? Me? Not on your life. It'll be a great presentation." I tried to sound confident, all the while deep down I was doing my best to believe the words I was saying, especially given my aforementioned fear of speaking in front of people.

She patted me on the top of my and said, "Good boy." Just like you'd say to a dog. No getting around it, now that I think about it. Why beat around the bush? She was a jerk.

I was worried I was going to botch my talk and Ellen the head-patter would be mad and take it out on me by not giving me a much-needed bump in my salary come performance review and raise time, so I did my best not to let my nervousness get the better of me. And, miracle of miracles, I also managed to stay sober and clean for nearly a week leading up to the event, with only the occasional lusting glance at rows of kumquats on display in the food line of the company cafeteria, newly arrived bing cherries at the grocery store to tempt me, which I'm happy to say I valiantly fought off. And that was a good thing. I was pretty proud of myself, thinking maybe I had finally become strong enough to fight for and maintain my fruit sobriety.

The dinner was an occasion to celebrate the end of the company's fiscal year. It was held at the beginning of October and was historically a chance for salespeople and managers to celebrate and blow off steam. The Big Wigs at Lakeside rented a huge banquet room at the four-star Hilton Hotel in downtown Minneapolis. There were twenty-five round tables with twenty employees seated at each - salespeople, managers of all levels, and support staff, including us technicians.

The atmosphere was festive with classic rock music piped in through overhead speakers. Food and alcohol were flowing freely and in no time everyone in the room was happy and relaxed and loudly on their way to becoming intoxicated. Everyone but me. Not only was I a committed teetotaler when it came to alcohol (I just didn't like the taste of the stuff), but I was also too nervous to even eat.

Sitting next to me Sam Jacobson, programmer extraordinaire and my best friend at work, slugged down half a bottle of

Budweiser and let out a loud belch before slapping me on the back and laughing loudly. "Hey Jesse man, lighten up will, ya? Have a drink and get with the party. Don't be such a friggin' stick-in-the-mud."

In response to being slapped, I choked on the water I was trying to swallow and sputtered. "I'm just thinking about that damn presentation. You know that talk I have to give?" I coughed and cleared my throat. "I'm worried about it, that's all."

"Hell!" Sam expostulated. "You've got nothing to worry about." He looked around the crowded banquet room as he downed the rest of his Bud. I followed his gaze. The place was packed with people laughing, eating, drinking, and talking at the top of their lungs. The music was cranked to ten or eleven. The entire party was amped up loud and getting louder. "No one cares about what you have to say anyway," he yelled in my ear. "They're all too loaded." He laughed long and hard before collapsing in a fit of coughing. Then he grabbed another bottle of beer from a passing server and took a long, deep swallow, definitely on the way to becoming loaded himself.

Funny guy, I thought to myself as I turned away and back to trying to control the panic rising in my chest. Real funny. I wished I could believe him. But I was a loyal little trouper. Ellen was counting on me to give a professional presentation, which, of course, I hoped to do, and, beyond that, I wanted to do a good job, if not for her and the few people who would be paying attention, at least for myself. In short, I didn't want to come across as a complete idiot.

If I could only get a little help. Something to help build up my courage. Something to help settle me down and calm my nerves. I checked my watch. The time for my presentation was rapidly drawing near. My nerves seemed to have suddenly taken over and were kicking into high gear, causing my stomach to turn cartwheels and my throat to constrict. I coughed to clear it, but it didn't help. This was not good.

With my heart rate going up and sweat beginning to bead up on my forehead, I scanned the room looking for an escape; a way out. Who was I kidding? I was trapped. If I bolted, I'd never hear the end of it and Ellen would have some harsh words for me at the very least, plus a probable demotion and dock in pay at the very most. I had no alternative. I had to suck it up and give that damn presentation.

The sweat began in earnest, seeming to pour out of every pore.

A commotion behind me suddenly caught my attention. Through the swinging doors leading into the room came a parade of at least a dozen servers, each dressed in white and each pushing a heavily laden cart. I was about to turn away from them when I looked closer. I couldn't believe what I saw. Dessert was being served and it wasn't just any old dessert like your traditional bowl of melting orange sherbet or microscopically thin slice of dark chocolate cake. Not even close. It was much, much better. Laid out on those carts were thick individual slices of pie - blueberry pie to be exact, the sides of each slice dripping in berry juice pooling on its plate in purple puddles of splendor. The crusts were shining in a sugary glaze under the bright lights of the banquet room, glistening like diamonds in a high-end jewelry case.

My eyes locked onto them. Hundreds of plates of pie were being paraded through the room right before my very eyes. They were beyond gorgeous - they were a dream come true. I was unable to stop myself as I started to slip, at first just a little, then a little more, then a lot (Damn!), before finally falling off my sober wagon and tumbling headlong into a heap of wanton desire. I wanted each and every one of those beautiful berry-filled delights. And I wanted them now! I grabbed the edge of the table with both hands and held on tight, fighting the good fight of sobriety as I tried to hold firm to my resolve to stay fruit-free.

It occurred to me that while everyone was enjoying their scrumptious dessert, I was going to be standing at a podium on the stage in front of them, speaking into a microphone, talking about *The Future of Automated Servers* which is what my talk was about. Even I got bored thinking about it. I needed some of that pie to help get me through the arduous task that lay ahead.

My eyes zeroed in on individual slices as the servers went around to each table, setting down plates of pie - lovely, mouth-watering pie. Each plate of ambrosia was calling to me like the sweetest of dreams, one slice of pie to a plate, one plate to a person. Over four hundred of those beauties were sharing the room with me. My, my, my. My delectable blueberry pie. From table to table, the servers went, dispensing heavenly gifts around and around the room, until all the tables were laden with dessert - slices of blueberry pie that, each and everyone, seemed to be calling to me. It was a cacophony of fruit, so beguiling, so enticing.

A server set a plate down in front of me. Oh my god, the temptation was so strong I almost gave in to my need and dove in, headfirst. But I didn't. I was still fighting the good fight. Still battling to stay clean. Still holding onto the table with all my might. By now my knuckles had turned white, my hands nearly numb. I pried my eyes away from the pie in front of me and turned to watch my fellow Lakeside employees, wanting to savor vicariously the delicious eating of the pie, the tasting of the beautiful fruit, the wolfing down of that tantalizing dessert.

But what was this? No one was eating! Everyone was neglecting their pie, paying no attention to it at all. I couldn't believe what I was seeing. People had the chance of a lifetime to partake of this luscious, fruit-filled experience and, instead, what were they doing? Well, they weren't eating, that much was for certain. No. Instead, they were (of all of the fool-hearty things) just sitting around talking and laughing and drinking and carrying on as if nothing stupendous was happening. But something was happening: they were giving up their chance to top off the evening with a taste of heaven, a taste of blueberries. A taste of fruit!

In my increasingly confused and befuddled state, I wondered why no one was having their dessert. What was the delay? Were they waiting for me to begin my talk? I looked up to the front of the room where all the top-level managers were seated at a long table. Ellen was holding down a place of honor near the middle and was animatedly talking to Larry Munson, vice-president of operations, her immediate boss and second in command of the company. They seemed very friendly with each other.

During a break in their conversation, she sat back and smugly looked out over the banquet hall, enjoying the opportunity of lording over all of us minions. Her gaze passed over me, and I could tell she refused to make eye contact. It was just the kind of thing she'd do. I checked my wristwatch. I knew it was time to begin my talk; she had told me I was to start when the dessert was served. I was confused. Wasn't she going to introduce me? That was the plan. Should I just get up and go to the stage and start talking without any introduction at all? What did she want me to do?

Sweat beaded on my forehead and started running into my eyes. Next to me, my friend Sam was turned away from me and talking to one of the other technicians. I overheard something about the Vikings, our professional football team. Sam was a diehard fan. God, once some people started talking about sports there was no turning back. He was gone. I knew he'd be no help.

I took a chance and loosened my grip on the table with one hand and wiped the perspiration from my brow. My vision blurred for a moment before it cleared. Then I detected a motion from the front of the room and looked. Ellen had risen and was making her way to the podium. She was wearing a brown suit and sensible shoes. Her short hair had been cut even shorter for the occasion. She looked like a librarian on that fifties television show, *Leave It To Beaver.*

I gripped the table more tightly. As she walked, she looked to her left, her beady eyes making contact with my rather blurry ones, and I swear she snapped her fingers at me. Maybe that's what did it. Maybe something in my brain snapped (well obviously it did, as you are about to find out) because I couldn't help it. Seemingly in another world, I loosened my hold on the table and slowly rose to my feet. I straightened my back and adjusted the lapels of my sports coat with what I felt sure was an air of confident resolve.

Then, instead of walking with a firm and determined step to the front of the room and the awaiting podium and microphone, where I was supposed to turn to the assembled crowd of my peers to offer up my speech in a flowing, melodious voice, what I did, instead, was this: I lost my compose. I lunged to the table next to me and, like a squirrel frantically gathering nuts for the winter, I grabbed one slice of pie, then another, and then another and another, and stuffed each piece in my mouth until my cheeks bulged. I chewed frantically, swallowing as fast as I could to keep from choking, stuffing in more and more fresh pie until my mouth was jammed, the blue juice running down the sides of my face, dripping onto my shirt on its way to the floor.

When I couldn't get any more in, I started stuffing pie into the pockets of my sports coat, and when they were full I stuffed pie into the pockets of my pants. When they were full I somehow ripped open my shirt and started stuffing pie down my front as from one table to another I went, around the room, grabbing slices of pie and stuffing them in my shirt.

When I was done at one table I went on to another one, stuffing pie wherever I could put it, in my shirt, my pockets, and my mouth, gathering slices of pie like a manic squirrel (or a manic Fruitaholic).

When my pockets were full and my shirt bulging, one would think I had nowhere else to put any more pie. Except I did. All the pie I had been and stuffing in my mouth I had swallowed and my mouth was empty. So I casually grabbed a big slice from the nearest plate, opened my mouth wide, crammed it in, and chewed the pie deliberately, masticating it on and on and on until I was finally finished. Then I swallowed and turned to the front table where Ellen and the Big Wigs sat. I gave them a salute, which flung blueberries in a purple arc out in front of me and started walking toward them. What I planned to do, to this day I still have no idea, but as I took my first step, I felt a firm hand on my shoulder. I turned and saw it was Sam.

"Buddy..." he said, anxiously. "Jesse, get a grip on yourself. Calm down." He turned me around so I was facing him. Not a pretty picture I'm sure. Me, with my manic eyes staring back at him. Me, covered in blueberries and blueberry juice and pie crust. Me, completely out of my mind. "Come on, Jesse," he said, firmly gripping my shoulder. "Let's get you out of here."

And that's all I remember.

I awoke in the emergency room of Hennepin County Memorial Hospital in downtown Minneapolis early the next morning. I thought I was alone. I deserved to be. But I wasn't. My long-suffering wife, the ever-patient Iris, was sitting in a chair next to the bed, right by my side.

"Jesse, thank god you're alright. You don't know how worried I was." She stood up, leaned over, and gave me a big hug before sitting back down. She took hold of my hand and looked at me compassionately, taking the measure of her pathetic husband.

It took a minute to get my bearings. When I realized I was in the hospital, I was overwhelmed by a tidal wave of guilt. I had not only let myself down again but also my loved ones. As if reading my thoughts, the next words out of Iris' mouth were these: "Jesse, I'm so afraid for your physical and mental health. You really need to get some help."

I nodded my head contritely and said, "I know." I looked at Iris and tried to convince her with my eyes and my chagrined expression that I meant what I said. "I know," I said, again. "I will."

I must have been successful because, for the first time in a long, long time, my wonderful wife smiled at me as she leaned over and gave me another big hug. "I'm glad," she told me, her lips brushing my neck. "Really glad."

She believed me!

And I wanted to believe in myself. Too bad I was going to let her down. But it would be a while before that happened. Until then, I really did make an effort.

At the time of my company party fiasco, I'd been addicted to fruit for almost ten years and it was obvious that I couldn't continue to try any longer to manage my addiction on my own. And if I ever needed a reminder that I needed help there were dozens of photos and videos posted on social media of me binging on pie, blueberries running down my face, sticking to my clothes, stuck in my hair and hands...blueberries everywhere. Believe me, it was a sight better off not contemplating for long, if at all. (Although the images of me with my purple face smeared in crushed blueberries with blueberry juice dripping off my chin occasionally pop up in my mind, even to this day. Unfortunately.)

But my predicament was made even more disturbing because over the rest of that year and into the next, I still was not able to make myself get the help I needed even though I told Iris I would. Can you believe that? I still can't. And I still can't believe that Iris didn't boot me out of the house. But she didn't. She stayed by my side, ever faithful, trying to help in any way she could, all the while hoping I'd get better.

But I didn't get better because the fact of the matter was that I hadn't hit rock bottom yet. That low point took another year to attain. Another year of binging on whatever fruit was available, and then quitting, and then binging some more, and then quitting, and then binging some more...well, you get the drift. I still can't believe it took that long. And more to the point, I'm surprised anyone close to me (specifically Iris and my kids) continued to have anything to do with me. But they did, and for me to say I'm eternally grateful doesn't even begin to describe the depth of my true feelings.

The final straw came at my youngest daughter's wedding. I had been clean for a few weeks leading up to the big day and feeling pretty good about myself - confident that I had finally turned the corner and could handle any fruit temptations that came my way. I should also say this: I dearly love my children. My oldest boy Joe is twenty-four and works as a graphic arts engineer for a local media design company. Karen is twenty-two and has just started teaching second grade in south Minneapolis. Kate is twenty and works in a used bookstore. She was born with Guillain-Barre syndrome, has limited use in the left side of her body, and has trouble moving her arm and leg, but her affliction has not stopped her from leading a complete and rewarding life. She loves books, loves to read, and has a 'can do' attitude that I'm envious of. She definitely gets it from her mother.

Kate had been working at Old Thyme Books near Macalester College in St. Paul for nearly a year when she met Caleb, a twenty-four-year-old graduate student in American Literature when he came into her bookstore looking for an obscure book by Ralph Waldo Emerson. Kate knew some sources online that Caleb was unfamiliar with and helped him find the book he needed. That was over a year ago. One thing led to another, they fell in love and decided to get married. They wanted an outdoor July wedding and the beautiful Minneapolis Zen Garden near picturesque Lake Harriet in southwest Minneapolis was the perfect location. Iris and I were overjoyed for them.

The day dawned bright and sunny, the kind of picture-perfect Minnesota summer day that makes you feel glad to be alive. The Zen Garden is a contemplative five-acre secluded spot nestled between Lake Harriet and a nearby bird sanctuary. It's also just across the street from the renowned Minneapolis Rose Gardens, and the sweet scent of hundreds of roses in bloom filled the air adding to the splendor of the day. The wedding was set to begin at three in the afternoon. The kids (that's what Iris and I fondly called Kate and Caleb) had written the words for their ceremony and a nondenominational minister would officiate. Three of their friends would provide music - a fiddle, a guitar, and a standup bass.

Everyone was having so much fun and in such good moods, talking and catching up, that the ceremony didn't begin until nearly 3:15 pm. There were maybe forty people there, most of them friends of Kate and Caleb. Iris and I stood in front and off to the side, both of us smiling proudly at this, the first wedding of our three children. We couldn't have been happier.

Did I mention earlier I had been fruit-free for a few weeks? I had been and was feeling pretty good about both my sobriety and myself, confident in my ability to remain on the straight-and-narrow path of zero-fruit indulgence.

About halfway through the wedding, the musicians started a quiet version *of Seven Bridges Road*, a favorite song of mine. My mind started wandering and my eyes followed suit. My gaze traveled across the Zen Garden with its beautiful polished stones, reflecting pool for meditation, and the simple but elegant plantings of yew, cypress, and blue spruce. I felt my heart lift with joy for my daughter. This is what Iris and I wanted for all of our kids, for them to be happy, and it looked like Kate was on her way.

Perhaps I let my guard down. Perhaps I let my overconfidence in my short, few weeks of sobriety get the better of me. I don't know for certain, but what I do know is that I let my gaze travel outside of the peaceful Zen Garden, away from the charming wedding ceremony, and over to the big community garden down the street. It was about fifty yards away, but even from that distance, I could see where people had planted row after row of colorful annuals, verdant vegetables, and...(oh, be still my beating heart) fruit. Luscious fruit. Lovely, gorgeous, scrumptious fruit. I could see canes of blackberries and raspberries and bushes of blueberries; all swollen and ripe and gleaming in the sun. Near to them were rows of strawberries with bright red jewels hanging by their stems, bursting with sugary sweetness. The entire garden was swollen with fruit in abundance and it was all out there waiting, beckoning for me to come to it and indulge.

I know my mind started to go blank and, looking back, I should have been able to control myself. But I couldn't. My heart rate sped up and my body was suddenly bathed in perspiration. I could feel sweat running down my back. I clenched my fists and forced them to my side. Then I put them in my pockets. *Stay the course*, I said to myself. *You've been sober for two weeks. You can't afford to give in. Not now. Not at Kate and Caleb's wedding. Get a grip. Be strong. You can do this.*

I fought a battle with my desire. I fought valiantly. But, I'm sad to say that I was unable to fight hard enough. I was too weak and, in the end, succumbed to my need for fruit.

Iris told me later that she tried to help. "I knew something was up when I looked over at you and saw you weren't even paying attention to Kate's lovely ceremony. I followed your line of vision and when I saw that community garden with all the fruit I knew something bad might happen. I grabbed you by the arm and tried to get your attention. I told you to try and get a hold of yourself. But you were in such a state you didn't hear me. You were already mentally gone.

"Then you bolted from my grasp and ran. You ran faster than I'd ever seen you run before, straight for the fruit in that garden. On the way you even knocked down a little six-year-old girl who was playing in the grass with her puppy. You didn't even stop to see if she was injured. Thank goodness she wasn't. You just ran like a man possessed, straight for that garden. At that moment I was afraid I'd lost you forever."

She told me all of this later that night at the hospital, just before she left to go home after finding out I was going to be alright.

"Will I see you tomorrow?" I asked. I felt horrible. I'd ruined the wedding. I'd let down Kate and Caleb, and I'd disappointed Iris.

"I'll be back to pick you up at nine in the morning and take you home. Then we're going to have a talk." Her voice was firm and no-nonsense. She shook her head in what I could only imagine was disgust, or maybe pity, as she turned on her heel and left my hospital room, saying nothing more, leaving me alone and all by myself.

Oh, shit. I'd really messed up this time.

That night in the hospital was bad and not only because I was dealing with my fruit hangover. I was the loneliest I'd ever felt. I also had a ton of guilt about how poorly I'd acted; how I'd ruined Kate's wedding and let down Iris. But, I have to say, I still felt I was going to get through it okay; that the consequences of my behavior would be negligible, just like all the other times in the past. After all, Iris was coming back the next morning to pick me up and take me home right? If she was going to do that she must have already reconciled herself towards me and what I'd done. Perhaps she'd even forgiven me, just like she'd done so many times in the past.

Shows you how stupid and self-absorbed I really was.

Iris showed up to my room right on time that next morning. She and the nurse got me situated in a wheelchair and Iris pushed it down to the hospital entrance and loaded me into our car. She said nothing to me from the time she entered my room, up to and including the entire forty-five-minute drive home to Orchard Lake. I tried to engage her in conversation but she was having none of it. By the time we arrived home, I was finally beginning to realize that things weren't the way they used to be or were supposed to be. Not by a long shot.

Once inside Iris sat me down on the couch in the living room. I barely had time to get settled when she stepped back, stood up straight and tall right in front of me, and delivered her ultimatum. "This is it, Jesse. We've been married for twenty-five years and nearly half of them you've been an addict. You are addicted to fruit and you say you want to get better, but you don't do anything to try to help yourself. I love you but I'm exhausted and worn out. I can't take it anymore."

She was honest, blunt, and to the point. I'll never forget her words. She didn't cry. She didn't rant and rave or scream and throw stuff which were all things she'd done in the past. No, what she said was, 'I can't take it anymore.' Well, I thought to myself, she's pissed and I don't blame her. But I can deal with that. In fact, how much worse can it get?

Plenty, I found out, because then she added, "If you don't get help, I'm going to leave you. I promise." She pointed her finger right at me to make her point. "I'm done putting up with you and your addictive behavior. You can't get better on your own. You've proven that time and time again. You need professional help and you need it right now."

And here's me, still not convinced I've got that bad of a problem, spreading my arms wide, giving her a big smile, and making a joke out of what she was telling me by saying, "Hey there, honey, it's not so bad. I was sober for two weeks. Give me a chance. I can do it again."

I'll never forget what she did. She said nothing. Instead, she pulled out her iPhone and brought up some photos and videos that people had sent her taken the day before at the ceremony. She held the phone right in front of my face so I wouldn't miss a thing.

As she showed the pictures to me, I was no longer embarrassed by my behavior. I was appalled. The image of a tornado sucking up everything in its path of destruction is an apt vision of me decimating that poor community garden, ripping raspberries and blackberries and blueberries and strawberries from their vines and bushes and branches, gorging myself whether the fruit was ripe or not. A shark tearing into a school of fish is also apt.

But the real-time images of me in a tuxedo on my hands and knees crawling through the dirt, wolfing down any fruit I could get my hands on as if my life depended on it (and in a way it probably did), is an image that will haunt me from the rest of my life.

I looked up from my seat on the couch and gazed into my wife's eyes. She had put up with my behavior for eleven years now. I knew it was time to stop and stop for good. "I will quit, Iris, I swear to god, I will. But please, please, please don't leave me."

I stood up to hold her, hug her, and gain strength from her presence. Iris would have none of it. She put up both her hands to stop me.

"You get sober and stay sober, Jessie. Then we'll talk about what comes next." She put both her hands on my chest and pushed me backward. I fell back onto the couch and watched as she walked out of the room, saying over her shoulder, "You've used up all the extra chances I'm going to give you, buddy. Get help, and get it now."

She walked into the kitchen and slammed the door, leaving me to myself.

Years ago I had quit going to my shrink. Don't ask me why. But I called Dr. Rosenblum that day and had my first session with him two days later. I was willing to do anything to save my marriage.

We did a quick catch-up that lasted about a minute before the good doctor got down to business. The first thing he reminded me of was this: "An addict feeds his addiction, whether it's booze or drugs or, in your case, fruit, to not only satisfy his graving but to give his life meaning."

"That's all?" I asked, thinking there had to be more.

He got mad, his eyes shooting daggers at me. "Of course not."

Well, at least I was right.

"There are all kinds of factors contributing to your addiction," he continued. "And we will look into all of them. But, for you primarily, Jesse, your entire life is focused on fulfilling your hunger and desire for fruit. It has become the focus of all you do. Your wife, your family, your job, they all have become secondary to your figuring out ways to satisfy your desire. Do you understand what I'm telling you?"

I nodded my head. "I do," I said. I meant it. He was right. I saw that now. And if I ever forgot, I had the video taken of me at the wedding ceremony as a reminder.

"If you don't make a change. You will lose everything."

I started perspiring. I didn't want to give up all that was precious to me; Iris, my children, even my job. I had to make that change he was talking about. "What do we do?"

"We will begin right now."

So I started going to regular, weekly, sessions with Dr. Rosenblum, once again, just like eleven years earlier. But this time it was different. This time I really was committed. And, I have to say, it was just like being in school again. Kind of like with Noah. I won't bore you with the details, but the more I understood that not only did I want to change my behavior, but that I was capable of doing it, the better I felt, and the more things began to make sense. It all boiled down to winning back my respect in the eyes of Iris and my three kids. In short, I began making an honest effort or, as we stay in treatment, 'putting in the work.'

I've only just begun and I'll say this: I know I have a lot of work to do, but I have too much to lose if I don't. It may take the rest of my life. I'm told it probably will, but I'm committed to changing my behavior, dealing with my addiction to fruit, and winning back the love of Iris and my children and the respect of the people I work with. It's what my life is all about now.

It was Dr. Rosenblum who introduced me to Noah.

"I believe we are ready for the next step, Jesse," he told me after I'd been seeing him for about seven months. "I've got someone I'd like you to meet." He handed me a slip of paper with Noah's phone number on it, "I think he can help you and do things for you that I can't."

Later that week Noah and I met for the first time. It was at Jumping Jack Java and we were sitting at a table by the window, having coffee and getting to know each other. When he started telling me about Fruitaholics Anonymous and suggested that I start attending their meetings I coughed into my mug before sputtering.

"You've got to be kidding me!" I started laughing as I wiped French Roast from my face, "What kind of a lame group is that, for god's sake?" I took a big bite of the ginger cookie I was eating to make my point.

Nonplussed, Noah said, "It's a group dealing with the same issues you are, Jesse. They're good people." He looked me in the eye and smiled. "I think they might be able to help you," he added, calmly.

After talking about it for a while, I reluctantly agreed, mainly because I was willing to do anything to get a handle on my addiction, even if it meant hanging around with a bunch of...Wait a minute. I was going to say, "Losers," but these were people who had the same problems as me. Perhaps I shouldn't be too quick to judge a book by its cover. I might want to look inside first. Maybe they knew something I didn't. Well, that was obvious, but maybe I could learn from their experiences. I decided to give it a try. And, as long as I was trying, I was going to try to keep an open mind.

***

That was five weeks ago and brings me to where we are now, me sitting in Jumping Jack Java talking with Noah after my first Fruitaholics Anonymous meeting, planning my future. I look across the table at his calm demeanor and say, "Dr. Rosenblum believes he's done all he can for me and I believe him. I'm smart enough to get that I have a problem - a problem that has not gone away in the last eleven-plus years. In fact, despite the effort of Dr. Rosenblum and the extreme patience of Iris and my kids and even people at work, it's only gotten worse. Much worse. And it's all because of me and whatever flaw there is in my makeup that leads me to act the way I do when I'm around fruit." I look at Noah and he is silent, unwilling to interrupt what I'm saying. It's one of the many things I like about him. He's thoughtful and not judgmental.

"What's Rosenblum say?"

"He believes I can get better, I just have to learn to control my desire for fruit." I take a moment, shake my head sadly, and add, I really want to, but it's hard, really hard." I look Noah right in the eye and say, "I'm being as honest with you as I can be. The issue is this: My shrink tells me that I can eventually control my addiction. I tell him that I've tried countless times to get clean, but I can't. Then he reminds me, 'If you don't find a way to fight your addiction, then you will lose your wife and children - those whom you love and care for. Is that what you want?' And when it's put that way, the answer is, of course, no."

I stop talking and shake my head again, wishing suddenly for a wand to make my addiction magically go away. But it's not to be. There's no easy way out. I've got to put in the work and do this on my own. I shake my head again, conscious that all my head shaking is giving me a headache. I could use an aspirin. I fall into a deep funk.

My silence must have lasted for more than a few minutes because I'm startled back to reality when Noah clears his throat. I look up at him. His kind eyes let me know he understands my predicament. He smiles and says, "You seem to be deep in thought, Jesse, where did you go?"

I have no idea and tell him. "I don't know. It's just all so confusing. I want to get better. I couldn't stand it if I lost Iris. I've made a fool of myself with my kids, especially Kate. I'm a joke at work. My life is a mess.

I look into my coffee cup. It's empty. So is Noah's. I stand up and stretch, my knees cracking, and say, "Let me get you some more coffee, my friend. My treat. I can see a long night ahead for us. We've got a lot to talk about. Can you stay and help me?"

Noah nods and says, "I've got all the time in the world."

On my way to the counter, I passed by the kid with the piercings who was at the meeting. He's with a girl with short, dark hair and purple streaks in it. She's about his age and dressed completely in black. They are drinking coffee and talking. No iPhones or earbuds or anything to distract them, just talking.

As I pass by he glances up and recognizes me. He gives me a nod and says, "Dude." Then he goes back to his conversation.

I nod back, smile cordially, and continue walking to the counter. The connection with him is a little thing, but it gets me thinking: There are people out there like Piercings and Ponytail and Green Dress and Mr. Marathon and Mr. Goatee who are fighting the fight of addiction, just like I am. If they can find ways to stay sober, find ways to cope with their desire for fruit, and learn to live full and useful lives, maybe I can too. In the final analysis, it all comes down to the fact that I have too much to lose if I don't.

Right then and there I decide to go to the next meeting. In fact, I promise myself that I'll take it deadly seriously this time and tell them my real story, the one I've just told you - the one that includes the company party meltdown and the wedding disaster.

I'm nervous but relieved to finally be taking my first, honest, small steps toward sobriety. I find myself at the counter and order two coffees and a couple more cookies, pay for them, and then hurry back to our table. Noah grins when he sees me walking his way. I grin back at him. I'm eager to get started.

Too Quick To Judge

The first time I saw him I was making my way through the jam-packed crowd in terminal A on my way to find Number 33, the departure gate for my flight from Missoula to Denver. I was in my usual self-important hurry and he was walking so incredibly slow that I had to pass him on my right. Silently cursing this rude jerk for having the gall to be in my way, here's what I noticed as I came up from behind: He was an old guy with a cane. He was wearing a sharp-looking gray Stetson under which flowed long white hair down to the middle of his shoulder blades. He had a stocky build, a good four inches shorter than me, and was wearing black jeans, hiking boots, a cream-colored, pearl snap button, a long-sleeved shirt with brown, black, and red Navajo designs on it, and a dark brown leather vest. I glanced at him as I passed and noticed his beard was long and white, too, just like his hair. He had a small backpack slung over one shoulder and, to be honest, he looked like an old, but clean, miner from the 1840s California gold rush era.

A few minutes after getting by him I found my gate but continued walking all the way to the end of the terminal before turning around to head back. I was restless and was trying to burn off some nervous energy. I stopped to use the restroom, went into a gift shop where I bought two small bags of healthy snacks and browsed around, pondering longer than necessary whether or not to buy a Mad magazine before deciding not to, and then got a drink from a drinking fountain - all before making my way back to Gate 33 where I found a place to sit down. I put my lightweight jacket in my small carry-on, took out a paperback, and stuck my nose in it, unsuccessfully trying to lose myself in the story of a mountain man crawling across the great plains in 1823. It was a good story, a good "read" as they say, but I'd been having an unsettling past twenty-four hours which I'm sure contributed to my inability to focus. In short, I didn't get much reading done. I'd also completely forgotten about the old guy.

When my boarding group was called I stood up, positioned myself at the end of the slow-moving line and five minutes later showed my ticket to the agent, making sure to avoid eye contact even though he greeted me with a friendly, "Hi, there." I gave him a curt nod in return. I fly a lot and like to keep my interactions with people to a minimum when traveling, just on general principles. Or anytime else, for that matter. Then I made my way through the boarding tunnel, onto the plane, and down the aisle scanning the row numbers until I finally found mine, just in front of the wing. I stowed my travel bag in the overhead bin and sat down in the narrow aisle seat, glancing to the left at the man next to me by the window. It was him.

He had been studying something outside, but turned as I seated myself and acknowledged my presence with a nod and a friendly smile. "Hi," he said, as I fastened my seat belt. He pointed out the window. "Nice day," he added. He said it like a statement, not a question.

I took a look, just to be polite, although I knew what my response would be after having just an hour and a half earlier come in from outside where the sun was shining and the temperature was a balmy sixty-three degrees. What I saw now was that it was late afternoon, and the sun was about an hour from setting. That's all I noticed.

"Yeah, it is," I said, cryptically, only wanting to keep this interaction as brief as possible. Who knew what kind of a fruitcake this guy was, looking like he did?

I opened my book to make my intentions clear. No more conversation would be forthcoming from me.

He seemed to get my point as he, too, settled back and reached for a book (one of two I hadn't noticed until just then) that he had slipped into that pouch thing on the back of the seat in front of him. Now, I'm an avid reader and, I couldn't help myself, but I was suddenly interested in what it was. A novel, perhaps? Non-Fiction? Mystery? Self-help?

So curious that I nearly popped my eyeballs out of their sockets, keeping my head straight ahead pretending to read, while casting my eyes to the left to see what the title was as he transferred his book from the seat back to his lap. Two things struck me. One, he didn't, like ninety-five percent of the other passengers on the plane, immediately plug into an electronic device of some sort and immerse himself in a mind-numbing game of solitaire or *Grumpy Cat* or something. And two, the book wasn't a novel like I was reading or anything even remotely close to what I had only moments before taken a wild guess at. Instead, it was a book of poems by a Native American poet - a guy semi-well known and popular enough that even I had heard of him. I was intrigued and, I have to say, more than a little interested.

But interested enough to start a conversation with him after I had surely somewhat rudely put him off with my curt comment about the weather? Yes or no? That was the question. One I had no immediate answer for, so why belabor the point? I put the matter aside, kept my mouth shut, and settled in with my own book while trying to ignore the chatter of the flight attendant, the incessant gabbing of the couple across the aisle, and the baby two rows back who was crying non-stop. It was shaping up to be a long and arduous flight, not only stressful but also nerve-wracking.

The plane taxied to the runway and eventually took off, lifting us into a sky that, when I casually glanced out the window to look, was so stunningly blue it was almost surreal. It even impressed me, and let me tell you, I'm not easily impressed by Nature. This time, however, I was and, despite my somewhat cantankerous mood, I spent more than a few pleasurable moments enjoying a panoramic view of the surrounding snow-covered mountains that unexpectedly took my breath away.

I'm from Minnesota, known as the land of ten thousand lakes. The highest point in our state is Eagle Mountain (2,391 feet), located in the Boundary Waters on the Canadian border. The only way to get to it is by canoe in the summer or snowshoe in the winter which eliminates it being seen by nearly everyone in the world except only the few hardy souls willing enough to brave the elements to get there, a group I am not a member of. So the view out the window was spectacular, that was for sure, and I watched the vistas unfolding with increasing wonder as the plane climbed to thirty-five thousand feet. My ears popped three times. But the point is, I liked the scenery, and I might have even consented to talk to the gold miner next to me about the majestic mountains and pristine snow and the very wondrous beauty of Nature and the natural world and all of that, but I couldn't. He had fallen asleep before we'd taken to the air, his book of poetry resting in his lap, hence my opportunity to enjoy the view privately, unencumbered by human interaction, an opportunity I gladly seized upon.

When the plane leveled off I realized I was tired so I closed my book and my eyes and rested while next to me the gold miner peacefully slept. I was left alone with my thoughts which usually wasn't a good thing but this time was surprisingly benign because, I have to say, there was something comforting about being next to the guy. Something calming, I guess, would be the way to put it, which was strange because I don't normally feel that way toward other people. Well, never felt that way is closer to the truth, so I took it for what it was, an anomaly, and didn't think too much more about it.

I was on my way to visit my brother in Arizona after spending a quick trip the day before driving around Flathead Lake in northern Montana. This was the fifth year I had made such a journey from

Orchard Lake, my little hometown in Minnesota, something I was finding myself doing yearly. The main reason to go to Flathead was to touch base (as I referred to it) with my mother, whose ashes, my brother, two sisters, and I had scattered on the lake as part of a request she had made of things to do for her after she had died. A request we dutifully honored. That was six years ago.

I'd flown into Missoula the day before, rented a car, and driven up the east side of the lake to Woods Bay, the spot where we had chosen to scatter her remains. I spent the afternoon in a meditative mood, sitting at a picnic table in the bright sunshine, listening to the waves lap on the rocky shore, and remembering my mom, the lady who singlehandedly raised me and my younger brother and two younger sisters after our dad left when we were all below the age of twelve.

In my mind, she was a remarkable woman who not only was a single parent but who also worked long hours as a receptionist for a successful law firm in Minneapolis, all the while trying to teach her children the value of hard work, something she demonstrated both in her words and her actions. She also believed in helping those less fortunate than we were and for many years donated four hours a week to the Braille Institute of Minneapolis. She thus instilled in us at a young age a strong moral compass. I never once heard her complain. She died at the age of seventy-eight from congestive heart failure, and she is still missed by the people she came in contact with, family, friends, and co-workers alike. I never tire of remembering her and if I sound like I'm still mourning her and still miss her, I can't help it because it's certainly true. The fact that I probably haven't lived up to her high standards is my fault, not hers.

Yesterday was a little different from previous visits because I'd found myself spending more time than usual contemplating my life, a life that has, to be honest, been unremarkable in every possible way that there is even though I spend a lot of time and mental energy trying to convince myself that it isn't. But it's true, and that sad fact once again reared its ugly head, this time while I was standing on the shores of picturesque Flathead Lake, the largest freshwater lake west of the Mississippi.

I am fifty-three, work as a sales rep (it says *Sales Consultant* on my business card) for a nationally recognized pharmaceutical company that I'm not going to name because of pending lawsuits regarding one of our blood pressure medications. I can't stand working for them, yet I still do because I don't have the gumption to get off my butt and look for something else.

I've been married and divorced twice and have three grown children from my first marriage that I have only distant relationships with. Now that I think about it, that's being generous, because I hardly ever talk to them let alone see them, so I guess no relationship would be closer to the point.

Let's see: hate my job, divorced twice, and a lousy father to boot. In short, I'm your typical middle-aged American male failure.

I had spent the night in Big Fork on the north end of the lake at a Holiday Inn where I made the unfortunate decision to alternate drinking local craft beers with Black Russians at the Lakeview Restaurant while watching a boring early-season baseball game on the big screen television that took up most of the wall at one end of the crowded, noisy bar. I can't remember who won.

Also, I should say that I spent the last part of the evening in the company of a lovely young woman named Jenny whose last name she never told me but who was gone when I woke up in the morning, leaving me with a splitting hangover and two hundred dollars poorer. I also found myself, once I started coming around and begun sipping on the first of many cups of bad coffee, feeling strangely alone and out of sorts because the fact of the matter was, I was - on both counts.

So, I was in a glum and somewhat depressed mood when I drove back to Missoula to the airport, dropped off my rental, and made my way inside, through security, and eventually to look for my gate. For some reason seeing the slow-walking old guy looking like a gold miner just pushed me over the edge and got me going. Who was he to take up space and impede my progress to my gate, acting so hippy-dippy, and, as they say, "Together?"

I'm sure he bothered me because I was such the complete opposite, with my slightly wrinkled khakis, button-down powder blue dress shirt, dress shoes, neatly trimmed short brown hair, and clean-shaven face. I know I shouldn't have been thinking like that but I was. And, sure, I'll give you that the view of the mountains during take-off had truly been spectacular, but that was beside the point. Now all that pissed-off mood from earlier was coming back to me and, let me tell you, it was getting my blood boiling. Here he was dozing in the seat next to me, smelling of Patchouli and being super mellow, making my life miserable. The more I thought about it the more pissed off I became. I glanced over at him and gritted my teeth. Thank god he was still asleep, or I might have really given him a piece of my mind.

To try to get out of my bad mood, I leaned over to look out the window again, hoping the view would calm me. But, instead, it did the opposite. The crystal clear blue sky was gone, replaced by a socked-in world of clouds. And not the nice, smooth, pillow-like clouds you sometimes see when you're cruising above them at a high altitude and the sun is shining down on them making the world look soft and peaceful. No. These were thick, gray clouds and the plane was flying right through them so all I saw were wet wisps of gray streaming by the window. My thought was that they might have rain in them and could potentially be dangerous. And then, as if to verify my suspicion, the plane at that very moment went through heavy turbulence, bouncing and shaking, causing more than a few passengers to gasp.

The fasten seat belt sign came on. I held my breath and tried to maintain my composure. It wasn't easy but I did my best and was rewarded when, a few moments later, all returned to normal. I looked out the window once again. One thing was certain, the clouds hid my view of the mountains and made the world look depressing and closed in. Claustrophobic. I couldn't see a thing. Then the plane started shaking again and dropped a couple of hundred feet. My stomach turned over and I grabbed both armrests. Saliva flowed into my mouth as a precursor to throwing up. I certainly wasn't going to do that, no sir. I held on and got control of myself. In a minute the feeling passed and so did the shaking, both the plane's and mine, much to my relief.

With the plane leveling off, I began to regain my composure, but one was certain that any chance for me to mellow out like my neighbor on my left had vanished. He was still peacefully sleeping and breathing deeply. How the hell could he do that with all the shaking and rattling and rolling and dropping and whatnot that had been going on? I felt my blood pressure rise. He was beginning to piss me off again. Then I had the thought that maybe it'd be raining in Denver where I was to pick up my connecting flight to Las Vegas. Perfect, I thought sarcastically, that's all I needed to add to my already bad mood. A rocky, bumpy ride for the rest of my trip; both into and out of Denver. *Go ahead,* I thought to myself. *Make my day and rain on my friggin' parade while you're at it.* What a messed up flight, not to mention the past twenty-four hours.

I turned back to my book, hoping to lose myself in the story. The baby two seats back, who had mercifully quieted down during take-off now started up crying in earnest, wailing at the top of its lungs with barely a letup to gasp for breath. *Sure,* I thought to myself, gritting my teeth and shaking my head at my continued bad luck. *Why not?*

Before attempting to read, though, I glanced at the gold miner once more. He was wearing something on his right wrist I hadn't noticed before - a bracelet made of big, amber beads, each one separated by a smaller, dark red bead. The contrasting colors were kind of pretty, I had to admit, but on a man? Come on, who was he kidding? I shook my head and sighed, wondering what the hell could possibly cause some people to do the things they did.

Then I went back to my book, trying unsuccessfully to ignore the ever-greater pissed-off feeling growing in my chest. After a while, I gave up and gave in to being just plain mad and shut my eyes to escape from the messed up world I was in.

I must have dozed off.

"Hey, buddy."

From somewhere nearby a voice was calling to me.

"Hey, there. Hey, buddy."

I felt a gentle, but nevertheless irritating poke in the left muscle of my arm, interrupting, I might add, a rather risqué dream that included Jenny from the night before and a chocolate ice cream sundae. In a quick momen I came to, waking up with a start. My first thought was: *I'm going to kill that friggin' idiot next to me. That crazy old gold miner.*

Now I'm not a violent person, but I had not been having a particularly good day and I guess I was set to explode. His gentle nudge lit my fuse and it was like everything suddenly seemed to come to a head all at once. I clenched my fists, tensed, and jerked my head to my left, ready to rain some serious hurt down on the old guy, starting with giving him a huge piece of my mind.

But I never got around to it. Something happened right then at that very instant to suddenly change the mind that I had only moments before been so eager to give up a piece of, and I held back.

I blinked and blinked again, feeling myself calming down. I felt my fists involuntarily unclench. It was something about the old gold miner. He wasn't reacting to my sudden rather aggressive motions at all. In fact, just the opposite. He was doing nothing but smiling. That's all he was doing. Just smiling at me and, I have to say, it was quite disarming.

If that old guy knew the thoughts that only moments before had been running through my brain, I'm sure his grin would have vanished in the blink of an eye. But I made an instantaneous decision not to say anything, and the reason I did was that instead of engaging me in a dreaded conversation he did exactly the opposite. Without a word he silently motioned to his left and leaned back to make room, encouraging me to look out the window. I followed his calm instruction and looked, surprised to find that while I had slept the sun had set and evening had begun to settle in. Through the vanishing twilight, I could see that the clouds had disappeared and the sky had turned a soft, muted magenta, a pinkish and purple wash of color that was quite beguiling. Once my eyes adjusted, I could see there was enough residual light left outside to view a range of snow-capped mountains stretching all the way to the horizon, mountains rolling on and on off into the distance as far as the eye could see. The last, fading light of day was illuminating their snowy summits, brushing them with a mellow golden afterglow, softly like an artist might finish a canvas with a gentle flourish.

I might have gasped a little as I came fully awake and began to look in earnest. It really was a stunningly beautiful sight, one both otherworldly and profound. Something unexpected clicked inside me. I was suddenly glad he had taken a chance to awaken me. Me, a fellow traveler who had previously been so dismissive and rude, and certainly not deserving of the kindness put forth by him to awaken me to enjoy this once-in-a-lifetime experience.

But instead of being gracious, me being me, all I could think of to say was, "Nice," even though I was unable to pull myself away from the spectacular view thousands of feet below. I did, however, feel my unwarranted dislike of the guy vanishing somewhat, mitigated by the relentless beauty parading by outside the window.

"If you think that's nice," he said, "check out the lights." He leaned close to the window and pointed past my head.

I looked. Way below down in a valley between the mountains, where it was already getting dark, a single light was illuminating the ground around it with a soft glow that looked like a Dickensian street lamp at dusk. It was the last thing I expected to see. What was the deal with it?

He tapped me on the shoulder and pointed. "Look to the right."

I did and guess what I saw? Another light, and again, all by itself. And then I looked further and saw more of them, single solitary lights spaced a mile or maybe more apart, scattering throughout the mountain wilderness standing all by themselves with no outbuildings or any kind of inhabitation to be seen.

"Interesting," is what I said, suddenly at a loss for words due to my conflicted feelings. Here I was five minutes earlier preparing myself to go crazy all over the guy, but now, instead, I was finding myself slowly but ever so surely warming to him.

"What do you suppose the deal is with them?" he asked, exactly echoing my thought of just a minute earlier. Maybe we were sort of on the same wavelength, a thought which I found not so much troubling as slightly intriguing, given the obvious fact that we were so completely different.

"I don't know," was all I could think of to say.

I sat back, pulling my eyes away from the lights and the mountains, this one-of-a-kind spectacle I'd never witnessed before, and for the first time took a seriously good look at his face. It was weather-beaten and serene, that was for sure, and tan, too, like he spent a lot of time outdoors; no doubt happy times, I imagined, tromping through sunny mountain meadows past rushing mountain streams. His eyes were blue and friendly and, I kid you not, they actually twinkled when he smiled, kind of like Santa Claus is supposed to do when you're a kid and you're wrapped up in the wonder of Christmas and the spirit of the season. I caught myself, right then, wondering if there was something wrong with me because I don't normally think thoughts like that. But I couldn't help it, his face had broken into the friendliest smile I'd seen in a long, long time. If ever.

"Me, neither," he said, giving his shoulder a shrug and smiling some more. "It's kind of fun to imagine all kinds of reasons though, isn't it?"

Just hearing his soft but rich and luxurious voice was having an effect on me. I could feel myself relaxing more and more, becoming calmer.

I thought about what he'd said for a moment and then responded, breaking my vow never to talk with strangers and opening myself up to further conversation. "It is. But I can't imagine what it'd be like to live out in the middle of nowhere like that."

He nodded his head sagely, agreeing. "I hear you. It'd certainly be a challenge that's for sure." He looked for my affirmation and I tipped my head in agreement. He smiled some more and then stuck out his hand. "Nice to chat with you. My name's Josh. Josh Jacobson."

An hour ago, when I first sat down, you couldn't have paid me to even interact with the guy, let alone shake his hand and touch him. But now without the even slightest hesitation I took his hand and shook it.

"Larry," I said. "Larry Craig."

"Pleased to me you, Larry," he said. He had a nice, straightforward handshake, not the macho-hand gripping power-playing routine my customers (or even my few friends) typically laid on me.

"Same here, Josh," I told him.

He smiled again, an open friendly smile and I couldn't help it, I smiled back and immediately felt like I'd done the right thing.

Now I'm not one to actively go out and engage people in idle conversation. I mean, really, what's the point? Sure, I'm in sales, and I'm pretty good at making small talk and all the BS that goes along with it if I do say so myself, but that's because it usually leads to a sale, a commission, and money in my pocket. But right then, ensconced in my narrow seat in a narrow Boeing 727 on the way to Denver International Airport, maybe I was at a low ebb, especially after my melancholy time the day before on Flathead Lake thinking about my mom, and my mental meanderings thinking about my pointless life, and my less than satisfying night with Jenny. But Josh had a way about him, that was for sure, and I found myself being drawn into the warmth of his persona and personality.

"So you're heading for Denver..." I said, stating the obvious, leaving an opening for him to take the conversation any way he wanted.

"Yes, I'm on my way home," he told me.

"You were in Montana on vacation?"

"No. I'm on spring break. I work up north of Missoula at the Salish Kootenai College." He smiled, a cross between both sheepish and proud. "I teach math."

Well, I don't know what I expected, but for him to say he was a teacher at a Native American college in northern Montana was pretty far down toward the bottom of the list of things I would have guessed. Even though I tried to hide my surprise, I guess I wasn't successful.

He chuckled and added, "Not what you'd expected, right?"

I felt my ears redden. "Well..."

He bailed me out. "Don't worry, Larry. You're not the only one. It's not the first thing most people think an old guy like me would be doing."

Now I was really embarrassed. All I could think to say was, "I'm so sorry. I didn't mean anything..."

He held up his hand and cut me off with that disarming smile of his, "Don't sweat it. Really. It's no big deal." Then he turned to look out the window. It was nearly dark now.

"Look," he said, mercifully changing the subject. "It's easier to see those lights now."

I leaned over to look as he sat back to give me more space, being courteous and nice and giving me a chance, I think, to make up for my being so quick to judge him. It was an opportunity I appreciated. I'm positive I wouldn't have had the grace and certainly not the temperament to do the same thing if the roles were reversed.

"I can see a few more," I told him. Then I pressed on, picking up the thread of our earlier conversation, eager to put my faux pas behind us. "Really," I asked, because now I sincerely was curious about those lights, "what do you think is going on down there with them?"

Josh chuckled, a soft expression full of warm mirth that must have been extremely comforting to the students in his class struggling with calculus or advanced algebra or whatever else could possibly be taught. Math was never my strong suit in school.

"I haven't the faintest idea," he said.

For some reason, I found his answer and the way he said it like he really didn't have 'the faintest idea' and was honest enough to admit it, pretty funny. I laughed out loud, and he joined me, and with our combined laughter any residual tension between us completely melted away and dissipated, leaving a companionable calm in its place.

I pulled myself away from the window and sat back in my seat feeling more at ease and relaxed than I'd been since my drive to Flathead Lake the day before. It was a nice, comfortable feeling, one that I owed all to Josh. The more I thought about it, the more it occurred to me that I hadn't felt as calm and tranquil as I was now feeling in I couldn't remember how long. I took a deep, cleansing breath, enjoying this new, unexpected experience.

With the ice broken, Josh turned toward me and started talking about his life and I surprised myself by being more than a little interested in listening to him, something I don't ordinarily care to do, not unless I get something out of it like a sale or something. He told me he'd held several jobs, all of them what I would refer to as "A Little Different." He'd been a surveyor with the Department of Natural Resources for the state of Oregon and spent his free time out there working with an organization to protect the spotted owl. He'd been a construction worker in Louisiana and, in addition, had donated his time to help rebuild homes in New Orleans after Hurricane Katrina. He'd been a sous-chef for an organic restaurant in New York City, taught sixth grade to inner-city kids in Los Angeles, and, most recently, volunteered as a caregiver for a hospice organization in Milwaukee.

"My wife is a craftsperson who makes miniature furniture for doll houses," he said, again with that friendly smile and twinkle in his eye. "She has an on-line shop and more than a few loyal customers, so she doesn't have to stay in one place, which is good because she likes to move around and, as she puts it, 'Feel the inspiration of different places.' I'm glad to follow her because I love her and want her to be happy." He paused and laughed to himself. "Plus, I'm interested in lots of things myself, and I'm lucky that I can usually find work wherever we end up, you know, something to do to earn a living."

God, how interesting! He and his wife were free to do pretty much whatever they wanted to do and follow their own passions. It made my life seem excruciatingly boring and pointless. I'd had the same mind-numbing sales job for thirty-five years, ever since I'd graduated from the University of Minnesota with degrees in chemistry and biology and had taken the only job I could get, working for the big, pharmaceutical giant I'm still with, selling prescription drugs under the guise they would help people.

"How'd you get the job teaching math at the college?" I asked, wanting to hear more, and (to be honest) try to put some mental distance between his life and mine.

"Well, it was something I'd always wanted to do. My wife is happy where we are now in Milwaukee. We have our daughter and her kids living nearby and our son is only an hour away. She's ready to put down some deep roots as she calls it. I tried retirement for about three months after we moved there, but it didn't suit me. I like to be busy, like to be doing things - doing something good or helpful for other people." He laughed at himself a little self-consciously. "This is my second year teaching at the college," he added. "I like it a lot."

It was now my turn to contribute to the conversation, but what could I say? Tell him how much money I made selling drugs so doctors could prescribe medication that ninety-nine times out of a hundred didn't do one single thing to help their patients? That they were really just super expensive placebos that ended up making more money for the pharmaceutical industry not to mention the insurance companies? No, it didn't seem like the right thing to do.

I'll open my heart up to you right now and tell you why. I didn't want to talk about my job because the true fact of the matter is that my job was impossible to justify. It's a pointless occupation that does not do one little bit of good except make the users more dependent on medication while doing barely anything to improve their quality of life. On top of that it makes the executives for the company I work for filthy rich.

I don't mean to get all philosophical here but I do get a little wound up about it from time to time (like right now) but really, the truth of the matter is that the drugs I sell are legal. However in both the short and long run are of so little value to people that it's ridiculous. And the fact that I am a small cog in the pharmaceutical wheel that perpetuates it all is embarrassing to admit. So there.

On the other hand, my job pays my bills, that is true, and it allows me to make a pretty good living, which is also true. So the sad fact of the matter is that my job was all I had, as much as I hated to admit it. I just didn't feel like talking about it right then or about myself either because to be blunt, there wasn't much worthwhile to say. Especially when compared to Josh and the variety of interesting and worthy jobs he'd had.

So I did the next best thing. I threw the conversational ball back into Josh's court. I asked about his wife and his family and he told me his wife's name was Lynn and they'd been together for forty-eight years. He was seventy-one. They had the aforementioned son and daughter and seven grandkids, all of whom they saw regularly.

A successful marriage, a successful family situation, and, as far as I was concerned, a successful life. If I compared the two of us (which, believe me, I was doing throughout our entire conversation) I was coming up exceedingly short if not woefully lacking.

He showed me the book he was reading by the Native American poet. We talked about the author for a while and he showed me a few of his favorite poems. I even read one. It was about a golden eagle that was killed after flying into the propeller of a wind turbine, which I was surprised to find very moving and poignant. Then he showed me the other book he had with him, a biography of Carl Linnaeus. "He's the guy who invented the system for classifying organisms in the natural world," he said with a sheepish grin. "It's an interesting book, especially the biology side of it." He paused for just a tick and then added, "I enjoy gardening and kind of dig plants. No pun, intended."

I couldn't help myself, but I laughed out loud. It had been a long time since I'd met such an engaging person. I could have talked with him forever.

Just then the flight attendant's voice came over the intercom telling us to prepare for our descent into Denver. I checked my watch. Our half-hour conversation seemed to compress into about five minutes, time literally having flown by.

We readied ourselves and soon the plane began its final approach with Josh and I comfortably taking turns looking out the window, watching the lights as we drew near to the outskirts of Denver, all the while chatting together amiably about the sights we were seeing and whatever else popped into our minds.

Does everyone compare themselves to others when they first meet and get to know someone new or was it just me? But the more I talked with Josh, the more the feeling returned that my life had been a total and complete waste. I didn't have a close relationship with a woman. I wasn't close to my three kids let alone my grandchildren. I not only didn't like my job, I resented it. All in all, it was rather depressing, to put it mildly. I closed my eyes and involuntarily shuddered, perhaps subconsciously trying to rid myself of the fact that I was a pretty feeble excuse for a human being.

Maybe Josh sensed my mood because just as the landing gear set down and the wheels hit the runway, the plane rattled and shook and for the briefest of instances I thought we might crash.

My eyes flew open in panic. He gently reached over and placed his hand on my arm, calming me and relaxing me. "Don't worry, Larry," he said. "It'll be all right."

What a nice man. He was worried I was freaked out about a crash due to the rough landing because he was a kind and sensitive person. But a plane accident was the furthest thing from my mind right then and it certainly didn't even come close to the feeling I had, a feeling, not of fear, but one of profound dejection coupled with complete and utter worthlessness. We might also add in a dash of loneliness while we're at it. I looked over at him, at those gentle eyes and caring expression. His thoughtful words struck a chord in me that I didn't know I had, and I don't why, but at that moment I did something I hadn't done since I was a young boy; I started to cry. Not a lot I should be quick to point out but, believe me, there were some tears there.

Now, I'm not an emotional guy. You can ask both my ex-wives and my three kids if you don't believe me, but trust me, I'm not. I can't tell you why I broke down that night while taxing across the runway at the Denver International Airport. But I will tell you this, if the roles had been reversed, I certainly wouldn't have done what Josh did next, but that's what he did. He did something nice and tried to calm me down. That's right. Me, this complete stranger he had only just met a few hours earlier.

And maybe he had intimated enough in our brief time of getting to know one another not to make a big deal out of it because he didn't. He simply put his arm around my shoulder (which, coming from this person I'd only known for such a short time, was strangely comforting) and did the best thing he could have done. He just sat with me calmly and didn't say or do anything. He didn't need to. His mere presence was good enough.

We stayed that way as the plane taxied across the runway. Once at the gate, he removed his soothing arm, patted me once on the back and we both sat back in our seats. I was rattled by my behavior, both shaken and a little embarrassed. He kept a careful eye on me as we waited until most of the passengers had disembarked before rising from our seats. I was slowly getting myself together, feeling less guilty about my little tearful episode, but still kind of out of it. He grabbed our bags from the overhead bin (I had completely forgotten about mine) and we joined the last stragglers. I was a little unsteady on my feet but Josh stayed close beside me. The slow walk did me good. In a few minutes, we were off the plane, down the enclosed walkway, and through the door into the boarding area in the terminal.

If you've never been to Denver International, I'll tell you this, the place is one huge, crowded, chaotic madhouse. I made my way through the boarding area, jam-packed with humanity impatiently waiting for the next flight, and out to the fifty-foot-wide concourse. It was divided in the middle by a conveyor belt used for the convenience of hauling travelers back and forth up and down the entire length of the long terminal. Most people, however, chose not to participate in such a passive activity and instead hurried along the wide aisles, pulling luggage, carrying bags, tried to manage crying children, singles and pairs, and groups of travelers, young and old, most of them all-the-while talking loudly on their smartphones, while the intercom blared non-stop with pending flight departures and what to do if you found any unattended baggage. Barely controlled chaos would be the way to put it. In addition to my rather tenuous emotional state, I immediately got a splitting headache.

Josh stayed with me as we made our way along the edge of the concourse until we found one of the flight arrival and departure big screens. His flight to Milwaukee left in two hours from terminal A, mine in four hours from terminal C, the one we were presently standing in.

I have to say that I was still a bit undone by what had happened on the plane. I'd never broken down like that before, and certainly not in front of a stranger, even one with the gentle, soothing nature of Josh. It was all I could do to man up and try to pretend it didn't happen but, believe me, pretending it didn't happen was hard because it had. I leaned up against the wall with my pounding headache, closed my eyes, and set about the business of trying to collect myself.

"Are you alright?" Josh asked. We had moved off to the side, out of the way of the crowds streaming by, more for our safety than anything else. "We could go get some coffee or something."

God, he was such a thoughtful person. I had never met anyone like him before in my entire life. Every guy I knew leaned toward the category of *Macho man,* always trying to outdo someone else and prove they were better than the rest. You probably know a few of them yourself. Josh was completely different. He was calm, mellow, kind and caring. The type of person there needed to be more of in the world (in my opinion.) Then I had an intriguing thought, a rare moment of creative thinking for someone like me. Maybe there *were* more people like him around. Maybe I just hadn't taken the time to notice them. Maybe the problem was me. Maybe I was the one who needed to change and be more observant as well as more accepting of others.

Well, who knew the answer to such a broadly sweeping philosophic question? I sure didn't and I definitely wasn't going to be pondering it on this particular night in this particular airport. But the more pertinent question was this: Was it possible for someone like Josh to have a positive effect on someone like me in such a short period of time?

In my bitter, jaded mind I knew the answer was no. Why should he? Or even could he? He was a man, not a magician. I was the way I was and that was it. End of story. The easiest thing right now would be to just shake his hand, say goodbye, and be on my way. Change is hard and takes an excruciating amount of time. I know. I tried to learn Spanish a few years ago, thinking it would help me make more sales. I finally gave up after a few weeks, finding it too hard and time-consuming.

"Larry. Larry, are you Ok?" Josh finally asked, since it had been a few minutes and I still hadn't answered his question about going for coffee. He put his hand on my shoulder, comforting me again, wanting to help me. Help I decided I didn't need.

I quickly opened my eyes and turned to him, puffing myself up a bit, regretting that I had broken down in front of him in the first place. "Yeah, I'm fine," I told him. "Just a bad day is all. I'll be OK once I board the plane and get out to Arizona to see my brother." It was the best excuse I could come up with.

Josh removed his hand and looked at me carefully. I swear I could feel his kindly eyes as they probed deep into my soul, checking my emotional well-being. He was such a sensitive person - totally at ease with himself and on a wavelength far removed from mine. His peaceful aura extended outward from his inner spirit like warm sunrays, a calming balm to those willing to accept it. Was I one of those people? Good question, and one I pondered for about two seconds before coming up with my answer. No.

I was suddenly uncomfortable with all the touchy-feely stuff and wanted to be rid of him and away from him. "I'm good," I told him, cryptically, deciding I needed to put an end to this kind of thinking and this kind of conversation. I stepped back to put some space between us.

"You're sure?" he asked, clearly not believing me, but intuitive enough to know I wasn't going to budge.

"Yeah, I am," I said, reverting to my old self and my curt behavior and speech.

"Well, Ok, then," he said somewhat reluctantly, his eyes blinking rapidly while he searched his mind. I got the feeling he wanted to say more, to stay and be helpful in any way he could, but, in the end, accepted that I didn't want or need him to. After a disquieting moment, he finally said, "I guess I'll be going then."

We shook hands and said our final goodbyes. I appreciated that he didn't make a big deal out of it, or, heaven forbid, try to hug me. Instead, he simply turned away and walked slowly to the center of the concourse and got on the conveyor belt. When he was situated he turned and waved once with his cane. I waved back and, I have to say, I was sad to see him go, but tried not to let it show in my face. I think I might even have mustered a half-hearted smile. In a few minutes, the conveyor belt had taken him away and he had disappeared into the crowded terminal.

Wow! What an experience! It had been both exhilarating and unnerving. Talking to Josh had exposed feelings I never knew I had, or if I did know I had them, I'd kept them nicely hidden deep inside for many, many years. My entire life. Which was probably a good thing. If this is what it took to contemplate changing my life to try to become a better person, I was having nothing of it. It was too exhausting.

I dragged my eyes away from the crowd where I'd last seen Josh. It'd been a trying day and I was overly tired not to mention emotionally wrung out. I needed to find a place to sit down and collect myself. At least my headache had mysteriously vanished.

I hunched up my shoulder bag and started walking in the opposite direction from where Josh was headed. In a few minutes, I found my gate but my flight didn't leave for nearly four hours so I had a lot of time on my hands. I walked past it looking for a place to sit down and spend some time reading. Unfortunately, the airport was packed, even at this late hour, so finding an empty seat was not easy. I checked my watch. It was nearly nine pm. I slowed down and took my time walking, not thinking about much of anything, trying to put thoughts of Josh and my encounter with him out of my mind.

Way down toward the far end of the terminal was a short row maybe seven seats with their backs set up against the protective guard rail of the conveyor belt. This put them in the middle of the concourse, not the best spot to sit for quiet introspection, but it was the only seating available. At least I was by myself. I sat down, careful to keep my feet placed under my seat and out of the way of travelers hurrying by in both directions. I took my book out with the intention of reading but couldn't bring myself to do it, my thoughts were too disjointed. Instead, I just sat and stared into space, oblivious to the crowds around me until the noise and the din eventually melted into the background, a kind of silent scream.

I came back into consciousness with a sudden start, momentarily disorientated. Then I heard a voice over the loudspeaker paging someone, reminding me I was in the airport as if the people walking by in front of me with luggage and backpacks weren't enough.

I yawned and casually checked my watch. What the hell? I had fallen asleep for nearly an hour. My heart rate sky-rocketed and I sat up with a start, silently berating myself for not being more vigilant. Unbelievable. Who knew what could have happened to me? Someone could have stolen my travel bag which contained all my money and personal possessions.

I quickly checked under my seat. My bag was still there. Good. I also noticed my book had fallen to the floor so I picked it up, thankful no one had kicked it down the concourse or taken it. I reached into my pocket and checked my boarding pass. Still there. Good. My breathing started to return to normal as did my heart rate. All was well. I looked around, noting that the crowds had thinned remarkably. Good.

I settled back, beginning to calm down. I still had nearly two hours to go before my flight to Arizona was called so all was good. I even felt a little refreshed and more like myself after my nap. I opened my book and settled back to read. Soon I was able to escape for a while to the western plains of long ago. After the day I'd been having, it felt remarkably pleasant to go there.

But my good feelings didn't last for long. I had hardly read a few pages when a young couple with a small child and a baby bustled in with a harried rush, trailing a scent of dirty diapers and something sweet and probably sticky. With an entire airport at their disposal, they chose to sit down in the same row of seats I was in. Right next to me. How rude. The man couldn't have been more than twenty-five and was muscular and fit. He had a shaved head and was wearing a white tee shirt, military green cargo pants, and heavy work boots. He also had purple, red, and black tattoos up and down both arms along with something serpentine tattooed on his neck. My immediate impression was: Oh, oh, this guy's trouble. My immediate thought was: Get out of here quickly before something bad happens to me.

I was frantically thinking how I could get up and leave without causing a scene when Mr. Tattoo made it a point to catch my eye. "Sorry, man," he said, "My wife and I and the kids have been traveling all day and we're pretty tired. Mind if we crash here?" He had an unexpectedly soft voice, one that had a pleasant tone to it even though he also sounded completely worn out.

"Daddy, I'm tired," said his little boy at that moment. He was a cute little towhead, maybe five years old. He was wearing bib overalls and red tennis shoes, an innocent-looking little kid, especially compared to his dad.

The father looked at me again. The fact that he even asked for my permission to sit next to me counted for something in my book. Most people wouldn't have given a crap.

I thought of Josh. I thought of how I had misjudged him based on his tattooed appearance. He had turned out to be completely different from what I imagined him to be. Then I had another, somewhat more troubling thought, one that came back to me from earlier when I'd said my final goodbye to Josh. Maybe it really *was* me that was the problem.

I made it a point to move one seat over to the end of the row, giving them more space. "Absolutely," I said to him. "No problem. Sit right down." I tried to smile, but I'm sure I failed miserably and ended up cracking, at best, a slight, half-assed grin. Like I've said, I'm not comfortable with much in the way of social interactions, even on the best of days, and this certainly wasn't one of my better ones. My encounter with Josh had kind of taken a lot out of me.

Josh...

With a look of relief, the young man turned to his wife. I'm assuming she was, anyway. "Let's crash here, Amber," he said. "This guy seems good with it."

Amber gave me a thankful look and said to her husband, "That's good, Hank. I'll get us settled. While I'm doing that, could you please get some bottled water for us? I'll stay here with baby Emma and little Wyatt."

"Got it," Hank said, shaking off his tiredness and mustering his energy. He was a big man who seemed to take up the space of two people as he stood up. He turned to me and said, "Thanks, mister. Like I said, it's been a long day."

No kidding.

I looked up at him from where I was sitting and said, "Seriously, like I said, it's not a problem."

He looked relieved and gave me the thumbs-up sign. He turned to his wife, bent down and gave her a quick hug, kissed the baby and his son, and then took off into the crowded concourse.

I don't know why, but watching him with his children made me start thinking of my own kids, all three of them adults now, and all three of whom I had basically fallen out of touch with. Had any of them been in a similar situation to Hank and Amber? Traveling with their young families, off on their own in strange surroundings? Maybe in need of a little friendly assistance?

Then I had a more immediate thought. I had bought snacks at the airport in Missoula and hadn't touched them, engaged as I had been in talking with Josh. Maybe the little family would like them.

I leaned over to the young mother and said, "Excuse me."

Amber was cradling the baby Emma in her arms. Little Wyatt was sitting quietly next to her holding a stuffed dog and playing some kind of game with it, pretending to ask the dog questions and then listening with a serious expression on his face to the dog's answers. Maybe I was overly tired or something, but I had to admit that it was kind of cute.

At my query, Amber looked up at me in surprise. She was about the same age as her husband and had big brown eyes accented with dark purple eye shadow, short black hair, and a small red heart tattooed on her right forearm. She was wearing a long, colorful floral skirt, a dark green tee-shirt, and black combat boots. I couldn't tell how many piercings she had in her ears, but I will tell you this: there were a lot. She looked up and met my eye but didn't say anything, just waited to hear what I had to say.

"I have some snacks," I told her. "Healthy ones, with nuts and raisins and things."

Just then the boy said, "I'm hungry, Momma."

"Little Wyatt, hush," Amber said to her son, who immediately quieted down. Then she looked at me. "That's very kind, mister, but you really don't have to do that."

I don't know why, but a vision of Josh flashed in my mind. I knew what he would do. "I understand," I said, "But I don't have to do it. I want to do it."

"Please, Momma, please can I have the nice man's snack."

Amber gave her son a quick look and he was silent again.

"I don't mean to cause a problem," I said, backpedaling a little. "But they're unopened. I reached into my travel bag and took one out to show her. I held the package upside down and shook it a little, "See."

Little Wyatt blurted out a laugh. "He's funny, Momma."

Nice to have a child who was so easily entertained. I smiled at him and shook the bag again, causing him to laugh some more.

"Well, all right. Thanks, mister," Amber said. She took the bag of *California Treats* and inspected it and found it to be to her liking. I could see her visibly relax, "Okay, that's great, mister. Really great. Thank you."

She opened the bag and poured a small amount into little Wyatt's palm. He immediately started to pick out individual raisins and pop them into his little mouth, chewing contemplatively. He even offered one to his doggy. Like I said, he was a pretty cute little kid.

Amber looked at me and smiled a tired smile, "You hit it big, mister. He loves raisins."

"Yeah, I can tell," I said and sat back, feeling good about doing something nice for this young couple. "I've got some more in here if he finishes those off."

I made it a point of reaching down into my bag, while Amber smiled at my poor attempt at a little joke. Then she went back to cuddling her new baby who couldn't have been more than a few months old and was dozing peacefully.

I found the snack bag I was looking for but I also found something else. My fingers came upon a smooth but bumpy object shaped like a donut and I jumped a little in surprise. What the? I'm sure a puzzled expression appeared on my face because Amber looked at me with concern and asked, "Is something the matter, mister? Are you all right?"

I carefully took the object out of my bag and held it in my hand. It was Josh's bracelet. The one he'd been wearing on the plane. The one I'd noticed before we'd begun our conversation which had led to us becoming friendly with each other. The one I had negatively and erroneously classified as feminine. How'd it get there? Then I remembered him handing me my bag from the overhead bin when I'd been in such a befuddled state that I'd started to walk down the aisle without it. He must have put it in the bag when he took it down. I rubbed my fingers over the smooth surface of the beads. I was touched and somewhat blown away because it was so unexpected and such a thoughtful remembrance of our encounter and our brief time together. And, the more I thought about it, the more I realized that maybe it was something more.

I held the bracelet in my hand and showed it to Amber. "It's from a friend of mine," I said.

Amber took it from me and admired it before returning it to me. "I can tell it's handmade. It's really quite lovely," she said. "He must be a very good friend."

I didn't have to think. Although I doubted I'd ever seen him again, I answered, "He was...er...is," I said, slipping it easily on my wrist with its elastic band. "He's a really good guy."

Little Wyatt was admiring my bracelet when a few minutes later Hank came back with a bag of four bottles of water and some more snacks. He took a glance at the bracelet as he sat down and nodded, "Cool." He gave me a bottle which I accepted, but I declined to share their food, thinking that the young family needed it lots more than me.

We began chatting amicably back and forth. It turned out they were heading to Seattle, going to Amber's aunt's funeral. They'd been traveling all day from Vermont where they lived and Hank had his own small business as a carpenter and cabinet maker. He spent more than a few minutes telling me all about the different kinds of woods he used for the different projects he was working on and the various 'Tools of the trade' as he called them to work on those projects. I have to admit it all sounded interesting and creative and, like with Josh, I was more than a little envious that Hank was doing work that he liked (if not loved) and believed in.

I declined to talk much about my life and my job, those being the last things I wanted to waste anybody's time hearing about. Instead, I helped the young parents out by playing with their son while they took care of baby Emma. Little Wyatt introduced me to, and let me play with, his stuffed doggy whose name was Skipper. We fed Skipper raisins and pretended to talk to him for a while and then we went for a walk (with his parent's approval, of course) in the airport. Then we rode back and forth on the conveyor track about a hundred times, killing time before their flight was called. I enjoyed it all.

When their flight was announced we went to their gate and I stood with them in the boarding area, keeping them company and helping out as much as I could. Little Wyatt even held my hand while we walked there. I stayed with them until they got checked in and Hank, Amber, and little Wyatt all waved as they entered the boarding tunnel. I waved back and made a weird face at little Wyatt that caused him to laugh. He waved harder and I smiled back and waved some more, watching until they were finally gone from view.

They were a decent little family and it was nice to have gotten to know them. At one point I even thought about giving either Amber or Hank the bracelet Josh had given me, just to be nice, but decided against it, thinking maybe it would seem strange to them -

a little too much overt friendliness, maybe. But putting that aside, all and all, I have to say that the time I spent with them was pretty fun.

A little while after they boarded my flight was called, and I walked down to the gate to get ready for the final stage of my day's long journey. I rubbed my fingers over Josh's bracelet, thinking about something I'd been thinking about since I'd met Hank and Amber and wondering what Josh would suggest. Well, there wasn't much to ponder since I knew what he'd tell me to do, so I decided I would do it. I decided that the first thing I was going to do that next day when I got to my brother's was to make three phone calls. I hadn't talked to any of my kids in years and wouldn't blame any of them if they didn't want to have anything to do with me, but I figured if only one or two consented to talk to me I'd think of it as a win. I wouldn't fault them, though, for holding my lack of interest in their lives against me after so many years of neglect, but I wanted to try to rebuild some bridges. Hopefully, it wasn't too late for me to change. Hopefully, it wasn't too late for them to let me.

I boarded the plane and found my seat, by the window time. I was a little chilled so, along with my book, I took my jacket out of my travel bag before stowing it in the overhead bin. Then I got myself buckled in. When I was all set, I looked outside, watching the loading process for a while, wondering where all those bags were heading before finally realizing they were all heading to the same place I was, Las Vegas. I guess I was a little distracted.

Then I looked to my right and waited expectantly for the person to come and sit down who would be my traveling companion. Maybe it would be someone interesting to talk to. Someone like Josh. I waited and waited and then heard the flight attendant announce that the door was closing and we were to prepare for departure. The two seats next to me remained empty -

no one was coming to sit down. I was going to have the row all to myself and I have to say, I was a little disappointed.

The flight attendant came over the intercom and told us about fastening our seat belts and all that but I wasn't paying attention. I was suddenly really chilled so I put my jacket on and pulled it close, thinking I might ask for a blanket later. I lay my head against the window staring outside yet seeing nothing.

Feeling suddenly lonely, I touched the bracelet Josh gave me and wondered what he was doing right now at this very moment. Had he made his flight okay? Was he looking forward to seeing Lynn? How would it go for him to teach his math class at the college when he got back to Montana after spring break? It was weird. I don't normally think about other people much, and certainly never with people I'd just met. What was happening to me? Maybe I was just overly tired.

The plane taxied out to the runway and soon took off, climbing into the night and leaving the bright city lights of Denver far behind. At cruising altitude, we leveled off and I looked out the window. Down below I could see the dark outline of what I guessed were the Rocky Mountains. I even saw those tiny lights that Josh and I had seen and talked about. It was a wonderfully clear night. I could even see stars. Stars above and lights below. I wondered what Josh would have to say about that.

I checked my watch. It was just after one in the morning and the plane was dark, everyone sleeping or trying to. I'm sure I was the only one awake. My brother would meet me in Vegas in a couple of hours and then we'd drive 2 1/2 hours south across the desert to his home in Lake Havasu City. It'd be dawn when we arrived.

I turned on the overhead light and opened my book but only glanced at the pages, not able to read at all, suddenly feeling quite lost. I turned the light off and looked out the window some more, watching the nighttime world go by. Now and then I'd see a light or lights down thousands of feet below, maybe a random ranch or farm, sometimes a small city, places where people lived and were tucked in safe and warm for the night. But not me. I pulled my jacket closer, not able to shake the chill that had come over me. I picked out some bright stars and watched them, marveling at how they filled the void of the universe. I wondered...Could they perhaps be symbols of something like hopefulness, or a belief in a brighter future yet to come, a journey into the unknown where the mysteries of life are waiting to be revealed? I chuckled a little at my sad attempt at poetic imagery and then wondered what Josh's Indian poet would think about such musings. Probably not much.

I closed my eyes, eager to forget my loneliness and feeling of being adrift, but I couldn't. Images flooded into my brain of the people I'd recently met. My new friend Josh (for that's how I now thought of him, as my friend) and his long, white hair and beard. Hank with his shaved head and colorful tattoos, and Amber with her black hair and combat boots. Their kids, baby Emma, and little Wyatt. I was glad I'd gotten to know all of them and I silently wished them the best in their journeys on this long night. They were all such nice, decent people, and it was difficult to admit, but here was the hard, cold truth: they were all nicer people than I was, a lot nicer. It would probably be a long time before I'd ever forget them, if ever. I wondered if they even bothered to think of me. My guess was probably not. Why should they?

As the night dragged on and as my thoughts kept swirling I realized that there were a lot of good people out there. People I hadn't ever bothered to notice before, or if I did, had formed quick and erroneous judgments of. People who were a lot better at this business of living a good life and being a decent person than I was.

Because of my job, I'd flown many times in my life, hundreds for sure, maybe even a thousand. All of those plane rides were different, of course, but on each one of them, there was one thing that was a common factor. On all of them, I'd been able to eventually fall into a deep and restful sleep. But not tonight. Sleep never came for me on that late-night flight to Las Vegas. I guess I had a lot on my mind.

The plane landed in Las Vegas and I met my brother. We drove across the desert and other than semi-truckers we were the only cars on the road. The east was just turning light when we got to his place. We sat outside on his back patio and watched the sunrise, sipped coffee, and talked. I told him about the events of the last day going all the way back to Flathead Lake and then meeting Josh, and then Hank and Amber and their kids. He listened but didn't say much. I appreciated that in him. Frankly, it was just nice to talk and try to make sense out of how I was feeling.

To make a long story short, I'm still staying with him, my more than generous brother, Charlie. It's been five weeks now and he tells me he doesn't mind. He's been a bachelor his whole life and tells me enjoys the company. I make it a point of trying to believe him. He works as a mechanic for a garage in town that specializes in building high-performance engines for people who race jet skis on Lake Havasu and around the country. His talents are in high demand, and he works long hours, so I try to make myself useful by helping out around the house and in the yard. He seems to appreciate my effort.

I called my work shortly after I arrived at Charlie's and told them I was taking a leave of absence from my job. I wouldn't be surprised if they fired me, and to be honest, I don't think I'll mind if they do. My apartment in Orchard Lake was a tiny, one-room studio above the hardware store. I also called my landlord and told him to rent it if he could and he said he would. So I guess I'm not coming back to Minnesota any time soon. I'm probably done with my job, too, now that I think about it, even though I've heard nothing from them since I called.

I made good on my promise to myself and called my kids that first day I was at Charlie's. Only my oldest daughter, Zoe, consented to answer my call but that was OK. It was good to talk to her and we've slowly been renewing our relationship ever since. I'm still committed to keep trying with, Sara and Jack, my other daughter and son. It's what Josh would have counseled me to do and it's what I sincerely want as well. After all, I'm their father and I have neglected them for far too long. It is up to me to do the right thing and try to show my kids that I care about them and wasn't as bad a person as they thought I was, even though I probably was. But one thing is certain, time isn't slowing down and it certainly isn't going to wait for me. I know it's something I'll be working on for the rest of my life, gaining my kid's trust and rebuilding our relationship. The important thing is that I have to start somewhere. The next step is to start talking to Sara and Jack and working toward eventually getting together and seeing all my kids in person. The term baby steps comes into my mind a lot these days.

Every evening that we can, Charlie and I go out into the desert and go for a long walk. Sometimes we talk and recap what we've done that day, sometimes we don't say much of anything and just enjoy each other's company. Sometimes we stay out and watch the sunset. Sometimes we even watch the stars come out. I like the peacefulness of the desert, the wind blowing across the wild land, the sense of complete emptiness. My brother says I'm getting pretty healthy and tan. I don't know, maybe I am. I do know that I like being out in the wide open spaces and walking, letting my thoughts wander and go free.

Is it weird to say that I want to change and become a better person? I hope not because I'd at least like to try - try and take the measure of all that was special about Josh and Hank and Amber, even little Wyatt, and learn from them. Try to emulate what was so good (if that's the right word) about each of them. It seems like the right thing to do and, like I said, I've got to start somewhere. It'll be an interesting journey, that's for sure. One I am looking forward to taking. It's been a long time coming.

What Gene Told Me

Ever since I've known him, my best friend Gene has always been a storyteller. He's good at it, too, most of them having to do with things that have happened to him at work on his job as a carpenter. Like uncovering a nest of garter snakes. "There must have been ten thousand the friggin' things." Or the time he almost got hit by lightning. "I couldn't hear a thing for the rest of the goddamn day." Or the time he shot himself in the foot with a nail gun. "Hurt like a son-of-a-bitch." Stuff like that. He was pretty funny, too, how he told his stories, and I enjoyed listening to him. He always made me laugh.

Last summer we had gotten in the habit of sitting on a couple of lawn chairs in his garage on Sunday afternoons, having a few beers, and listening to the Twins game on the radio. Gene wasn't always a carpenter. Twenty-seven years earlier, for a brief time, he played first base and batted fifth for the Quad City River Bandits, a Class A baseball team affiliated with the Houston Astros. On that July afternoon during the game between the Twins and Kansas City, he told me a story with a different tone to it. One that wasn't funny at all. One I'll never forget. It was about when he visited a prostitute in downtown Rock Island, Illinois.

"Yeah, it was on my nineteenth birthday," he said, turning serious as he lowered the volume on the radio. Then he cracked open a cold can of Hamm's. I half expected him to switch gears after setting me for something heavy and start telling me a funny story, like when there was once a rain delay and the ball diamond turned into a lake and the fans in the stands as well as both teams went skinny dipping. You, know, making a joke, out of things. It was the kind of thing he might do.

But he didn't.

"My friends from the River Bandits were behind it all," he said, using finger quotes around friends to make the point that, even though they were teammates, his friends weren't really his friends. "There was Stinky, Fred, Jorge, and Harper, all..."

"Wait a minute," I interrupted, "Stinky?"

"Yeah." Gene looked at me like I was dense. "You know, cuz of his feet." He crinkled up his nose, remembering, I suppose, the noxious aroma emanating from his teammate's baseball cleats. Probably not the most pleasant memory in his arsenal of memories, I wagered. Then he took a sip of beer.

In my mind, I went, *Oh, well, sure. Feet. Of course.*

"I guess the smell is caused by bacteria on the sweat glands," he informed me, pointing to his boots propped up on a milk crate. "In Stinky's case he must have had twice as many as everyone else, cuz, man, they were always pretty ripe..."

I put my hand up. "Stop, stop, stop! Way too much info."

"Well, you asked."

"Right. Well never mind. I get it."

"So, can I get back to my story?"

I waved my can of beer at him. "Go ahead."

"As I was saying, those guys set the whole thing up. We were at home playing a doubleheader with the Lansing Lugnuts."

I coughed out a laugh, spewing a mist of beer. "The Lugnuts?"

Gene was getting exasperated. "Yes, and they were damn good. Do you want to hear my story or not?"

I did. "Sorry. Go on." I wiped my nose. A little beer had gone up it.

"We lost the first game in the afternoon. But we won the second in the evening, so I was in a pretty good mood." He smiled, thinking back to that night. Gene's team had been based in Davenport, Iowa, and he'd told me many times that they were, 'Marginally Ok,' as he put it, finishing in the middle of the seventeen-team Midwest League each of the two seasons he was with them. "Harper was twenty-eight, the oldest guy on the team and the ring leader. He organized everything. The guys borrowed a car, made the arrangement with Jackie, and..."

"Whose Jackie?"

"Geez!" he exclaimed. He stopped talking for a moment and stared at me for a long couple of seconds before asking, "Who do you think?"

"Oh," I said. " Yeah, right."

I was pretty excited to hear his story. Most guys would be. After all, that first time always sticks in your mind, doesn't it? At least mine always has - a misfire of mammoth proportions on my part with my college sweetheart, the ever-patient and long-suffering Molly Henderson.

"So they had me set to go. All I had to do was follow their lead. Problem was, I guess I wasn't ready."

"A bit of a premature issue?" I asked. This time it was me using finger quotes around premature. I was sympathetic to what I imagined might have happened.

"Something like that."

Damn. I was hoping he'd had a more successful first time than me, but I guess I was going to be disappointed.

"What happened?"

"After we won that second game, we were all pretty stoked. We went to a bar across the river in Rock Island. It's a college town you know, and the place had some weird name like The Smiling Toad or something like that. It was just off the interstate in Illinois and down near the river bottoms of the Mississippi. It looked like it was an old roadhouse of some kind because the parking lot was dirt and there were trees all around, like it was carved out of a forest. It was pretty secluded and the place was packed. Anyway, we were going to have a few beers to celebrate the win, my birthday, and my pending present from the guys." He stopped talking for a moment before continuing. "I have to say, talking about this...it's embarrassing."

Well, he started it. Ten minutes earlier, I was happy just listening to the Twins playing the Royals.

"You don't have to tell me if you don't want to," I told him.

"No. I kind of want to. Need to, actually."

It dawned on me that he was agonizing over this. I liked Gene a lot and I wanted to be supportive. "Go ahead, man, it's happened to millions of guys," I told him, surmising that millions was probably way too low an estimate.

"The bar was loud. Some local band was playing Led Zeppelin covers, and I was tossing back those brewskies like I was drinking glasses of water." He looked at the can of Hamm's he was holding, grimaced, and set it down on the cement floor. Then he continued. "When I was pretty well on my way to feeling no pain, the guys got me to my feet, held me steady, and led me outside. I remember stumbling down the steps into the parking lot and falling down at least once on the way to the car - probably a lot more than that. Not my finest moment, that's for sure."

He looked at me and I just shook my head. No, it wasn't. Nowadays, Gene is a pretty sober guy, a hard worker, and a devoted family man. But back then at nineteen...well, hell, we've all done stupid things when we were young, right? I told him, "Don't worry, man, we've all been there."

I think he appreciated that I understood the limitations inherent in his intoxicated state. He continued. "I guess earlier one of the guys had moved the rental to the far side of the parking lot, over by the forest and away from the floodlights. It seemed like the walk took forever. Stinky put his arm around me as we made our way up to the car and said, 'Here we go, Slugger, it's your big night. Get ready for the time of your life.'

"Talk about adding to the pressure, right?" I asked.

"No kidding. When we finally got to the car, Harper opened the back door leaned in, and said, 'Here he is.' Stinky gave me the tiniest shove, and told me, 'Good luck.' I went tumbling inside, not knowing what to expect. Then they slammed the door."

"Man…" I said, just to say something. "Not good." What a bad situation. I was beginning to really feel for the guy.

"No kidding. Not good is putting it mildly."

"What happened then?"

"The guys I was with, my friends (finger quotes again) just laughed. The window was down and Stinky leaned in and said to me, 'Her name is Jackie. You all have fun,' and then they left. I could hear them laughing all the way across the parking lot back to the bar."

"Not the best beginning," I observed.

"No. Not at all," Gene said, turning to me. "And it didn't get any better from there." He paused again, picturing, I'm sure, how events played out. It was not a pretty picture I was guessing, more Jackson Pollock than Claude Monet if you catch my drift. It turns out I was right (about it not being a pretty picture, that is), but I was way wrong about what happened. In fact, I've been wrong about a lot of things in my life, but never more wrong than when it came to Gene and Jackie. He continued with his story, turning even more serious. "Here's the deal, Ed. When I finally got up the courage to look at her, I couldn't believe what I saw. In my mind I was picturing a sexy woman in her late twenties, with wavy blond hair, blue eyes, and a great build, wearing a short, tight, red dress and perfume that smelled like vanilla. You know, some weird preconceived sexist image." Yeah, I thought to myself, something a nineteen-year-old horny guy (if not a lot of other guys) with an overactive imagination and no girlfriend might have. He continued. "But the person I was sitting next to was nothing like that. Not at all." He looked at me, imploring me to believe him.

I did. His seriousness and tone made what he was telling me quite believable. In fact, I'd never seen him as upset as he was. For some reason, I lowered my voice almost to a whisper, "What was she like?"

He was clearly agitated. Beads of sweat had broken out on his forehead. "Ed, she was so young! She looked like she was only fifteen. She reminded me of my sister, of all things." He twisted his hands and then rubbed them on the thighs of his jeans.

Shit. Not good. I'd seen enough news coverage about underage prostitution rings to know how horrific they were.

"That absolutely sucks," I said.

"No kidding," he shook his head some more before sucking in a breath of air and letting it out. "It made me sick back then and it makes me sick now, just thinking about it." He looked me in the eye. "She was nothing like I'd imagined. She..." He shook his head, at a loss for words.

I understood where he was coming from. "Unbelievable," I said. Then I thought to clarify. "Fifteen you think?"

He shook his head some more, chagrined at the memory. "I'd guess, yeah. She looked lots younger than me, that was for sure. She had short dark hair and bangs and was wearing blue jeans and some kind of white peasant shirt with embroidery on it. I remember she wore a thin gold chain necklace that had a little gold heart on it." He was quiet for a moment and added, almost in a whisper. "She looked like a little kid."

The garage fell quiet except for the muted game in the background. We were both lost in our thoughts. Finally, I said, "Well, you did the right thing."

"What do you mean?"

"You left right away didn't you?"

Gene's face turned beet red. "Well, no."

"What!?"

"But I should have," he was quick to add. "I mean, I would now. I mean...," he was flummoxed.

"What happened?" I asked.

"Well, remember, I was pretty drunk. Plus, I was looking forward to this happening, so I tried to ignore her age and rise to the occasion, so to speak."

Man, I couldn't believe what he was telling me. I got mad. He should have just left. Taking advantage of an underage person (a girl!) was not cool in my book. It wasn't in Gene's either, he just didn't know it then.

"How'd that go for you?" I asked sarcastically. "Did you get your birthday present?" I didn't even bother with the finger quotes. I was disappointed in him. And myself. I averted his gaze and looked into the corner of the garage where the radio was playing. The Twins were batting in the bottom of the seventh, but I wasn't paying attention anymore. The unsettling thought had just occurred to me that I might have done exactly the same thing if I'd been in his situation. Believe me, it was not a pleasant character trait to have to face, but there you had it. Then I remembered he was only nineteen (me, too, in my imagination.) We all make mistakes. I know I certainly had. Have. Did. I calmed down a little to let both him and me off the hook."Sorry," I said. "It's just out of character for you, is all."

He smiled a wan smile, "Yeah. Well, thanks for that. I was stupid and deserved what I got. So, no, I didn't get my present. Not even close. Let's just say that too much beer and too much guilt...well, they just don't make for a happy ending, if you know what I mean."

I nodded, unfortunately having been there in the beer scenario way too many times. "Yeah," I said. "I definitely know what you mean."

Gene was silent for a moment, listening to the Twins. He turned up the volume a little. Buxton has just hit a triple. We both smiled. Gene picked his beer up from the floor and we taped our cans. But my friend wasn't done with his story. Not by a long shot.

"I have to tell, you, though, she was very nice about it. I remember she patted my shoulder and said something like, 'It's OK, Slugger, it happens more often than you think,' which didn't make me feel any better, but she was so sweet about it that I almost believed her."

I thought that it was nice she tossed him a lifeline. In fact, she sounded like she was a decent person. I was curious, though, and asked, "Then what happened?"

"The weirdest thing. I pulled up my jeans and was getting ready to leave, but she stopped me, put her hand on my arm, and said, 'Do you have a cigarette? Your friends have already paid. We could just sit here and talk or something.'

"You're kidding!" I said. Then I remembered her age. Maybe she just wanted a break in what I could only imagine was a god-awful life. A few minutes of peace. Plus, even back then I'm assuming Gene was a nice guy, like he is now. Maybe she was being honest with him.

Gene started shaking his head again. "I just wish I hadn't drunk all the beer. I would have enjoyed just sitting there with her. I didn't have a girlfriend. I'd always been shy and didn't date much, so it would have been nice to be with her and, you know, just talk.

Given all that had happened that night, I could see his point. "So, did you?" I asked. "Sit and talk?"

"No. Didn't get a chance," he said.

"Why?"

"Right about then, the cops showed up."

I coughed and choked on the mouthful of beer I had just drunk. "What!?" I managed to quite literally spit out. "You've got to be kidding me!"

"Yeah. Well, no, I'm not kidding. We were in the back seat remember? Just sitting there. I was wondering what to do next and trying to sober up. Jackie was offering to talk. Then, all of a sudden two cop cars came tearing into the parking lot, sirens wailing, lights flashing, tires spinning. The dirt was flying everywhere. My first thought was that I was going to get busted."

"What'd you do?"

"Well, I started sweating like a pig."

"No. I mean the cops. Did the cops surround your car and arrest you or something?"

I'd watched enough television to have a crystal clear picture in my head of the events unfolding. I could see the squad cars skidding to a stop in a cloud of dust right next to Gene and Jackie. I could see the cops jumping out, pulling their guns and surrounding the car, pointing high beam flashlights at them and shouting for them to 'Get out of the car! Get out of the car!' Or 'Down on the ground! Down on the ground!' Or 'Don't move or else!' Or something like that. My imagination was working overtime.

"Man, that's not good. Did you get arrested?"

"Arrested?" Gene laughed, "Not on your life."

I was confused. What about the police surrounding the car and pointing their guns and all the yelling and all that stuff. "Well, what happened?"

"We ran."

"Ran?"

"Yeah. It was Jackie's idea. As soon as the cops pulled into the parking lot, she took one look and said something like, 'Shit, let's get out of here.' She opened the door on her side, got out, grabbed my hand and pulled me along with her. We ran in the opposite direction."

"What the hell?"

"Yeah. Remember we were at the edge of the parking lot? Well, she opened the back car door on the other side of the cops and pulled me into the underbrush. Then she grabbed my hand and we ran as fast as we could, busting through the woods, falling down, getting smacked in the face with branches and all scratched up. Eventually we made it made a quarter of a mile or so to the Mississippi, slid down the bank and right into the river. Man, I'll tell you, that muddy water sobered me up quick." He laughed at the memory and looked at me. I'm sure my mouth was hanging open. This stuff only happened in the movies, didn't it? "It was a blast," he added, smiling some more and taking a healthy drink of beer.

"Weren't you scared?"

"I was too drunk to be scared. Besides, it turned out the police weren't there to bust an underage hooker and a misguided, drunken, nineteen-year-old guy. They were there to break up a big brawl in the bar". He laughed. "They didn't have a clue about us."

"Amazing." It was all I could think of to say, because, you know what, it really was. Amazing, I mean.

Gene sat back and took another swallow of his beer. "Yeah, I totally agree. And you want to know the really amazing part?"

There was more? "Absolutely."

"Well, Jackie and I sat on the bank of the river all night long, just talking and getting to know each other. It was first time that'd ever happened to me with a girl."

Shit. It was just like in the movies!

"Turns out she was a great person." Right then I started picturing that movie with Richard Gere and what's her name in it, the prostitute he befriends. Gene set his beer aside and leaned forward. So did I. He continued. "She told me her story. She was eighteen and she and a few of her friends were 'Hooking,' as she called it, for extra money that summer. She was going to use it when she started college in Decorah that fall. I'll tell you this, Ed, we hit it off right off the bat. No baseball pun intended." Pun or not, he gave me a big, silly, grin.

"Are you going to tell me you not only became friends, but you started going out?"

"Yeah, and then some."

I was finding this increasingly hard to believe."What more could there be?" I asked somewhat skeptically.

"We became friends. We started dating and..." he said, drawing the statement out. The garage went quiet except for the radio. In the background Polanco singled home Dozier. The Twins were up 5-2.

"And then what?" I asked, despite my skepticism, I was drawn in by his story and anxious to find out what happened.

"Three years later we got married."

"What?!" I blurted out, choking on the mouthful of beer I'd just drunk.

He looked at me. "Yeah. Jackie is BJ, my wife."

Oh. My. God.

***

Gene and I had become friends twenty-one years earlier when our girls started playing soccer on the same team in the Orchard Lake Under-Seven soccer league. We were both in our late twenties, enjoyed doing stuff with our kids, and shared a common philosophy regarding children's athletics: the main thing was to have fun when you were playing the game. Learning new skills, learning how to play as a team, those kinds of things were good, too. Winning was way down on the list. That first year our kids' team challenged that philosophy by only winning two games out of fifteen and finishing dead last in the league. But we bought the team, The Orchard Lake Lady Lilies, dilly bars at DQ after every game, and the little girls were happy and had fun, so that's what counted.

Anyway, back then Gene had just started working for a general contractor in the western Hennepin county area. He was busy a lot, so I ended up car pooling his daughter, Samantha, along with my daughter, Ellie, to a lot of the games. To make up for it, he'd invite me and my wife, Chris, and Ellie and our son, Ethan, over on Sunday afternoons to barbeque brats, toss the Frisbee around and hang out. Over that first summer not only did Gene and I get close, but so did my wife and his wife, Beth, or BJ as he called her.

BJ worked part-time at Ridgedale, the big shopping Mall seven miles east of us, at Macy's in the jewelry department. Chris made hand-crafted place mats and table runners on her loom in our basement that she sold on-line. They both were devoted mothers, and they both enjoyed gardening and reading, so they had more than a few things in common. To make a long story short, over the years we all become close friends, eventually working our way up to spending the occasional Thanksgiving together, along with ever single Fourth of July and Memorial Day and Labor Day for the past twenty years. It was as good a friendship as four people could ever have.

Gene was a big man, standing six-three, and towering over my five-ten. He outweighed me, too, by probably fifty or sixty pounds, all of it muscle, not like my jelly belly flab. And that man was strong. I've seen him carry a forty-pound bag of concrete mix under each arm like it was nothing. Me? One bag and two hands and I could barely lift it, let alone carry it.

He dressed in blue jeans, work boots, and flannel shirts most of the time except for when the Minnesota summers turned hot and humid. Then he ditched the flannel for white tee shirts but kept the jeans and boots. He wore his dark hair long, tied it back in a ponytail, and kept his salt and pepper beard neatly trimmed. He kind of reminded me of a mountain man.

Anyway, the point of all of this is that he was one big guy who could have used his size to intimidate people but he didn't. He was one of the kindest people I'd ever met. He gave money to numerous environmental organizations, donated his time at the local senior living complex by helping out doing odd jobs, and even kept the grass cut on his next-door neighbor's lawn, Mrs. Halverson, an eighty-two-year-old widow, who Gene said reminded him of his mother.

Last fall he told me he wanted to tear down his old, single-story garage and build a new one. "Yeah, it's going to be double wide with space in the back for my workbench and tools. I'm even going to make room for us so we can sit and visit and listen to the games. Like a clubhouse." He tapped his temple and smiled. "I'm thinking all the time, buddy. I'm even going to put in a stove for heat and a refrigerator, you know, in case we want some beers."

I liked how his mind worked.

Initially, he was going to do the construction himself but I ended up helping, which was an experience in and of itself because handy with any kind of tools I'm not. Even the simple task of hammering a nail straight gives me problems. They always bend. Early in our marriage Chris kindly put up with my lack of skill in the home maintenance department, saying encouragingly on many occasions, "That's Ok, Eddie, at least you tried." Nowadays she simply says, "Ed, don't waste your time. Just call Gene." So I do, and the job gets done, done fast, and done right.

So after twenty years or so of him helping me out, I felt I owed him more than the occasional gift card for a dinner out with BJ or a case of Hamm's (conveniently, both his and my favorite beer.) "How about if I help with the garage?" I asked him that afternoon when I was over watching as the bobcat demolished the eighty-year-old structure in about ten minutes, "It's the least I can do after all you've done for me."

Gene looked at me askance. "Carpentry, Ed? Are you sure?"

I understood his reticence. After all, my job as a Life Science teacher at the local middle school was a far cry from what Gene did for a living. But I was eager to try. "Sure, what not?" I said, adding quickly before he could say 'No,' "I take orders well, just ask Chris." Which was true. I may not possess the greatest number of skills when it comes to practical matters, like fixing a leaky faucet or replacing a screen on a window, but I was willing to tackle any project. (Then I'd call Gene.)

"All right," he said, after considering it. "Who knows, it might be fun."

It was. Working one day a week, we got the demolished garage debris cleared out and hauled away by the end of October. Then he had a crew come over and pour the slab. After it cured for a couple of weeks, we started the framing which we finished by New Year's. We had the siding on in the middle of February, in time for the first day of spring training for the Twins. Then we put a small wood-burning stove in the back to heat the place during the rest of the cold Minnesota winter while we finished the inside.

We usually worked either Saturday or Sunday and it was fun just like Gene suggested. I even learned to drive a nail straight, and Gene taught me how to use a nail gun. By the time April and the Twins first regular season game rolled around, we had the two-car space complete, and with extra space added on in the back, we were ready for the radio, some beer, and baseball.

All well and good, right? Well, the thing was, during the time we were doing the construction, a good six months, I noticed something changing in my friend. He'd always had energy to burn and could easily outwork me. But as the year ended and this new year began, he started to slow down a little, took more breaks, and just didn't seem to have the pep he normally had. When I mentioned this to Chris in February she said, "Why don't you ask him about it?"

Novel idea, and not one that guys are usually comfortable with. But after I hemmed and hawed for a few weeks, trying to figure out a way to bring it up without it looking like I was prying (and coming up with nothing), I said to myself, to hell with it, I'll just ask him. So, I did.

"Say Gene, how are things going? You feeling OK these days?" It wasn't as hard as I thought it was going to be.

He turned to me. "Sure. Why?"

"I was just wondering is all."

"Nope. All is good, buddy." Then turned and looked past me to the section of wall I was working on, giving it a critical eye. "Make sure you get that tape sanded a little smoother, Ed, It looks kind of rough."

So there you go. Back to work we went. Everything was Ok.

When I told this to Chris that evening she gave me an incredulous look and said, "That's all you did? Just asked him and left it? You didn't push him and ask for some more detail. You know, maybe probe a little," she said, raising her voice and poking me in the chest with her finger a few times to make her point. "God, Ed, you a such an idiot."

"What?" I said, a little defensively, rubbing the spot where she'd poked me. "What else could I have done?"

"Not let him off the hook, that's what. Haven't you noticed that he's lost weight, too?"

No, I hadn't. "Not really."

"Men!" Chris exclaimed, and stomped off, saying over her shoulder, "I'll call BJ. and find out what's going on."

"No, you don't have to do that," I said, hurrying after her.

But she did anyway.

Gene had been feeling poorly, is what BJ told Chris and what Chris relayed to me later that night. "He just doesn't have much energy," BJ told me.

"Yeah, like I said."

She ignored my comment and continued. "His doctor's keeping an eye on him. BJ thinks we should carry on with Gene like all is well. I guess he doesn't want to make a big deal of it." She paused and looked at me and then added, "She thanked me for my concern and for calling her." She smiled faintly. "She told me it was good to talk."

Chris's take-charge attitude made me feel a little defensive, but I let it ride, knowing I was never going to win an argument with my headstrong wife.

"Sounds good to me," I said, happy to have avoided a confrontation. Besides, not getting into feelings was something both Gene and I were good at. So we left it at that.

***

And that brings me to where we were now, sitting in the finished garage on an August afternoon, drinking a few beers and listening to the Twins play Kansas City. I had been a little surprised by Gene's out-of-the-blue prostitute story but was happy to play along, more curious than anything as to what happened, and, you know, what the final outcome had been. Now this. The reality of the situation was that the prostitute, Jackie, was really BJ, Gene's wife, and they were happily married and had been for many years. Wow!

Did his telling me the story have something to do with his illness?

"Ed, there's a little bit more I need to tell you about," he told me.

Asked and answered. I guess I was about to find out.

He stood up, went to the workbench, and fiddled around with a jar of screws before going to the radio and lowering the volume. Then he walked over to his chair and sat down again. "You might have noticed I haven't been myself lately." He picked up his beer, swirled it around, and then set it down without taking a swig. He looked at me with the most serious expression I'd ever seen on him. I waited, now wondering what the hell he was going to tell me. I have to admit that, like him, I myself was struck by a sudden urge to get up, walk around and fiddle with stuff, but I didn't. Something told me what he was going to tell me wasn't going to be good. I stayed right where I was, took a sip of beer, and nervously waited, watching him.

Finally, he sighed and took a breath, mustering himself before looking at me and saying, "Well, the thing is, Eddie, I've got a tumor. It's in my brain. I've got a friggin' brain tumor."

Shit, I was right. It was bad.

I don't know about Gene, but for me the world suddenly stood still. For about a minute. I was aware of nothing except maybe the game on in the background. I don't know. The surroundings turned blurry while I tried to process what he'd told me. I do know that the bottom fell out of my stomach, and I felt like I was going to be sick. I needed to say or do something. Fast. So I did both.

"What the hell, man?" I said, standing up and hurrying over next to him. I knelt down so we were eye to eye. What do you say in a situation like this? I knew nothing about brain cancer. Could it be treated? Was he going to die in a few weeks or was he going to be able to live a long and fulfilling life? I had no clue, but I did know this - my heart went out to the guy. I put my hand on his arm in a show of solidarity and said, "I'm so sorry, man. Is there anything I can do to help?"

And he looked at me, his eyes sad and a little tearful, and said, "I was wondering if maybe you could drive me to the treatments. It'd be a big help. Jackie's pretty freaked out."

And then, almost as if it was scripted, his wife's voice came from the entrance to the garage. "I take it you told him," she said, racing across the floor to us. "Good." I stood up, my knees a little weak. She looked at me and said, "He's wanted to tell you for a long time, Eddie. It seemed like now was as good a time as any."

My first thought was (swear to God) is she talking about him telling me about her being a former prostitute, or about his brain tumor? I took a chance on the latter. "Yeah, he just told me about the tumor," I said. My heart went out to her, too, like with Gene, and I embraced her. "I'm so sorry."

Gene broke the tension with some levity, motioning towards himself. "Hey, what about me?" And we both knelt down and hugged him, which is how Chris found us. BJ had called earlier and told her to come over. She joined us in a four-way hug fest. I have to say, it was pretty emotional.

***

That was last summer. By February, the dead of winter, Gene was doing pretty well. His type of cancer is referred to as low-grade (diffuse) astrocytoma. The five-year survival rate for a man of his age (forty-eight) is 43 % so we are hopeful. Throughout the rest of the summer and into the fall I gladly did what he asked of me and took him to the University of Minnesota Hospital for radiation treatments. He had six of them and they were spaced far enough apart so he could rest and recover in between. We completed them in the beginning of December. The next step is surgery, but his lead doctor (well, doctors. He has a team of them) is holding off on that. They're monitoring all kinds of factors relating to my friend's condition, of which I only understand a little bit, and, remember, I'm a science teacher. It's pretty complicated.

For the rest of the year, he got progressively weaker. The doctors attributed it to the radiation treatments and it looks like they were correct, because I'm glad to say that around the first of the year, Gene turned the corner and started getting a little stronger. In fact, he seems to be getting a little bit better every day. He's lost maybe thirty pounds and most of his hair has fallen out. The ponytail is long gone. So is the beard. At least he's not as weak as he was. I prefer to think of him as not dying but getting better, and the weight loss and hair loss are just part of that process, but then I've always been a glass half full kind of guy. I'm just not ready to lose him yet, so I'm not planning to. He's the best friend I've ever had.

Anyway, the point of this story is really not about dying and death. It's about Gene and his stories. See, the interesting thing about his form of brain cancer has to do with one of its side effects. Gene has always been a talkative guy and way more expressive than me. If he was a good storyteller before the brain tumor...well, let me tell you, he's an amazing storyteller now. We've taken to spending one or two evenings a week together out in the garage with the wood burning stove cranked up. It's deep winter, so we're listening to the Minnesota Wild hockey games, drinking herbal tea, which believe me, we are still getting used to, but it's supposed to be better for him than beer, and I guess neither of us can argue with that.

Anyway, I swear, put a quarter in him these days and he just won't stop talking. He's telling stories about playing minor league baseball, stories about hiking both the Appalachian and Pacific Crest trails, stories about training to ride the Tour de France, stories about when he was a Peace Corp Volunteer in Sierra Leone, and on and on and on.

I asked his doctor about it and he told me not to put too much stock in the stories Gene is telling - that they're probably not true and just a crazy aspect of how his mind is working and a unique side effect of the tumor. Like a hallucination. I guess the doctor's the expert and I'm supposed to believe him. Maybe I should but, hell, whatever the case, Gene's stories are fun to listen to. Besides, it's great to be with him and hang out together and listen to him talk. It's just like the old times, back before the tumor.

But it's gotten me thinking back to that day when it finally came out that Gene had a brain tumor. He had just told me about his encounter with the prostitute, Jackie, and how they had talked, became friends, then lovers, and how it turned out that her name was not Jackie, but Bobby Jean, BJ, who eventually became his wife, and Jackie was just her stage name if you know what I mean. The thing is, was the story real or not? Or did Gene make the whole thing up?

The logical thing, of course, would be to ask BJ, but man, that seems like an insane thing to do. I can just picture that conversation:

"Hey BJ, I have a question for you?"

"Sure, Eddie, what is it?"

"Gene tells me you guys met when you were a teenage hooker. Is that true?"

I can just imagine the look on her face. It wouldn't be pretty. In fact, my guess is that it'd be pretty scary. Anyway, she's got enough to deal with now taking care of Gene without having to deal with my idle curiosity. Plus, I really can't think of a good way to broach the subject without offending her. And, to tell the truth, what good can come of It? I do know that their story has always been that they met at a bar after one of his ball games in Davenport, started talking, started dating and the rest was history. Which, in a way, is close to the truth. The more I've thought about it, the more I think, *who really cares*? Gene and BJ are happy together. They've raised a fine daughter in Samantha and now are dealing with the most challenging event of their marriage - Gene's brain tumor. I'm going to help out as much as I can, be the best friend to him I can possibly be, and leave the story of her being a prostitute alone. True or not.

Besides, for the last few visits he's been telling me about playing goalie for the Hamilton Bulldogs, a minor league affiliate of the Edmonton Oilers. My favorite sport when I was growing up was playing hockey so to me they're highly entertaining. You see, when Gene was with the Bulldogs one of the guys on his team was an eighteen-year-old hockey phenomenon, the soon-to-be hockey legend (get this), Wayne Gretzky of all people! Since I've always liked (well, loved, maybe is a closer word) hockey those have been some great stories to listen to.

But when they run out, I'm optimistic there will be more. Who knows where his mind will take him? But Gene is definitely on a roll - it's hockey this and Wayne Gretzky that, and I'm more than happy to sit there and be with him, spending time together, him telling me his stories and me listening. Hopefully, it's something we'll be doing for a long, long time, because, I mean, really, what better way is there to help a friend deal with a crisis like Gene's going through than to hang out and talk and listen to him tell his stories? None that I can think of.

Besides, when he tells me about being in the nets playing goalie and stopping the greatest hockey player of all time on breakaway after breakaway, time after time again, well, hell, I could listen forever.

The Fight

"What's happened to you?" my wife asked, standing calmly at the door of the bathroom with her arms folded, watching.

"What the hell do you mean?" I answered, slurring my words, just before vomiting again into the toilet for what seemed like the tenth time that night. "What in god's good name are you talking about?" I added for good measure when I was done, trying to show her I was in control of my situation. Then I slumped to the floor and rested my burning forehead against the cool base of the porcelain sink. It felt good. Comforting. I waited for Linda, my wife of forty-four years to come and get me up, help guide me to bed, and get me settled like she'd done so many times in the past. But she didn't. She left me laying there for the first time in my life.

I awoke the next morning, curled next to the bath tub, freezing to death on the cold tile floor, hugging a towel that I must have pulled off the rack. It took a few minutes to come around and collect myself. Then I made an attempt to stand, weaving to my feet before grasping the tub and trying to sit on the edge where I promptly fell backwards, knocking my head on the wall and causing my stomach to heave once again. I felt a cauldron of bile bubbling around down there but nothing came up. I decided to rest. Five minutes later, after I had climbed out, rinsed my mouth in the sink, made my way down the hall, down the stairs and into the kitchen, it dawned on me that the house was eerily empty. Suddenly I was worried. Where was Linda?

It took a minute for me looking around through blurry, watery eyes before I saw the Post-it note on the counter next to the coffee pot. *Enjoy your life, Dave. I've moved out to start over. Don't bother calling.*

What the hell was this all about? I read the note over and over again, not believing what she had written. With shaking hands, I took a filter out of the box, fit it into the basket, added the coffee and water, and turned the pot on. Then I went to the kitchen table by the window overlooking the backyard. I looked outside, barely registering the blue sky and bright October sunshine. Then I saw the other note she left me, this one on the table right in front of where I usually sit. It read: *Whatever happened to you?*

Through the fog in my brain, the words she had written seemed to ring a bell. Did she say the same thing to me last night? Outside the window, chickadees were feeding at the feeder and juncos were scratching around on the ground. I watched them for a while. For a long while, actually, before I realized I was crying.

In all of our forty-five years of marriage, I never told Linda about Danny. I don't know why. A few months earlier I gone (against my better judgment) to my fiftieth high school class reunion and bumped into him and we'd started talking. Danny was still as lean and muscular as he was back in twelfth grade when his nickname was The Snake because he was so quick to strike. He was a fighter, is what he was, and was tough to boot, often taking down two or three guys when his little gang fought other gangs in the Minneapolis area. Rumor was that he never even carried a knife, preferring to use his fists instead, liking, I guess, the idea of man-to-man combat where the toughest and quickest usually won. And that's what Danny was: The toughest and the quickest.

I should be clear here - he and I were never friends, but we knew each other due to an incident after gym class when three guys from a rival gang in our school bushwhacked Danny in the boy's locker room. When I came upon them, they were pounding the crap out of him as he valiantly fought back, barely holding his own. I didn't like that it wasn't a fair fight and I jumped in to help. It turned out to be my first and only fist fight in my life. I landed a lucky punch to the jaw of a jerk named Ed, knocking him on his ass. It also broke my middle finger. But that punch turned the tide in Danny's favor, and he went after them with a renewed and sustained furry that caused the three hoods to run off like their lives depended on it. Danny chased after them and I, grimacing in agony, gamely followed behind, unable to do anything more than not scream due to the pain.

"Fuck off," he yelled, flipping the bird at them as they ran through a door that lead outside onto the grounds that surrounded the school. Then he stopped and turned to me with a big smile, the beginnings of a shiner and a little bit of blood dripping from his nose. "Wow!" he exclaimed. "What a bunch of assholes, right Dave Baby?"

I was shocked because I didn't realize he knew my name. "Yeah," I said, groaning gingerly cradling my hand. "Real assholes," I managed to sputter.

Danny took one look at the hand I was babying and said, "Well, buddy, let's get you to the nurse. I think you broke that motherfucker.

Profanity aside, I appreciated his concern, and let him lead me to Miss Borgman's office where she put a split on my finger and taped it up, looking a askance at each of us, fortunately not questioning too much my story that I'd broken it falling down the stairs. Nor about the tiny bit of blood still leaking from Danny's nose.

When we left and were out in the hall, he laughed good naturedly, slapped me on the back, thankfully respecting my throbbing hand, and thanked me again before heading off in a different direction. That was it. We never hung out together after that since we weren't even close to running in the same crowd. He and I did nod and say "Hi" to each other occasionally in the hallway between classes, but that was all. After I graduated I never saw or heard from him again. Not for fifty years.

The reunion was held in the banquet room of the International Market Square in south Minneapolis. I'd made my rounds, greeting the few people I knew, finding I didn't have much to say and nothing in common with any of them (other than graduating from the same high school), wondering why I'd even bothered to come to the thing in the first place. The answer was that I guess I was just curious about the people I'd gone to school with back in the late sixties. What had they ended up doing with their lives? What were they doing now? That kind of thing.

If it sounds like a fool's errand and a waste of time to you, you are not alone. Linda, for her part, could have cared less. Not only did she go to a different high school, but she wasn't a fan of those kinds of reunions anyway, finding them a tedious waste of time, and preferring, as she often said, to 'Live in the present.' Now, standing by myself against a wall off to the side, watching the crowd start to get loose and loud, her words were beginning to ring true and make a lot of sense.

I was looking toward the bar wondering if I should get my third JD and coke, chug it down, and then go home, when someone clapped me firmly on the shoulder. "Dave Baby, is that you buddy?"

I turned and faced a tall, lean-looking man in clean jeans, boots, and a black tee shirt that revealed a series of tattoos on both of his arms. He was smooth-shaven and had swept-back gray hair with a prominent widow's peak. He smiled, showing white teeth against a tan, outdoorsy complexion. He looked healthy and fit. It was Danny.

"Yeah, it is," I stammered. "It's me, Dave," I added, clarifying my name. I never really cared for Dave Baby, like in Dave 'Baby' Cortez, a '50s musician I actually kind of liked. "How are you doing?" I smiled a little, not knowing what to expect from him, and politely put out my hand.

Danny shook it firmly and smiled back at me, friendly like, "Life is good, my man. Real good. It's nice to see you." Then he stepped back, frowning, and looked me over once or twice, seeming to make a decision as he did so. "Let me get you a beverage, Dave, you look like you could use it."

Well, that was unexpected. I laughed a nervous little laugh. "Why's that?"

"I can just tell," he said and motioned to the guy behind the bar. "Could you please get him..."

Danny looked at me and I said, "A JD and coke."

He made a motion to the bartender. "JD and coke. And I'll have a bottled water."

When our drinks came, he put his arm around my shoulder and guided me to an empty table where we sat down. He looked around, the crowd building, music blaring, people glad-handing long lost acquaintances, laughing and cutting up, just like half a century earlier when we were naive kids in senior high. It was beginning to remind me of a high school dance after a Friday night football game except fifty years had passed.

As if reading my thoughts, Danny said, "Man, what a zoo, right?"

"Agreed," I said. He smiled again, and we clinked our drinks. Then, with that common ground established, we started talking and catching up.

Danny had served in Vietnam, married a Vietnamese woman while stationed there, came home, settled, had two kids, raised a family, started and ran his own business, and lived a complete and full life. I had gone to college, avoided the draft with a student deferment, graduated with a degree in business, got a job working for a nationally known insurance company, had three kids, raised a family, and lived a complete and full life. Almost like Danny's right?

Well, not quite.

After we had talked for a while, filling each other in on how our lives had played out, Danny sat back, took a sip of his water, and looked at me. In my mind, I pictured him seeing a balding, jowly guy about fifteen pounds over the optimum weight for my five-foot ten-inch medium build frame. I must have looked soft to him and I probably was. Well, forget probably, I *was* soft, not ever feeling a need to exercise and keep in shape. Not like Linda, who regularly jogged, did yoga, and worked out with her girlfriends at the health club she'd attended for years. But Danny ignored my appearance and instead got to the point. "I've got one question for you, Dave."

"What's that?" I asked, feeling loose and more friendly now with our conversation and the accumulative effects of the JD and no food. I was also glad he had dropped the "Baby" from my nickname, letting us off the hook to be able to move away from our high school years.

"Are you happy?"

Well, whatever question I'd been expecting it wasn't that and it definitely caught me by surprise. "Sure," I answered quickly. "Why wouldn't I be?" I added, feeling a little defensive.

And there was the rub. The big question. It's the question that came back to me now that I was sitting alone in my kitchen with a note from my dear wife telling me she was leaving me. I'd given Danny what I told myself at the time was an honest answer. I'd told him I was happy, my reasoning being simple: I had my job, my wife, my kids, even a few grandkids. Who wouldn't be happy? The thought came back to me now two months later, and through the alcohol fog in my brain, I realized the question had some merit. A lot of merit, actually. Was I happy with my life?

I crumpled up the note Linda left me and tossed it on the table. *The hell with it*, I told myself. I suddenly felt the need to quit thinking and probing too deeply into the inner mysteries of my existence. I needed to do something. Anything. Anything to escape my thoughts, which were rapidly turning into a whirlwind of conflicting arguments.

I turned off the coffee maker, poured a mug, and drank down a couple of scalding gulps, instantly regretting my rash move. Trying to ease the burn, I rinsed my mouth under cold water from the faucet in the sink. Then I went outside to take a walk only to return in a few moments when I realized how disgusting my vomit-stained, filthy clothes were. My shirt and pants were streaked with the remnants of last night's toilet bowl-hugging experience and, on top of that, I didn't smell too good. I went upstairs to change and glanced at myself in the bathroom mirror: bags under my red eyes and gray stubble on my ashen face. The verdict? I did not look good. I decided to take a long, hot shower, hoping it would help me improve my mood and ease my sadness at Linda having left me.

It did neither.

Linda and I have lived in Orchard Lake, a small town of just under two thousand located about twenty-five miles from downtown Minneapolis, for over thirty years. Our home is a story-and-a-half bungalow built in the 30s. I love it and so does (did?) Linda. It has stucco siding with sky-blue trim around the windows and doors painted golden yellow. Trust me, it looks nice. We converted the front and back yards to flower gardens during the first couple of years after we'd moved in with only a slight nod to islands of green grass for accent. People often stop on the street to admire how pretty everything looks and I have to agree with them. Our married life together has been a labor of love and commitment and it's been reflected in our quaint, well-kept home and our beautiful, colorful gardens. I couldn't believe it was all starting to implode - just because of me.

I was thinking about all of those things after I was finally as presentable as I was going to be on this first morning of my life without Linda by my side. I went back outside, made my way down the driveway, and turned left, walking slowly, still getting my bearings after last night's drunken debacle. The sunny day helped. So did the cool October weather. I guessed the temperature was in the high forties. Was I really going to have to give up everything Linda and I had worked our entire marriage for? Our home together? Our security of being with each other? Our love? OK, sure, she'd left me, so I could keep the house and maybe find a way to carry on by myself, but what would be the point? Would it be worth it to go on the living rest of my life alone in the home Linda and I had shared for so many years, reliving all the memories of our life together? A life I was now finding out she wasn't happy in. At least with me it. It was an experience I didn't savor. The truth of the matter was that I liked being married to Linda. She, however, was now making it clear she no longer liked being married to me.

Thirty minutes of walking brought me to a small, secluded park on the south shore of Orchard Lake, the lake our town is named after. It measures a mile long by a quarter of a mile wide and the park I was in was as good a place as any to mull over my fate. I went to a wooden bench and sat down, staring across the water, seeing nothing but my own swirling thoughts. Thoughts that weren't helping me find any answers as to what I should do next.

When I had talked with Danny at the reunion a few months earlier one thing stuck out more than anything and that was this: when he had asked me if was happy, I felt I had stumbled with the answer. In retrospect, I can say that I honestly wasn't sure if I was all that happy, even though I'd told him I was. But here's the thing. When Danny said he was happy, he really was. He honestly and truly meant it. He'd started his own auto-rebuilding business when he'd come back from Vietnam and it had flourished. His specialty was working on classic cars from the 50s and 60s, and he apparently was good at it although he didn't toot his own horn about his success at all. (Sorry about the pun).

"When I started it was just me and my shop in the garage attached to our home," he told me that night. "Now I own a good-sized garage in south Minneapolis and have three employees, plus my oldest son who pretty much runs things now." He sat back and sipped his water. "He's a way better mechanic than I ever was."

I liked that he loved his work and took pride in what he had accomplished and I told him so. "Sounds like it's been a good life, for you," I said. Did I detect a little envy in my voice? I hurried to add, "Things seemed to have worked out well."

He grimaced at my observation and told me he'd had his share of 'issues' as he put it, using his fingers to make quote marks in the air. "I don't want to belabor the point," he said, "but I had problems with drugs and alcohol when I came back from 'Nam. I had anger issues, too, with my temper and fighting and all that. Thankfully Kim (his wife, he'd told me earlier) has stuck by me. I wouldn't be here if it wasn't for her."

I couldn't believe his candor with me; I was only a guy, a person who, more than anything, was a lucky punch and a broken finger away from being a complete stranger to him.

I reached for my JD and coke and then stopped myself. He looked at me and smiled. "Go ahead, it doesn't bother me. I've been clean and sober for thirty-two years."

Something about the way he said it, though, made me stop. He wasn't judging me, but the way he looked at me made me think that he knew something I didn't. Maybe I was drinking too much, and, more to the point, relying on it too much. I pushed my drink aside and didn't touch another drop that night.

I liked that Danny had his own business, something he believed in and had a passion for. When I was younger, growing up around an uncle and grandfather who enjoyed fishing and hunting and spending time camping in the woods, I was influenced enough by them to want to have a career working outdoors. Like them, I enjoyed being outside and saw myself going to college and becoming a Wildlife Biologist or something like that. I could be outside, work at a job I enjoyed, and earn a living while I was at it.

Nice idea but it never happened. Why? Nothing went wrong per se, but life offered me another path and I took it. When I was at the University of Minnesota I met Linda and we got married right after we graduated. Then we had three kids in quick succession. I decided while she was pregnant with our first child that maybe the best thing I could do was to get a job making more money than a Level 1 Biologist working for the State of Minnesota could make. I answered an ad for an entry-level sales position for the largest insurance company in the upper Midwest and was hired immediately. The work was steady, I was good at it, I earned a decent salary and, just like that, I was on my way. But, now, sitting on my bench by the lake, I remembered at the time Linda had questioned my decision.

"You're sure you want to give up your dream?" she had asked me. "You don't have to, you know. After the kids are older, I'll go back to work. She was just starting her teaching career as a fourth-grade teacher and was good at it. "We can get by until then if we're diligent with our spending. I'm sure we can. We'll just budget a little bit tighter, that's all. Above everything else, I want you to be happy."

Linda's prophetic words were now coming back to me. I hadn't so much as forgotten about them in all these intervening years, as ignored them. When the kids were old enough, she had made good on her promise. She went back to her teaching job and enjoyed a long and successful career in the Minneapolis school system. She was beloved by both her students and other teachers, once having won Minnesota Teacher of the Year, an award that said it all. She was exceptional, but humble, saying in her acceptance speech that she owed it all to the amazing students she was privileged to teach and to the wonderful school she worked for. She was bright and modest - two characteristics worthy of admiration.

On the other hand, I had chosen to stay with the security of my insurance job, telling myself that I was doing the right thing for my wife and kids. I was neither bright, nor modest, and certainly didn't win any awards. I just did my job, telling myself everything was fine and I was happy.

But was I?

A little while after Danny and I had begun talking, a nice-looking dark-haired woman came up and poked him jokingly in the muscle. "Hey there, big guy," she grinned at him. He turned to her and smiled a bright smile.

"Well, there you are. Hi, sweetheart." He turned to me. "Dave, I'd like you to meet my better half." He stood up and gave her a big hug. "This is my wife, Kim."

I stood, too, and we shook hands. She was warm and friendly, and I could tell there was still a connection there between the two of them, even after all these years. I could see it in their eyes and how they were with each other. Their love and affection was still strong. It was good to see.

They started talking about how crazy the reunion was getting, and I sat back and watched them, appreciating how happy and comfortable they were with each other. I was glad for them, but also slightly envious. I realized I was missing Linda. What was she doing right now at home? Probably working on a knitting project or one of her other many hobbies. I felt myself smiling inside, looking forward to going home to be with her. She was a wonderful person and I was lucky to have her.

Danny had told me earlier that Kim was the rock of their family.

"She's the glue, man. Without her, I'd be nothing." He looked hard at me then, making me remember the way he'd fought those three hoods in the locker room all those years ago. Then he told me something that now came back to me as I was sitting all alone on that bench by Orchard Lake. "A good woman is hard to find," he told me. "I know it sounds like a cliché, but too bad. It's the truth. If you find one, don't let her go. That's what I've done with Kim. Sure, I made mistakes, but I've tried to deal with them and put them behind me. And I've tried to do everything I can to be a good husband to her and do everything I can to keep her."

I'll never forget the look in his eye as he stared at me - the look of a fighter. It was deep. It was clear. And he meant every word.

It came to me now as I watched some ducks swimming along the shore that Linda had also been the glue for our family. She had been there for each of our three kids' birthdays, PTA meetings, sicknesses, marriages, and one divorce. Everything. Me? I had deluded myself that I was the *bread-winner*, an archaic term if there ever was one, and taken a backseat to family life, letting Linda shoulder the burden: one she accepted without complaint, I might add, because she had loved the kids and had loved being a mother. Plus, on top of all that, she had worked full-time. God, I'd been a jerk.

Why was all of this coming to me now? I think that Danny had helped put things in perspective. He had done something I hadn't done. He had acknowledged his faults as a person with his temper and dependence on drugs and booze, accepted them, done something about them and, as a result, become a better person for it all. He had realized that there was more to life than just himself; he had Kim, his kids, and his business, things to be proud of. But, more to the point, he realized how important they all were to him.

I, on the other hand, had hidden my unhappiness by withdrawing from my kids and my wife, eventually choosing to *drown my sorrows in alcohol* as they say. I had missed the point completely. What a pathetic, selfish idiot I was. No wonder Linda had left me.

I sat back and looked at the lake. The water was like glass and a flotilla of mallards had just landed nearby, probably to rest up on their way in migration south. A flock of geese flew overhead, their boisterous honking filling the air. The fall leaf change was in full swing with trees dotting the hillsides exploding in kaleidoscope colors of reds, yellows, and oranges. Late blooming purple asters shown in the sun and cattails along the shoreline were bursting with seed. Life was happening all around me, something that I used to appreciate, even love when I was younger, and, it seemed, spent years and years forgetting how to do it. Instead, here I was, sitting alone, feeling sorry for myself, on the verge of losing the most important person in my life.

I didn't like that I was such a pathetic figure. No wonder Linda had said goodbye to our marriage, our home, and me, and moved on to start a new chapter in her life - one that didn't include her husband. I pictured what Danny would say if I called him and asked what I should do. He'd say, in no uncertain terms, "Get your head out of your ass and call your wife and apologize."

It was the best advice I'd ever heard, and I silently thanked him for it.

I reached for the phone in my pocket, took it out, and dialed Linda's number, ignoring what her note had said about not calling, wondering if the fact I did so would count against me. The hell with it. I had nothing to lose. I listened nervously as it rang once, then a second time. On the third ring, she picked up only saying, "What?"

I tried to gauge her mood, but couldn't. Was she mad at me, or sick of me, or just plain tired of me? Probably all three, but I just couldn't tell.

"Hi. It's me," I said and rushed on before she had a chance to hang up. "Please hear me out. I just want to apologize for everything. I've been an idiot and I know I don't deserve you, but I'm so sorry about so many things. I want to talk with you. I want to change. I want to try and make it up to you. I love you and don't want to lose you. Please forgive me." My words spilled out without my thinking or planning. I only knew they came from my heart, and every one of them was true.

I was quiet then, not sure what else to say. The silence over the line was deafening. Out of the corner of my eye, I caught a movement. It was a beautiful orange and black monarch butterfly, landing delicately on one of the nearby purple asters. I knew it was there to feed and then rest for a few moments before continuing on its remarkable journey thousands of miles across the country to Mexico where it would spend the winter before beginning its journey home.

The monarch butterfly's beauty, frailty, and strength have always been a wonder to me. I took it as a sign, a sign that maybe Linda would forgive me and we could pick up the pieces of our life and start afresh. Together. Was that too much to ask for? Or was I deluding myself? Had I drifted too far from the core of our marriage and the love we once had?

I saw in my mind an image of Danny nodding his head, saying, 'You did the right thing by expressing yourself like you did. Now you have to show her. Remember, actions speak louder than words.'

Yeah, I know it was another cliché' but that didn't matter – those words would be right. Danny's life had been all about action. First by fighting with his fists when he was young and then by fighting with his heart by changing for the better as he got older.

Could I do that? Could I change? I needed to and wanted to and it was clear I was going to have to if I wanted to become a better person and better husband and keep Linda in my life.

I pictured myself talking to her in the near future, listening closely to her, and learning to appreciate anew her and the life she had created for herself (irrespective of me) with her friends, interests, and hobbies.

I pictured myself paying more attention to her, learning to listen to her concerns, and doing what I could to make her life better.

I pictured taking her to her favorite restaurant more than once a year (and finding new ones that she would like.)

I saw myself doing whatever I could to show her that I still loved her and wanted to be the kind of guy that she married and believed in all those years ago.

I wanted to prove to her that I would never drink again.

I wanted to be her friend.

And, especially, I wanted to show her that she could count on me to be a dependable and trustworthy husband for the rest of our lives together.

If she would only give me one chance, I was sure I could prove it to her.

My hand began to sweat as I held the phone. I'm not even sure I was breathing as I sat there, waiting for her to say something.

Finally, she spoke, "Dave?"

"Yes?"

"Didn't you read my note?"

And she hung up.

***

I read somewhere once that the pathway to hell was paved with good intentions. Was I naive to think I could talk my long-suffering wife into believing that I could change my life and be a better person on the strength of a fifteen-second phone call? Most definitely the answer was "Yes," I was that naive and probably stupid to boot, as was born out by her quick and decisive answer.

But I saw Danny's face in my mind's eye encouraging me not to give up. Was I man enough to step up and fight for my wife and our marriage?

The answer? An unqualified, YES!

I got up from the bench with fresh resolve and left the park, my footsteps moving ever faster as I headed home. I had a lot of work to do: I was going to clean the house from top to bottom, dump out all my booze bottles, and have a long talk with myself. I had to figure out the next steps in my fight to win Linda back. To that end, I planned to call Danny. He'd encouraged me to do so, but two months ago I didn't think I needed to. Now I did. I had a feeling he'd be able to help. I was going to need both help and a friend. I'd call him today.

I knew the road wouldn't be easy, but that was all right. I was willing to face the future. I wanted to change. I wanted to learn how to be a better person, one Linda would want to be with. This was a fight of a different nature than when Danny and I fought those hoods back in high school. Back then it was for some misdirected idea of pride. Now it was my wife, for the person I valued most in my life. My decision was made. I was committed to doing all it took to win her back. I didn't want to lose her.

I hurried on, eager to move forward. The fight had just begun.

Why I Don't Run Away Anymore

I've run away from home twice.

The first time I was five years old. It was right after my sister was born and I guess I was feeling sorry for myself what with the attention my parents were paying to her and all. I remember I put some plastic dinosaurs in my pocket, tied a cape around my neck (a raggedy old towel, actually) like Superman, my favorite superhero, put on my Minnesota Twins baseball hat, and left home. My jerk older brother just laughed at me. I got two blocks away before Mrs. Nelson, a kindly kindergarten teacher out working in her garden saw me, figured something wasn't quite right, and brought me home. I don't believe I could sit down comfortably for a week after the spanking my father gave me.

The second time, seven years later, I should have known better.

"God damn it, you big bully!" I yelled at Sean. He grabbed me in another head-lock and ground his knuckles over my skull, giving me a knuckle rub, just one more torture in his bag of tortures he was forever dishing out on me, his unfortunate little brother. Then he threw me to the ground, punched me in the back, rubbed my face in the dirt, and walked away, laughing. It was just another normal day.

Older than me by three years, Sean outweighed me by fifty pounds, was almost a foot taller, and was becoming the horror, the absolute terror of my existence - something I certainly didn't need. Mom had left home with her boy friend the year before, never to be heard of again, leaving me and Sean and my younger sister, Lea, under the care of my poor excuse of a father and his girlfriend Sally who my dad, I kid you not, always called Sexy Sal. Geez.

Now when I say that the two adults responsible for taking care of me and Sean and Lea left something to be desired in the parenting department, that would be putting it mildly. Dad worked for some kind of auto parts store and drove a delivery truck between our home in the little town of Orchard Lake, located twenty miles west of Minneapolis, and St. Cloud, seventy miles to the north. Sexy Sal worked at a cut-rate (no pun intended) hair salon in Brooklyn Center, about thirty miles away. I think it was called the 'Cut n' Go' so you could probably imagine what it was like.

Sexy Sal wore her bleach blond hair in a bee-hive style like it was the year 1965, smoked Kool cigarettes, and liked to drink any kind of beer that was available. Dad wasn't much better but without the hair. He was a large man - a camel straight smoker with a big beer belly who shaved his head when he started going bald ten years ago and had grown his beard out so he looked like an outlaw biker. Maybe that was his fantasy. Who knows? All I can tell you is that he didn't own a motorcycle. I knew that for a fact. Being an outlaw? Well, not that I knew of but you'd have to ask him if you really wanted to know.

I'm telling you all of this to let you know they were gone from home a lot, leaving us to supervise ourselves, and let me tell you, the end result wasn't pretty. Especially that summer. I guess Sean at fifteen was supposed to be in charge but he was a mean little kid when he was young and the older he got, the meaner he became. My belief, from the time I could think at all, was that he was born mean and nothing in my life up to this point contradicted that idea.

I suppose, in the long run, I should have counted myself lucky to be just getting knuckle rubs from him. After all, at the beginning of the summer he had started carrying a Buck 110 folding knife with a four-and-a-half-inch blade that locked in place and the things he used to do to frogs and toads and the occasional baby bird...man, it still makes me sick just thinking about it. It was my ever-growing fear that he could easily start doing the same to me. Or worse.

Fortunately, he didn't bother with my poor little sister Lea. I guess he thought that being a girl, she wasn't worth the time. She mostly stayed in her room and played with her dolls, smart enough to stay out of the way of her two older brothers who fought all the time and, in general, made life around the house pure hell.

Add to that the fact Dad and Sal liked to party a lot when they were home...well, like I said, they weren't going to win any prizes when it came to parenting, that was for sure. More than once I heard them talking late at night, beer bottles rolling around on the floor, watching some late-night talk show, and smoking a final bowl of weed. Something to the effect of:

Dad: "God those friggin' boys are a major league pain in the ass."

Sexy Sal: "No shit, Sherlock. Losers, both of them. Give me another hit."

My teacher last year in sixth grade used to read to us from a book the final half hour of the day on Fridays. We ended the year with *Tom Sawyer* and I have to tell you that I liked the main character a lot. The two things I got from the book were one, even though Tom was a hellion (big word, huh? I might have gotten it from the book), he at least had his aunt who loved him, and two, sometimes running away was a good idea.

So that's what I did.

School had ended in early June and by the middle of July, I'd had it with Sean. He was supposed to be working that s,ummer at Jorgenson's hardware store, a place near enough to us so he could walk or ride his bike but, he kept getting to work later and later until finally Mr. Jorgenson the owner just up and fired him. I heard that his final words to Sean were, "Send Quinn back here when you get home. He's ten times the worker you are."

Now, how he knew that I had no idea, but it pissed off Sean to no end and when he got back to our house he beat me up, apparently just on general principles. He must have enjoyed it too, deriving some perverse, sick pleasure in pounding on me because it started him on his campaign of terror, tormenting me every day, beating me up whenever he had the chance, and making my life miserable. And for no good reason either, I might add, other than I was small for my age and couldn't fight back. He was just as mean to me as he always had been and getting meaner with each passing day.

I remember the last time he did it very clearly. It was a Tuesday morning and he'd caught me in the backyard by the garage cleaning the spokes of my bike, not paying attention or being on the lookout for him like I normally was. He jumped me from behind and pounded the crap out of me, twisting my arm up behind my back just for good measure while I begged him to stop. When he was finally done with me he threw me to the ground and stomped on my back while I lay sprawled out in the dirt.

He sneered at me and said, "I'll see you later." Which of course meant he'd beat me up again. Then he sauntered away inside to play on the Atari set up in the living room.

I sat up and wiped the blood from my nose and wondered how I was going to ever survive until school started because now with him not at work, Sean seemed to take it as his new job to torment me a will. Full time! Not a pleasant future for me at all. Fall looked to be a long time away.

You might wonder, 'Why doesn't this kid just tell his dad?' That's a very good question. I momentarily thought about it that day but had a feeling it would be as fruitless as the approximately five hundred other times I'd told him over the years - about Sean and how he made my life a living hell on a daily basis. But there wasn't a lot of sympathy for my plight from dear old Dad on that front. 'Just suck it up and deal with it, Quinn,' was his basic answer, often followed up with, 'Be a man, for Christ sake,' tacked on for good measure. Thanks a lot, Dad. So no, I didn't spend a lot of time that day thinking about telling my dad anything about Sean and what he was doing to me. I figured I'd just have to find a way to learn to live with it.

I was struggling to get to my feet, get on my bike, and go for a ride just to get away from that big idiot of a brother for a while when something happened that I'll never forget. Lea quietly opened the back screen door, walked across the thread-bare patch of grass we called a backyard and sat down in the dirt next to me. She was seven years old and a skinny little snip of a thing. She had long, stringy blond hair and liked to wear soft cotton dresses that probably were colorful once but were now faded away to gray after so many washings no matter what the color they'd been. And, like I mentioned before, she liked to stay in her room and play with her dolls. Barbie's. I think she had three of them. She and I were pretty close, maybe because of Sean. I liked her and she liked me and I even gave her rides on my bike now and then, you know, just goofing around.

Anyway, she never talked much and she didn't this time either, but she did something then that I later thanked her for over and over and over again in the years to come. She reached her hand into the pocket of her dress, pulled out Sean's knife, and handed it to me only saying, "He left it on the kitchen table. I don't think he's missed it yet." Then she got up, brushed the dirt off her dress, skipped back to the house, and went inside. It was the most she'd ever spoken to me in I don't know how long.

Stunned, I held the knife in my hand. It had a golden brown handle and when I snapped it open its shining, razor-sharp blade gleamed in the sun. Sean had brought it earlier that summer at the hardware store with his first paycheck and was as proud of it as anything else in his life. Probably more than the Atari even. I knew it was only a matter of time before he noticed it missing and why Lea gave it to me I could only guess at. Maybe for my own protection. But if I kept it and he found out...Man, I pictured him beating me up in a way so bad that I quickly had to erase the image from my mind because it was too disturbing. Then I imagined him coming at me with his knife, using the blade on me like I'd seen him use it on those poor defenseless creatures...

God, why was I thinking about those kinds of things right now? *Stop it!* I told myself. So I did.

But what I did think about right then and there was this: Now is the time to go. Now's the time to get away from this hell-hole and move on to "greener pastures," (another phrase I'd heard once in school, maybe even in Tom Sawyer). And that's exactly what I did.

I stood up, put the knife in my front pocket, crept to the back door, and listened through the screen. I could hear Sean playing *Space Raiders* on the Atari so I knew what little mind he had was now completely occupied by his make-believe world of outer space aliens and whatnot. I quietly opened the door, holding my breath when it screeched a little and tip-toed across the kitchen floor, glad I was wearing my Converse sneakers. I crept to Lea's room and went inside, closing the door quietly behind me. She was sitting on the floor with her dolls arranged in front of her in a half circle. She looked up at me with her big eyes and greeted me with a little smile. I went to her, knelt, and gave her a hug.

"I just wanted to tell you goodbye," I said, holding her tight. "I'm leaving and I'm taking the knife with me." I couldn't think of what else to say. I sat back, looked at her once, and then hugged her again. She held me close and I almost didn't go then, not wanting to leave her all by herself, but I forced myself to pull away and stand up. I quickly stepped back before I could think too much about what I was intending to do and maybe talk myself out of it.

I went to her door and opened it, looking back once when Lea said, "Be careful."

I waved to her and whispered, "I will," as I stepped out of her room, watching as she waved to me while I closed the door behind me. With the sound of it latching in place I felt like I was not only saying goodbye to her, but saying goodbye to part of myself, too. I have to admit, it was pretty emotional. But since I now had the knife I had a strong reason to get away or else face Sean's wrath - my desire to run away stronger than doing the smart thing which would have been to put the knife back on the kitchen table and forget the whole thing.

Lea's image would come back to me again and again that day. Dad and Sexy Sal? I never thought of them once.

I snuck across the hall to the room I shared with Sean. It was a mess. I had made the beds that morning and picked clothes and stuff off the floor like I always did because it was one of my jobs around the house, but after pounding on me Sean must have decided to trash the room just for good measure. It didn't take much to set him off. I looked around, thinking to myself that I should pick it up and straightened things out again. Then I almost slapped myself on the forehead. *Who's the idiot, now?* I thought. Not me. Nope, not anymore. The hell with it. It's his room now and he can do whatever he wants to with it. And to hell with him, too, by the way. I'm outta here.

I reached under my mattress where I kept my wallet hidden. It had seven dollars and thirty-seven cents collected from the odd jobs I did for my next-door neighbor and I figured I could use the money on the road. I put the wallet in my back pocket and then glanced in the mirror, choosing not to dwell on my small size and skinny build, concentrating instead on what I was wearing. I had on a tee shirt that once was white but now was kind of gray (like my sister's dress) and cut-off blue jeans. I wondered if I should maybe bring a jacket. Naw, I thought to myself, it's too hot out. I'll get a job somewhere if I need more clothes. The idea of traveling light appealed to me. Just like a hobo or something.

I took one last look around and said goodbye. I was really going to do it. I was going to run away. I was both excited and nervous, but not that nervous. "Goodbye forever," I whispered, and then I was gone.

I snuck out of my room, down the hall, through the kitchen, and out of the house. I ran to the garage, jumped on my bike, and rode it through our little town out to the highway where I stopped, looking back and forth in both directions. Right, would take me past the lake our town was named after and eventually all the way to the big city of Minneapolis. I really didn't want to go there so I started riding my bike west, in the opposite direction, out toward the country. Besides, there were a lot of cars on the road going that way and I figured I had a better chance of catching a ride.

A mile of riding brought me to the far outskirts of town. I hid my bike in a weed-choked ditch and climbed back onto the highway. It wasn't even noon yet but the sun was burning hot and I was already sweating. I stood on the side of the road and put my thumb out, just like I'd seen them do on the television. I had no idea where I was going or what I was going to do when I got there. All I knew was that I was running away for real this time. I felt in my front pocket. The first time I ran away I brought toy dinosaurs. This time I had Sean's knife. It gave me a sense of security and I liked that feeling. It was a feeling I wasn't used to. It felt good.

***

Highway 12 is a two-lane road that leads west to the Minnesota border with South Dakota and beyond that to Montana and I think eventually the Pacific Ocean. He pulled over after I'd only been standing there for maybe fifteen minutes, long enough to get hotter and sweatier than I already was and to start looking longingly at the Texaco station about a quarter mile down the road, thinking maybe I could find a hose or something and get a free drink of nice, cold water.

He was driving an old, faded red, and slightly rusted pickup truck with a big dog kennel in the back but no dog. There was also a roll of dark green canvas tied up with rope. I bent down and peered in the side window as the truck rolled to a stop.

He leaned across the seat toward me. "Hi there, young man," he said. "Need a lift?"

He seemed nice and polite. He was maybe thirty years old, clean-shaven with light brown hair that fell across his forehead. He was wearing tan-colored slacks with a sharp crease in each leg and a clean white, short sleeve dress shirt, open at the collar. For some reason, I remembered his shoes as being fancy. They had tie laces and were shiny and black. Coming from where I was coming from with a dad who was big, bearded, and scary looking, this guy looked like a choirboy.

I was hot and frankly starting to get bored. "Sure, "I said, happy to get out of the sun and trusting he was as innocent as he seemed. I opened the door. "Where're you going?" I thought to ask, not that I cared. Anywhere away from my home and Sean was good enough for me. I climbed in and settled onto the front seat.

"Anywhere you want," he joked, laughing, showing me a row of small front teeth stained brown. He put the truck in gear and carefully accelerated back onto the highway.

His response to my question seemed odd, and right then and there my rather cavalier attitude about hitting the road and living on my own began to diminish. I started to get just the tiniest bit nervous. In rethinking my actions that day, I should have jumped out while I had the chance. But I was just a kid who didn't know any better. I'd made my decision earlier that morning and right now it was up to me to live with it and make the most of it. *What the heck?* I finally thought to myself. *What have I got to lose? He seems nice enough. Everything should be OK.* I set my suspicions aside and settled in on the bench seat of the truck thinking I might as well enjoy my ride and whatever lay ahead, just like a real adventure.

"What's your name, young man?" he asked as he brought the truck up to speed. The wind blowing through the cab was hot, but it felt lots better than standing on the side of the highway baking to death. He had a soft voice with kind of a southern accent and seemed very well-mannered.

"Quinn," I told him, wondering if I should tell him that my last name was Charles. Nah. I decided not to. I'd taken enough ribbing in my life for having a first name as my last name. "What's yours?" I asked instead.

He told me his name was Ronny. "Like Ronny Milsap," he said laughing. "You know, the blind country singer?"

I had no idea what he was talking about. Dad was a big Lynard Skynard fan. Ronny Milsap? Never heard of the guy.

"Don't know him," I said.

Ronny just shrugged and grinned with those brown teeth which for some reason were starting to irritate me. How hard was it to take a minute and brush your teeth every day, anyway? Even Sean did that, and he hardly had the gumption to get dressed in the morning. Plus, now that I was in the truck, and even though the windows were down, the day being so hot and all, there was a stink inside that was starting to make me a little sick to my stomach. Maybe it had something to do with the dog that kennel was for. But there was no dog around. To take my mind off the stink and my nausea I asked him where he was going.

"Out west, Quinn. Got a job lined up."

That sounded great. I'd never been further away from home than Minneapolis, and once up north to Duluth. Out west? Never.

"What kind of job?" I asked, just to be polite.

"Anything they want me to do, young fella. I'm a self-made man. I do a little bit of this and a little bit of that."

Well, that sounded good to me and I turned completely toward him, interested. Dad was always complaining about his job and the delivery truck he had to drive. At my young age doing a little bit of this and a little bit of that sounded like a pretty good deal.

"Does it pay good?"

He laughed long and hard at that one. "You bet it does, my boy. You bet it does."

My boy? I shifted a little in my seat. The stink was starting to go away, or maybe I was getting used to it. I looked at Ronny thinking that the guy was a little strange but, all and all, he seemed pretty harmless. At least he wasn't mean like Sean or ignoring me like my dad always did. That counted for something. I felt myself relaxing a little bit more. My stomach was a little better, too. *This ride might not turn out to be so bad after all*, I thought. In fact, it might turn out to be pretty good.

Ronny liked to talk. He told me he'd grown up in Oklahoma on a ranch. I guess that's why his accent sounded so different. He'd worked at a bunch of jobs of which I'll list a few: cowboy on a ranch in Montana, maintenance worker on an oil rig in the Gulf of Mexico, forest ranger in Idaho, gold miner in Colorado, and a riverboat captain on the Mississippi River. I think he also had been a bush pilot in Alaska and worked on a lobster boat up there, too.

So he'd done a lot, and I remember being impressed - my imagination running away with me, picturing myself in each of those scenarios. Despite my initial misgivings I was beginning to warm to the guy. Not once did I think for a moment that he might be making all those jobs up to impress me, relax me, and get on my good side.

Around mid-afternoon, we stopped for gas in western Minnesota near the town of Atchison. I got out and stretched my legs. The temperature had to have been around ninety. The heat reflecting off the pavement looked like rippling waves and even the tar in the parking lot felt soft under my tennis shoes. I looked west out across a big cornfield toward the horizon. There was nothing out there but corn and more corn. The stalks looked shriveled, and the leaves shriveled and faded. The wind blew hot air from the south. The only thing alive were some crows across the highway, feeding on something on the ground. It was pretty humid too. Even though I'd never been in one before, I got that feeling that being outside right now felt like what it must have felt like to be in a sauna.

I was picturing myself swimming in a nice, cool lake somewhere, floating on an inner tube, when Ronny asked, "Quinn, are you hungry?"

His voice startled me. He'd finished filling the tank with gas, come up beside me, and put his hand on my shoulder. I was surprised to see him not sweating at all. But I was. Perspiration was running down my back and I could feel it beading up on my forehead under the brim of my baseball cap. I looked toward the gas station, still conscious of his hand on me. It felt a little strange. My dad never did stuff like that, but to be honest, it didn't feel too bad either. Next to the gas station was a little cafe with a sign that read, *Ma's Place*. It looked good to me.

"Sure," I said, thinking suddenly that I really was hungry. Visions of pancakes with butter and syrup dripping off the sides and an order of sausage filled my mind. All I'd had to eat that day was my usual breakfast of a bowl of cheerios and I'd had to eat them dry since Sean had taken the last of the milk. It occurred to me that

I was beyond hungry, I was starving. "That'd be great!" I turned and smiled at him

Ronny smiled in return and said, "Be right back." I watched as he went to the truck. I had a sudden clutching feeling inside that he'd take off and leave me stranded in this little town all by myself out in the middle of nowhere. But to my relief, he didn't. He simply started the engine, pulled away from the pumps, and parked by the cafe. Then he got out, came over to where I was standing, put his arm around my shoulder, and led me inside. I have to admit, I was relieved he had stayed with me.

The cafe was air-conditioned and the cold air hit me so hard it took my breath away. We sat in a booth with red vinyl seats that were slippery but comfortable. I quickly cooled off and entertained myself watching the sweat dry on my arms. The waitress was young and, to my inexperienced eyes, really good-looking. She had dark, wavy brown hair that fell past her shoulders just like my mom used to have. She brought us an icy pitcher of water and I drank down a glass in about ten seconds. The water was so cold it made the sides of my head hurt.

We sat across from each other and Ronny made small talk with the waitress whose name tag read *Annie*. He even turned around and chatted with the people seated behind him - an elderly couple who looked to me like they just stepped off the farm. I tried not to stare at the ring of white around the farmer's hairline and forehead that was probably from the hat he wore when he was working outside driving his tractor, or something. The lower half of his face was deeply tanned and he had on a plaid, short-sleeve shirt and a clean pair of bib blue jeans. His wife wore a pretty floral dress and a bonnet. I got the feeling this was a special outing for them. I caught a faint aroma of manure, maybe from the guy's boots, that I have to say wasn't all that unpleasant. For some reason, I liked seeing them in the cafe with us.

I ordered three pancakes which, when Annie set them down in front of me (I think she might have even given me a wink along with her smile), blew me away. They took up the whole plate. I drowned them in maple syrup and slabs of butter and wolfed them down along with my side order of sausages. Just like I'd imagined! Man, they tasted fantastic. Ronny didn't order anything. He just sat and watched while I ate and smiled at me. I was so hungry it never even occurred to me how strange it was that he didn't order or eat anything. He barely drank any water.

After I finished I excused myself to go use the bathroom. When I was done, I washed my hands and splashed cold water on my face. As I was drying off I looked at my reflection in the mirror. I couldn't believe how red my face was and my freckles stood out like crazy. I was a little sheepish about my looks. Most of the boys I knew and went to school with had nice, shiny, longish hair - long enough to blow a little in the wind. Dad had something against that kind of hair, probably because he'd lost most of his, so whenever he used his electric razor to shave his head he also did me and Sean. Buzzed us right down to the nub. So, along with being outcasts in town because of our family situation, we were also outcasts on account of how different we looked because of our hair, or lack of it being a more accurate way of putting it. *Now that I'm on the road,* I thought to myself, *I'll let my hair grow ou*t. Smiling into the reflection in the mirror at my great idea, I finished drying my hands and joined Ronny back at the table.

He greeted me with, "All set, there, Quinn?" He had been using my first name ever since he'd picked me up. The fact that he was getting so familiar with me was kind of odd, but not all that bad. At least he was talking to me like a person. Not like my dad, who just ordered me around, getting him beers and stuff, or Sean, who didn't talk to me at all, preferring instead to push me around and, of course, beat me up. Ronny talking to me was different but in a good way, like I was a real person, and that was just fine with me once I got used to it. In fact, it was kind of nice.

"Yeah, I'm good."

He pointed to my water glass. "Drink up, my boy. We might not be stopping again for a while."

"Ok."

I dutifully finished off my water and stood up. I noticed Ronny hadn't left a tip for my pancakes and sausage. I thought about using some of my own money from my wallet, but Ronny seemed in a hurry so I didn't. He hurried me out of the cafe and hustled me to the truck. I've always felt bad I didn't leave the nice waitress at least a quarter.

We got in the truck and I got settled. Ronny started the engine and drove out of the parking lot onto the highway. I was pleasantly full and feeling really good, thinking that running away was the smartest thing I'd ever done and that life on the road was the perfect solution to all my problems at home. But after a few minutes staring at cornfields, cows and the occasional farm house and barn, the heat must have started to get to me, because I began to feel kind of groggy. I put my hand on my forehead and was surprised that it felt cold and clammy instead of hot which was weird because I was sweating heavily under my tee shirt again.

"Quinn, are you feeling Ok?" Ronny asked, looking at me with a strange expression. One I can only describe as both concerned and excited.

"Not really," I said, feeling my words slur.

He patted the seat. "Just lay your head down here, my boy. Rest. I'm sure you'll feel better soon."

He sounded like he cared about how I was feeling so I trusted him and did just as he suggested.

"Ok," I said. And I lay my head down.

The next thing I knew I was waking up. Well, coming to was more like it. I was lying completely stretched out across the front seat of some sort of vehicle with my head jammed under the steering wheel. I was looking at the foot well and saw a brake pedal, an accelerator pedal, a steering column, and a bunch of wires. It took a minute for me to work it out, but when I did I remembered I was in Ronny's pickup. Then it all started coming back to me: the hitchhiking, the truck, Ronny, the cafe. But why was I here by myself? Where was Ronny?

I sat up and rubbed my eyes, feeling dizzy and disoriented. I looked out the driver's side window and saw cleared spaces on the ground, grass, a few trees, and some picnic tables. I looked out the front window and saw I was about fifty feet from a big, muddy river rimmed with brush, bushes, and some tall trees. It dawned on me that I had to be in a campground somewhere. The river looked to be about a hundred feet across and, if I had to guess, I thought it might be the Minnesota River since we'd been heading in that direction the last I knew. I looked to my right and there seated at a picnic table about thirty feet away was Ronny. And of all the things to be doing in a camp ground by a river, the thing he was doing was reading. It looked like a magazine. What the heck?

I watched him as I took a few moments to get my bearings. I was really kind of out of it. My head felt fuzzy and it was hard to think. My mouth was dry and felt full of cotton. My eyes were caked with sleep and crap and I rubbed them as clean as I could. My stomach ached too, pretty awful, like the flu. I'd been sick bad in my life before but not much worse than this. Then my stomach heaved once and I fought back an urge to throw up. Thankfully both windows were down, not only because of potential vomiting, but also because it was still hot out and it helped to have a little air movement in the truck. I could see out the front that we were pointing west. The sun was above the trees on the other side of the river but starting to go down, it's rays shinning into the cab, adding to the heat. I was woozy but sitting up seemed to be helping. I was slowly starting to feel better.

For some reason I had the feeling I should be as quiet as I could be, so instead of yelling out and greeting Ronny with, "Hi there. I'm awake," I scrunched down and peered over the edge of the window, spying on him and getting a feel for my surroundings. He had set up a tent near the picnic table. It was one of those old-fashioned dark green, canvas ones with no windows that looked just plain hot inside and it occurred to me that it must have been what I'd seen in the back of the truck when he'd first stopped for me.

From my seat in the cab which now with the sun shining in was starting to burn a little, I carefully looked all around outside, expecting to see other campers. But the eerie thing was that I didn't see anyone else. Not a single solitary person. This was really surprising considering it was the middle of summer and everyone in Minnesota knew this was the height of the camping season, even me and I'd never been camping before in my life. So maybe that's what we were going to do, I thought. Me and Ronny were going to go camping together. That would be fun. But it was strange that Ronny really didn't appear to be camping. He didn't have a fire going, or any firewood, or fishing poles, or a cooler, or anything. All he was doing was sitting at that picnic table reading a magazine. What was going on?

I watched him turn a page. The magazine looked worn out and old. I thought most people went fishing or something when they were camping. And, the more I thought about it, the more the way he was acting seemed doubly odd because I hadn't seen any luggage or camping gear or anything like that when he'd picked me up other than that roll of canvas which turned out to be the tent.no

Looking around the area some more I noticed he'd put the big dog kennel next to the tent. He must have moved it there from the back of the truck. Maybe he had camping stuff in the tent, but if he did, where had it come from? I was confused and beginning to get both nervous and suspicious. What was he up to?

Just to be sure, I cautiously turned around and looked out the driver's window and then out the back window. I saw no vehicles anywhere and then it dawned on me - not only were we all alone, but I was here with this guy who all of a sudden was starting to seem kind of creepy, just like when he'd first picked me up and I'd gotten in his truck. That feeling I had back then was coming back to me now all over again. My heart thumped a little in my chest. Something wasn't right.

I scrunched down again and went back to watching him over the edge of the passenger side window. For a few minutes, he just read, turning the occasional page. Nothing strange about that. I started feeling a little better about my situation. Maybe I was making things up in my mind. Maybe it was only my imagination getting the better of me. After all, he'd been nice to me, getting me lunch and all. He'd been friendly the whole time I'd been with him, and he'd even talked to me like I was more than just a kid. Like I was a real human being. Maybe things really were OK.

I was about to call out and greet him and get on with this camping business, when all of a sudden he reached down, ran his right hand along his right thigh, and began moving it back and forth. Back and forth. Back and forth. Then he casually moved it into his crotch, massaging and rubbing it, keeping his hand there for a long time - like he was playing with himself or something. Then it hit me. Oh, no! A feeling of dread washed over me that made my entire body go weak. My friends at school sometimes talked about weirdos who played with themselves and other stuff. I wasn't sure if that's what he was doing right now but whatever it was it didn't seem right. And I'll tell you what - it scared the hell out of me. My heart jumped and started racing. Call it a gut feeling or a premonition or what have you. It was the same feeling I'd get when Sean looked at me a certain way, just before he started to chase me hoping to catch me and beat me up. But this feeling I had now toward Ronny was a thousand times worse. It was a feeling of stone-cold fear.

I quickly ducked down. My heart started pounding away like there was no tomorrow, and a wave of terror washed over me. I had to fight back an urge to scream. Then it occurred to me that if I screamed no one would have heard me anyway and, I couldn't help it, but knowing I was so alone just made it worse. I was so scared, so terribly scared. I didn't want to anything bad to happen to me and I made myself hold back my fear and tried to think. I had to do something, but what? My whole body started shaking. I kept my head lowered below the window and searched in my mind for what I should do next. I came up with nothing. Absolutely nothing. I realized I was trapped. The shaking got way worse after that.

And who knows...I might have lost it right then and there and surrendered to my fate with Ronny except for one thing. My mind went to the safest place I knew, my home. I saw Dad and Sexy Sal and Sean and Lea. I focused on Lea, my sweet little sister who I cared for more than anyone else in the whole wide world. Then I remembered: Lea had given me Sean's knife. I had it in my pocket. And it wasn't so much the knife (although that was certainly comforting in a totally bizarre kind of way) but it was the thought of Lea giving it to me that helped calm me down. I centered my mind on my last vision of her - my little sister playing with her dolls, nice and safe in her bedroom, and I made myself keep that vision in my mind as I tried to reason out what I should do. There was one thing for sure. Ronny was some kind of weirdo, there was no doubt about that, just like my friends at school used to talk about. I wasn't safe and it was only a matter of time before he came for me. I had to figure out how I could get away.

My first idea was this: Maybe I could just climb out the opposite window on the driver's side, slide to the ground, and make a break for it. But then where would I go? And what if he saw me? What if I couldn't outrun him and he caught me? Then what? Oh, man, 'Think Quinn,' I told myself, 'Think!' But I was so scared my mind was starting to go blank.

I took a chance and snuck a peek over the edge of the window frame to check on him and that was my undoing. Ronny suddenly looked up from his reading and, seeing me staring at him, grinned and closed his magazine. I froze.

'Well, well, well. Look who's awake," he said, smiling and standing up, "It's my little pal, Quinn. How are you doing, young man? Sleep well?"

He took a last look at his magazine and then started walking slowly toward the truck, all the while staring straight at me.

My mind started racing, grasping for an idea. Any idea. I had to do something. My fear was so overwhelming I almost wet my pants. But I didn't. Instead, I did the only thing I could think of. I put my hand in my pocket and took out Sean's knife. I carefully held it below the sight line of the window and opened the blade, waiting, watching as Ronny came toward me, his smile confident. But, I have to say, holding that knife didn't help all that much. I had no idea what I was going to do with it.

And that creep took his time coming for me, that was for sure. One step after another, slow and steady, while my heart pounded in my chest like a kettle drum. And with every step he took my fear grew and grew until my mind almost went blank. It didn't, although I almost wish it had, because instead I was left with watching him while my mind whirled out of control, knowing that if didn't do something there was no doubt that this guy who had once been so nice and kind to me, now was going to do something bad to me.

As he walked he kind of sauntered, swinging his hips a little, which freaked me out even more. Then half way to me he took a length of thin rope out of his back pocket and dangled it from his right hand, twirling it in a circle. With his left hand, he raised it a little and started moving it back in forth like he was waving at me.

It took him maybe half a minute to all total to cross to me. Both were the shortest and longest half minutes of my life and as he got closer, my fear turned to panic. I knew for sure I was going to die. When he was a few steps from the truck, he started beckoning to me with his index finger like that witch in The Wizard of Oz. 'I'm coming to get you.' God, I couldn't help it - I started shaking all over again.

When he reached the truck he put his right hand on the handle, rope dangling from it while he paused waiting, toying with me I guess, looking at me to see how'd I react. We were less than three feet apart - my only protection the door of the truck, but with the window down that wasn't much. I took a deep breath to try to quit shaking without much success. He was so much bigger than me and he acted so confident. Like he could do anything he wanted to me. My eyes welled up and I fought back tears as I tried to get myself ready.

"Here I come, Quinn," he said, smiling with those brown teeth. "I'm glad you finally woke up."

With his right hand, he pushed in the latch, opened the door wide, and held it there. He suddenly seemed to grow taller right before my eyes, growing until he was gazing down upon me, looking me over while I crouched and cowered. And he just stood there, silently tormenting me with eyes that now started to look like some sort of weird, slimy reptile's eyes. I tried not to faint dead away with the worst fear I'd ever felt in my whole life - I knew right then that once he was done doing whatever despicable things he was going to do to me, he was going to kill me.

I'm sure he was thinking that I was just a small for my age kid so I'd be easy prey for whatever sick thing he had in store for me. Holding the door open he put his left hand out toward me, reaching for me, thinking god only knew what unthinkable horror he had planned for me.

But I wasn't going to wait. I had kept the knife in my right hand hidden behind me and I didn't hesitate. I fought through my fear as adrenalin took over. I screamed as loud as I could as I lunged out at him, stabbing at his hand with my knife. I might have been small, but I was quick and I must have startled him because he moved at just that same moment I lunged and I missed his hand and instead slashed that razor-sharp blade right across his forearm. Deep.

He stopped, startled, and looked at the cut. So did I. For an instant nothing happened and I remember thinking, *Oh, my god, I'm in for it now. What did I do wrong? Why wasn't he bleeding?*

But then the blood came. In torrents. Streaming out of the gash, running out of his arm, covering it like he'd dipped it in a bucket of red paint. Big drops started falling to the ground, followed by a river of blood. Ronny screamed in shock (and, hopefully, pain) and fell back against the wide open door of the truck as he tried to stop the flow of blood with his right hand. He wasn't having any success. His knees sagged a little and he looked at me with disbelief as he tried to collect himself. But only for a moment. Then his eyes pierced me with an anger and hatred so deep I almost froze again. But I didn't.

In an instant, I slid off the seat, pushed past him, and hit the ground running. He tried to grab me but I was able to push his bloody arm away and he screamed again. I bolted to the back of the truck, around it, and then ran like hell to the river. I slid down the embankment and jumped into the muddy water thinking for some reason how refreshingly cool it felt. Then I fought my way out to the middle where I started swimming and floating downstream with the current. Was Ronny yelling and screaming and running after me? I don't know. My world had closed in and all I thought about was survival. But I'll tell you this: I never looked back. And I didn't know where I was going, either, but I didn't care. I was getting away and that's all that mattered.

It was many minutes later I realized I still had the knife gripped in my hand. I rolled to my back and floated, closed it, and managed to stuff it in my front pocket, thinking that Sean would kill me if I lost it. Funny what can come to your mind sometimes, especially considering who I was trying to escape from. Anyway, once the knife was safely put away, swimming became a lot easier.

I stayed in that river for as long as I could, my fear that Ronny was going to catch me becoming less and less the further along I dog paddled and swam. But I was still frightened and might even have floated in that muddy water all the way across the state of Minnesota to St. Paul if a farmer hadn't been tending to some cattle on the shore and seen me, called to me, and waded out into the water to drag me to safety. I realized then that I was close to being drowned, and that my fear of Ronny and what he might do to me if he caught me was the only thing that was keeping me going - keeping me afloat so to speak.

The farmer was old, strong, and kind enough to bring me up to his farmhouse (in fact he carried me most of the way in his arms). It was a big two-story white home with a wide porch - just like you see sometimes on the television. He brought me through the back door, right into the kitchen, and set me down on a rug by the door, saying, "Greta, look at what I found."

Whether he was making a joke or not I didn't know but his wife, who was stirring something on the stove, took one look and ran straight to me, smacked at her husband with her wooden spoon, and told him to get some towels which he did. Then she took over, helping me to the kitchen table where she sat me down, knelt on the floor, began drying me off, and fussing over me which, I have to admit, even to this day the memory of still makes me feel really good.

The farmer looked on, his eyes topped by white eyebrows that I swear stuck halfway up his forehead, giving me the once over while his wife worked on pampering me.

At one point she looked over her shoulder and said, "For pity's sake, Clive, don't just stand there dripping on the rug, get a towel and dry yourself off. I'm sure not going to do it for you." And he did.

When he was finished, he took a pipe from a pipe rack, filled it with tobacco, and lit it, taking his time, puffing away. When he was lit to his satisfaction, he said to me, "Your name wouldn't be Quinn by any chance?"

What the...?

"Yes sir," I told him. "It is," curious as to how the hell he knew that. Then I immediately got suspicious and frightened all over again. After what I'd been through, who wouldn't? "Why?" I looked toward the back door as I wondered if I'd stepped into another bad situation and I'd have to make a run for it. Again.

"Clive, quiet down and don't bother the boy," his wife, Greta, told him. "Can't you see he's frightened enough?"

She turned to me and smiled, reassuring me, "Don't let him scare you, young man. His bark is way worse than his bite." She looked past me toward the old farmer and I could almost see daggers coming out of her eyes.

Clive, I guess that's what his name was, shuffled his feet on the rug, shook his head, and said, "Didn't mean anything by it." He sucked on his pipe some more and conscientiously blew the smoke outside through the screen door. By this time got the feeling his wife pretty much ran the show in that household.

Greta made sure I was comfortable in my chair at the table, and after she'd dried me off she went and got a big quilt that she wrapped around me. It smelled clean and fresh, just like the out of doors. Then she went to the refrigerator and took out a bottle of milk. "You're all over the news," she said, pouring me a big glass."We've been listening on the radio. The police have been looking for you. We heard you'd been kidnapped."

She brought me the milk and a heaping plate of chocolate chip cookies and set them in front of me. Suddenly I was famished and I started eating them right away. They were the best cookies I'd ever tasted. Then or since.

While I was eating, Greta stood next to me, watching over me with a concerned expression. She was a large woman with her gray hair pinned up on top of her head and she wore an apron over her dress. She knelt down and felt my forehead. It didn't bother me at all - her attention felt kind of nice. She had blue-green eyes that I especially noticed when she peered closely and asked softly, "Are you OK, Quinn?" Her breath smelled sweet, like peppermint.

"Yes, ma'am, I am," I told her, swallowing after finishing off my third or fourth cookie, "I'm fine. I really am." And for the first time since I'd run from the truck I truly believed I was and, I have to say, with the relief I suddenly felt, my eyes filled with tears and I almost started to cry.

She pulled me to her bosom and hugged me tight.

Well, I never...

Then she released me like she'd had a sudden thought and turned to her husband. "Lordy, Lordy, Clive," she exclaimed, "What in heaven's name's the matter with you? What are you waiting for? Get on the phone right now and call Sheriff Nelson. Quick. Tell him we've got that boy they're looking for. Tell whoever answers that he's OK and that he's sitting right here in our kitchen."

Clive, who I got the impression wasn't the fastest man alive, moved pretty darn quick under his wife's command and made the call.

That night I spent in the hospital in Ortonville. The next night I was home and I'll tell you this, after all I'd been through, even seeing Sean felt pretty good.

The morning after I got home Dad and Sexy Sal went to work. Sean and I were alone in the house for the first time since I'd been back. Everybody wanted me to rest so I had our bedroom to myself while Sean had to sleep in the living room on the couch which I don't think he minded too much because he could be close to his precious Atari. I'd given his knife back to him the evening before and received nothing in return but a menacing scowl.

That morning as soon as Dad and Sexy Sal left, he came into the bedroom. I immediately got nervous, my stomach tying itself all up in knots.

"So you stole my knife, huh?" he asked, sitting down on my bed and moving close.

I didn't answer right away. If I said no, he might find out Lea took it and gave it to me and I didn't want her to get in trouble. If I said yes, well...My imagination took over, leaving me with nothing but an unhappy ending. But hell, I'd had to deal with Ronny and I got through that all right. I figured I could take on anything - even whatever Sean had to dish out.

I puffed up my chest a little. "Yeah, I did," I told him, trying to sound tough. "So what?"

I looked at him and he looked right back at me. Two days ago the next move would have been me trying to get away and probably not succeeding, suffering Sean's version of justice with him proceeding to pound me into a bruised and battered, bloody little pulp before walking away with a self-satisfied smirk on his face.

But Sean surprised me by doing nothing violent. Instead, he put his hand on top of the covers on my leg, and not in a mean way at all. I only flinched a little.

"You don't have to lie for her," he said. "I know what happened with the knife. Lea told me."

"What?!" I screamed. "Is she all right?"

I tried to get up, but he held me back. I pictured my sweet-natured little sister submitting to his wrath. The image was more than I could bear. Then I had a thought. Wait a minute. I'd already seen her when I got home. She'd been perfectly fine. She'd even given me a big hug and everything before retreating to her room with her dolls for the rest of the evening.

"Relax, man, she's OK" he smiled. I accepted that Lea really was unharmed, but now Sean was smiling at me, which was creepy in and of itself. He never smiled at me. What was up with that?

"Seriously, she's just fine." He sounded almost like he was trying to reassure me. Like he knew I cared about Lea and he didn't want me to have to worry about her. Weird, was the word that popped into my mind. He was acting veery weird.

And he was also confusing me. Big time. He was right about my sister, of course, she truly was OK, but his behavior was so different from how he normally acted that I have to admit I was stunned. I looked at him like he was nuts and he must have seen the disbelief in my eyes because he waited for me to say something. But I didn't. I couldn't think of anything to say. I was speechless.

Maybe a minute went by before he continued. "I admit I was mad. Pissed as hell is more like it. I honestly was ready to kill you." I involuntarily shuddered, I don't think he noticed. He continued. "But then you were gone and no one knew where you were and someone found your bike up on the highway and called Dad who got mad and worried and he called the cops and..." He stopped and shrugged his shoulders. "And everything else happened so I just sort of forgot that I was mad at you."

What the hell? Was this real life or had I stepped into a fantasy world where nothing bad ever happens and there's unlimited ice cream and hot dogs every night for dinner and there's always a happy ending?

I was pondering the significance of such a world and finding it to my liking when I sensed a movement at the bedroom door. I pulled myself back to reality and looked. There was Lea, peeking around the doorframe. She was safe and unharmed and she looked great. She took a tentative step into the room. "Hi," she said, shyly.

"Lea!" I grinned and shouted. "Come here." I patted the side of the bed as I moved over.

She smiled and ran to me and hugged me so tight that for a moment I wondered where she got the strength for such a little thing. It almost hurt. Almost. And it felt great.

Sean stayed and sat on the bed with us and it suddenly came to me that it was the first time we all three had been together in our room before in I didn't know how long. If ever. And without fighting or anything. Like a normal family. I have to say it felt pretty good.

We talked a lot. Sean couldn't hear my story enough, especially the knife part, and he had me tell it over and over again until I finally got tired. I had been through a lot and it was still catching up to me. Finally he stood up, telling me that Mr. Jorgenson from the hardware store had called the night before and offered him his job back. "Yeah, he told me that when he'd heard what you had gone through and what you had done to get away, he thought maybe there was something in me that he'd missed. What do you think he meant by that?"

I had my own idea that Mr. Jorgenson hadn't missed anything, but I certainly wasn't going to tell Sean that so all I said was, "Maybe he was just being nice."

Sean shrugged. "Maybe. Anyway, I'm going down there now." He glanced at the clock on the nightstand by my bed. I followed his gaze. It read a few minutes after nine. "Shit. I'm late. I'm supposed to be there right at nine. See ya.'"

I watched as he ran out of the room. Then I caught Lea's eye. We looked at each other for a moment before my little sister pointed to Sean's disappearing back, then pointed to her head with her finger and twirled it around like 'he's crazy' and rolled her eyes. I couldn't believe it. She was making fun of Sean and it was funny! I laughed out loud for the first time in I don't know how long. It was right then and there that I had this thought: It was actually great to be back home.

***

You know what? They never found Ronny. When the sheriff came and picked me up at Greta and Clive's place, he talked to me on the way to the hospital. I was able to give them an idea where I had been and he immediately sent some deputies to search the area. The car, the tent and the dog kennel were all still there and surprise, surprise, no camping gear. But Ronny was nowhere to be seen. They searched the river, sent out hundreds of police type bulletins, dragged the river; everything they could think of. They never found him. My fervent hope is that he followed me into the river, the current got him and he drowned and was eaten by some big ugly fish with dull teeth. It would have served him right.

Dad and Sexy Sal pretty much acted the same as ever to me after I came home and I don't really want to talk about them.

But Sean and I got along better with each other. A lot better. I think the job at the hardware store helped - made him feel older and more responsible maybe. Anyway, he didn't pick on me so much afterwards, only sometimes joking with me, pretending like he was going to hit me, but he never did. I guess he just started to grow up some.

Lea and I became closer. I couldn't then, and still can't now, ever thank her enough for giving me Sean's knife that day. But maybe I was able to in some small way. She got me to play dolls with her a lot the rest of the summer right up until when school started (and even after that) and I didn't really mind. She was fun to be with and she had a really good imagination, especially when it came to using her dolls to play a game she called Family. I never did understand why she never had a lot of friends. Well, any, to tell the truth. Maybe she just liked being by herself. But she was a sweet kid and I figured playing with her and being kind of a friend to her was the least I could do after what she'd done for me, even if it had been inadvertent (another word I learned about in school.) I'm positive I wouldn't have escaped without what she'd done.

Next year in seventh grade in the fall my teacher, Mrs. Rademacher, had us studying *The Adventures of Huckleberry Finn*. Now there's a lot of fancy imagery and stuff in the book that I didn't understand, but there were some other things that I kind of got what she was saying. Like at one point she talked about how at the end Huck sort of is rescued from his life on the river and ends up living with his Aunt Sally and everything is fine for him. But he doesn't like being civilized and decides light out for the west. One of the points she was trying to make was about how life sometimes works in mysterious ways and there's no accounting sometimes for why things happen the way they do. Huck was rescued and had the good fortune to have the easy life all laid out for him: good food, clean clothes, a roof over his head, someone to love and care for him, and he chose to give it all up.

Mrs. Rademacher looked at me when she talked to us about that but didn't mention me or refer the class to my story from last summer about how I'd run away from home and what had happened and that I'd returned safe and sound. Thankfully most people didn't talk to me too much about it. But when she said it and I thought about I had to agree. I think I might even have nodded my head at her because I think what she meant was this: If Sean hadn't bought the knife and if Lea hadn't stolen the knife and given it to me, I wouldn't have been able to use that knife to get away. Weird, huh? Or lucky. But yeah, I think I got what she was saying. Sometimes life does work in mysterious ways.

By the way, Mrs. Rademacher was really nice to me that whole entire year.

And the knife. Later that first day I was home, Sean came in from his first day of working at the hardware store and sat down on the bed next to me and woke me up from a nap. "Here," he said. He handed me his knife. "I've been thinking about it all day." Which was surprising to me. Was I still dreaming? I actually pinched myself a little. No, I was wide awake. I'd never thought of Sean as much more than a bully. A thinker? I didn't think so. Maybe he was changing. In one day? I doubted it but I guess stranger things could happen. He looked at me like he meant what he was saying. "Seriously," he said. "I want you to have this." He reach over, gently took my hand and put his cherished knife in it.

I was shocked. I watched him to see if he was kidding, but he put his hand over mine and said, "Really. After all you went through, I want you to have this. You deserve it."

I took his knife and held in my hand. I opened the blade. The sheriff's department had wiped it down for traces of blood before they gave it back to me. They must have cleaned it too because it was gleaming. I looked at it and saw my image on the blade reflected back. I looked tired. Real tired. Then the image changed and I saw something else. For the briefest moment I thought I saw Ronny smiling at me with those ugly brown teeth of his. Grinning at me like I was all his and he could take me and do anything he wanted to me.

It freaked me out. I might have screamed. I don't know. But I do know that I quickly closed the blade and handed the knife back. I swear it felt hot to my touch like maybe it was possessed or something. I knew one thing. I didn't want to touch it again. Or have anything to do with it again. Ever.

I tried to compose myself and told him, "That's OK, Sean. But thanks. I think I've had it with knives for a while."

He looked at me for a moment or two before putting the knife in his pocket."All right. If you're sure. I think I get it."

Well, that made only one of us because I certainly didn't 'get it.' But I didn't make a big deal out of it and just let the matter drop. Sometimes, though, still to this day an image of Ronny will appear in my mind. And when it does, it's scary. People tell me that it's normal for that to happen, especially after all I had gone through. But I have to say, others have been through a lot worse. A way lot worse, and for the rest of my life I always counted myself as among one of the lucky ones. I got away.

Now I'll tell you one last thing. In the summer three years later Sean started driving a delivery truck for the company my dad worked for and I began working at the hardware store. Even though I was still small for my age, Mr. Jorgenson was happy to have me, saying, "Sean turned out to be a good worker, but I'll bet you'll be lots better." Well, Sean had changed and actually gotten to be a pretty good guy and I didn't want to say anything against him so all I did was tell Mr. Jorgenson that I'd do my best.

The first thing I did with my first paycheck was to take my money and go to the knife display case. I'd spent many long and enjoyable hours looking at the knives in there in those three years since Ronny, picturing myself having one of my very own. One like Sean's except a little bigger. I knew exactly the knife I wanted and so I bought it, snapped open the blade a few times, getting the feel of it and the balance of it. It felt good. Finally, I closed it up and put it in my pocket, said goodbye to Mr. Jorgenson and went outside to get my bike.

Now, I'm not sure I really understand it all that much, but ever since I escaped and came home, Lea started not to like to go outside the house alone. She took the bus to school and it was hard for her, but she was able to build up her courage and do it, but that was about it. Once she was back home she pretty much just stayed inside. So I sort of made a commitment to myself to be with her as much as I could. To be a friend to her. After all, if it hadn't been for her, I wouldn't be here to tell my story. So I told her that morning that when I got home from work I'd take her to the park, which was referred to by the locals as the City Park. It was located a short bike ride away on the shore of Orchard Lake and it was something we had started doing pretty often over the last three years. We liked to go there and goof around and play. She liked swinging on the swings and so did I. As I rode my bike home that afternoon I looked up at the sky. It was bright and blue with a few puffy clouds. A perfect day to play outside. I rode faster and got home in record time.

Lea was standing at the back door waiting for me. She ran outside, jumped on the back of my bike and we rode down to the park. We spent an enjoyable hour, swinging on the swings, playing on the merry-go-round, climbing on the jungle-gym and running up and down the slides, acting silly and goofing around. We had a fun time. She even laughed out loud a few times.

Before we came home we found some purple and white wildflowers that Lea liked so I cut a bouquet of them for her with my new knife. She carried them carefully in her hand all the way back to our house and then put them in a small juice glass that she filled with water from the kitchen faucet. Then she took them to her room and set them on her window ledge.

"My dolls like them, Quinn," she told me. I was standing at her door watching, happy that she was happy. She looked at me and said, "So do I." And then she smiled and waved as I closed the door. Standing in the hall and listening, I heard her saying, "Come on now girls, let's play family."

I went into the kitchen, got an apple and went outside and sat on the back step to eat it. I used my knife to cut it up. It sliced really good. Tasted good, too. When I was finished, I cleaned off the blade on my jeans and put it in my pocket. I've kept it there ever since.

After all these years I'm not sure if it helps or not, but I have to say that I like having my knife with me. It gives me a sense of security that I just can't explain. But when those images of Ronny appear and I start to freak out a little, I put my hand on my knife and they go away. I like knowing that I can do that - that I have a some control. And it gives me a little sense that I might not be a victim after all. Or ever again. But, I carry it with me every day. Just in case.

And you know what? I never once thought about running away from home again.

Rodent Control

Diane and I had been dating for a few months when she called. "Kyle, do you mind doing me a favor?" she asked.

"Sure," I said. "What's up?"

"Remember I told you about my brother, Johnny?"

Yes, I did remember her telling me. Among other things, I remembered that apparently Johnny had a bit of a drinking problem. Hold on. Let's be honest, here. He had accumulated multiple DWI's over the past twenty years, and he'd also been encouraged by a Hennepin County judge to do a few stints in rehab. So, I'd say he had more than a bit of a drinking problem. He had a major league drinking problem.

"Yeah, you told me about him. Is he okay?" I left her brother's aforementioned issue with booze hanging unspoken between us.

She paused before answering, and in that moment I knew Diane needed my help. I liked her a lot, maybe even loved her, and certainly was more than happy to oblige. I just needed to know what was going on.

"Well..." she slowly began. "Johnny's been sober for six weeks now and has just started a new job."

"Good for him." I was thinking, that's fine, I'm glad to hear for Diane's sake that her brother was staying sober, but there had to be more. "His new job...tell me about it. Does he like it?"

"I think so," she said, a little cautiously. "I'm happy for him. It's good to see him working."

I picked up on the hesitation in her voice and my concern went up a notch. "What's he doing?"

"He's with Simonson's Pest and Rodent Control. They're training him in on the rodent side of the business."

Oh, so that was it. My mind immediately went to a cable television show a few years back, *World's Worst Jobs*. The vision of

Diane's brother fooling around all day long with bug infestations and rats nests wasn't a pretty sight. But, she was my lady friend. Part of being her boyfriend was so show interest in her family, something I was not only happy to do, but wanted to do.

I was divorced and my three kids were grown and living in different states. My two younger sisters resided with their families on the each of the coasts, one in California and the other in Maine. My parents were both dead. I lived by myself, but I wouldn't say I was lonely, just alone. Those of you living by yourself probably can relate and understand the difference. The closer I got to Diane and her family the better, as far as I was concerned.

I knew how much Diane cared for Johnny. Like me, her family all lived far from Minnesota. Her younger sister lived in Florida, her son in Seattle, and her daughter in Kentucky. And, like me, her parents were both dead. She was by herself with only her brother to call her immediate family. Meeting with him would be an opportunity to show Diane I was not only committed to our relationship and also wanted to be close to the things that mattered most to her.

With all that in mind, I was completely on board with having him join us. Besides, I'd never known an animal control, or more specifically, a rodent control guy, and I prided myself on trying to keep an open mind when it came to experiencing new things. Plus, truth be told, I really was sort of interested in his new line of employment. I worked at the local hardware store, which was an alright job, just not the most exciting way to spend my time and earn a living. Dealing with what I imaged were rabid skunks and pesky chipmunks on a day-to-day basis? Well, that sounded way more interesting than directing Fred Jamison to the isle where the six inch hex-bolts were located.

"How's he like it?" I asked.

"Well, that's why I called. He had a pretty traumatic day today and wanted to talk to me about it. When I told him I was going out with you tonight he said, 'Cool. Kyle's a good guy. I don't mind telling him, too.' So I kind of suggested that he could met us."

We were going to dinner at Black's Ford, a nearby restaurant know for healthy, locally sourced foods. It was a cozy and well run place that featured live acoustic music on Saturdays. We were going tonight, Thursday, on what was turning out to be a much anticipated weekly date night for us. The restaurant would be quiet and peaceful, a good place to talk to Johnny. He lived in the small town of Delano, ten miles west of where both Diane and I lived in Orchard Lake. I'd met him two or three times before when he'd driven his motorcycle to his sister's home w I'd while I'd been there. I liked him. He was friendly and gregarious, a vastly different personality type from me, but that was no big deal. We got along just fine. In fact, I was looking forward to seeing him.

"Sure," I said. "Sounds good to me."

Diane sighed with relief. "Thanks, Kyle, you're the best."

Well, I wasn't sure about that, but it was nice to be appreciated. I'd been married once before for nearly twenty-four years, and it had ended contentiously. What can I say? My ex and I both had our issues and were better off apart. In fact, I'm sure she still hates me and won't be handing out compliments about me anytime soon, if ever. It had been a long time since I'd been anybody's 'Best.' Diane's words made me feel appreciated. It was a good feeling.

"I'll bet you say that to all the guys," I said, joking with her.

She laughed. "Only the ones I care about." Then she laughed again, making me feel even better."See you at seven?"

Only the ones she cared about? I liked the sound of that and grinned. "Seven it is."

A few hours later, I was home from work and standing in the bathroom of my little one bedroom apartment getting ready for our evening out. I glanced in the mirror, grimaced and shook my head. I learned long ago not to spend much time contemplating my reflection for too long. I'm what you would call an average guy, both in looks and general overall appearance; certainly not remarkable by any stretch of the imagination: five-eleven, brown eyes, thinning hair, neatly trimmed beard, maybe ten pounds heavier than I should be and a propensity for wearing work boots, jeans and plaid, flannel shirts. I'm more introverted than not and like to read, walk, bike ride and identify birds. Like I said, not remarkable. But Diane likes me and that says something. Just what, I'm not sure.

I enjoy being outdoors and that's what drew me away from Minneapolis, the large metropolitan city where I'd lived my entire life, to Orchard Lake, a quiet little town of less than two-thousand people, located twenty miles to the west. It's is a peaceful place to live and for years has been home to blue collar workers, happily putting down deep roots in well constructed ramblers built in the 20's and 30's. Most of the people who live here tend to stay put, and homes hardly ever go up for sale. For being so close to a large city, it's an area verdant with rolling hills, forests and fields. In short, it's as pleasant a place to spend one's life as anyone could hope for. But all that's changing.

For the last twenty years or so, builders have been buying up land and constructing huge, three to four thousand square feet homes on pristine, three acre lots. The locals refer to them as McMansions. It's been a sort of 'Build it and they will come' philosophy that could have had a disastrous impact on the area, especially when rich, well off people started purchasing the gigantic houses at an alarming rate. Surprisingly, though, their effect has been minimumal. In general, the new owners have jumped on the Green bandwagon and have been pretty environmentally conscious. They even helped develop the area's first natural foods coop, Great Harvest Moon. So, even if there are less fields and forests than there used to be, at least the area hasn't lost too much of its natural beauty and charm.

An unexpected and somewhat pressing issue has arisen, however. The influx of new homes has drawn the unwanted attention of resident critters, the kinds that are better off kept outside where they belong rather than wandering around inside brand new, multi-million dollar mansions: box elder bugs, carpenter ants, bats, mice, shrews, voles, even bull snakes, to name but a few. And they all had to be eradicated. That's were Simonson's Pest and Rodent Control came in. I Googled them. The company has been serving the western Hennepin County area for over half a century, and business has been on a decided uptick, especially in the last ten years or so. Apparently, the new McMansion owners are more than happy to have professional help when it comes to dealing with the unwanted invasion any living creature, flying, walking or otherwise. Simonson's now employed eight full time Control Specialists and, as their website says, 'We're always looking for new, highly motivated team members.' That's where Johnny came in. They were hiring, and he needed a job, so they put him on the payroll. Was he highly motivated? Well, I wasn't sure about that. I wasn't even sure how hard of a worker he was. I guess we'd be finding out at dinner.

My apartment is within a stone's throw of picturesque Orchard Lake, the narrow, mile long body of water the little town is named after. In fact, if I stood in the far corner of my living room and looked out the window, I could just make out a sliver of water and the local public access. I'd moved from Minneapolis after my divorce five years ago and wouldn't think about leaving. I'm forty-nine years old and happily moving on with the next phase of my life. That's where Diane comes in.

We met a few months ago on a warm Sunday morning in the beginning of June. I was riding my bicycle along one of the many rustic trails in the area maintained by the county park system when I came upon her. She'd had a flat tire. I always carry a tire repair kit in my little saddle bag and a hand pump on my frame for just such an occasion. In no time flat (No pun intended. Well, maybe just a little.) I patched her tire, pumped up it up and got her all set and ready to be on her way.

"Good as new," I told her as I packed away my repair stuff.

"You're pretty handy with that," she said, pointing to my patch kit and tire pump. "I like a man who's prepared."

Hmm. Was she flirting with me or just being nice? Hard to say. Anyway, I liked her easy going, friendly manner. She'd introduced herself while I was working on her bike and we'd immediately hit it off. She was just over five-feet tall, had long auburn hair and a pretty, oval face, with high cheek bones, green eyes and full lips. Her name was Diane Swenson. She told me she'd lived in Orchard Lake for twenty-five years in one of older ramblers on the west side of town. She was my age. She had been divorced for eight years and had two kids, each of whom were living on their own. She worked at a local bakery. She like to read. She liked to garden. The longer we talked, the more I was drawn to her. We had a lot in common, yet were still different enough to find each other interesting. Before we parted, I asked if she'd like to go for coffee sometime and she replied, "Sounds good. How about tomorrow?"

I said, "Sure," and we did. We've been dating ever since.

I took one last look in the mirror, fluffed my hair a little and then shrugged my shoulders. What was the point? I was going bald, no use hiding behind the thinning hair ruse, so I might as well accept it. I grabbed the keys to my seven year old Ford Fiesta and headed out the door. Fifteen minutes later I had picked up Diane, and we were in downtown Wayzata on the east end in a little strip mall, a couple of blocks from Lake Minnetonka, the largest lake in the county and home to the fashionably wealthy of the western metropolitan area. I pulled up to Black's Ford and we both got out. I looked in the big window facing the parking lot and could see only a few patrons inside. It was going to be a nice, quiet dinner for us, the kind I'd come to expect. I hoped so, anyway. We'd have to see how Johnny's presence affected the evening.

Black's Ford was just the kind of place both Diane and I favored. It was busy enough to let you know the food was good, yet intimate and cozy enough to let you carry on a quiet conversation without having to raise your voice to be heard. It had twelve tables and could seat maybe forty people on a good night. Jerry Black was around my age and the owner. He was also the cook and a super talented chef, serving up tasty fried brown rice, chickpea salad, spiced pasta and roasted vegetable dishes that were the talk of the town. His wife, Rhonda, was the outgoing hostess, head waitress and general all around fount of positive energy for the establishment. Where Jerry was quiet and meticulous, Rhonda was effervescent and outgoing. Together, they made for a great couple as well as purveyors of a tasty dining experience. In its fifth year of business, the restaurant was going strong. *More power to them*, I thought, as we walked through the door.

Rhonda waved a greeting and showed us to a table by the window.

"So, Kyle, how's life in the hardware business?" she asked, as Diane and I took our seats.

"Doing good, Rhonda. Repaired a tricky screen door today. Put a new window pane in, too. Fun city, as always," I said, joking with her.

Rhonda grinned at Diane and said, "How do you keep up with this guy?"

Diane laughed, "Yeah, I know what you mean. It's hard."

Rhonda handed us our menus and smiled, "The special tonight is vegetable pot pie. It's absolutely to die for. The veggies are fresh today, right out of our garden."

It sounded so good, I couldn't help it, my stomach started growling. We were in the last week of August. The weather was hot and local vegetable gardens were filled to overflowing. Black's Ford took full advantage of a myriad of fresh produce when it came to preparing their tasty home cooked dishes.

"Sounds great," Diane said, opening the menu and perusing it, "Just let me have a quick look here. I've been thinking about that veggie pizza of yours since we were here last week."

"Oh, yeah. The Mediterranean flatbread with pesto? I don't blame you. No sweat, Di. You guys take your time. I'll have Marybeth bring your water. She'll take your order, too." Then she winked at both of us, "She's new, so cut her some slack, okay?"

Diane and I both laughed. "Don't worry, we will," Diane said.

See what I mean? Friendly but not overbearing. What was not to like about the place?

After Rhonda left, Diane reached across the table and took my hand. "Thanks for doing this with Johnny. I really appreciate it."

I gently squeezed her hand. "No problem," I told her.

I liked how we were becoming close and that Diane felt she could depend on me. My feelings for her were strong and getting stronger every day. I was happy to oblige. Plus, I didn't expect having dinner with Johnny would be any big deal. In fact, it would be good to get to know him better. I didn't have many close male friends. Well, none, actually.

She squeezed my hand in return, her finger tips lightly caressing my palm. I looked up, and she smiled at me. I smiled back and we held each other's gaze. It was a nice, intimate moment and could have gone on for a while as far as I was concerned. Then I saw her eyes slide past me toward the front door. I turned. Johnny was just coming in. I was so lost in the moment, I didn't even hear his Harley when he drove up.

Johnny was four years younger than Diane, and, like I said, I'd met him a couple of times before. He was a large man, at least six-two or three and he must have weighed easily two-hundred and fifty pounds. He had a full beard, and long, wavy, black hair he wore pulled back in a ponytail. He looked like a mountain man, although I'd been told he wasn't an outdoorsman at all, preferring to spend his time building model airplanes and battleships from World War II. He had deep set eyes, a round face and a pleasant smile if you didn't look too closely at his teeth; he was missing a few.

Tonight he wore a clean white tee-shirt, black leather vest, blue jeans and motorcycle boots. Each arm was covered with tattoos. If you didn't know him, he was a formidable looking character, definitely exuding a biker vibe. But he was actually very sweet natured. Diane told me he almost never got mad and that he had a fondness for little kids and small dogs. With those traits in mind, if it wasn't for his alcohol problem, he'd be a model citizen. At least to my way of thinking, anyway. Unfortunately, he did like his drinks, there was no doubt about it. The fact that he'd been sober for six weeks was cause for a minor celebration. But that's not what this meeting was about.

"Hey, Di," he greeted his sister and bent to give her a big, warm, hug.

Then he stood up, turned to me, and spread his arms. "Kyle," he grinned. " Hey, my man." He gave me a high five, which I returned, something I'm not prone to doing, but with Johnny, you kind of got drawn into the force of his personality.

He grabbed a chair, sat down between us and Marybeth brought him a menu along with a glass of water. We chatted back and forth, making amiable small talk for a few minutes while

Johnny looked over the menu. Finally, Diane asked, "So about your new job...how's it going?"

"Oh, man, it's unreal," Johnny said, setting his menu aside and shaking his head. He was clearly distressed.

"In a good way or a bad way?" I asked.

He managed to cough out a laugh. "Well, not in a good way, I can tell you that." He took in our perplexed looks and turned quiet, thinking how to proceed. Finally, he said, "How about if I tell you about what I did today? Then you guys can judge for yourselves."

We were more than curious. "Sounds good," Diane said.

"Fire away," I added.

So he told us and I'll never forget what, to this day, is still a remarkable story.

"First of all..." He turned to me. "Kyle, let me ask you a question. What are you most afraid of?"

"What do you mean?" I asked. I was guessing he wasn't getting at the big universal fears like death and dying, speaking in public, or dreaming you were wandering around a shopping mall in your underwear.

"You know. Like spiders, centipedes, whatever."

I was right. Those kinds of fears. Well, here's the deal: I like to think I'm a mellow, love thy neighbor and all god's creatures kind of a guy, but, honestly, I'm not. Spiders, beetles and cockroaches kind of creep me out. So do most reptiles, with salamanders being right up there.

So that's what I told Johnny. He nodded sagely, agreeing with me and letting me know he understood what I was saying. But before he could comment on what I said, though, I was quick to add, "But right at the top of the list are snakes. Ugh. I know I should accept them for what they are, and how they're important to the environment and everything, but I can't. One crawled into my sleeping bag once when I was a kid and it freaked me out so bad I just about died. It was just a harmless bull snake, but, man, it was huge, at least ten feet long." I spread my arms wide to indicate how long it actually was and, at that moment, an involuntary shiver ran through me, just from that long ago unpleasant memory. Even now, talking about it was traumatic. I forced myself to continue. "I honestly can't help it. They one-hundred and ten percent weird me out. I'll run for the hills before I'll ever touch one. Which I've never done. Touch one, I mean. Ugh." I sat a moment, thinking, and then said, lowering my voice somewhat shamefully, "Well, to tell the truth, I actually have run away from them. A few of times, anyway." I glanced at Diane. She gave me a sympathetic smile and reached for my hand in a show of solidarity. God love her. I gladly gave it to her.

Johnny had been listening carefully and nodding along. When I told him about my fear of snakes he smacked his hand hard on the table, causing the glasses and silverware to rattle. "Right on, man. Me, too. Big time." He looked at Diane and pointed. "Di here has a thing for snakes, too, but also mice and rats. Pretty much all the Rodendia family in fact, isn't that right, Sis?"

Diane shuttered. "Don't even mention it."

All this discussion about fears and reptiles, besides making me uncomfortable, was also having another effect. It was making me more curious than ever. "So what's the deal, Johnny? What happened today?"

Just then Marybeth stopped by our table and we gave her our orders. I was hungry and ordered a black bean burger with sweet potato fries. Diane suggested to her brother that they split the large Mediterranean flatbread and he agreed. Orders were placed, but if Diana and I had known what Johnny was going to tell us, we would have just skipped trying to eat and gone straight for the doggy bags. Neither of us felt too hungry when he was done with his story.

"Last week was my first week," he began. "I rode with Larry Swartz, just to get the lay of the land. He was kind of training me on rodent control. We checked a lot of traps for mice." He glanced at his sister, knowing her aversion to them, and added, "Not the most thrilling job, but it wasn't too bad. At least they were all dead."

I looked at Diane. Was she turning just the tiniest bit pale? Maybe. I reached for her hand but she gave me a little, 'Thanks, but I'm alright,' pat on the wrist and, instead, took a sip of water.

Johnny continued. "Most of our jobs were in those big houses south of Orchard Lake." He pointed out the window even though the area he was telling us about was five miles away. "Lots of mice out there, I guess. Larry told me they were all over the place, you know, in the fields and such."

I got the drift. Mice, mice, and more mice. I personally didn't mind them but didn't need to dwell on the image of herds or hordes (or whatever you'd call them) of the little buggers running rampant over hill and dale, nosing around and searching for ways into people's homes. "So what happened today?" I asked, hoping to move the story along.

He easily shifted gears. "This week I got to go out on my own. Let's see, it's Thursday, right? Monday, Tuesday, and Wednesday weren't too bad. I took over part of Larry's route, checked mice traps, and laid down some new bait. Dealt with a raccoon in the rafters of someone's garage and a possum living under somebody's deck. Even some chipmunks that had taken over a tool shed. You know, basic stuff."

I didn't know, but that was okay. I got what he was saying. "So you were out on your own?"

He nodded. "Yeah, I was. There was lots of paperwork, too, that I had to learn about." He stopped and grinned enthusiastically. "Well, not really paperwork. They've got these cool hand-held computers..."

I glanced at Diane. She rolled her eyes. I guess her brother had a propensity for going on and on about things he was interested in, and it seemed like Simonson's hand held electronic record keeping devices were one of those things. She smiled at me, letting me know, I think, that she appreciated my patience.

But, still...let's get to the story. What happened today that was so all fired up weird or crazy or whatever, that caused Johnny, this big mountain of a man, to cave like a pile of wet sand and call his older sister? I looked at Diane, and she nodded a silent, 'Go ahead,' so I turned to her brother and said, "So, come on, Johnny, tell us what happened today."

"Oh, yeah, right." He took a big gulp of water and wiped his hands nervously together. I guess in retrospect he was just trying to delay the inevitable. After what he told us, I could understand why. His expression turned serious and he choked up, his nervousness causing him to lower his voice. Both Diane and I had to lean in close to him to hear what he was saying.

"It was early this afternoon. I was thinking about lunch and just driving back to the office after spraying for termites at a huge house on Willow Trail. I should explain, even though I'm rodent control, our pest control guy, Freddy, had called in sick, so we were all covering for him."

He looked at us like, did we understand? and we both nodded that, yeah, we got it. In the back of my mind I was thinking, at least Diane's brother likes to keep his facts straight. That had to be a good thing. Right?

He continued with his story; his voice more confident as he spoke. "Anyway, I got a call from our dispatcher. She wanted me to head over to White Oak Road. A lady had called in about a noise under the floor in the family room in the basement. I was supposed to go and check it out, so I drove over. The house was pretty new, maybe only a few years old. It was on a two or three of acres of land, woods all around and a driveway maybe two hundred feet long. It was built toward the back of the property on a slight rise with a nice view of the front yard all the way out to the road. The backyard was overlooking a big swamp. I mean, it was huge. I think it's called Marsh Lake, but it didn't look like much of a lake to me. It was a swamp, no doubt about it. Cattails, reeds, muskrat houses, and not much open water. A good place for ducks, maybe.

"I parked my Simonson's truck and got out. The owner hurried up to greet me like she'd been waiting for me. She was maybe mid-thirties, one of those tall, thin, and in-shape kinds of women that you see living out that way. Anyway, she was nice enough. She told me her name was Susan Mackelmore and that she and her husband and three children had been living there for two years. And, I was right, they'd had the house built brand new for them.

"She also told me that it was supposed to be their dream home, but that it'd been anything but. Her very words were, 'It's been a nightmare.' I was about to find out why.

"She took me inside and we went downstairs. God, you guys, maybe I'll take you out there and show it to you sometime. It was one of those huge mansions with white walls, big rooms, tall ceilings, and windows everywhere. Nice, I suppose, if you like that kind of thing, but, man, definitely not for me. Too much of everything."

I looked at Diane. She was following her brother's story carefully. I was, too. Nearly a brand new home? What could have been so bad that they had to call for help?

"She took me downstairs to the family room. It was on the ground level and covered with wall-to-wall, light gray carpeting. It was a huge space with a big-screen television at one end and a couple of those big sectional couches taking up most of the rest of the area. It looked comfortable to me, definitely a party room, you know, a good place to hang out," he looked at both of us. Diane and I nodded, letting him know we got the picture.

Diane said, "So..."

Johnny grimaced and continued. "There was a sliding glass door that led to a small backyard. It slopped down to the swamp about fifty feet away. I have to say, it had a nice view, but it wasn't the view she wanted me to see. We walked into the middle of the room, behind the couches, and stopped. She pointed to the floor and told me to listen. I did. I held myself still, didn't talk or anything, and listened carefully. After a few seconds, I told her I didn't hear anything. She told me to be quiet and wait a little while longer, so I did. I squatted down and concentrated. After a minute or two I finally heard a noise. It sounded like something was shuffling around down there. Like 'swish', 'swish', 'swish'. Something like that. Anyway, when I adjusted my feet to keep my balance the swishing stopped. When I kept still for a minute longer, the swishing started up again. Then I moved my feet a little bit, and it stopped. I stopped moving, and it started up again. Something alive was definitely down there.

"I looked at the owner. At the sound of the swishing, she'd backed away to the far end of the room where the stairs were and was holding onto the banister for dear life. She looked frightened. 'What do you think it is?' she asked. I stood up and walked over to her and told her that I had no idea."

He looked at us both. It seemed like his eyes were sad. Or frightened. Or something not normal, anyway. He was certainly still shaken up. After a few moments, he took a sip of water, cleared his throat, and continued. "I really didn't know what was down there, but, I have to say, I had my suspicions. I thought it might be a raccoon, a skunk, or even a possum. The guys at work told me it was common to find them holed up in crawl spaces. They liked the protection and, in the heat of the summer, like now, they liked the fact that it's a nice, cool place to hang out. Whatever was down there, though, I needed to check it out and find out what was going on.

"I told Susan I needed to look under the floor. She took me out the sliding glass door to the backyard and around to the side of the house. There was a small door in the foundation that was the entrance to a crawl space. I took out my flashlight and then grabbed the handle of the door so I could take a look inside. It was kind of stuck because it had never been opened before. I yanked and yanked and after a couple of tugs, I was able to free it. I swung it open, bent down, shined my flashlight in, and saw what was in there. And, man oh man...

He stopped talking and took another drink of water. Then he looked at us and said, "It was like nothing I'd ever seen before."

Just then Marybeth brought out dinners. She set the plates down, and even though I was ravenous, my appetite had disappeared entirely. I glanced at Diane. It appeared she felt the same way because, after she'd taken one look at the pizza that she and her brother had ordered, she'd pushed it away. Johnny gave her a quizzical look, shrugged his shoulders, and took a slice. We watched as he wolfed it down in half a minute, savoring every bite. I was incredulous that he could eat after what he'd just told us, but he was a big guy and, I guess, had to fuel the engine. But, I was impatient and wished he'd hurry up and finish eating. I was anxious to find out what he had seen.

In less than a minute he'd chomped down his second slice. I couldn't wait any longer and said, "So, back to the story. What was in there? A raccoon like you thought? Or a rabbit? Maybe with babies?"

Johnny let out a laugh and wiped his mouth on his napkin. "That's funny, Kyle. And I wish, I really do wish it had been little baby bunny rabbits. At least they'd have been cute. But, no, they weren't rabbits."

The heck with it. I was hungry, myself. Whatever was under the floor of the house, how bad could it be? I was reaching for my black bean burger, getting ready to sink my teeth into it when Johnny said, "So, Kyle, my man, no. It wasn't a cute little bunny rabbit with her cute little babies. Not even close." I paused on my way to take a big bite.

Diane, who'd been silently listening, asked, "Well, what then, Johnny? What?" Did she sound just a little petulant? Was she losing patience with her brother? I looked at her, but I had misjudged her reaction. She seemed fine, just a little on edge. Well, I could understand that feeling. I was, too.

Johnny hesitated for just a moment, maybe to build drama, but he didn't need to. He had Diane and I hooked with his story. Finally, he took a deep breath, let it out, and went ahead and said, "Okay, I'll tell you. You know what it was? It was the last thing I could have ever expected, and way worse." His eyes got wide and he spoke softly. "It was snakes, you guys. Garter snakes. A shit load of them. Like an ocean of them. A huge, tangled up, mass of garter snakes and they were all alive and slithering around all over the place under that house like there was no tomorrow. It was freakin' unbelievable."

Thankfully, I never got to bite into my burger. I put it down. In fact, to be honest, I haven't touched one since. Remember earlier I'd told Johnny of my fear of snakes? Well, my body reacted to what he'd said, and a surge of adrenaline flooded my system. My hands began shaking and sweat started running down my chest. The image of those snakes filled my brain; a slimy mass of them ready to slither out that crawl space door, wind their way through the woods all the way to Black's Ford, find me, and start crawling all over my body. NO!

I nervously rubbed my hands on my thighs and glanced at Diane. She'd gone pale. I'm sure I wasn't looking much better. I took a gulp of water. Diane used her napkin to dab some perspiration off her brow.

Johnny took a look at each of us, noticing our reaction. "You guys okay?" he asked, sympathetically. He was genuinely concerned. We both nodded our assent, a little dourly, I might add. He waited a few moments for us to get our bearings, then said, "I know it's hard, but there's more. You want me to go on?"

I looked at Diane. She had her face set, grimly resolute in her desire to offer emotional support for her brother. After all, that's what we were there for, and that's what we had to do, no matter how hard it was. Plus, we'd already come this far. We needed to put our fears aside and support him, the slithering, slimy, mass of garter snakes notwithstanding.

"Sure," I managed to croak. "Go on." I'd almost lost my voice.

Diane didn't bother trying to say anything, she just nodded. Then she took another sip of water and dabbed her forehead again. "Yeah, go ahead," she finally managed to say, her voice barely a whisper.

Johnny sighed, "Okay." It was then that I realized how hard this must be for him, reliving the experience all over again. He was as afraid of snakes as Diana and I. Maybe more so. But he dug deep, found the fortitude to go on, and continued,

"At the sight of all those snakes, I jumped back and slammed the door shut. I think I startled Susan, because she jumped back, too, and screamed, 'What? What's in there?'"

"I took a moment to compose myself and then told her what I'd seen. I tried to keep my voice steady. I'm supposed to be a professional, you know, but man, it was hard. My hands were shaking." He held them out to make his point. I looked. Was that the tiniest little tremor I detected? Yes, it was. I looked at Johnny, and he nodded. "Yeah, I'm still freaked out a little bit."

No kidding. Me, too. Same with Diane. And we hadn't even been there! I felt for the guy. What a hell of a position to be in. His second week on the job. He wants to make a good impression. Now, this massive invasion of snakes to deal with. Plus, he was as afraid of them as I was. And his sister. God, what a horrible position to be in. How do you begin to deal with something like that?

I went ahead and asked, "So what'd you do?" I was trying to put my fear of snakes aside, and I must have been successful because, suddenly, I was curious...very curious. After getting over the shock, I have to say, I really did wonder, what did you do in a situation like that? How do you get rid of, as Johnny had said, a shit load of garter snakes? I was about to find out.

"After I told Susan what I'd seen, she sort of freaked out herself. I can't say that I blamed her. I mean it was a mess. There were hundreds of them in there. Maybe thousands. It was hard to count." He looked at us and managed a little grin, like a smirk, a vain attempt at humor. We just stared back at him, speechless. I didn't find the situation humorous at all. He shrugged his shoulders and went on. "She told me she had to call her husband and ran back inside for her phone. Me? I called the office right away and explained the situation. They told me what I had to do."

I found my voice. "What?" I managed to say, "Seriously, what'd they tell you to do?" My mouth was dry, my discomfort palpable, but my unease was overshadowed by my curiosity. I could tell Diane was wondering, too, despite her earlier misgivings.

"They told me to trap them," Johnny said.

"Trap them? What the hell?" I immediately pictured a steel trap, the kind with jaws that you pried open and put on the ground and then some poor animal stepped in it and got caught. I was incredulous. Is that what they used for snakes? "I don't believe it," I told him, "I've never heard of such a thing."

"Yeah," he said, warming to the subject, "I set traps for them." He saw the perplexed look on my face and hurried to add, "Maybe not the kind you're thinking of." He leaned forward and put his arms on the table. "Here's what I did. I went out to the truck, found the box they told me would be there and carried it back to the crawl space. By this time Susan had talked to her husband and they decided that they wanted me to get rid of the snakes. 'No matter what the cost,' were her exact words. So that's what I was going to do. The dispatcher walked me through the steps I had to take. Let me tell you, guys, it was the worst thing I'd ever done in my life."

I could only imagine. I'm sure my eyes had never been so wide open, picturing what Johnny had gone through. I looked at Diane. Her eyes sure were.

"We use what they called, 'Sticky Traps.' They're like fly paper. You peel off the back and set the sheet down and the snakes crawl over them and get stuck. Then you come back later and you remove them."

"What!" I exclaimed, more loudly than I'd intended. I sheepishly looked around the restaurant. I'd started a few of the diners. I half-heartedly waved my apology to the room. But really, sticky traps to catch snakes? It sounded insane to me. I turned my attention back to Johnny. "I can't believe it."

"Yeah, sounds crazy, right?" he said, "But, I guess it's supposed to work. I'm told that's what everyone uses."

Everyone uses them? I sat back kind of stunned. Asked and answered. So that's how you got rid of snakes. Who would have thought it? Well, well, well. You learn something new every day.

"So what'd you do?" Diane asked, finally having found her voice. Though Johnny was forty-five and an adult, she was older than him by four years and still considered him her little brother. Plus, I could tell how concerned she was for him. I smiled to myself, the first time in a long while that evening it seemed. He was easily twice her weight and over a foot taller, but the fact that she cared so much about him was refreshing to see.

"That was the worst part, Di." He pointed to himself and grinned, "You know I'm kind of a big guy." At six-three and at least two-hundred and fifty pounds, the statement was self evident. "It was a tight fit getting into that space, that's no lie. I had to get down on my hands and knees and crawl in there with my sticky traps. The clearance was about two feet so it was a tight fit. Plus, there was no light; it was pitch black. Thank god for my flashlight. I had to carry it in my mouth like this." He picked up a fork and put it between his lips to show us. He didn't need to. We got the drift. "Anyway, I had to lay on my stomach so I could use both hands to peel the back off and lay the traps out. I figured the best way was to start at the far wall and work my way back out. Let me tell you, crawling through those snakes was no walk in the park. It was a bitch. I was scared of them anyway, so it was taking all I could to not lose my mind. You know, it's hard not to think about snakes when you've got snakes crawling around right next to you." He paused, trembled a little, and looked at us to make his point. We both nodded. We got it. Point made.

He went on with his story. "Some of them even crawled over my arms and legs. A couple even got caught in my hair." He shook his head and let loose a gigantic shudder at the memory. (Both Diane and I did, too.) Then he continued. "The hardest thing was trying not to think about what I was doing while I was doing it, you know?" He shook his head some more. "But, I managed to put all those snakes out of my mind and made myself keep working until I was finally able to get the job done. Thank god. If I hadn't been able to ignore what I was doing, I doubt I'd be here right now talking to you guys. I'd probably be in a hospital somewhere with a heart attack or some bar somewhere getting drunk, trying to forget."

I found myself nodding along with him. Yeah, what he had done was not only hard, it was courageous. Hugely courageous, at least as far as I was concerned. I looked at Diane. I'm sure she felt as I did, but it was hard to tell. By now, she was pale, really pale. I took her hand to connect and be close to her. In spite of our reactions, though, we were both still hanging on every word.

Johnny took a deep breath and exhaled. "Not all of them wanted to move. I had to push some of them out of them away." He made a sweeping motion with his hand. "Man, I'm glad I had my rubber gloves on."

The fact that he was terrified of snakes, yet crawled in amongst them, all in the name of getting the job done, was incredible to me. In fact, the vision of it has stayed with me to this day. But, at the time, all I could think of to say was, "Geez..." I literally was speechless. Johnny had ten times more courage than me. Maybe a hundred times. And the fact that he had been able to push past his fear of snakes to get the job done? Well, that was truly amazing. Me? I'd have slammed the door to the crawl space shut and let the snakes do their thing. I'd have packed away my flashlight and sticky traps, dropped off the Simonson's Pest and Rodent Control truck back at the office, quit right then and there, and never looked back. Then I'd have gone home and started applying for jobs in a different line of work. Safer jobs. Cleaner jobs. Easier jobs. Jobs like...Like...Well, like anything.

Diane was back to being speechless. I was, too. Johnny, for his part, took another slice of pizza and casually ate it, wiping his hands on a napkin when he was finished. Then he took a drink of water. It came back to me about his alcohol problem. Apparently, his drinking was under control for right now. No beer or alcohol for him tonight, just water. I had to give him a ton of credit for that, even though in the past it had been easy for him to fall off the wagon. For now, though, he was under control and sober. It was good to see.

We were all silent for a minute. Johnny worked some more on the pizza while Diane and I held hands, silently supporting each other, trying to rid our minds of the images Johnny had painted of his 'Incident with the snakes in the crawlspace,' as I was beginning to think of his experience as.

After a minute or so I asked, "While you were in there with them, where'd the snakes all go?"

Johnny finished chewing and swallowed. "Where do you think? Most of them went right out the crawl space door. You should have heard Susan scream when that started happening." He smiled at the memory. In spite of myself, so did I, imagining the scene; a mass of snakes slithering out, rushing toward the unsuspecting homeowner. I looked at Diane. She was grinning, too. I think we were both thinking, though, better Susan than us. Johnny added, "A lot went under the ground, though, under the foundation. It was pretty hectic in there for a while."

No shit, Sherlock. I could only imagine.

Diane put aside her ill-at-ease feelings of snakes and began to get in the groove of supporting her brother, wanting to show an interest in his work. "How long did it take to get the sticky traps put down?"

"About two hours. Pretty much all afternoon."

I glanced at the clock on the wall. It was nearly eight o'clock. While I'd been showing Frank Becker a new fixture for his bathroom vanity, on my way to finishing up my shift at the hardware store, Johnny had been on his hands and knees with a flashlight clamped firmly in his teeth, crawling around in a dark, dank, two-foot high crawl space, laying out sticky traps for hundreds if not thousands of garter snakes. God, what a job.

All of a sudden, I had a thought."So you've got the traps out. Now what happens?"

Johnny sat back, took another slice of pizza and bit into it, chewing contemplatively, and said, "I'm not done yet. I've got to go back there tomorrow and see what there is to see."

"What!" I blurted out. I let go of Diane's hand and sat straight up in my chair. I couldn't help myself. I never imagined that he'd have to go back into that crawl space, but, of course, that's exactly what he'd have to do. How else would he get rid of the snakes? Diane patted my hand to calm me. I looked around and saw Rhonda watching. She looked at me questioningly, and I waved, 'It's okay,' to her. Then I turned back to Johnny.

He spread his arms wide smiled a big smile and said, "What can I say, man? It's my job. Somebody's got to do it."

Oh. My. God. He wasn't done yet. He still had to go back tomorrow. Unreal. I looked at Diane. Her eyes were downcast and her expression had turned inward. I could almost hear the wheels in her brain grinding away, working overtime. I knew she was wondering if the stress of this new job would be enough to cause her brother to go back to his apartment and start drinking again; you know, turn to alcohol to bolster himself with some liquid courage for the task that lay ahead of him tomorrow. That being said, though, I have to say that I kind of got it. When my marriage fell apart, I admit that I turned to Jack Daniels to drown my sorrows, a habit that could have gotten out seriously of control if I hadn't put the brakes on and quit cold turkey. Sober, now, for over five years, I was sympathetic to what he was going through.

Johnny must have known his sister well because he rushed to allay her fears. "Don't worry, Sis. I'm good. I've got it all under control." By which I'm sure he meant his drinking. "Besides," he added, "I have to say, dealing with the snakes and all is kind of a challenge. I kind of dig it. In fact, I'm looking forward to going back tomorrow to see if I got any of the damn things."

He smiled a big smile, took another piece of pizza, and bit into it. Then he looked at Diane and changed the subject. "Hey, Sis, better grab a slice. I'm kind of hungry and might finish the whole thing." There was only one piece left. Then he laughed loud and long. The other diners looked at us and then quickly turned away. It occurred to me they might have overheard parts, if not all of, Johnny's story. If they had, I wondered how could they have been able to continue eating. Me? I'd totally lost my appetite.

Just to be polite, later on when we left, I asked Marybeth for a bag for my black bean burger. It never made it into my home. I tossed it in the trash container outside my apartment before I even considered going inside.

The problem was that Johnny's story wasn't over. That next day he had to go back and complete the job, doing, as he'd told us, 'What he had to do.' For our part, I knew this: Johnny wasn't far from either Diane's or my mind all that next day, with both of us wondering how the horrific task of snake removal was going with him.

Later that Friday night, Johnny called his sister to talk. Diane called me right after. "Yeah, Kyle, I just got off the phone with Johnny. He was in a really good mood. He said that it was great being with us last night, and he really appreciated the support we gave him. He wanted to see if he could take us out to dinner next week at Black's Ford. 'On him' he said. Then he'll fill us in on what happened today." She paused, playing around with me, "If you're interested, that is."

I couldn't get the words out fast enough, "Yes, yes, yes!" I told her. "Of course I am. Big time."

I was beginning to like Johnny. I enjoyed being around him. Plus, truthfully, I'd spent more than a few minutes at work that day wondering how it had gone for him, getting rid of the snakes and everything. In fact, when I mentioned the snake infestation to the people I worked with, they were all adamant in telling me that dealing with garter snakes coming into homes was becoming a big issue in the area. Almost epidemic.

My boss Larry Jorgenson pointedly said, "Yeah, they come up from the swamps. If they get inside someone's house, it's trouble. A huge pain in the ass. Once a snake lays its eggs and hatches its young, that owner's home becomes their home. Well, den is the correct term. Anyway, when that happens, it's almost impossible to get them out."

Wow, I didn't know it could get that bad. Needless to say, it was not a good situation at all, and, in the case of the mansion out on White Oak Road, Johnny and his sticky traps were stuck right in the middle. (Pun intended.)

So, of course, I wanted to hear what happened. "Can you call him back right now and tell him that for sure we'll be there?" I began picturing a myriad of possibilities as to what might have happened with the garter snake roundup. Then I stopped myself and asked, "By the way, did he give you any hint? Any clue as to how it went?"

She laughed. "Hold on, Kyle, not so fast. First of all, I've already told him we'd be there. I figured you'd want to. Was I right on that?"

"Absolutely. My mind's going a mile a minute imagining what it was like." Again, though, an involuntary shudder coursed through my body. After all, it was potentially hundreds and hundreds of dead and dying snakes we were talking about here.

"Good." I could picture Diane smiling into the phone, and the image made me feel warm inside. I hope that statement doesn't sound too sappy, but, I can't help it, that's just the way I felt. In fact, being with her was fast becoming the best I'd felt in years.

Her voice came into my ear, just then, and interrupted my thoughts of love and romance. She continued, "And, no, no hints at all, thank you very much for asking. My brother's playing it close to his chest about how it went, having some fun with us, I think. But that's okay. I'm glad he's staying sober. That's the main thing. Plus, I think he likes this job."

Back to the reality of the here and now and Johnny and the garter snakes. "So we wait until next Thursday?"

"Yeah. But that's a long way off. Do you want to get together before that?"

"Of course," I said.

"Ok. How about we fire up the grill at my place tomorrow night and then go for a bike ride on Sunday?"

"You're on," I told her, grinning like there was no tomorrow. Except that there was, and I'd be spending it with Diane. And the next day. Perfect.

So we spent the weekend together and had a wonderful time. Saturday after work, I came over and we made up our own black bean burgers and did them on the grill on the back patio. They were scrumptious, juicy, and flavorful. Then we stayed up late outside, sipping iced tea and talking, enjoying a quiet evening together before turning in. We both had Sunday off, so we slept late, had a leisurely breakfast, and then went for our bike ride.

Out of the trail, we saw early-blooming white asters and I even spotted a barred owl. When I pointed it out to Diane, she was visibly excited. "I've never seen one before. It's so cool." She snapped a few pictures with her phone, and I broke into a big smile, one that she immediately returned.

It was a simple moment, sure, as was the entire weekend; one that might not seem like much in the bigger picture of things, but we were stockpiling a lifetime of those special moments and it felt wonderful. Moreover, it was the sharing of those kinds of uncomplicated times, I think, that was helping to build a strong foundation for our relationship. That's certainly what ours was becoming, anyway, one based on friendship as well as mutual attraction and respect.

From my standpoint, I was very happy. So was Diane. For each of us, having been through a divorce, we had started by taking our time, wanting to get to know each other before committing emotionally. But that was back at the beginning, when we'd first met, nearly three months earlier. Clearly, now, all of that was changing. It was obvious that we were not only enjoying each other's company but were also building a strong emotional bond. It was fun to experience, especially coming from the disaster that had been the end of my first marriage. I could tell the same was true for Diane. She and her ex, both eighteen at the time, had married far too young and had, over the years, simply grown apart. "The divorce was mutual. He's moved on with his life and so have I," she told me early on when we'd first started dating. Another time she told me, "As far as I'm concerned, getting divorced was the best thing to do. It gave me a chance to have a better life." I understood completely.

For me, being with Diane...Well, I counted myself lucky, that was for sure, if not extremely fortunate. For us, things started good and have steadily improved as our feelings for each other have grown. In fact, recently, when I was over at her house grilling corn on the cob, she came up out of the blue and gave me a big, passionate hug. "I'm happier now than I've ever been," she said, holding me tight.

"Me, too," I told her in return, and hugged her back, almost (but not quite) forgetting about the corn smoking away on the grill. I understood where she was coming from.

One thing was certain, we could talk about anything that was on our minds. She was opening up about her family, her marriage, and her kids. I was, too. I'd even told her about my past issues with alcohol. In return, she confided that she'd gone through a period of opioid dependency to oxycodone ten years earlier after fracturing her pelvis in a car accident. She was clean now, as I was sober, and we both intended to stay that way.

In short, our relationship was becoming closer and stronger every day. I hadn't been as happy or fulfilled in a long time, if ever.

So, we had a good week, but Thursday evening couldn't come soon enough. When it did, I picked up Diane and we drove to Black's Ford in time to meet Johnny at seven. He was at the same window table as before, carrying on an animated conversation with Rhonda. She turned as we walked in. "Hey there, you two," she greeted us with a sly smile. We sat down and she handed each of us our menus. "Johnny, here was just telling me about his job and what he's been doing this week. Here to talk about snakes again?"

Whoops. I felt my ears turn red. I guess lots of people in Black's Ford last Thursday could overhear our conversation.

"I'm so sorry..." I began to apologize, but Rhonda waved a hand in my face.

"Don't worry about it, Kyle. It's a public space after all." Then she winked. "Besides, I'm looking forward to hearing what happened. Johnny here's keeping mum on the outcome." She grinned at her little rhyme and then ambled off to chat with some customers a few tables over.

While Diane and I watched her walk away, I laughed nervously. Johnny just grinned and asked, "So...before I fill you in, should we order first?" Then, before we could say anything, he answered his own question. "Sure, let's do that. I'm starving. And remember, you guys," his grin got wider, if that was possible, "It's on me." I couldn't tell if he was enjoying being generous, or simply enjoying dragging out the end of his 'Incident of the snakes in the crawlspace' story.

I decided to give him credit where credit was due and went with both possibilities.

We perused our menus until Marybeth came to drop off water and take our orders. At this point, after Johnny's story last week, I felt I had a handle on what might be coming and figured I could listen to the outcome and still enjoy a tasty meal. Diane did too so we ordered: a rice curry dish for me and baked summer squash for Diane. Johnny went with the vegetarian lasagna. We chatted amicably while waiting for the food to arrive. When it did, Johnny hungrily dug into his meal. Inhaling might be a better word. Man, that guy could eat. After finishing half of the lasagna, he set his fork aside and looked at us. "So," he smiled mysteriously, "are you ready to hear about what happened last Friday?" He knew that, of course, we were, he was just goofing around and playing with us.

Diane grinned back at him, playing along. "Sure. Anytime you're ready, little brother."

Johnny laughed and made it a point of getting himself set. He took a big bite of his lasagna and chewed away happily. In fact, he ate most of the rest of it right then and there while we waited patiently, letting him have his moment. When he was finished, he wiped his hands (rather symbolically, I thought) on his napkin, and said, "Okay, here goes..."

We were all ears.

"I went back early Friday morning. The guys at work told me that because snakes are reptiles and reptiles are cold blooded, in the early morning their body temperature is low. That means they're sluggish. Not so active."

Honestly, I was interested, but the image of a sea of sluggish snakes lolling around in a tangled, reptilian web was not a good way to begin a nice meal. In fact, my appetite, ravenous five minutes earlier, was suddenly beginning to fade. I looked at Diane. She must have felt the same way because she was only half-heartedly nibbling at her summer squash. I had a private mental talk with myself along the lines of, 'Man up, Kyle, and get with the program. It's only a bunch of harmless garter snakes, for Pete's sake.' To that end, I picked up my fork and took a big, healthy bite of my rice curry. I'm happy to report that I was able to continue to listen to Johnny, as well as chew and swallow, with only a minimal amount of choking.

"I got there around seven in the morning," he continued. "Remember, when I left the day before I'd put the sticky traps down, but the snakes had all slithered out, so the crawl space was empty. I had no idea if the traps would work like they were suppose to at all. In fact, I wasn't even sure there'd be any snakes there when I came back."

That was that. The picture of all those garter snakes slithering out the crawl space door heading for who knows where did it for me. I put my fork down. So much for my pep-talk to 'Man up.' I figured I'd just wait for the end of his story. Then maybe, just maybe, I'd be able to continue with my meal without getting the dry heaves. I looked at Diane. She gave me a wan smile and set her fork down, too. For both of us, dinner was on hold.

Johnny stopped and looked at us with a slight grin. I could tell he was just loving our reaction.

Loss of appetite notwithstanding, I was still inordinately interested in what happened and didn't mind playing along. I asked, "So were there any snakes there? Anything stuck in the sticky traps?"

He smiled, enjoying the moment, I'm sure, before answering, "Oh, yeah. The traps worked great. There were snakes in them alright. Lots of them. Tons of them. Even more than last time, I think. Maybe a double shit load."

I shoved my meal away. No more rice curry for me for a while. To take away my queasy feeling, I felt I had to make some sort of comment."So the sticky traps worked?" I managed to say.

"Yeah, they worked great. The floor was covered with them. Wall-to-wall dead snakes."

I was glad I hadn't eaten anything. My stomach literally did a complete somersault and I put my hand over my mouth, just in case. Diane reached over and took my other hand and held it tight. She was ghostly pale. I was queasy. What a couple we made. But, hey, at least we were there for each other and doing our best to look out for the other one.

In fact, in looking back, I think that it was right at that moment that our fondness for each other reached a deeper level. A level where, bound by our fear of reptiles in general and snakes specifically, we tumbled over the edge into the abyss and fell in love. Yeah, strange as it may seem, I'm pretty sure that's when it happened, right in the middle of a sticky trap-covered, snake-infested crawl space. But I'll always say, simply, that it was at a nice dinner with Johnny at Black's Ford and leave any mention of dead garter snakes out of the discussion. It sounds way better.

Romance aside, however, back to Johnny's story. Without getting too graphic, here's what he told us happened: I guess when the snakes got stuck on the traps, they couldn't move much and eventually died from shock or something. Most of them, anyway, but not all. When Johnny got there he had to clean out not only the dead ones but, also, the still barely alive ones. He and his big bulky self worked his way into the crawl space like the timr before, flashlight firmly clenched between his teeth, dragging a large leaf bag that he used to stuff the snakes into. This time he worked from the front entrance to the far back wall. And remember, this is a guy who was terrified of snakes. 'Thank god,' he told us, 'that had my heavy-duty rubber gloves on.' Anyway, it took all morning. He filled one bag, hauled it out to his truck, and then went back in for more. The image of a heavy-duty black plastic leaf bag, filled with writhing, still living snakes, is another image that continues to haunt me to this day.

He filled five bags all total. When he was finished he took them back to the office where they buried the dead ones in a landfill. The live ones? They gassed them with the exhaust from Johnny's truck. Then they buried them.

Man, alive.

When he finished his story, Diane sat quietly. Me, too, both of us stunned speechless. We were still holding each other's hand, though, and that was nice, but we were also both processing what Johnny had told us: me, the picking up and hauling out of five garbage bags full of snakes, some of them still wriggling around. Diane, as she told me later, imagined crawling around in a confined space in the dark with the only light coming from a small flashlight. (That's when I found out she had an issue with claustrophobia.)

"Well, I'm in the mood for dessert," Johnny said, finally, clapping his hands together after a minute or so of silence. "How about you guys?"

When he looked at us and asked if we wanted dessert ourselves, we looked back at him incredulously. 'No, no dessert. Not tonight, thank you, very much,' was the essence of what we told him. Food was the last thing on our minds. We hadn't even been able to eat our dinners.

Johnny shrugged both of his big shoulders and went ahead and ordered himself some dessert, a big slice of fresh apple pie topped with two scoops of ice cream.

Finally, Diane found her voice and said, getting to the main point as far as she was concerned, "So you got rid of the snakes, little brother, and I'm glad for you, but what do you think? Is this the kind of job you want to keep doing?" She shivered and added, "Personally, I won't be surprised if you quit. In fact, I can't believe you haven't hung it up already."

Me? What did I think? Honestly? I found Johnny's job, even though it wasn't something I'd want to do, I found it fascinating. I mean, to know there were people out there doing that kind of work - work that us ordinary folks wouldn't ever dream of doing - well, more power to them, I say, and more power to him, too, specifically when it came to Johnny.

Diane pressed her point. "So what are you going to do, little brother? Stay at Simonson's or hang it up?"

Johnny sat back and grinned. "Well, this might surprise you, and honestly, it kind of does me, too, but I'm staying, Di. I really am. I like it. I have to say that I enjoy the work. Yeah, I know we get called out to deal with some pretty disgusting things sometimes, but, hey, that's alright. I'm doing something most people would never consider doing, and I kind of dig that. In fact, my boss is thinking of putting me in charge of snake disposal. Kind of like a promotion."

Promotion? Yikes, was he joking? That seemed to be stretching things a bit. I looked at Johnny, though, and it was clear that, indeed, he was serious. Deadly serious. It was also obvious he was happy with his job. The more I thought about it, the more I thought that maybe Diane's brother had found his niche. I pictured the company's trucks with new lettering on the side reading 'Simonson's Rodent, Pest and Reptile Control.' At least there'd be more bases would be covered, from an animal control standpoint, and more work for them, too. Hmm. The future was looking bright, for both Simonson's and Johnny. Well, I thought, good for everybody.

"Plus..." He stopped for a moment and looked at us both to make his point, "I'm staying sober. And that's a good thing, right? The most important thing, really, you know?"

Both Diane and I nodded our heads in the affirmative, "Right," Diane said at the same moment I said, "Absolutely."

Just then, Marybeth brought Johnny's pie and ice cream and cleared out plates. Doggy bags for both Diane and I. Again. I secretly hoped this wasn't going to become a habit. I promised myself that, this time, my leftovers would make it inside my apartment when I got home, and that I would I eat then and enjoy them. For sure.

"So all's good, right?" Johnny asked, enthusiastically digging into his pie.

"Yeah, it is," Diane said, agreeing with her brother.

I could tell she was very happy for him. A little skeptical, maybe? Sure. You kind of had to be when dealing with chronic drinkers. For now, though, she was ready to cut him some slack and give him the benefit of the doubt. And that's what siblings did, right? Tried to be there for each other? Well, at least in this family they did. The point was, if Diane was happy for Johnny, then I was happy for her.

"So, what's going on now?" I asked, my appetite was returning as I enviously watched him destroy his huge piece of apple pie nearly buried under the two generous scoops of vanilla ice cream, "What are you working on now?"

"Right now I'm assigned to a house that's in the process of getting over run with mice. It's pretty challenging. Want to hear about it? It's a real mess."

In spite of ourselves, both Diane and I nodded.

"Sure," I said.

"Why not?" Diane added.

He looked at our nearly empty place settings, with only a water glass each, and set his fork down. "Come on you guys. I feel bad you didn't eat anything. How about if I at least order you some desert? Maybe we can celebrate not only my new job, but the fact that I'm staying sober." He lifted his plate in a mock salute and intoned the essence of the Alcoholics Anonymous Creed. "Here's to taking it one day at a time."

Diane and I looked at each other and smiled. Johnny was happy and sober and we were happy for him. Plus, we were happy with each other. Three times happy. You couldn't beat that. So, why not? Why not celebrate?

In the end, that's exactly what we did. I waved Marybeth over and ordered a bowl of salty caramel ice cream for each of us. Two big scoops each. We chatted a little until our bowls arrived and when they did, Diane and I dug in hungrily while Johnny settled back to begin another captivating tale, this time about, as he put it, 'A shit load of mice.'

After he began his story, Diane and I looked at each other and made eye contact for a long moment. Each of us smiled warmly at the other. Then she reached over and squeezed my hand, and I squeezed hers back. I didn't know about her, but for my part, I was getting the feeling that this could become habit forming, meeting her brother like we were on a weekly basis, just chatting and getting the low down on his job. You know, getting caught up and staying in touch. It's something I wanted to do. I felt like I was being drawn into this little family of a brother and sister and it felt good, all three of us being together and talking, subject matter aside. In fact, I couldn't think of a better way to move on with our lives; Johnny with his new job and staying sober. His sister and I moving forward with our relationship as we continued to forge a new life together.

"...and those mice, man, they aren't just downstairs, they're all over the place, especially in the kitchen, in the cupboards and everything. Everywhere. Mouse crap like you wouldn't believe. I guess they got into the walls somehow and are starting to overrun the house. Man, it's going to be a horrendous job. I've got to..."

Diane and smiled at each other, content and at peace. We ate our ice cream and held hands and listened to her brother's story. We couldn't have been happier.

The Lucie Line Trail

Mike McCormick loved his horse. He was a Tennessee Walker of such a deep, rich, chestnut color that it made Mike's eyes hurt sometimes if the sun hit the stately animal's coat just right. In preparation for his ride, Mike gently placed the worn, blue, and red Navajo patterned wool blanket onto the horse's back as the animal quivered in anticipation, muscles rippling. Then he picked up the saddle, admiring for the thousandth time the ornate, floral carving in the leather, and with a practiced, confident motion, lifted the saddle, settling it perfectly in place.

"There you go, old boy," Mike said, taking a moment to run his hand over the horse's withers before tightening the chinch and securing the end through a ring on the skirting. "Looking forward to going for a ride?" The horse's name was Paint, a name given to him by a previous owner, one who thought the white blaze on the animal's forehead looked like someone had painted it on. Mike didn't mind the name, and it seemed Paint didn't either, so it stayed.

Mike smiled when Paint nodded his head in the affirmative. Whether it was in answer to the question or to get rid of a persistent horsefly, it didn't matter. There was a connection Mike felt with his horse that began the moment he'd laid eyes on the animal four years ago. Four years and two months and sixteen days to be exact. The day he'd been driving his family home from the funeral of Jessie, his seven-year-old son. He'd spied the *For Sale* sign on a fence post next to a country road and the horse standing by himself out in the pasture. The sleek animal had turned its head, watching as Mike slowed his car, pulling off onto the grassy shoulder where he coasted to a stop. He got out and walked toward the fence, the brown expressive eyes on the big horse following his every movement. The day was warm for April and a light breeze blew from the south, ruffling the horse's black mane and tail.

Suddenly it started walking toward Mike. Their eyes met, and in that moment it seemed like fate was suddenly intervening, driving a wedge into Mike's grief and sending a wave of warmth through him that he was unable to explain.

" I think it's something Jessie would want me to do," he tried to explain to Lauren, his wife, who, along with their two daughters, was waiting patiently in the car. "It's like he's trying to communicate with me. I think our son would have wanted me to have this horse."

Lauren, who was grieving in her own way and really didn't want to deal with her husband at that particular moment, waved a hand at him to end the conversation. "Then go ahead and get him. Just be careful."

'Being careful' became her mantra from that day forward, and who could blame her? Jessie had died after being hit by a car while riding his bicycle. He'd been on one of the many quiet, tree-lined neighborhood streets in the area, only a few blocks away from home. He shouldn't have been riding where he was, but Jessie always had a mind of his own. 'Willful' some would say. 'Independent' was how Mike looked at him. But, whatever the term, his son was gone, gone for good and Mike began to use his time on his horse to help alleviate his grief which, now, after four years, was still there but much less so, thanks, in no small part, Mike felt, to the time he spent riding his cherished horse.

"Let's go, boy," Mike said, stepping into the stirrup and lifting himself up into the saddle, wiggling his butt, enjoying the feel of the leather through his jeans. He was fifty-five years old, clean-shaven, with a slight paunch and a stocky build. He had short cropped dark hair, speckled with gray, a narrow chin, and droopy dark bags under his brown eyes. His appearance was unremarkable and he knew it, but when he rode Paint, well, he felt on top of the world. Something about being on the horse made him feel happy and carefree. He loved the muscular motion of the animal, the warm mixture of horse sweat and leather that filled his nostrils, and the freedom of movement, pretending when he rode that he could head off in any direction he wanted, and go anywhere in the world he felt like going. And even though he knew he was only pretending it felt good to go somewhere, anywhere, in his mind and escape, if only for a little while.

"Let's go," he said, making a clicking sound, tapping the horse with the heels of his cowboy boots. Off they went, Paint breaking into a smooth trot; the trot Tennessee Walkers were known for.

The horse kept a steady almost metronome pace as Mike steered him down the driveway. It was paved with crushed red limestone and easy on the horse's hooves. Little puffs of dust hung in the still air as the horse trotted along, the early evening sun reflecting off soft clouds of red like a colorful, floating mirage. At the end of the drive was Old Orchard Way, a paved secondary road that ran north and south through the county. He took a left, careful to stay off the gravel shoulder. Paint moved happily at a steady gait as Mike acknowledged with a nod and a tip of his hat the few cars that sped past, careful to keep off to the side, 'Being careful,' just like Lauren had asked.

In five minutes, they met up with the Lucie Line Trial, a state-maintained, ten-foot wide, hard-packed dirt track that ran east two miles to the town of Orchard Lake and then twenty miles further on toward Minneapolis. In the other direction, the trail ran west out one hundred and fifty miles to Blue Heron Lake in the middle of the state. Usually, Mike turned left, heading back toward town, but today he was feeling adventurous. He checked the traffic and then turned to the right onto the trail toward the west, finally allowing himself to relax, slowing Paint to a walk and feeling himself unwind and start to enjoy the serenity that came with riding his beloved horse.

June blooming wildflowers of white Campion and purple Dain's Rocket adorned the sides of the trail, vying for space with purple vetch and yellow trefoil. Wild cherry blossoms filled the air with a scent so sweet it made Mike's mouth water. Off to the left, in a thicket of wild cranberry bushes, a finch sang a warbling song. From a clump of wild sumac, a wren chattered back, as if in accompaniment. The sky was cloudless blue and the sun was moving down toward sunset, nearly level with the tree tops and leaving a burning orange glow on the horizon. The day had been hot but now was cooling and Mike was glad he had chosen to wear a red plaid, long-sleeve, pearl snap-button cowboy shirt. He waved a few deerflies away from himself and Paint with his old, straw cowboy hat, and concentrated on enjoying the horse's easy saunter as they made their way down the trail, careful to stay toward the center.

The Lucie Line Trail was an old railroad bed that had been reclaimed by the state in the early 1980's. It passed through five counties and a mixture of forests, fields, and marshland, and was elevated, with thick, brushy sides dropping away nearly ten feet in some cases. The trail was popular for walking, jogging, and bike riding, but was rarely crowded. Only a few used it for horseback riding and that was fine with Mike. He liked to get out and enjoy the peace and quiet, listening to the birds singing, immersing himself in the natural world, and letting his mind go wherever it wanted. He rarely thought about work. (He had an office job as an assistant sales manager for Heartland Controls, an international electronic controls manufacturing company.) Today, instead of thinking about work, he used the time on Paint to unwind and relax. Lauren had taken the girls, Emma, fourteen, and Chrissie, twelve, to their evening lacrosse game. Ever since Jessie's death, she had thrown herself into raising their daughters. She had quit her job at Mount Olivet Hospital in Minneapolis where she had been head of Administration, telling Mike that they could use her savings to help make ends meet. Money wasn't a problem. His job paid him well; they had bought their home nearly twenty years earlier for a fair price a few years before housing values had begun to shoot up. They lived in the western part of the Hennepin country in an area that was nearly rural with rolling woodlands, marshes, and small ponds as the predominant features. Like most of the homes in the area, they had three acres, enough property to have a corral, and a small barn built for Paint. On paper life was good. However, Mike was often plagued by vague feelings of unease, sometimes even mild depression. But he wasn't one prone to considering using drugs or drinking to escape his problems. Instead, he chose to be alone and spend time with Paint and get away from what he sometimes referred to as "life" for a while.

Like he was doing now, not thinking about if it was the right or wrong thing to do, but, rather, that it was something he had to do. So, to that end, he sat back in his saddle, soaking in the sights and sounds of the oncoming evening. There were only a few people on the trail. He let Paint have the lead and the horse walked along with an easy, undulating motion that was almost like a narcotic. Time slowly slipped past, Paint's hooves clip-clopping down the trail, the sun moving further below the horizon, twilight turning to ever-increasing shades of dark purple.

Mike awoke with a start from a deep sleep. Night had fallen completely, the sky above nearly blocked by the tops of tree branches forming a high arching cathedral over the trail. There were stars out but any starlight was dim due to the thickness of the leaves; he could barely see where he was going.

"Whoa, boy," he said, shaking himself alert and reigning Paint in. "We need to get back to home base. Lauren will be worried."

Mike was upset with himself; his wife didn't need more worries due to his negligence. The Lucie Line was running through a thick forest. Up ahead he could just make out an opening to the left, probably a marsh or pond. The trail at this point was straight as a stick, but he could only see a little way due to the near complete darkness, sight being more of an impression of things than true vision. The forest on either side seemed intent on hemming him in, trapping him. He fought back a vague feeling of claustrophobia as he turned the horse around.

Paint nodded his head as he made the turn, chomping the bit in his mouth. "Come on, boy," Mike said, touching the horse's sides with his cowboy boots. "Let's head for home." They were just straightening out and Paint was about to break into a trot when, unexpectedly, up out of the brush popped a coyote, right onto the trail and only ten feet in front of them. The scruffy animal planted its paws and stopped dead. It took a second to stare at the horse and rider before it snarled, baring canines that gleamed in the low light. It looked like it might leap at them. Mike froze in the saddle, fear taking hold. Then the coyote barked a few short, yipping bursts and snarled once more before sinking into a crouch and running across the trail, where it dropped into the underbrush on the other side and scurried to safety.

The movement startled Paint so badly that he snorted and reared high on his hind legs, whinnying and baying out of control, eyes wild. Panic caused the horse to step backward, his hooves flailing, looking for purchase in the air. There was none. He lost his balance, falling off the trail, tumbling down the embankment, and sliding and twisting through twenty feet of brush all the way to the bottom. When Paint finally came to rest, Mike's left leg was crushed and pinned beneath the big animal.

It all happened so fast that both horse and rider were momentarily stunned. Then Mike became aware of a sharp pain in his leg at the same moment Paint instinctively made a sudden move to stand up, his body pushing off of his rider's leg, magnifying the intensity of the pain, ratcheting it up to an unbearable level. Mike screamed in agony as a wave of nausea overwhelmed him. It was probably fortunate that he passed out.

Paint rose to his feet, shaken but unhurt, reigns hanging loose. The horse shook his head, stomped his hooves, and looked around, snorting once or twice, distressed. The night was deep and dark, the woods silent. After a minute he got his bearings, settled down, and moved to the prone body, stepping carefully on the uneven ground. He bent down and nuzzled his rider. Mike didn't move.

It was probably the mosquitoes feasting on his face that finally caused Mike to regain consciousness a few minutes later. "Damn!" He slapped them away and then immediately screamed. The pain in his leg nearly made him throw up. He'd never felt anything like it before - sharp pulses surging through him like a tide of burning needles. Stupidly he tried to move, ratcheting up the pain to an unbearable level. He nearly passed out again. "God..." His breath was labored. He closed his eyes, but the mosquitoes buzzing around and feeding on any exposed skin forced him to stay awake. He feebly waved at them. He was on his back, his head facing down the slope, his crushed leg at an odd, unnatural angle. He had cuts on both his hands and it felt like something like a stick had punctured through the skin under his right shoulder blade where his shirt felt wet against his back. Blood, no doubt.

He adjusted himself as comfortably as he could and was closing is eyes again when there was a loud snort, startling him back to reality. Panicking, he remembered the coyote, wondering if it had come back to try to feed on him, a thought too gruesome to contemplate. There had been rumors of black bear sightings in the area too. Frantically he raised his head, trying not to move his leg, and looked around, eyes slowly adjusting to the darkness, readying himself to fight to the end if need be. With his fingers on his left hand, he groped through the leaves and plant debris on the ground looking for a stick or anything he could use as a weapon. A movement over his shoulder caught his eye and he dared to look, expecting the worst. He immediately calmed down and smiled. It was Paint. His old horse was standing right behind him at the bottom of the slope, swishing his tail and shaking his head to keep the bugs away.

Mike couldn't help but be touched. The animal had stayed with him rather than run off. "Hey there boy," he said affectionately, gritting his teeth, trying to ignore the unrelenting pain. He reached his hand up to pet the horse. "How are you doing?" Paint nodded his head and snorted again, stepping closer until he was near enough that Mike could reach out and touch its leg. The connection felt good. Mike ran his eyes over the horse's body as best he could in the dark, judging him to be uninjured. "You look good to me, boy," he said. "You look real good." He patted the horse's leg again and then lay back down, exhausted by the effort. He closed his eyes and passed out again.

***

Lauren put the phone down with an exasperated sigh and said to her friend, Kali, "Still no answer." She shook her head, resigning herself to her husband's uncharacteristic behavior.

"What's up with him, anyway?" Kali had invited Lauren and her daughters back to her home for lemonade after their lacrosse game. She didn't have a high opinion of Mike, thinking him at best inattentive, and at worst, selfish and self-centered. "Why doesn't he answer?"

"I don't know," Lauren sighed again. "He's probably busy." With what she had no idea. He was supposed to be on the trail with Paint but should be back by now. "Maybe he's out in the barn. He should at least have his phone with him." She was tired and wanted to relax with her best friend and not think about Mike right then. The girls were on the same team lacrosse team as Kali's daughter, Heather. They were letting off steam after the game, playing tag in the pool, laughing, and shouting. The night air was cool and refreshing, the sky brushed with a white wash of stars. Lauren leaned her head back in the lounge chair, put her feet up, and closed her eyes with a grateful sigh. She could stay like this forever. "I'll call him again in a little while," she said.

Kali was concerned for her friend. Lauren was just over five feet tall and wore her auburn hair cut so it was just long enough to pull behind her ears. Her eyes were brown and her complexion dark. Over the last four years, ever since the death of Jessie, her expression had taken on a more severe look; frown lines had formed around both sides of her mouth, and she rarely laughed anymore.

Kali reached over and patted her friend on the arm. "You just relax. I'll go freshen up our drinks. Do you want something to munch on? Veggie's and hummus?"

Lauren opened her eyes and looked gratefully at Kali. She shook her head. "No, thanks. Just the lemonade is fine." Lauren watched her blond, tall, slim friend walk slowly toward the sliding glass patio door that led inside the sprawling ranch house. Kali was a confident, no-nonsense person - someone who Lauren depended on to talk with and confide in. *What would I do without her?* Lauren thought to herself, not the first time today, or any other day for that matter. Then she turned back to the pool and waved at Emma and Chrissie goofing around in the water, tossing an oversized blue and white beach ball.

Lauren smiled a rare smile. She loved to see her girls having fun and secretly wished she could join them. But she didn't. Instead, she lay her head back and allowed herself to close her eyes again; except her mind wouldn't shut down. Sure, she and Mike had drifted apart somewhat after Jessie's death, but she still loved him and was convinced he still loved her. All couples had to find ways to cope with tragedies, didn't they? She and Mike were working through their grief in their own way and in their own time. She had the girls and Mike had...what? Well, work and Paint, a horse she really did adore. She knew others felt she and Mike should be focusing on their own relationship, working toward reestablishing the bond they once had. Sometimes, though, like now, it was easier to make the best of things the way they were, letting time heal their wounds, to paraphrase the old adage.

They'd been to couples counseling off and on and Lauren felt they were making progress; moving ahead with their lives. She had nothing to complain about and could cope with her husband's occasional distance. In truth, though, she longed for them to be closer and for him to communicate with her more. To that end, she was planning a surprise. She recently had been thinking about getting a horse so they could go riding together. She'd found a pretty little mare for sale at a ranch just west of them. Her color was a mixture of warm honey and cream, and she was named Butterscotch. The owner was willing to hold her for a least another week.

She could picture herself and Mike going for long, relaxing rides together, following their whims and riding wherever they wanted; being spontaneous for a change. The image came into her mind of her on Butterscotch ridding next to Mike on Paint out on the Lucie Line. The thought made her smile. She'd plan to talk to him about it tonight. Why didn't he answer his phone?

"Here's some more lemonade," Kali said, interrupting her thoughts. She walked across the flagstone apron of the pool and plopped down on her lounge chair, handing over an icy glass. "Drink up and relax."

"Thanks." Lauren glanced at her watch and took a refreshing sip, appreciating the icy, sweetly sour taste of the drink. It was a few minutes after 10:00 pm. She was starting to get worried about her husband. Where was he? Then a splash from the pool caught her attention. Chrissie had exploded into the water with a huge cannonball off the diving board. Lauren laughed and applauded. She turned to Kali. "This is nice. The girls are having so much fun. It's just the kind of evening we all need." She settled herself more comfortably on the lounge and took another sip from her glass. *Just a few more minutes*, she told herself. *Then we'll get going.*

***

A young boy was standing next to him when Mike regained consciousness.

"Geez!" he yelled, startled, trying unsuccessfully to sit up, pain shooting trough his back and leg again. "What the hell are you doing here?" He lay back, groaning.

"I heard your horse, mister, and then saw you." The kid eyed Mike quizzically. "What happened to you? Are you OK?" he asked. Then he carefully stepped past Mike and moved over to pat Paint on the nose. The horse stood still, accepting the boy's gesture, lowering his head, encouraging him to continue. "Hi there." He started petting the horse, now using both hands, working up around his ears and under the straps of his bridle. Paint whinnied softly in obvious pleasure.

"Coyote scared my horse," Mike said, answering the boy's question. He forced the words out and raised his head to get a closer look at the boy. From what he could tell in the dark, he was a skinny little kid dressed in a white tee-shirt and baggy, dark colored basketball shorts. He had on a baseball hat (Mike assumed the Minnesota Twins), worn backwards and he appeared nearly five feet tall. Mike guessed that he was maybe ten or twelve years old. Suddenly his vision fogged over momentarily, then cleared, and he started to have trouble breathing. He realized there might have been more damage done to him that he wasn't aware of. The unrelenting pain was dulling his senses.

The kid kept petting Paint, moving now to run his hands over the horse's shoulder and through his mane. "I like your horse. What's her name?"

"She's a he and his name is Paint," Mike panted. His back hurt, and his leg felt like it was asleep, which was good, he figured. The pain was less but still a constant throb. He lay his head down and closed his eyes.

The kid moved over to him, swatting away misquotes. "Mister, mister." The kid shook Mike's right shoulder, causing him to scream "OW!" in pain. "Sorry," the boy said, backing away, looking scared.

"Hold on, there." Mike had come to and was holding up his hand as best he could. "Don't leave me."

"I'm not. I'm just going to get some bug spray."

Thank God, thought Mike. The mosquitoes were swarming all over him, hungrily feeding. He watched the kid shuck off a small backpack and take out a can. "What have you got there?"

"Northwood's Off with Deet," the kid said. "Best stuff in the world." He shook the can, the aerosol rattle strangely comforting, and moved closer. "Close your eyes, mister." Mike did as he was told and in a moment the cool mist of the spray drifted over his face. It felt wonderful. The kid then sprayed Mike's hands. Then himself. When he was all done he put the can in the pack and sat down on his heels, peering into Mike's face. "You alright, mister? You don't look so good. Do you have a cell phone to call for help?"

Mike shook his head, groaning. He'd intentionally left the damn thing on his dresser at home. So he could have some uninterrupted privacy. Stupid. The pain in his back now seemed to encompass the entire upper part of his body. He felt the kid carefully move some leaf debris and dirt from his clothes and then gently caress Mike's right leg, the one that was undamaged. The touch was remarkably soothing.

"Where are you from?" Mike finally asked. "From around here?" Speaking was getting exhausting.

"Naw," the kid responded. "Not from around here."

"How old?" Mike could barely speak. The pain was returning but something about the kid made him curious.

"Eleven," the kid said. "Just finished sixth grade."

Geez, Mike thought to himself, he's the same age as Jessie would have been. Then he had a thought. "What the hell are you doing out here this time of night, anyway?" The effort to speak sapped his strength. He lay his head down, closed his eyes, and started to drift into unconsciousness.

Dimly aware, he heard the boy say, "I just went for a bike ride and ended up here."

"Really?" Mike asked skeptically, senses on alert. Despite his pain and ever diminishing capacity to think clearly, at heart he was still a father. Something didn't ring true. "At this time of night?" He stared at the kid. "Where are your parents?"

"Oh, they're around," the kid responded quietly. He looked into the forest, avoiding eye contact. "They're busy with some other stuff," he added evasively.

Right, Mike thought to himself. It sounded exactly like what the girls would say or even Jessie would have said when pushed for the truth. He might be severely injured, but he'd been a parent long enough to easily see through the kid's lie.

Right now, though, he was too exhausted to argue. Instead, he played along, thinking it was probably good to keep talking. Besides, having the kid around was giving him hope that he was going to come out of this okay. He changed conversational gears, getting more to the point. "So are you going to help rescue me or what?"

"Sure!" The kid almost shouted. He was enthusiastic and happy to be needed. He opened his pack again and took out a bottle of water. "Here, mister," he said, unscrewing the cap. He held it to Mike's lips. "Drink this."

The kid tilted the bottle, cupping the back of Mike's head as he drank thirstily, excess water running down his chin. The cool liquid felt wonderful on his overheated body. The kid seemed to sense this and he poured some into his hand and washed Mike's forehead and face. Mike sighed a silent, grateful *thank you*. The kid then took a drink before capping the water and putting it back in his pack.

With the water washing off the mosquito spray on Mike's face, he went through the spraying process again. By now, they both could see pretty well-their eyes finally having adjusted to the darkness. "What else do you want me to do?" the kid asked.

"Go get help," Mike said, shifting up on his elbow. He could tell shock was setting in: the pain had come back into his left leg and was now a throbbing dull ache that was never-ending. He needed to do something quick. "How'd you get here anyway?"

The kid pointed up onto the trail. "My bike."

"Can you ride and get someone to help me?"

The kid looked around. "Maybe me and Paint can pull you up to the trail. They do stuff like that in the movies all the time."

In spite of all the pain he was in, Mike grunted out a laugh. "And then what? I get on the horse and ride home?"

"Damn, mister. I was just trying to help."

The kid got up and made a move up the slope. "Hold on, hold on!" Mike after him, "Don't get all bent out of shape."

He stopped and spat out. "What?" He was angry.

"Look, we need to work together..." Suddenly, Mike screamed. He had moved just slightly to try and get more comfortable and was leaning back when the point of a dead branch went right into the wound under his right shoulder blade. "God damn it!" was all he was able to say. Sweat popped up all across his forehead, beads of it running down his face.

The kid quickly bent down to help him, looking at what little of Mike's back he could see. "Man, mister, you're bleeding a lot. I'll see if I can help." He pushed the sharp branch out of the way. Then he reached into his pack and pulled out a tee-shirt. "Here, let me see if I can stop the bleeding." Their argument was forgotten.

Working together over the next few minutes, the kid was able to use the shirt to staunch the flow of the blood. He took off one of his shoes and used the lace to wrap it around Mike's chest to hold the shirt in place. The effort exhausted the injured man and he lay back with a groan, grateful for the padding of the kid's shirt. But the pain was still there. They needed to do something fast. "You've got to go for help," Mike groaned. He was lying flat out on the ground, gasping for breath. God, maybe he'd punctured a lung.

"Where should I go?"

"Do you live around here? Can you go to your home?"

"No, I'm from back toward Minneapolis."

Well, that answers part of the mystery, thought Mike. "Fine. Go back the way you came." Despite his labored breathing, he was able to explain how to get to his house.

When he was done the boy asked, "Why don't I just take Paint? Wouldn't he know the way?"

Smart kid. "Maybe. First, you have to get up onto the trail." He was losing the strength to talk.

"I'll do my best," the kid said. He spit on his hands and rubbed them together in preparation.

Just like in the movies, Mike thought, as he struggled to maintain consciousness, mentally crossing his fingers that the plan would work.

It took about two minutes. The kid grabbed hold of the reigns like he was born to the task. Together they scrambled up the slope, clods of dirt flying from the big animal's hooves, both of them slipping and sliding and fighting through the brush until they finally reached the trail. Paint shook himself, took a moment to get his bearings, and then immediately turned to the right and started walking toward home.

"Whoa," Mike yelled, using the last of his strength. Yet as he watched the whole process, he was impressed beyond words. "Tell him to 'Whoa,'" he gasped to the kid.

Between the two of them yelling, "Whoa," Paint finally stopped. The kid positioned himself on the side of the horse, grabbed the saddle horn, and jumped up, scrambling and kicking his legs, fighting himself into the saddle, his feet dangling above the stirrups. Paint, to his credit, stayed standing perfectly still through the whole process.

"I'm ready, mister," he said. At the sound of the boy's voice, the horse started walking down the trail, heading for home.

Mike suddenly had a thought. "Hey, kid," he yelled, using the last of his strength.

"What?" They were beginning to move away at a steady pace.

"I'm Mike. What's your name?"

"Jacob," came the reply, fading into the distance. "They call me Jake."

Geez, thought Mike. That was Jessie's middle name. Then he passed out, but not before saying a silent prayer that the kid, Jake, would make it down the trail okay, find where he lived, and bring help.

***

"Come on, girls, time to head home!" Lauren waved to get their attention. Emma was just diving into the pool.

"Aww, mom," Chrissie complained. "Can't we stay a little longer?"

"Nope. Go inside and change. We leave in five minutes." Honestly, she didn't want to go and said to Kali, "The girls always have such a good time here."

The cooler temperature brought out the scent of a Japanese Lilac, its sweet aroma filling the air. The night was so quiet that when the girls weren't yelling and laughing she could hear a chorus of frogs down in a nearby marsh. Off on the edge of Kali's property near where the forest started, fireflies were out. Lauren had spent the last fifteen minutes distracted in her conversation with her friend, watching as they blinked trails through the darkness, trying to guess where the next flash of light would appear, never successful, but not caring either. It was a silly little game, but it was fun to play. Plus, it took her mind off her worry: she had been unable to get a hold of her husband.

"Want to stay overnight? The kids would love it if you did," Kali leaned over, smiling in encouragement.

"Tempting as it sounds..." Lauren checked her watch. "It's nearly eleven thirty. Mike will be wondering where we are."

"You think? He could always call you, you know." Kali not too successfully tried to keep her low opinion of her friend's husband out of her voice. "All he seems to care about is that stupid horse."

"Yes, well..." Lauren's voice trailed off. She could see her friend's point. Lots of people felt Mike, even though it'd been four years, wasn't handling the loss of their son too well. But from her perspective, he was doing as well as could be expected. If you haven't ever lost a child, don't be too quick to judge how parents cope, was how she looked at it. She began to shake off her relaxed mood, gearing up to head home. "At any rate, we should go. I'll call you tomorrow."

Lauren pushed herself out of the lounge chair and stood up, taking in the quiet, peacefulness of the night one more time. But thoughts of Mike were now intruding. It was time to get home and find out what was going on. In a few minutes, the girls returned, dried off, and changed into shorts and tee shirts. Lauren pulled a white cotton cardigan closer to ward off the night's chill. "Let's go girls," she called to them. She and Kali embraced goodbye as Emma and Chrissie waved to Heather and then joined their mom. The three of them walked side by side to their Suburban.

"Is Dad home?" Emma asked.

"He should be."

"But is he?" Emma was a persistent, exacting child.

"We'll find out, honey." They got in, slamming doors, and Lauren started the engine. She carefully turned around and drove down the long driveway, thankful for the illumination of her headlights. She paused where the driveway met the dark county road and looked both ways before turning onto the night. She switched the headlights to high beam and accelerated cautiously to twenty-four miles an hour. Then she carefully drove home.

In five minutes they were pulling into their driveway, head lights cutting a path through the darkness. Up ahead a few soft lights from inside the house shone the way. Off to the right was the barn with an outdoor security light on over its double wooden doors. Lauren was concentrating on driving the car up to the garage, wondering to herself where Mike was, when suddenly Chrissie called out, "Mom! There's Paint!"

Lauren stopped the car and looked. Standing next to the barn was Mike's horse. He was nosing at the closed door, trying to get in, stomping his feet, and impatiently shaking his head. Probably hungry, Lauren thought herself. Then, a more immediate thought hit her, and a rising panic set in. Where was Mike?

She jammed the car into park, turned the engine off, and got out, running to the horse. Paint turned and took a step toward her. He was comfortable with the members of the family; they all rode him. He nodded his head up and down and snorted, loose reigns flopping. He was sweaty, dirty and had burrs sticking to his tail and mane. Otherwise, though, to Lauren's eyes, he appeared to be alright. As she approached him she saw something attached to a leather lace on his saddle. Emma raced ahead and got there first.

"Mom, it's a note," she said, opening it.

"What's it say?" Lauren was worried about her husband but tried to hold her emotions at bay, not wanting to upset the girls any more than they were. A tiny part of her hoped this whole thing might be some kind of joke. But she was a realist. It couldn't be. She had a strong feeling something was very wrong. She was right.

"It says 'On the trail To the west. Hurt,'" Emma said, handing the note to her mom, who quickly scanned the tattered piece of paper, concurring with what her daughter had said. It didn't look like Mike's writing, but if he was hurt...

"Girls, go and check the house for your dad," she commanded. As they ran off, she took out her phone and dialed 911. It was 11:45 pm. Her feeling was something was horribly wrong.

By 12:20 am Hennepin County Search and Rescue was on the Lucie Line Trail, heading west, looking for Mike. One guy was driving a county pickup truck, headlights on high beam, while four officers rode in the back scanning the sides of the trail with high-intensity flashlights. Behind the truck a line of hastily assembled volunteers spread out on foot, carefully peering into the underbrush, their flashlights in constant motion.

Lauren sat in her living room with Kali. "Mike's gone missing. I'm scared," was all she had said into her phone when she had called earlier. Kali came right away prepared to hear her friend's husband had left home or something. Anything idiotic Mike would do at this point wouldn't surprise her in the least. She immediately downplayed her opinions, however, hearing Lauren's tearful telling of her story. "I just hope he's alright," Lauren said sobbing when she'd finished. "The girls and I need him safe and sound and to be here in our home. Where can he be?"

Kali moved close and rubbed her friend's back. "He'll be home soon. He'll be fine, just wait. Mike's pretty strong." The words spilled out in a rush. Whether that last statement was true or not only time would tell. Kale hoped for Lauren and the girl's sake it was. She moved closer to console her friend and hugged her tightly.

Emma and Chrissie were out in the barn, their concern for their dad's safety running on overdrive, adrenaline flowing. They were cleaning Paint, their nervous pacing back and forth making the job take twice as long as it normally would. "Do you think Dad's going to be OK?" Chrissie asked. She had sprayed the horse off with a hose and was now wiping him down with a towel, rubbing it over his coat and rinsing it in a bucket of clean water. After a few minutes, the repetitive motion began to have a calming effect on both her and the animal.

"I don't know, how would I know?" Emma spit the words out. She was mad that her dad was causing them grief, but, more than that, she was worried. Losing Jessie was hard enough, but the thought of losing their father was too much to bear. "Let's just get Paint cleaned up, alright?" She was running a curry comb through the horse's mane, taking out the burrs and smoothing the stiff hairs with her fingers as she worked. Working on the orderly task of cleaning the horse was calming her down as well.

When Chrissie was done washing Paint, she hung the towel on a post to dry, picked up a soft bristle brush, and started working it over Paint's coat. She stood on the opposite side of the horse as her sister. After a minute they both made eye contact. The barn was silent except for Paint occasionally stomping one of his hooves. Outside of the open door of the barn, darkness seemed to spill in. It had a sinister feel to it. Where was their father?

Tears welled up in Emma's eyes. Chrissie saw them and then she too started crying. Something made them join hands and lean across the horse's back. The heat of the big animal warmed them. The closeness felt good. In a few minutes, their tears subsided and they both went back to work in silence, bonded by the mutual hope that their father was going to be home soon and that he was going to be fine and life, as they knew it, would get back to normal.

They worked into the night until much later the job was done. Then they put Paint in his stall with a bucket of fresh oats and clean water and went inside to join their mother, exhaustion had finally set in.

At 3:10 am Lauren's phone buzzed. She hadn't been asleep, but, instead had been talking to Kali non-stop about how much she loved her husband how much Mike meant to her, and how she couldn't live if something had happened to him, not after what had happened to Jessie, and what would happen to the girls if their father wasn't there with them... And on and on.

When the phone buzzed, Lauren fumbled once but was able to get a hold of it, hands shaking. Kali watched as her friend nodded her head. Then she smiled, sighing with relief, covering the phone. "They found him! He's going to be OK!" On the floor where they had fallen asleep, the girls stirred, coming awake.

"Mom?" Emma asked, rubbing her face.

"Dad?" Chrissie said, not taking her eyes off her mother.

Lauren held up a finger 'one second,' and listened some more. After a minute she hung up and held out her arms. "Come here girls," she said. Her two daughters crawled quickly across the floor, came to her, and were enfolded into their mother's arms. "They found your dad out on the trail. He's injured, but he's going to be OK." She grinned over the heads of her daughters at Kali who smiled back at her, thinking that it was about time her friend had something good happen in her life. She obviously cared about her husband and, hopefully, one day he would reciprocate the feeling.

"What are you going to do now?" Kali asked.

"The girls and I are going to the hospital," Lauren said, standing up. She pulled the girls, who were instantly wide awake, with her. She was happy and excited. "I guess Mike's been asking for us."

Kali got to her feet, catching Lauren's energetic mood. "Let's go, then," she said, grabbing her purse and leading the way to the door. "I'll drive."

***

Two days later Mike was home from the hospital recuperating. Lauren had set up a bed for him on a couch in the family room: a big, open area, with the kitchen at one end and the living area at the other, separated by the couch Mike was on and an informal sitting area in between. A double set of sliding glass doors along one wall let him see the backyard. Before he'd come home the girls had talked Lauren into going to a local garden store where they'd purchased overflowing pots of red and pink geraniums, white trailing bacopa, orange and yellow marigolds, and bright blue cascading verbena. They'd carefully placed the pots on the patio outside the glass doors so Mike could see them.

All the colorful flowers lifted Mike's spirits, which were pretty high anyway. When the sun was shining, like it was this morning, the family room was the most cheerful place in the house. The open floor plan made it easy for Mike to see everyone and be a part of the day-to-day activities of Lauren, Emma, and Chrissie. Which is what he wanted more than anything.

"I don't want to be away from any of you ever again," he kept saying, over and over again, both in the hospital and once he was home, obviously shaken by his experience.

Lauren thought it was sweet for him to be talking like that; something he hadn't done in the last four years. Nevertheless, the sentiment was starting to lose some of its punch after hearing it so many times. "Honey, we aren't going anywhere, are we girls?" Lauren had told him time and time again, hoping he'd eventually believe her.

"No, Dad, never," Chrissie would say to him, rushing to hug him.

Emma was by nature somewhat reticent but still thankful her father had returned from his accident safe and relatively unscathed. His left leg tibia had a hairline fracture, and he'd strained some tendons. The puncture in his back only did muscle damage and would heal nicely. Mike's oldest daughter had appointed herself an entertainment coordinator and had been enjoying some much-needed quality time with her dad. They had been playing cribbage almost non-stop since his return, chatting and laughing like old times.

There was a definite change in him, that was for sure. A change for the better as far as Lauren was concerned.

"I love how nice the walls look in here," Mike remarked. It was his first morning back home and it was as if he was seeing the color of the room for the first time. He had slept well the night before, felt rested and ready to put the "ordeal" as he put it, behind him. "What would you say, Lori, light green?"

Lauren smiled at him calling her "Lori", a term of endearment he hadn't used since Jessie had died. "Don't you remember?" she chided him. "It's sea-green. We picked it out last year."

Mike shook his head, grinning. "I've been kind of in a fog for some time, now, haven't I?"

That's certainly an understatement, Lauren said to herself. *Try four years.* But she kept her thought to herself, preferring instead to enjoy the novelty of having her husband more like himself than he'd been since Jessie had passed away. "We've all been trying to deal with Jessie's death in our own ways," she told him.

"But you've been doing such a good job holding things together," he countered. "The girls are doing great," he shook his head, chagrined. "I haven't been much help, have I? I'm going to try to do better, starting right now." As if to prove the statement he made a move to get up and suddenly grimaced, the pain still evident. "Well, maybe I'll take a rain check," he groaned lying back down.

Lauren smiled to herself. She had been sitting in an easy chair next to him, keeping him company, having a cup of tea, and glancing through a home improvement magazine. She was enjoying the homey sensation of starting to feel like a complete family again, and, even though it only had been a couple of days, she was daring to let herself think that maybe their situation had turned around. Maybe Mike would become more of the man she needed him to be: more involved in raising the girls and more of a husband who helped rather than hindered around the house. She allowed herself to hope Mike really was changing and that it would be for the better and that it would last. She set her magazine down, stood up, came over sat on the couch, and ran, her fingers through her husband's hair. It was thinning, had been ever since Jessie's death, but the intimate gesture felt good to her.

Mike responded, looking into her eyes. He took hold of her hand and kissed it, "I love you so much. I don't know what I'd do without you."

Lauren smiled and lay her head on his chest. She could feel his heart beating. She felt the warmth of his body. Suddenly, all of the chores she had planned: getting the laundry going, dusting and sweeping the first floor, and vacuuming the upstairs, didn't seem so critical anymore. She stretched out next to him. "I'm not going anywhere."

Mike sighed and smiled, looking up at the vaulted ceiling with its rough beams giving him a sense of security. He felt relaxed and was happy to be spending time with his wife. He put his left arm around her shoulder and kissed the top of her head. "I was wondering," he said. "Have you ever thought about getting another horse? Lately, I've been thinking it would be nice for us to go riding out on the trail. You know, do something fun together." He ran his fingers gently through her hair.

Lauren laughed, thinking he was wondering about something else. She reordered her thoughts. "Funny, I've been thinking the same thing, you know, about getting a horse." She briefly told him about the little mare Butterscotch she'd been looking at. When she was done she asked what he thought. Mike nodded and grinned in approval. Before he could say anything, she asked, "Where'd you get your idea?"

"I've been thinking about it for a while, but it really started coming together when I was out on the Lucie Line waiting for help." Then he stopped and slapped his forehead. "God, I forgot to ask you! What about Jacob? Jake? The kid. Where is he? What's happened to him?"

Lauren sat up, perplexed, "Jake? What in the world are you talking about?"

"Jake. The kid who rode Paint home. Skinny, little guy, but pretty friendly. Wore a baseball hat. Resourceful, too. He was the one who put that tee shirt bandage on my back."

Lauren smiled at him and went back to her chair and her tea and magazine. She'd heard an automobile drive up and car doors slamming, the girls getting dropped off from lacrosse practice by Kali. They'd be coming through the door any second and would probably give their parents no end of grief about being intimate together on the couch, as good as it had felt.

She smiled at Mike. "Sorry, honey. There was no Jake, no little kid, no nothing. Just the note you wrote, stuck in the saddle, telling us where you were. You were probably hallucinating seeing someone. The doctor said that happens sometimes if you're in a lot of pain." She opened her magazine and took a sip of her tea, chamomile, appreciative of its flavor and relaxing effect.

Mike wasn't ready to let it rest. He sat up the best he could. "I never wrote any note, he stated emphatically. "I couldn't. I was in so much pain I could barely stay conscious, let alone think to write something. The kid rode off to our house on Paint. I swear he was there with me ."

"Well, I never saw anyone." As far as Lauren was concerned, Mike was still suffering some sort of hallucinogenic after-effect from his accident. A little part of her wondered about what he'd said, though. *Could it have happened?* Too bad they'd lost the note in all of the confusion of that night.

Just then Emma and Chrissie bounded into the room and interrupted her thoughts, their strawberry blond long hair tied back in ponytails, faces glistening with sweat. They were laughing and joking, obviously in good moods. Whether it was from practice or having their father home, Lauren couldn't tell. She hoped it was both. "Girls, did either of you see anyone around Paint when he came back the other night? You were out at the barn with him. Your dad thinks there might have been a boy around somewhere."

Emma rolled her eyes, chiding her father. "No Dad, no one. I think you're making the whole thing up." Then she smiled a big smile and ran over to the couch and hugged him, putting that awful night out of her mind. "I'm so glad you're back and are going to be OK."

"Me, too," Chrissie added, plopping on the couch and hugging her dad as well. "Double glad." She looked at her sister, gave her a high-five, and they both started laughing.

Lauren was amazed how, in just a day, the girls had suddenly become more relaxed and less tense. *It must have to do with how Mike is behaving*, she thought. *He's being more attentive and thoughtful, talking to them, talking to me. It's a start. I hope he keeps it up.*

From Mike's point of view, all he wanted to do was whatever he could to bring his family back together again. He quickly decided to put the thought of Jake out of his mind, putting the arguments aside and willing to accept the kid was only in his imagination. After all, he'd been pretty banged up and had lost a lot of blood. It made sense that he imagined the boy, who really, did look a little like Jessie might have looked like if he'd grown to that age.

Stop it! Mike shook his head to get rid of that kind of thinking. He made a silent vow right then never to let thoughts of what may or may not have happened on the Lucie Line Trail ever cloud his mind again. It was time to put the entire experience behind him. All he cared about right now was his family and being home and safe with them.

He turned to his daughters. "Hey girls," he said, giving Lauren a wink. "Your mom and I have been talking. What do you think about us all getting another horse?"

And he smiled, then, at the response to such a simple idea when both the girls jumped up and down and clapped their hands, cheering and joyfully echoing each other. "Yes, yes, and YES!"

Mike watched as the girls danced around the room. He grinned a wide grin and looked over at Lauren who gave him a wink back and an encouraging smile. She was all on board. "Well, girls," he called out, "Let's do it then!"

***

That same day, when Mike and his family were talking about getting another horse, out on the Lucie Line Trail, right where Paint had reared up and fallen off the side, there was a movement in the underbrush. Suddenly a coyote jumped up onto the trail, paused, and looked both ways. In an instant, he realized he was all alone. He relaxed, sat down on his haunches, and bit at a tick crawling across the top of its paw. The coyote was a male in its third year and not yet attached to a pack. He roamed the woods and fields around the town of Orchard Lake, every now and then venturing into the well-kept, manicured yards common to the homes in the area, looking for any inattentive cat or small dog. He was always on the lookout for food and getting to be a good hunter; rarely did a day pass with him being hungry.

He chomped down the tick and took a survey of the trail and the woods around it. Then he sniffed, catching the faintest whiff of horse and human. In his brain, the memory came back of the commotion a few nights back with the truck and all the humans with their lights and all the racket they'd made. He remembered the encounter with the horse and the human. He had escaped the horse's hooves and scurried for safety into the brush, but he hadn't run away. No, instead, he'd circled back across the trail and hidden pressed to the ground nearby under a thick tangle of grapevine. He'd been curious and had watched the horse and the human.

After waiting for a while he saw the little human come along and a while later he and the horse left and went down the trail back toward town, and, a while later, he'd seen many humans come around and the big human get taken away. He'd stayed crouched out of sight after the big machine had left and the humans had gone until, finally, the night had become quiet once again. Then he'd come out of his hiding place and gone to where the big and little human had been with the horse and looked around, taking a few minutes to thoroughly sniff the ground. Finally, he had relaxed. The forest returned to normal with the night sounds of the measured hooting of an owl and the quiet murmurings of frogs and other amphibians in the nearby swamp. Satisfied all was well, he had left the area and gone on with his hunting.

But now, on this pleasant summer morning with the sun shining brightly in the sky, curiosity was starting to get the better of him. He put his nose to the ground and sniffed in the dirt. He picked an aroma, a scent of something familiar. He turned and looked away from the rising sun, out to the west. There was the faintest mark on the hard-packed surface. Narrower than his paw, the mark was nearly smooth with little bumps in it. The coyote bent and sniffed again. It had a faint odor, like the smell on the roads with the fast machines on them that he so carefully avoided, crossing over only now and then. There was the faintest scent of a human, too. Not an old human, but a young one. Experience had taught him the difference. It brought back the memory of the other night when there had been all of the commotions and the young human had been there. It was his scent.

The coyote thought for a moment about following it to see where it went but decided not to. He knew the dirt trail went away for a long distance, out toward where the sun would set later that day. Many miles. Today he wanted to stay close to the woods he called home. He'd picked up a trace scent of a female earlier that morning, just after sunrise. She was traveling alone, unattached like him. Maybe they could join up and start hunting together. If she was good, they could perhaps start a pack of their own.

Suddenly his ears caught a sound. Something was down in the brush on the other side of the trail. A rabbit, maybe. He crouched and ever so quietly made his way to the edge, sniffing, his nose to the ground. He paused, watching, his eyes quick to catch any movement in thick undergrowth. His heart beat rapidly, and his muscles tensed. He was ready. He made his move and pounced. In an instant, he'd disappeared into the underbrush.

The Cribbage Game

Tim shuffled the cards while watching Fred. Or his dad. He still wasn't sure what to call him. The old man was propped up in his hospital bed, having been moved into the hospice care wing of the nursing home the week before last. The same week Tim had been notified of the move. Also, the same week he had been notified that the father he thought had been dead all these years was, in fact, alive.

It was fifty years ago that Tim, then twenty, his mom, and his younger brothers and sisters had been told by Irv Lindenfelter, his dad's best friend, that Fred, who had divorced their mom and moved to San Francisco, had gone missing. Vanished without a trace, was the way it was put to them at the time. At first Tim and his family figured that Fred had just taken off and gone fishing or camping, his two fondest hobbies. But as time passed that notion proved to be unverifiable. He didn't return to his job at Tillotson and MaKray, the advertising firm he worked for. His phone went unanswered. Bills piled up in the mail box of the apartment where he lived. Finally the police were called in. Days turned to weeks and then to months with no answers forthcoming. Finally, the missing person case of Fredrick Clarence Beverly was put on the back burner and eventually filed away as "Missing-Unsolved". So that was that.

Fifty years was a long time to learn to forget and that's exactly what everyone had done. Tim and his brothers and sisters had gone on with their lives, having adjusted to life without their father anyway because of the divorce. After all, Tim, the oldest, was fifteen when his dad had left his mother and the life they had in Minneapolis and moved out to San Francisco to "start over" as he had put it.

The year had been 1964 and the loss of their father had devastated the family. But after about a week of moping around and collectively hanging their heads, their mother, Ann, had rallied the kids and told them to pull themselves together and quit feeling sorry for themselves.

"We are going to get through this," she had said, directing her fiery gaze at Tim and his brothers, Steven and Larry, and sisters, Kathy and Susan. "And we are going to be better because of it."

Their mom went back to work, the kids adjusted to the change in the household and they learned to live without having their father around. Life, indeed, did get better. For a while Fred maintained contact with his children with the occasional phone call and a card sent on their birthday with a twenty dollar bill in it. He never visited.

Over the course of the first few years the calls diminished in frequency until they only came once a year, at birthday time, piggy-backing on the birthday card and twenty dollar bill. After five years, Tim had pretty much put his father out of his mind. Then he went missing and Tim found himself strangely unaffected and detached.

"I really don't think that much about him anymore," he told his mom. "Honestly, I just don't care all that much." He paused and looked out the window. They'd been sitting in the kitchen, drinking ice tea together. Earlier, Ann had returned home and shared the news of their father's disappearance with her children. A detective with the SFP had contacted her at work that day and told her what had happened.

As she told them the news, all the kids had just sat and listened with a somewhat detached mood. Then they'd all talked about it for a while before the younger kids had gone their separate ways. Tim stayed behind with his mom to talk. They were close and had a good relationship. "I never felt I had the chance to know him, anyway," Tim added, somewhat cryptically.

Ann nodded. "I never want to disparage your father," she said, sipping from her glass, "but he was a hard man to get to know."

Tim looked at her. She was a thin woman of medium height in her mid forties, her shoulder length auburn hair streaked with gray. Her dark brown eyes were kind looking and had a tint of green in them. Her reading glasses were pushed to the top of her head. She wore a flowered sun dress and comfortable, canvas shoes and was unwinding after a long day working as secretary for a local manufacturing company. Outside the birds were singing as the sun settled toward the western horizon. It was August, the height of summer in Minnesota.

"Do you want to sit out back, Mom?" Tim asked. "Get some fresh air?"

Ann smiled at her son. "Yes, I'd like that."

Forty one years later, at his mom's funeral, Tim was asked by his brothers and sisters to speak about their mother. He had done so, delivering a heartfelt eulogy. Everyone had appreciated his remembrances but, being honest with himself, he never felt he had been able to capture her essence, the strength of character she exhibited throughout her life, as well as the tenderness and compassion she showed to not only her children and grandchildren, but others as well. She knew many people, and her life was one of giving to friends and family as well as caring for those less fortunate than her. She had remarried five years after their father had gone missing, out lived her second husband, and died in her sleep in her apartment at the age of eighty-seven. That was five years ago. He thought of her with fondness every day.

When Fred's lawyer called telling him about his father, that he was alive but dying and wanted to see his kids again, Tim was flabbergasted to say the least. He had gotten a hold of Steve and

Larry, and then called Kathy and Susan. All his siblings still lived within the seven-county metropolitan area and they decided to meet and talk about the news at Tim's house in Orchard Lake, a small town twenty miles west of downtown Minneapolis. The meeting took place five days after the lawyer had contacted him so they'd all had time to think about the request. They all had opinions on the matter, and they talked for an entire afternoon. The upshot was that no one wanted to see Fred.

"I've completely moved on," was how Kathy, the oldest daughter and now nearly sixty-five, had put it. "I can't tell you how little I think about him and how little he means to me."

All the others pretty much had the same opinion except for Larry, the youngest brother, who offered that he'd just as soon put a pillow over the old man's face rather than talk to him. So there was still some hurt and anger after all those years, even though, for the most part, everyone had gone on with their lives and learned to live without their father, or "Biological Father" as Susan put it, clearly distancing herself from the possibility of seeing the man.

In fact, that's how Tim's siblings talked about their father: referring to him in their discussions as Fred, not Dad or father or any other term of endearment common in families with a close relationship to their parents. Nope, Fred it was. A faded, distant memory of someone who left his family behind, eventually severing all contact with them. All contact that was until now, all these years later, when for some unknown and completely unfathomable reason, long lost Fred decided to try to come back and become part of their lives again.

A vote was taken whether to see him or not: Steven, no. Larry, a resounding no. Kathy, no. Susan, no. The verdict was unanimous. Everyone looked at Tim who hesitated. The years and their family's circumstance had drawn Tim and his younger brothers and sisters close together. Naturally, they didn't always agree, and big topic s like politics or religion were discussed more for fun than with the hope of changing anyone's views, but there was a closeness between them and a mutual respect for each other that included their differences. As Kathy put it once during a family get together, "We may disagree, but at least we know we have each other and can count on each other. We'll always have each other's back." Which was true. Tim couldn't count the number of times he'd helped with moving or baby sitting or what have you. And the help had be reciprocated. It was just something you did. Because they were family. Their mother had taught them that.

So why it was that Tim said what he said, he wasn't really sure. But Steve and Larry and Kathy and Susan all looked at him at first like he was nuts. But then, after thinking about it for a few moments, like maybe they understood, when he said, "Well, I think I'm going out there to see him. I can't tell you why, or what I hope to get out of it, but I just feel like it's something I have to do. Or should do. I don't know, maybe finally close a chapter or get some sort resolution or something like that."

He stopped and looked around at the table where they were all sitting. They were in the dining room, drinking coffee and munching on cookies Susan had made. Tim and his wife Emma had a calico cat named Frito who took this moment to jump up on his lap, and when he stroked its fur Frito started purring ecstatically.

Tim smiled and looked around the table. "I guess it's not really closure I want," he spoke thoughtfully, amending part of what he'd just said. "I did that long ago. I guess I just want to see why the guy left and what he's been doing with his life."

They talked about it for over an hour. No one tried to dissuade Tim from his decision, but they were curious as to why he wanted to do it, to go and make the journey. Kathy was afraid he might open up old wounds. Steve offered that he didn't realize his older brother had such a masochistic side. Of course, no one knew what would happen but the general consensus was that whatever happened, it couldn't be good. Tim, for his part, had no real strong answer to their concerns. Like he told Emma later that night as they got ready for bed. "It's just something I feel I have to do."

"Then do it," Emma said, kissing him and rubbing him on the back. "Just don't stay gone too long, though. I'll miss you."

Tim called Fred's lawyer the next day, the man who had contacted him in the first place, and arrangements were made. Fred was being cared for at Aurora Woods, an elderly care facility in Bellingham, Washington, roughly an hour and a half drive north of Seattle's SeaTac airport. Prior to leaving Minneapolis, and with the lawyer's help, Tim found a place to stay at a small but clean budget motel across the highway from Puget Sound and about five miles from Aurora Woods. He booked himself in for a week, not having any idea how long he was going to be staying. The visit could be short and he could be gone in a day, who knew? A week seemed reasonable. The thought of seeing Fred made him extremely nervous at first, especially in the initial planning stages, but after a while he started looking forward to it, once he got used to the fact that it was really going to happen.

Tim was a former school teacher. He had taught high school English at Southwest High School in Minneapolis for forty years. He was now retired. In the summertime he loved to garden, but August was a relatively slow period with all of the plants firmly established, so it was easy for him to free up the time to make the trip west.

Just a few days after he had made his decision at the family meeting, Tim stood on the front steps and hugged Emma good bye. Then he got in the cab to the airport where he boarded his plane to Seattle. Once seated, the thought of seeing Fred caused his nerves to kick in every now and then, causing perspiration to break out on his forehead. Other than that, the flight was uneventful.

Once in Seattle he picked up his rental car and drove up interstate 5 trying to adjust to his new surroundings. The day was sunny and mild. The air felt fresh and dry, not muggy like summers in Minnesota sometimes were. He'd never been to the west coast let alone the Pacific Northwest and was unprepared for the congestion and traffic. Interstate 5 was a crowded, five lane super highway and he forced himself to focus on his driving, only slightly aware of the scenery passing outside his window and the Cascade Mountains off in the distance on the horizon to his right. It had been two weeks since the lawyer had contacted him, and one week since he and his siblings had talked and Tim had made his decision to visit Fred. He took a deep breath and let it out slowly, surprised that he hands were shaking slightly. His motel on Puget Sound was called *By-The-Bay*. His map showed it coming up on the right in a few miles. He checked it watch. It was nearly dinner time. He'd see Fred tomorrow. He wasn't hungry at all.

What do you say to the guy who walked out on you and your mom and brothers and sisters over fifty years ago? Tim had no idea. Fred's lawyer, Vincent ("Call me Vinnie") actually helped. The next day he met Tim in the lobby of Aurora Woods. All in all the care facility was quite pleasant. It was relatively new, having been built five years earlier. To Tim's mind, it had a nice aroma inside, not institutional at all, more like a faint herbal scent. It wasn't bad.

Vinnie was about sixty years old, ten younger than Tim, and fit-looking. His head was shaved and he was very tan. He wore beige slacks with a sharp crease, a white short-sleeve button-up shirt, no tie, and sandals with no socks. He was definitely sporting a casual look. He took his hat off as he shook Tim's hand. It was a straw fedora and had a madras hat band. He smiled easily and his teeth were straight and white. He had the lean look of a long distance runner.

Tim was prepared to dislike the guy on sight but couldn't help being charmed when Vinnie said, "I've never in my life done anything like this before. I can only imagine how you feel." He was both honest and gracious and Tim found himself not minding him at all, maybe even starting to like him a little. "Let me show you to your dad's room." He pointed forward and started walking toward the elevator.

"I'd prefer to call him Fred if you don't mind," Tim said, feeling like he was coming across a little formal and stiff, but wanting to establish some sort of guidelines or boundaries nevertheless.

Next to him, Vinnie nodded quickly, not missing a beat. "Yeah, I get that. You're the boss. Fred it is."

The hospice unit of Aurora Woods was on the second floor of the two floor facility. They took the elevator up, got off, and turned left, Vinnie leading the way. The doors were sealed to the entrance to the hall that housed the hospice wing. "You need a pass code to get in." He punched in four numbers, the latch clicked, and he pushed through, holding the door open for Tim. They took an immediate left and when through another door. "This is the hospice wing," Vinnie said, lowering his voice to a whisper and looking around. "Mary is supposed to meet us. She's in charge here and wanted to meet you. Ah, there she is."

A trim woman in her fifties approached. Her dark hair was cut short and streaked with gray. She wore a green tweed skirt and jacket over a cream colored blouse. She carried a clipboard and smiled as she approached, putting out her hand when she got to the two men, acknowledging Vinnie with a faint nod. They'd obviously met before. "I'm Mary," she said, looking Tim square in the eyes. "You must be Tim."

"I am," he said, shaking her hand. She was confident but friendly. All of a sudden he became flustered. He realized the meeting with Fred was really going to take place and suddenly the whole thing seemed to be happening way too fast. Right up until now he thought he was ready for it. Maybe he wasn't.

"Would you like to have a little talk before you see your father?" she asked. Whether she was aware of his discomfort or this was protocol, he didn't know, but Tim gratefully accepted.

"I prefer to call him Fred if you don't mind," he said, as Mary moved a few steps down the hall.

She looked over her shoulder at him, her eyes probing. Finally she spoke with a slight smile. "I understand."

They moved to small conference room to the left of the entryway. Mary and Vinnie sat down at a round table leaving two chairs empty. Mary opened a small refrigerator and took out three bottles of water which she placed in front of them. Then she sat down next to Tim, looking at her clip board.

"Your father, er, Fred, has been at Aurora woods for just over five years," she said, turning to make eye contact with Tim. She had a firm, no-nonsense voice that also happened to be soft and pleasant. Tim appreciated her direct manner.

"I know some of his history," Tim said. "Vinnie filled me in."

Mary glanced at Vinnie and gave him a slight smile. *Was there something going on between the two*? Tim wondered to himself. His eyes moved to the ring hand of each of them, bare on both accounts.

She settled back. "Do you have any questions for me, then?"

Tim blurted out what was foremost in his mind. "How long's he got to live?" Then he caught himself. "Sorry. I didn't mean it to come out like that." He felt his ears reddening.

If Mary was shocked, she hid it well. "Of course," she said, shifting slightly in her chair, "Let me fill you in on what the situation is with, er, Fred."

"Vinnie said he has congestive heart failure."

"That's correct. His heart is functioning at about thirty percent capacity and it's very weak. He had a heart attack eight years ago which has contributed to its weakness."

"Fluid builds up, right?" Tim had done some reading on the internet.

"That's correct. Among other things it makes it difficult for his heart to pump the way it should." She stopped and waited. When she saw Tim had no questions she went on. "He also has had a series of what we call mini-strokes. They have affected his thinking capacity. Some days are better than others. He can't walk and has limited use of his limbs. He can still feed himself. He can still speak clearly. It's just that sometimes his mind is there and sometimes it's not." She paused and looked at Tim. Most of this Vinnie had told him. It was good to hear it from Mary, though, the person who now understood the most about Fred's condition.

"How's he doing today?" Tim asked, just to say something. He was starting to get a mental picture of Fred. He was also preparing to see him. After all, he'd come all this way. He might as well get on with it.

"He's good." She glanced at her wristwatch, which caused Tim to look at his. 9:30 in the morning. "He's just finished breakfast and the aid worker has helped him use the bathroom. He's doing pretty good today." She stopped. "He knows you are going to be here." She looked at Vinnie, who nodded.

"We've talked to him a lot about you coming to visit," Vinnie said, nervously twirling his hat. "He really wants to see you."

Tim sat for a few moments. He noticed a framed painting of a seascape on the wall. A wild ocean was crashing against a barren cliff wall. In the background, a tiny boat with two fishermen was being tossed on the crest of a huge wave. Would they capsize or not? Who knew, but Tim could sort of relate to their predicament. He took a deep breath and let it out slowly. "Okay," he said. "Let's go do it."

They stood up, the bottles of water all untouched. By force of habit, Tim pushed his chair in. Suddenly he realized he had to use the bathroom. "Is there a restroom around here?" he asked.

Mary pointed to a door Tim hadn't noticed. "Right through there. We'll meet you out in the hall."

Tim thanked her and went in. When he finished he washed his hands and splashed water on his face. As he dried off he studied his reflection in the mirror. He looked tired and haggard. His eyes were sunk from not having slept well the night before. Normally clean shaven, there was stubble on his chin from where he'd missed some spots that morning. He rubbed his hand over his bald head. He looked and felt old. Back home his brothers and sisters would be waiting to hear how his meeting with Fred had gone. Emma would be looking forward to his call tonight as well as him returning home. But before any of that could happen he had something to do. He had to go talk to Fred, his father (long lost?), and try to find out why, after all those years with no word, no nothing, the man suddenly wanted to contact the family he'd left behind over fifty years ago.

Tim took a breath and let it out. Time to face the guy. As he pushed out into the hallway and walked toward Mary and Vinnie he realized he'd not received an answer to the question he'd asked when he first sat down with her. The question that had been on his mind from the very beginning. He still didn't know how long Fred had to live.

"He's down this way," Mary said, walking next to him. Vinnie had elected to stay back, preferring, he said, to give Tim time alone with 'his father' as he put it. Due to his nervousness, Tim barely heard him and didn't bother correcting him this time.

The hallway was dimly lit. Classical music was playing, the volume turned so low Tim could barely make out the song. But then it came to him. Something by Vivaldi, he thought. There appeared to be five rooms on each side. "He's in the last room," Mary said, as was they walked slowly down the thickly carpeted hallway. "On, the right. All the rooms are private, of course," she added, whispering.

Tim noticed only a few rooms were occupied. As they approached the end of the hall, Mary indicated the room on the right. A placard on the wall indicated the name, Fred Beverly. The door was ajar. Tim peered in and could just make out the foot of a bed. He paused, knowing he had to go through with this but suddenly was unsure of what, if anything, he wanted to accomplish.

Next to him, Mary placed her hand on his shoulder. "It won't be so bad," she said. "He's pretty weak and doesn't have much time. A few days, maybe a week at the most." Well, that answered that Tim thought to himself. "He's very comfortable here. His body has just worn out. We are watching over him and treating him for pain as necessary." She stopped, letting the information sink in. "He's been asking for you. He's having a pretty good day. His mind is still as sharp as can be expected."

"I won't give him a heart attack or anything," Tim said, trying for a little joke to break the seriousness of the mood. He was immediately sorry for what he'd said.

Mary didn't seem to mind. She probably had seen her fair share of uncomfortable people in her time. People visiting a loved one at the end of their life and not knowing what to do. The *loved one* part of it wasn't necessarily the case with Tim, but still, the fact remained that Fred was dying. She squeezed his arm and pushed the door open. It was really going to happen. "Fred," she spoke quietly as she stepped into the room. "You have a visitor." She motioned for Tim to follow. He did. "Fred, this is your son, Tim," she said. "He's here to see you."

As Tim walked into the room the old man in the bed turned his head toward him. There was a momentary glimmer of awareness before it appeared the light went out of his eyes. At that moment Tim realized that this guy, this long-lost father, this man who had left his family behind without a word for over fifty years, had no idea who he was. Tim could have been anyone dragged off the street. He felt like an idiot to think something good could come from this meeting. He almost turned around and walked out of the room, but then the old guy blinked once and said,

"Hey there, Tim. How about a game of cribbage?"

And Tim knew right then that the guy did recognize him. After all, he'd taught Tim the game when he was ten years old, five years before he'd left home. It was the last thing Tim expected to hear from the old guy.

"Well, I'll leave you both to it," Mary said and glanced at Tim as she left, raising her eyebrows like, 'Are you Ok with this?'

Tim just nodded in response. "How long can I stay?" he asked her.

"As long as you want," she said, before quietly backing out the door, and giving Tim an encouraging smile before leaving him and Fred all alone.

Fred's bed was against the wall on the right-hand side of the room. Tim pulled up a chair and sat next to him. Outside the window opposite where he sat was a view of the Cascade Mountains. They were in the far distance, covered with green trees, probably some kind of evergreens. Their presence calmed him.

Tim turned to Fred who seemed to be waiting for him to say something. His face was what Tim would call grizzled. Worry lines were etched into his skin causing the sides of his mouth to droop down. A short, scraggly looking gray bead covered his face. Tufts of long white hair covered the few portions of his head that weren't bald. His eyes had a bluish-green tint to the iris and Tim was surprised to find that, after all these years, he remembered their color. Once over six tall and robust, Fred now was shrunken and withered. A sheet and blanket were pulled up to just below his chin, leaving a wrinkled scrawny neck exposed.

Tim had never met a ninety-two year old person before and had no idea what to expect. But now here he was. He his heart was beginning to beat rapidly and he felt the slightest bit of perspiration forming on his forehead. He took a deep breath to try to calm down. He had spent hours thinking about this first meeting. He'd talked to his siblings about it and talked to Emma about it too. He'd even stood in front of his bathroom mirror and practiced things to say. It all went out the window now that he was actually here with Fred. He said the first thing that came into his mind.

"How are they treating you here?"

"Fine, if you don't mind the fact that you're dying."

Geez, Tim thought to himself, *what a thing to say*. He forged ahead. "Are you comfortable?"

"I am," Fred said, and then just stared straight at him.

Tim had so many things he wanted to ask the guy, like what have you been doing all these years for starters, but suddenly it occurred to him, sitting right here in this quiet hospice room with the peaceful view of the mountains out the window and soft classic music playing in the background, that this guy didn't have much time to live. He could be gone from this earth at any moment. Tim shuffled in the chair and scooted a little closer to the bed. The movement caused Fred to look more closely at him. The guy was so old, so frail, so on the brink of death that Tim felt an unexpected wave of compassion roll over him. These were the last moments of the guy's life. Tim's being here counted for something. Plus, to be honest, he wasn't sure he wanted to get into anything heavy with the guy right off the bat. He decided to take an easier path. "So you want to play cribbage?" he asked. "Tell me where the cards are."

Fred pointed to a drawer on desk on the wall across from the bed. "Look in there," Fred said. His voice was rough and dry sounding. Tim stood up and offered him some water through a straw from a cup, which he gratefully accepted. When he was done drinking, Tim put the water off to the side on an end table next to the bed. Then he went to the desk and pulled out a worn deck of cards (red, Bicycle brand) and an old, two person cribbage board. Inside the drawer also noticed a small open box with some memorabilia in it which he figured would be interesting to look through. Maybe sometime he'd have a chance.

He pulled a rolling meal table on a metal stand that could be swung over the bed into position. He noticed how clean it was and wondered if Fred was eating. He sat down, shuffled the cards, set them on the bed, and then set up the cribbage board on the meal table. No one said a word while this was happening. Tim felt both nervous and relaxed at the same time. It was a weird feeling. Finally, he said to himself, *well I'm here. I might as well make the best of it.*

"Okay," he said, setting the deck of cards on the table. It was only a slightly awkward position. "Lt's cut to see who deals first."

***

Later that night when he talked to Emma, Tim was as frank as he could be with her.

"I was so nervous when I first met him, I almost turned around and left."

"But it went okay?"

"Yeah, it did. Once we started playing cards and had something to focus on other than each other we both relaxed. I have to say, though, it was one weird day."

"How long did you stay?"

"I got there around ten in the morning and stayed through lunch, which is at noon sharp." He chuckled. "Everything there is very organized," he added, with the emphasis on *very*.

"Well, I can imagine," Emma said. She had told Tim when he called that she was out working in the garden. "I'm going to sit down in the backyard and have some ice tea while we talk." He could picture her settling into a comfortable wooden rocking chair in the shade on their back patio. He was a little envious. "Went did you leave?" she asked.

"Later in the afternoon. I sat with him during his lunch. He had a cup of chicken soup, a few bites of a sandwich, and a little scoop of ice cream." He chuckled some more. "He really likes ice cream, I guess."

"Runs in the family."

"Really," Tim said, picturing Fred slowly eating his meal. Tim ended up helping him with the ice cream, spooning it for the old guy so it wouldn't drip on him. Plus, the guy's hand was shaking. Mary said it was all part of the body shutting down. "After lunch, he fell asleep. I was going to leave but decided to stay. Mary, the nurse came in to check on him and we talked out in the hall. She told me that in the five years he's been there he's never been a problem. He's very friendly. He had a few friends who used to visit him when he first arrived, but over the years they must have all passed away. The last year or so the only visitor had been Vinnie. So..." Tim said, summing up, "He's been by himself a lot."

"Sounds incredibly sad," Emma said. Tim could tell she had taken a sip of her tea. "What's his life been like? You know, after he left you and after he dropped out so to speak."

"Well, he rambles a lot when we talk. Vinnie's given me the best information. He told me that after Fred left the advertising agency he essentially went underground."

"Why?" Emma asked, noting that her husband still used Fred to refer to his biological father.

"Vinnie said that Fred started drinking heavily while he was in San Francisco working for the Ad agency. He wasn't happy at work and with life in general. He left us kids and mom for another woman, you know."

"I remember. You told me."

"I guess after a while she dumped him because of his drinking. Plus, she wanted kids and he didn't. This is all coming from Vinnie. He's been Fred's lawyer for over thirty years. I guess his best friend, the guy I've told you about, Irv, died of a heart attack a long time ago. Vinnie's been his closest friend since then."

"Knows a lot, I bet."

"He knows that Fred just up and quit work. That was in San Francisco in 1969. He left his car in the parking lot of his apartment off of Fulton Street in downtown and just essentially took off. Vinnie thinks he may have hooked up with a commune in northern California if you can believe that."

"Like he became a hippie?" Emma laughed. "Wasn't he a little old for that?"

"He was younger than Timothy Leary," Tim said, laughing with his wife. It felt good to talk to her. "No one really knows and Vinnie could never get it out of him."

"Sound crazy," Emma said, sipping some more tea. Tim could picture the whole scene back home. The peaceful backyard. Robins singing in the early evening. The aroma of freshly turned soil, the scent of flowers in bloom, and tomatoes ripening on the vine. The vision helped him relax.

"Really crazy," Tim agreed before continuing. "I guess he eventually ended up in Seattle working for a picture framing shop. He started doing drawings and art work of his own, if you can believe it. He lived in downtown Seattle for the rest of his life, working in the framing shop and doing his art work on the side. One of his paintings is even hanging in a conference room in the hospice wing. It's pretty good. A seascape. Reminds me of something Winslow Homer would have done if he lived on the west coast."

"I can't believe it."

"Me neither, but it's true. The guy's had a pretty interesting life."

They were both quiet for a minute, each of them thinking. Tim looked out the window of his motel room. Across the busy road was Puget Sound. There was a big barge on the water moving left to right. He watched it making it's slow progress wondering where it was headed. Emma's voice interrupted his thoughts. "How'd you two get along?"

"Not bad," Tim said. "He's pretty harmless. He even apologized."

"For what?"

"Everything, if you can believe it. He was pretty sincere."

"I can't believe it."

"Yeah, well," Tim said, pausing at least ten seconds before adding, "It's complicated, you know. I haven't seen him for over fifty years. I can't think of him as my father, since he hasn't really been in my life. But I sort of have feelings for him, probably because I'm related to him. Plus, we did have a history together. He was there for the first fifteen years of my life. I started remembering times with him like going hiking together, him teaching me how to fish, stuff like that. I'm still trying to work it out, but I can tell you this, I actually kind of feel for him. After all, he's dying. Mary said he has less than a weak to live. Being with someone at the end of their life is a strange experience. With Mom, it was what I wanted to do because of how much I loved her and what she meant to me and my life. With him, it's not like that at all. I don't even know him, yet I'm here." Tim paused and took a deep breath, letting it out slowly. "Like I said, it's complicated."

"I can certainly imagine," Emma said. She and Tim had been married forty-five years and they were very close. They talked about things and were open with each other. She knew exactly what her husband was getting at. She had known Tim's mom and had cared about her. She had never met the man who was Tim's father. She could only imagine what her husband was going through. Then she posed the question she most wanted to know the answer to. "Do you like him?" she asked.

Tim was quiet. She could picture him looking out the window at whatever was outside of his motel room. She felt for him. This couldn't be easy by any stretch of the imagination. Finally, he answered her. "The jury's still out on that," he said. And suddenly a wave of fatigue swept over him. He realized how tired and exhausted he was. He still had to call his sister, Kathy, who would relay the information to the rest of his siblings. "Look, it's been a long day. I should probably get going."

Emma told him she understood. They talked a little longer about what was going on around their home and yard before they rang off, agreeing that Tim would call the next day.

Emma sat in her chair looking over the beautiful backyard of their lovely home and wished with all of her heart she could be with her husband on this journey of his. A journey she knew he had to do on his own, but nevertheless, one she wished she could be with him for. *At least we can talk on the phone*, she thought to herself standing up and heading inside. The evening was beginning to cool and she had started to get a chill.

As she was washing out her glass she had a momentary thought about calling Tim back. But she didn't, knowing he needed time alone to get himself re-charged for tomorrow. Her husband was a kind man. She remembered the first time they ever had bluebirds nesting in their yard. Tim had insisted they turn a couple of chairs in their sunroom facing out into the yard. They spent every evening they could that summer, not watching television or reading, but watching the bluebirds as they first built a nest, then laid eggs and then hatched four new young fledglings. It had been a summer she'd never forget. That was the kind of person he was, gentle and loving.

But now this man had reappeared in his life. His father. Emma had no trouble calling him that, but if Tim wanted to call him Fred that was fine too. The guy was dying but to be perfectly honest, she couldn't have cared less. She had never met the guy and felt what he had done to Tim and his siblings was inexcusable. What she cared about was her husband and how he was coping with the situation. And then she realized she'd forgotten to ask him another question that had been plaguing her. She had forgotten to ask him if he was calling their long-lost father Dad yet.

Well, no, Tim wasn't calling the old guy dad or father or even Fred for that matter. It was amazing how much talking two people could do without calling each other by their names. That's what Tim had found out anyway. It was just one of the few things that were on his mind that night after he'd talked to Emma and gotten off the phone with his oldest sister, Kathy. It was after midnight when he'd finally gone to bed but sleep did not come easily. He'd lain awake most of the night, tossing and turning, listening to the whistles of the tugboats out on Puget and mulling over how the first day had gone talking to Fred.

He finally dozed off around five in the morning only to be awakened by the buzzing of his alarm clock at eight. He didn't know if he'd dreamt or not, but his mind seemed on fire when he woke up and it caused him to do something he'd never done before. He reached for his pillow, picked it up, and punched it. Punched it hard and watched it sail into the room. He was madder than he'd ever been before in his life.

He was mad at Fred for getting in touch with him. He was mad at himself for getting sucked into the old guy's drama. He was mad thinking about all the times his brothers and sisters had cried themselves to sleep because their father had left them. He was mad because his mom had been left alone through no fault of her own to raise of family of five kids by herself.

He was mad that for years and years he had worked to forget about the guy who had fallen off the face of the earth, and for all practical purposes was dead and gone, but he really wasn't. He'd just been living his life, not bothering to contact his sons and daughters, yet by some strange stretch of the imagination expected them all to fall back into his arms. Didn't he realize the effort it had taken each of his kids to, if not totally forget him, at least put him aside so they could go about living healthy and productive lives? Did Fred not understand the depth of the pain he caused- that it just didn't go away by wishing that it would? Was he that self-centered?

By the time Tim drove to the nursing home and ridden up to the second floor and let himself in to the hospice wing, he was fuming. He ran down the hall to Fred's room and pushed open the door with a fury he was unable to control. The old guy was asleep and awoke startled by Tim's sudden presence. He started to smile, like he was going to give out a pleasant greeting.

Tim cut him off.

"You wouldn't believe how pissed off I am at you," Tim yelled, leaning over the bed, his face only a foot from Fred's. "You ruined all of our lives. Me, Steven, Larry, Kathy, and Susan, and you don't even seem to care." He paused to catch his breath before continuing. "You're just a selfish, self-centered jerk." His heart was racing and his breath came in short spurts. He stared at Fred, daring him to say something. He didn't. He just looked at Tim, blinking. Tim was furious. "Say something you stupid old fool!" he yelled, not caring if anyone heard him. "Are you deaf or what?" He leaned closer, now only inches from Fred's face.

He felt a motion behind him. A nurse he hadn't met was pushing through the door. "Everything all right in here?" she asked, moving to Fred's bed as if to protect him. Tim stood up and backed away. She was heavy-set with her hair pulled back in a bun. Her dark skin shone. Her eyes were huge as she looked straight at Tim.

He stepped back from the bed and began pacing back and forth pounding a fist into an open palm. He was on the verge of losing control. He looked from the nurse to Fred, who now looked frightened. Then he looked out the windows to the mountains. The room was still and he felt the walls closing in on him. After a minute he became aware of the sound of classical music from out in the hall. The notes soothed him. He felt himself calming down.

He took a deep breath and let it out slowly. "No. Everything's okay," he finally said, feeling his heart returning to normal. He rubbed his hand over his head. "Sorry. I just lost my temper. That's all."

Though still looking concerned, she nodded. Her name tag said, *Annie*. "I know," she said symphatically. "It gets frustrating sometimes."

Tim looked at her, then at Fred. Then he looked out the window to the mountains again. The sky was clear and blue and it looked beautiful outside. He could feel the heat from the sun through the glass. A good day to be alive. "I'm really sorry," he said, to both Annie and Fred, raising both his hands in what he hoped was a peaceful gesture. "I had a rough night."

"I'm sure this can't be easy," Annie said. "But please believe me when I tell you that your father..." she smiled and motioned toward the bed, "truly wants you to be here."

Tim suddenly felt embarrassed. He reminded himself that Fred (not his father) had less than a week to live. "Yeah, I know," he said, wiping his hand over his forehead. "I'm okay now."

He looked past Annie to Fred. The old guy was watching him, but it was hard to tell what he was thinking. He didn't look scared anymore, only curious. Everyone said that Fred wanted him to be here and now he was. Yesterday had gone all right. He might as well make the most of today.

Tim moved carefully toward the bed so as to not startle the guy or frighten him, and asked, "Want to pick up where we left off on that cribbage game?"

Fred nodded and smiled. "Sure, just don't yell at me anymore." Was he making a joke? Tim couldn't tell.

He and Annie looked at each other. She seemed to be saying that it was Fred's way of forgetting that the outburst had happened. Time to move on. Tim felt like saying, *Yeah, easy for you to say*. He was still mad but had managed to get control of himself. Maybe he'd talk to Fred about it later. "Okay," he said, giving the old man the weakest of smiles. "Let's get that game going."

Tim took the cribbage board out of the top drawer of the small dresser where he'd left it the day before. Annie raised the back of the bed so Fred was better situated to play cards and then she left them alone, giving Tim an encouraging smile on her way out. Tim did his best to smile back but had the feeling he failed miserably. He turned his attention to the game.

Cribbage is scored by pegging points. The first one to get around the board and score 121 points is the winner. Usually, when a hand is played, seven or eight points are usually scored, meaning most games end after playing around fifteen hands. Yesterday Tim and Fred played three hands before Fred got tired and they quit for the day. They had agreed at the time, though, to continue the game, so they picked up today where they had left off. It was Tim's turn to deal, so he shuffled and dealt out six cards to each of them. Two were chosen to be put into the *crib* which was in Tim's possession this hand since he'd dealt. While they played Tim asked Fred a question.

"Do you remember teaching me how to play, back when I was about ten years old?" Fred studied his cards, apparently thinking. Tim watched him patiently. Through his mind raced all of the things he wished he'd asked yesterday. Reliving his history of playing cards with the guy who, back then, called himself his father, was low on that list. Finally he shook the old guys bony leg. "Hey, never mind. Why don't you tell me why you left us instead? And, while you're at it, tell me why you stayed out of our lives for all these years." He stopped talking and stared at the old man. Fred coughed a little, spit some phlegm into a Kleenex, and looked at Tim. Then his face reddened and he slammed his cards down.

"I left because I wasn't happy with your mom, okay? Marriage wasn't what I thought it was going to be, especially after you kids came."

"So you didn't have mom all to yourself, is that what you're saying?"

"Something like that," the old man stated simply. Then he lay back against his bed. His grizzled head looked small on the pillow. He closed his eyes.

Tim's anger reared up again and he wanted to smash the guy in the face. *What a self-centered creep!* He clenched his fists, fingernails digging into his hand. He took a deep breath and willed himself to calm down. "What do you mean, 'Something like that'?" he asked, trying to at least be civil. He set his cards down on the bed and looked out the window hoping the view of the mountains would help calm himself. It didn't.

"I just decided I didn't want to be married anymore," he finally said, his voice so low it was almost a whisper.

"And being a father..." Tim said, hoping Fred would finish the sentence. A minute went by, and when it became apparent he wasn't going to say anything, Tim added, "Being a father was something you didn't want to do anymore either. Was that part of it, too?"

Fred looked at Tim. His eyes were filled with more sadness than Tim had ever seen before in a human being. He looked genuinely contrite. But that wasn't good enough for Tim.

"In other words, you were just a selfish, self-centered, egotistical man, who had no place in his heart for anyone but himself. Is that it?"

"It's complicated, but, yeah, I guess that's about it."

Tim was sick of everything being 'complicated.' He pushed his chair back and stood up. "What a friggin' jerk you are!" he spat out. He turned, shoved the door open, and hurried out of the room, down the hall, and into the conference room. He needed to be alone. He'd often heard the term 'seeing red' and hadn't ever experienced the phenomenon until now. Yeah, he saw red, that was for sure, and if red signified out-of-control anger that's what he had. He had it in spades.

In the quiet security of the conference room he put his head against the wall, trying to calm down. He should never have come out here to try to reconnect with the guy who at one time was his father. The trip was more than a waste of time, it was deep down painful; like a knife cutting out his heart or needles jammed up under his fingernails kind of painful. It was so intense and overwhelming that he felt weak and nauseous like he was going to be sick. He should just leave, cut his losses, and chalk the whole thing up to a misguided idea.

Suddenly his mind went blank. He collapsed on a chair and stared into nothingness, numbness overwhelming him. When his senses returned, the first thing he noticed was the artwork on the wall. The painting Fred had done. He remembered it from yesterday. A seascape. Two guys were dressed in yellow foul weather gear, working the oars in a wooden row boat. It looked like they were fighting the elements and the stormy seas for their lives. Rain was pelting down and ominous cliffs were being battered by huge waves. The far horizon was dark and foreboding and the demise of the two men appeared to be imminent, but still, they hadn't given up. Fred had captured the mood perfectly.

Tim liked art. His brother, Larry, the one who was still angry enough to announce that he wanted to kill Fred, was a landscape painter of some renown in the upper Midwest. Tim liked his brother's work and the gentle, pastoral scenes he captured so well. Now he found himself strangely drawn to Fred's painting. He looked at the title, "Men Against the Sea." Not too original but it was certainly apropos.

Just looking at the painting allowed Tim some time to calm down. He suddenly felt emotionally exhausted. He leaned back in his chair. Should he stay or should he leave? He owed Fred nothing. Whatever he thought he'd get out of the trip, it wasn't going to happen. He honestly doubted Fred even knew who he was half the time. The guy was just an old, old man whose time on earth was coming to an end. Why did he even need to be around to watch him live out the last days of his life? Would Fred have done the same for Tim or any of his siblings given a similar situation? Not a chance. *The hell with it*, Tim thought to himself. He made his decision. He'd just leave, head home, and get back to Emma and all the good things that gave meaning to his life.

He was starting to get up when he glanced at the painting again. Without expecting it he felt himself starting to get drawn into the scene. There was life and energy painted on the canvas that was obviously done by a skilled artist. The more he looked, the more it seemed as if the scene was talking to him. Telling him something. Touching something deep in his soul.

Later, Tim realized he'd lost track of time. When he checked his watch he realized he'd sat in the chair looking at Fred's painting for over half an hour. Finally, he knew what he had to do. He stood up and left the conference room. Instead of turning right and leaving the wing and the hospice unit behind forever, he turned left and went back to Fred's room. He'd never get the answers to the questions he wanted to hear but at least he could try to understand the man whose genes he carried half of. He owned himself at least that much. Maybe he owed Fred that much too.

Mary met him as he walked toward Fred's room. "Everything okay, here?" she asked, looking at him carefully. Whether it was concern for Tim or concern for Fred, it was hard to tell. Maybe both of them. After all, she was a nurse and trained in being aware of things like this, people falling apart.

"No, I'm fine," Tim said, hoping he sounded confident. "I just needed to get myself together a little bit."

She nodded, like she understood, and patted his shoulder. "I understand. It's hard. Just let me know if I can help in any way."

"Thanks, I will," Tim told her, thinking that she didn't even know the half of it. He smiled at her goodbye and she gave him an encouraging look back. Then he went into Fred's room announcing, "Okay, I'm back. Let's get going with that cribbage game."

Fred had dozed off and awoke with a start. Tim gave him a minute to collect himself before asking, "Do you want to play some more?"

"Sure," he said. "Who's turn is it to deal?"

"Yours. Go ahead," Tim said, indicating the cards. He sat back while Fred shuffled and dealt the hand. They were halfway through the game and Tim was ahead by three points.

The decision Tim made to stay was not monumental at all. In a conversation with Emma a week later, after he'd come home, he tried to explain his reasoning. "I just felt I should stay," he told her. "To tell you the truth, I kind of felt sorry for the guy. That was my main reason."

At the time, they were sitting side by side in the backyard sipping iced tea. The sun was setting, the robins were singing and the flower gardens were blooming, just like the week before when Tim was at Aurora Woods with Fred, keeping the old man company and sharing the last moments at the end of his life.

"Even though he'd left you and your family and had no contact with you for over fifty years?" Emma asked. She reached over and caressed her husband's shoulder, happy beyond words that he was safely back home.

"You know, I resolved that issue years ago," he said, sighing. "Remember when my mom passed away and we were all there for her? She was loved and she felt everyone's love there for her at the end of her life."

Emma nodded. "I remember."

"Fred had no one. Just Vinnie, the staff at the facility, and no one else. It was sad. I just felt I should be there for the guy." He sighed a heavy sigh, blowing air out. "Just be with him. It was the end of his life. Someone should be there."

"You said he had Vinnie."

Tim was silent for almost a minute, framing his answer. "I was thinking more in terms of family," he finally said.

"Even though you didn't know him from Adam."

"Yeah, even with that. But I am, er, was you know. I was related."

"Well, that's a change, isn't it, you thinking of him like that."

"I know. I didn't expect it. It just happened. In fact, I almost left earlier that day."

"What happened?"

When Tim had gone back into the old guy's room, Fred seemed to have put the incident behind him. Or, more to the point, thought Tim, he'd just forgotten it'd ever happened. So they played cards, not saying much. Finally, Fred put his hand up. "Let's take a break. I'm pretty tired."

"Sure, that's fine," Tim said, setting the deck aside. The game was close, Fred up by two points. The old guy closed his eyes. He seemed to be breathing comfortably.

After a few minutes, he asked, "Are you married?"

Tim was taken aback. The old guy had never asked anything personal before. "I am," he said, recovering, thinking about his family. "My wife's name is Emma. I met her when I was in college at the University of Minnesota. We've been married for forty-five years." When the old guy just nodded, Tim went on and told him about the son and two daughters he and Emma had. Then he told him about their grandkids, eight in all. He deeply loved his family. Of course, they'd had their challenges like all family's but they'd worked through them. They were together and close and that was all that mattered.

But what really mattered was that, as he talked, Tim realized that Fred was a part of that family as well. Without Fred, there would have been no Tim. And without Tim, there would have been... well, nothing.

So he talked on and on, telling Fred stories about his wife and kids and grandkids and bringing the old guy some small understanding, he hoped, of the joy he had in his life and the joy his family brought him.

When he finished he told Fred, "The truth is, one of the reasons I wanted to see you was to tell you that by leaving us, you missed out on quite a bit, and that's putting it mildly."

"Life isn't always easy," Fred said. "At least after I left I had my freedom. I could do whatever I wanted to do, and I did. I had a pretty good life as it stands."

"You weren't ever lonely?"

Fred smiled. "No, I had friends, you know. I wasn't a hermit."

"Did you ever think about us?"

"A little. In the beginning. But honestly... after a while... not really... no. Especially as the years went by. I was happy with my job at the framing shop. With my painting."

"I saw the one in the conference room."

Fred smiled. "Two Men and The Sea."Not very original title was it?"

"I liked it. I should tell you that Larry's a painter. He does landscapes and he's pretty good. People buy his work."

Fred lay still. Tim wondered what could be going through the old guy's mind. He and his son had this huge thing in common, this shared ability to create artwork on canvas. Tim, for one, thought it was an exceptional gift they both shared. One that Fred may have passed on to his youngest son.

But did Fred acknowledge it at all? No. What he said was, "I think I'll take a little nap." He looked at Tim before adding, "Will you stay a while longer? I just need to rest."

Tim looked back at him. The old man's eyes were moist. Tears? He couldn't tell. The room was so quiet he could hear the classical music from out in the hall. Mozart? He looked at Fred who was waiting for an answer. "Sure," he said. "You rest all you want. I'm not going anywhere."

Fred closed his eyes. Tim stood up and quietly moved to the window. He pulled up a chair and sat down, looking out at the mountains, looking but not seeing, his mind turned inward thinking about the old man in the bed next to him. The old guy had lived so long but, to Tim's way of thinking, had missed so much. What is it that made him give up one life for another? Tim would never get an answer, he was sure of that now. He wasn't even sure Fred was able to tell him even if he wanted to. But what he did know was that he felt he should be her Why? Maybe it just came down to it being the right thing to do. To keep an old man company at the end of his life. He knew that's what his family would do for him when the time came. It was the least he could do for Fred.

Sitting by the window with his thoughts, Tim didn't notice Fred open his eyes and briefly look at him, trying to connect his mind with what he was seeing. Finally, he did. *That's the guy who's been playing cribbage with me,* he thought to himself. Then he smiled, remembering that he was winning. He looked around the room. The quiet sterile room where he'd spent the last few days. He liked how peaceful it was. He liked how he wasn't feeling pain anymore. He liked talking to the guy who was keeping him company. *Who did he say he was again?* He couldn't remember. Well, never mind. He seemed like a good guy. Maybe a little too emotional for him, but a good guy nevertheless.

Fred felt tired again and closed his eyes. His breathing slowed and he slipped into a deep sleep. A few minutes later his hand jerked one last time and then was still. His heart had stopped beating. Fred had passed away.

Tim and Vinnie made funeral arrangements. Fred had stipulated in his will that he was to be cremated. "There's a place he liked up on the Olympic Peninsula near the town of Moclips. That's where he wanted his ashes scattered," Vinnie told Tim.

Two days after Fred died they held a brief service in a small chapel in Aurora Woods attended by Tim, Vinnie, Mary, Annie, and a few other residents. Afterward, Vinnie and Tim each drove to SeaTac airport where Tim dropped off his rental. Then, together with Vinnie driving, they continued through Tacoma around the southern end of Puget Sound and over to the coast where they headed north up to the little town of Moclips.

Just north of town was a hiking trail that Vinnie knew about that would take them to an overlook on a cliff above the sea. They parked the car and got out to walk, Tim carrying Fred's ashes in a box in a brown paper shopping bag. The path led through a dense pine forest, needles on the ground softening their steps.

They walked the narrow trail in pleasant companionship, having become close, bonded by the events over the last few days. They didn't say much, but at one point Vinnie, who was leading, asked over his shoulder, "Hey, I never asked. You know that cribbage game you guys were playing?"

"Yeah?"

"Who won?"

"Fred did. He was up by two points at the end."

Vinnie grinned to himself before saying, "It was a good thing that you did, you know, being with your dad like that and keeping him company at the end. I'm sure it meant a lot to him."

Tim had nothing to say. Like so many things with Fred (he still didn't call him dad, but didn't mind Vinnie referring to him as that), whether or not his being with him was of any comfort was another thing he'd never know the answer to. Finally, he told Vinnie the only thing that made any sense to him. "I just did what I felt was the right thing to do. That's really all there was to it."

Vinnie stopped, turned around, and faced him. "You could have just left, you know, after that first day. You didn't even have to come out here."

"If I didn't come out, I would have always wondered about him and what he did with his life. Now I know."

"So you're glad you came?"

"Well, it was a long way to come to play a game of cards, I'll tell you that," Tim said, trying to lighten the mood. Vinnie just smiled and didn't say anything but turned and started walking. Tim followed along, talking. "But, honestly, when we were playing cards we were the most relaxed of all the time I was with him. We didn't even say much, just chatted a bit and were together. It seemed like that was enough. Maybe that's really all it needed to be. Just he and I playing cribbage, like in the olden days."

Tim walked along, enjoying the day, thinking about Fred. He'd walked this same trail who knew how many times. Now Tim was walking it, too, and seeing the Pacific Ocean for the first time. That counted for something.

The two men moved along the path toward the sound of distant waves crashing against rocks, carried to them on a fresh ocean breeze. "So, in the long run..." Tim said to Vinnie's back, "Yeah, I'm glad I came out here." Even though he couldn't see, he had the feeling Vinnie was smiling.

A few minutes later they came out through an opening in the forest where the trail passed right along the edge of a cliff, offering a panoramic view of the ocean. The day was bright and cloudless with sunlight glistening on the water. Gulls and terns soared above them calling back and forth, dipping and gliding on an off-shore breeze. Waves crashed on the rocks nearly one hundred feet below, kicking up a spray, rainbow patterns shimmering in the mist. There was a scent of salt and seaweed in the air. Tim was reminded of the scene Fred had painted. He had captured the essence of the ocean in a way that showed his understanding and awareness of the sea with all of its force and wonder. He was a talented artist.

Tim paused, looking out over the ocean. Fred had chosen to leave one life behind in Minnesota for a life out here on the West Coast. Vinnie told him that Fred would come up to the Olympic

Peninsula often to hike and paint. "He loved it up here," Vinnie told Tim more than once. "It was a special place for him."

Standing on the overlook, Tim could get it. He'd lived in the Midwest his entire life. The furthest west he'd ever been before was the Rocky Mountains in Montana. Seeing the ocean for the first time like he was now experiencing made him feel a little closer to Fred. The waves were so powerful and the sea so immense; he felt he could begin to get a sense of what Fred may have been all about. What may have driven him? He could have been trying to connect with nature to fulfill a desire to touch the beauty the world had to offer and to capture that beauty in his paintings.

Tim would never understand the man's need to separate himself from his family and turn his back on a wife who loved him and his children who needed him. But he could tell that within Fred there was a desire to live life in a way that was unique unto himself and to capture the essence of what life had to offer through his paintings. Yet, at the end of his life, Fred had reached out to try and reconnect with the family he'd left behind so long ago. Why had he done that? What had he hopped to accomplish? Did he not realize that some things once done could never be undone? Life went on.

Tim's brothers and sisters wanted nothing to do with the guy. Tim had chosen to come out to met him; taken a chance, really, just to see for himself what Fred was like and if he had any reservations about what he'd done. He hadn't. Fred had lived his life the way he wanted, yet, at the end, wanted something more. Maybe Tim had been wrong to journey to the coast to see him. Fred could have died all by himself with maybe Vinnie by his side. That's probably the way it should have been.

But Tim had been there. He and Fred had played cribbage and talked, and Tim found himself drawn into the last days of Fred's life, deciding to stay with him to the end. To keep him company. It seemed like the right thing to do. Did he do it because he suddenly had developed an affection for the old man? Not really. He didn't really know him well enough for that. But there was something there. A bond of some sort he felt toward the guy. It made more sense for him to stay with him to the end rather than leave him all alone. That much he knew for sure.

Vinnie tapped him on his shoulder interrupting his thoughts and pointed. "Look out there." Tim looked. Way out on the water, ridding the waves was a wooden boat with two people in it. They may have been fishing, but they certainly reminded Tim of Fred's painting, "Two Men and The Sea." He smiled at Vinnie. He had come to like the guy who had been such a good friend to Fred for all those years.

"You doing OK?" Vinnie asked.

Tim didn't have to think too hard. "Yeah. I'm doing fine." Then he asked. "How about you?"

Vinnie nodded and smiled. "I'm good. I like it here."

"Me too," Tim said.

The gulls were calling and the waves were crashing. It was a day he felt certain Fred would have enjoyed. Then he took the lid off the box, tipped it, and let the wind blow the ashes off the edge of the cliff out over the water and the rocks below, spiraling out to sea and forever becoming part of the ocean Fred loved.

After a moment's silent contemplation, the two men turned and headed down the trail away from the ocean and into the pine forest. Vinnie would be dropping Tim off at the airport and they had a three-hour drive ahead of them. Tim was heading home on the evening flight and he was ready to leave. He had done all he needed to do on his trip. Fred had his paintings. Tim had his family. Now all he wanted to do was to go home and see them and be with them. He'd been gone long enough.

Arnold and Tillie

I didn't mean to lose the Levendosky's dog, a cute little toy poodle named Tillie, but I did. I suppose I could claim as a reason my little problem with memory loss but I'm not going to because the fact of the matter is that the event had nothing to do with memory at all, but more to do with my general overall inattentiveness to detail. That, and the fact that I slowed to surreptitiously glance (well, gaze, actually) at Mrs. Jorgenson, the recently divorced fifty-something neighbor a few blocks down who was sunbathing along the south side of her house as Tillie and I walked by - that also might have had something to do with it.

The thing was, though, her lying there all oiled and supple in the summer sun had suddenly reminded me of when my wife Alice and I had taken our kids on a driving trip to the U.P. of Michigan one hot, humid July many, many years ago and we had stopped at an out-of-the-way beach called, I think, White Sand Cove. We were on the north shore of Lake Michigan on our way to Mackinac Island and had taken a much-needed break to let our young son and daughter wade in the water and cool off. Alice and I sat side by side in the sand watching the kids and holding hands, resting and talking quietly together. Oh my, she looked so young and fresh and happy sitting there in her blue shorts and white sleeveless blouse. After a while, she looked up at me with her bright amber eyes and smiled. She laid her head on my shoulder in a gesture of pure joy and happiness and...

Anyway, by the time I had dragged my mind away from Alice on the shore of Lake Michigan, Tillie had slipped her collar and bounded off, leaving me holding her leash along with a memory of my lovely wife from so many years ago. Apparently, my sun tanning neighbor had jumped started a journey into my past for longer than I thought.

Now please, I know what you're thinking: This guy is obviously an addled old coot who should have learned by now to keep his eyes to himself and I don't blame you. Hell, I'm seventy-eight and should have given up that ghost long ago and instead be preparing myself for a different journey - one to the great beyond, but there you have it. Sue me and take me to court if you want. The fact of the matter is that I'm still here, still alive and kicking, and there's not much I can do about it except make the best of things, which has less to do with taking an innocent, casual glance at my sun bathing neighbor and more to do with staying busy, which is what I was trying to do by volunteering to walk little Tillie.

"Arnie, do you mind terribly?" Janice Levendosky had asked a few weeks earlier, knocking on my door, interrupting my foray into the land of a thousand-piece Monet's water lilies jig-saw puzzle I was putting together on the card in my living room. "I don't want to be an inconvenience."

I am by far and away the oldest person in the neighborhood, as well as the person who has lived the longest in what they call the Lake Heights section of Orchard Lake, a little town in western Hennepin County, twenty miles from downtown Minneapolis. My name is Arnold but I go be Arnie. I've always been responsible and neighbors often call on me to help out whenever they are in need of assistance. The car won't start, the sink won't drain, the garage window was broken by little Johnny, you know, that kind of thing. Or did, anyway, until I seemed to have suddenly gotten too old for anything other than sitting around by myself working on jig-saw puzzles. Is it a coincidence that this less-than-neighborly attitude occurred shortly after my beloved Alice, my wife of over fifty years (fifty-three, to be exact), died three years ago last May or is it just me? I think not, but then who's around to argue the point?

Anyway, Janice and her husband and their three kids, all between the ages of nine and thirteen, were going on a driving vacation to the east coast and would be gone for two weeks and she was wondering if I could watch their dog, the aforementioned little Tillie.

Even though I'd always been a cat person myself, I jumped at the opportunity to shake up the routine and do something different. "Sure," I told her, trying not to sound as overly excited as I was. "Sure thing. Absolutely. No problem. You bet." I'm not sure how well I succeeded, but Mrs. Levendosky was happy with my effusive willingness to take care of the family's precious pet, so that was all that mattered.

We worked out that while they were gone I would stop at their house, one block over and one block down, twice a day to feed and water Tillie and take her outside to do her business. If I felt like taking her for a walk that would be fine.

"Just make sure you keep her on her leash," Janice told me a few days after our initial conversation when I'd gone over to meet Tillie in person and get the lay of the land. "She's a bit of a scamp, aren't you sweetheart?" She knelt down and made a kissy face at the little beast while I tried not to laugh. *Really*, I thought to myself, watching as Janice talked baby talk and made more kissy sounds. *Show a little dignity.*

All at once, the tiny animal turned away from her owner and looked at me with big blue eyes all innocent and sweet. Then she rolled over on her back with her feet up in the air and began kicking them languidly, yawning a gapping yawn and showing me more than I cared to see of the depths of her gullet, all the while looking at me, judging my interest, which was negligible at best.

Humph, I thought to myself. *This should be a piece of cake.*

"She looks like she'll be no trouble at all," I told Janice and reached down to scratch the white, curly-haired, little poodle behind her ears, something she seemed to like because her little tail started waging a mile a minute. Yep, no doubt in my mind. A piece of cake.

A week later the Levendosky clan left on their driving trip to discover the wonders of civil war battlefields and to garner a peak into America's past. Janice had told me before they left that they were, "Pretty excited." Me, I just pictured a drive like that with three kids at the ages of hers and I could only shudder at the thought, picturing boredom raising its ugly head by the time they hit the Wisconsin border, if not sooner.

But, then again, who was I to be such a grumpy old man? At least they were a family and were doing something family-orientated together. That was something, much more than I had going for myself. So I pleasantly wished them a bon voyage and for the next three days all was well between Tillie and me. It was the first week of August, the height of summer, and the days were warm and sunny and daylight seemed to last forever. The neighborhood was luxuriant with healthy green lawns, fragrant blooming flowers, and just enough mature shade trees to offer relief from the intense sun. In short, a great time of year for me to be out of the house and walking around with a little doggy who seemed as happy to be out and about and doing something different as I was.

I'm pretty sure Mrs. Levendosky would have been pleased with how well I was taking care of her precious pooch. I did as I was told, feeding and watering her two times a day and, after the first day, I even took the initiative of deciding that taking the little doggy for a walk was a good idea. And if I spent more time with her than Janice expected me to well, hey, I figured that I wasn't hurting anybody, Tillie included. Besides, I had a lot of free time on my hands so why not?

Now with her having run off there was a problem.

Before you think that this is a story about me wandering around the neighborhood, calling for a lost dog who's really not lost at all, only sitting calmly by the front door of her owner's home, patiently waiting for them to come back from their trip which wouldn't be happening for another ten days, but the person responsible for taking care of the little dog (me) is being corralled by the cops because some busy-body nosey neighbor called the local police concerned that the said person (me, again) was aimlessly roaming around the streets of Orchard Lake looking perplexed and confused...Well, it's not.

The fact of the matter is that I did think to go and check the Levendosky's house (I'm not that addled), and I did find little Tillie at the front door all safe and sound and happy to see me. So there, problem solved. End of story. Except that once I found Tillie I thought I'd take her back to my house for a little break in the routine, thinking maybe she'd like to sit out back and help me weed the hosta, and as I was on my way home I took a right on Grand Avenue when I should have taken a left on Lilac Way and ended up walking a little further than we intended, all the way down to the lake.

Our little town sits on the west shore of Orchard Lake, a relatively clean by today's standards body of water, a mile and a half long and a quarter mile wide. My neighborhood is about a ten minute walk from it. I've lived in the same small bungalow on Orchard View Avenue since 1964. Alice and I moved in a year after we'd married and shortly after we'd both graduated from the University of Minnesota, me in engineering and Alice in early childhood education. I had just begun working for the nationally known controls company, Heartland Incorporated, as a systems engineer and Alice had started her long career working in nearby Wayzata at Anderson Elementary teaching third grade. Within five years our son John and daughter Linda had been born and our lives were set.

Fast forward to now and you'll find me living by myself for the last three years, ever since Alice passed away after a heroic two-year battle with ovarian cancer. I've done my best to adjust. I see John and his wife and kids and Linda and her husband and kids every two weeks or so. I stay busy with my projects around the house and yard, keeping everything neat and clean and tidy both inside and out, just like Alice would have wanted. In my spare time, I do my jig-saw puzzles, and if I'm doing more and more of them as the months go by, well I can't help it if I'm becoming so efficient at doing my housework and yard work that I have a lot of free time on my hands.

I also try not to let my loneliness get me down. Maybe that's why I jumped at the chance to take care of Tillie, to give myself a chance to shake up my routine, even if it was with an energetic, seven-pound, four-legged ball of fur with a propensity to wander.

With the little Tillie safely back on her leash, the two of us walked down Grand to Brown Road where we took a right and continued on across the bridge over the Highway 12 by-pass and down the hill to the stoplight at County Road 112, the two-lane highway that runs through what is essentially the middle of downtown Orchard lake. We waited patiently to cross, watching the cars, trucks, and the occasional semi stream by heading east toward Minneapolis or west out to the country and points beyond.

I looked down at Tillie, sitting obediently beside me as she watched the traffic, her eyes missing nothing, and told her, "Good doggy." She cocked her head to one side and looked at me with her bright, intelligent eyes and I swear she was thinking...Well, I'm not sure what she was thinking, but I'll bet it was pretty interesting.

We crossed the street and walked past the liquor store on the left and the Quik-Mart on the right and continued a half a block down a slight decline to the west end of the lake where the public park is located. Now, believe me, the last thing I'd normally be doing on a sunny, warm, summer day would be what I did next, but what the heck. As long as I'd ended up at the lake, and as long as I had Tillie with me, and as long as she had been "Such a good little doggy," I said to her as I leaned over and scratched her ears for about the tenth time that day, I figured, why not?

The city has maintained the park and adjacent public dock since the 1930's. Earlier this summer they put up a chain-link fence in an area on the left side of the small parking lot as a place for people to exercise their dogs called, creatively enough, Lakeside Dog Park. Tillie and I walked up to the gate and let ourselves in. Other than Jerry Stevens who was strolling around on the far side with his mastiff Edgar (what a name for the poor dog!), we were the only people around.

"Hey there, Arnie," Jerry called out, waving. Edgar barked his own greeting.

Jerry was a stocky, forty-something man with a full, bushy beard who taught history and wrestling at the local high school. He was also a gregarious guy who liked to talk - to anyone about anything. He was off school for the summer and I'll bet had a good amount of free time on his hands because every single time I'd driven by the park I'd seen him chit-chatting with anyone who happened by to exercise the family canine. I think that taking care of Tillie the past few days had started something paternal going inside me. I was enjoying the responsibly of taking care of the little dog and, on top of that, it had definitely gotten me out of my head and away from my somewhat morose thoughts. Having lost Tillie earlier that morning had been slightly traumatic but at least I'd found her. I counted that as a win for the home team. It had also put me in a pretty good mood and I realized I was having a pretty decent day, way better than usual anyway. Why not be friendly with the bearded teacher?

I waved back at him. "What' up, Jer?" I figured I'd just open up the conversation and let him talk while I watched Tillie and Edgar play together, something they were already doing, running around with each other and hassling a beat-up, multi-colored beach ball someone had left behind.

Jerry gave me a big smile, walked over, and shook my hand. I tried not to grimace at his overly firm and enthusiastic grip.

"Not much," Jerry said in response to my question, smiling through his bead. He had on tan cargo shorts, red flip-flops, a purple Minnesota Vikings tank top, and a straw cowboy hat, a far cry from my clean-shaven face, faded khakis, faded blue work shirt, work boots, and old Twins cap covering my bald head. He was tan, brawny, and fit, while I was pale, tall, and skinny - not even remotely close to being athletic-looking. If I didn't already know he was a wrestling coach, Jerry's stout, muscular build would point me in that direction - it being one of my top three choices if I had to guess his occupation (along with steel worker and brick layer.)

He took a long moment and looked past me out to the east over the length of the lake. I turned and followed his gaze. There were a few boats slowly put-putting along, trolling for probably northerns way out in the middle, and a number of other boats were haphazardly scattered about at anchor, bobbing in a light breeze. There was a sailboat with an orange sail tacking back and forth, and two small kayaks, one red, one yellow, were being paddled along the far shore. It was quite a pretty scene, serene and bucolic, something an artist might paint if they wanted to represent an idealized summer day.

Most of the lake is surrounded by trees, with a few large homes and their subsequent green lawns cut into what was once forest land, but there are definitely more trees and forest than homes to look at. At the far end of the lake is a low swampy area where I sometimes see sandhill cranes nesting. People from the surrounding area enjoy coming to both the lake and our town because there's an old-time feel to be found despite us being only a twenty-minute drive from downtown Minneapolis. So we're a small town with a rural feel and a picturesque lake, a good enough reason that the people who move here tend to stay put, me and Jerry included.

"Nice looking day, isn't it Arnie?" he asked.

With the light breeze out of the south rippling the water and the blue sky overhead with a few big, white clouds drifting by and some seagulls squawking from somewhere behind me, I had to admit the scene was almost idyllic.

"Sure is," I agreed.

We nodded to each other knowingly and gazed some more over the water in companionable silence before Jerry broke the contemplative mood and asked, "What do you think about the new plan the city has to cut back the brush between the shore line and the highway over there?" He pointed off to the right where county road 112 ran close to the lake. It was a quarter of a mile away and easily seen from where we stood. "They're thinking of putting in a walking and biking path along the highway. I'm personally all for it. It'll bring more people into town and hopefully more business too."

I was pondering Jerry's question, wondering what I did, in fact, think about the city's plan to destroy (to my way of thinking) the natural shoreline, all in the name of progress, but I never had the time to formulate my answer. He hesitated only a moment before moving on to another topic. The term 'Put a quarter in the slot' came to my mind as Jerry jumped from the path project to the Corn Day Celebration coming up later that month and whether or not the city would have enough money for fireworks. When his opinions on that topic ran their course, he moved on to what might happen if the city council approved a proposal to put up an apartment building across from the Quik-Mart where the old gas station used to be, then on to whether or not the potholes along Brown Road were deep enough by now and shouldn't they be filled in before next winter, and on and on and on.

I just tuned him out, nodding occasionally and mumbling something unintelligible. I'm not kidding you, that man could talk. But I didn't mind - it was nice to be with someone other than myself for a change, so I stayed with him enjoying his company and watching the dogs play, all the while looking out over the lake and taking in the sun, which by now indicated it was early afternoon.

Eventually, Jerry moved away from the local happenings with our town and on to local sports and the ever-interesting but always frustrating topic of the Minnesota Twins and then on to national politics, a subject I tend to shy away from, especially in public. In the past, over at the local bar the Black Rooster, I'd been known to get into some rather heated conversations of a political nature, usually after a beer or two, but don't me started. Lesson learned. As an old song that my son used to listen to once stated, "The man hears what he wants to hear and disregards the rest." So instead of getting into anything political with Jerry and maybe ruining the pleasant mood set by the nice day and beautiful weather, I decided I'd better nip that little buzz kill (a phase my grandson taught me, which I rather like) right in the bud. Besides, by now I was feeling restless. It was time to move on.

"Ok, Jer...," I said, finally, putting my arms over my head and taking a big, long stretch before making a movement to signal my intention, "it was good to see you, but Tillie and I have to get going." I turned and called to my little charge. "Come on, girl." Tillie bounded over wagging her little tail and let me put her on her leash. What a good doggy!

I went out the gate and then turned and waved. Jerry waved back before making his way over to talk to Cindy Jackson who a few minutes earlier had entered the area with her little boy and their Irish Setter, Jax.

I have to say, it had been nice to have a long chat with Jerry, even though he did ninety-nine percent of the chatting. He wasn't a bad guy. Besides, I don't normally do much talking during my normal day except sometimes to myself (don't tell anyone), living alone the way I do, and I kind of enjoyed our conversation. But the novelty of so much verbal communication was tiring, that was for sure, and I felt in need of some sustenance. I figured Tillie might be too, what with all the running around and playing and chasing both the beach ball and their tails like she and Edgar had been doing. We made our way to the parking lot, took a right, and walked back up to County 112.

The Quik-Mart is the most thriving of the about ten businesses in town. When I'm out running errands I stop in if I need gas or milk, and sometimes, to be honest, I stop in for nothing other than the diversion, just to browse around and kill time. It has pretty much anything a person could need, even for an old guy walking around enjoying the sunshine on a bright, warm summer day with his dog. Tillie and I went inside and in a few minutes found just what I was looking for, a bottle of water for us to share. On a whim, I also picked up some slim-jims to munch on.

The kid behind the counter was a skinny, local high school guy with floppy hair and a lot of pimples that I'd seen before whose name tag said Lonny. I said, "Hi," to him as I paid, and he gave me a nod back along with my change and a non-committal, "Hey," and then went back to putting cigarettes in their slots above the counter. He seemed like an okay kid - especially, when, after he noticed Tillie, he stopped sorting the cigarettes and leaned over the counter and said, "Hey, there, little poochie," to her. She perked up her ears, stood up on her hind feet, and danced around in a circle, showing off her athletic abilities, while I held the lease out of her way. The kid smiled and coughed out a laugh. So did I.

Lonny lightened up then and asked me what it was like outside and I told him it was getting hot and he said, "Yeah, no doubt." We chatted a few minutes about the weather and the heat (like all good Minnesotans can do) before a young couple who Lonny knew came in and they all started talking and playing with brightly colored objects they held in their hands and spun around with their fingers they called spinners, so I figured it was time to go.

Tillie and I walked back to the lake and to the right side of the park, as far away from the dog playing area as we could get. We found some shade under a huge cottonwood tree and sat down at a picnic table to rest and enjoy the afternoon. The beach was about fifty feet in front of us and I was surprised that it was deserted. But not the dock, which was to the left of the beach and stuck out into the lake thirty feet. There were a couple of boys maybe ten years old on it casting lures out into the water and reeling them back in. I watched the two of them for a while, almost mesmerized by the repetitive motion of the casting and reeling, casting and reeling. I didn't see the kids catch anything but they didn't seem to mind. They were just fishing and talking, mostly fishing.

I opened up the water and cupped my palm to make a little bowl, poured some in, and offered it to Tillie who gratefully lapped it up. I poured out some more, which she drank, and then some more, and then some more. After a few minutes, her thirst finally seemed to be quenched. Then I had some (drank, not licked) and we shared the slim-jims. When we were finished, Tillie lay down in the grass at my feet in the cool of the shade and chewed on the pad of her paw. A few minutes later, she yawned and fell asleep.

Sitting in the shade was pleasant and I felt myself relaxing. It was getting to be enjoyable for me to be with the little poodle who had now been under my care for the past three days. I'd never had a dog before but being with Tillie felt like I imagined it would feel like if I had been young and was the proud owner of my own canine friend, like a German Sheppard or something, a companion to keep me company as a kid growing up like I did back in the forties and fifties in southwest Minneapolis. On such an idyllic summer day like we were having today, it was a nice image to be thinking about.

Well, who knows how things work, but one thought led to another and for some reason, my mind sent me back in time to when my grandparents had a rustic cabin they used as a summer getaway when I was young. It was on Big Sandy, a good-sized lake in Aitkin County, smack dab in the middle of the big woods of north central Minnesota, about a three-hour drive north of Minneapolis. I was the oldest of their daughter's two boys and two girls and they enjoyed taking us kids up to the cabin to, as my grandfather put it, "Learn about living in the Wild." I'm not sure how much of that we found out about or even did for that matter, but my younger brother and two younger sisters and I loved being up there.

Grandpa Quimby (we called him Grandpa Q) was an auditor and he and Grandma Helen lived in southern Minnesota in Fairmont, the farming-based town where my mom was from. Grandpa Q taught us all (even my sisters - no sexism in our family!) to hunt and fish along with lots of other handy skills like how to tie knots so the bows and arrows we made out of ash saplings would hold together and the fishing boat we tied up to the dock wouldn't float away. He bought me my first pocket knife when I was eight which I immediately used to start carving designs on the narrow willow tree I was making into a spear. It took me about two minutes to slice open my thumb prompting my Grandma to take the knife away from me for the rest of the summer, much to Grandpa Q's chagrin. Mine, too.

Anyway, Grandpa Q filled in for my father who was killed in the Battle of the Bulge when I was six and Grandma Helen picked up any slack not filled by Grandpa. She was a short, rotund, sweet-tempered lady who smoked Pall Mall red filter-less cigarettes and had the patience of Job to teach me how to play solitaire when I was only seven years old. They were good people. What my mom did with her time when my grandparents had me and my brother and sisters up at the cabin I have no idea, but I'm sure she enjoyed the peace and quiet while we were gone. She never did remarry.

One hot, windy, August afternoon when I was eleven Grandpa let my nine-year-old brother Eddie take the thirteen-foot aluminum fishing boat for a spin up and down the shoreline, about a hundred feet out from the front of the cabin. It had a five-horsepower Johnson motor on it and the rule was that he had to run it at half-throttle. However, my brother was a bit of a wild child and after only a few minutes of dutifully following instructions like he'd been told, Eddie cranked the throttle all the way up to full. I was playing with some water bugs along the shore next to the dock when I heard the whine of the engine as he jacked it. I casually looked up just in time to see him make a sharp turn into the huge wake coming up from behind. I remember the bow coming up high in the air, then smashing down hard on the water and seeing Eddie lose his balance just as another big wave hit, causing the boat to tilt dangerously to the side. It almost capsized but didn't. It did, however, toss the small-statured Eddie into the water. I stood up panicking, a sick feeling in my stomach, frightened for my brother, now struggling in the water. Of course, he wasn't wearing his life vest. My mind raced as I tried to figure out what I should do before failing me completely and going totally blank. I ended up standing stock still and paralyzed with my mouth hanging open, unable to do anything.

Grandpa must have been watching from the cabin because he ran out the front door and down to the dock, yelling to me, "Arnold, go to the shed and grab a rope. I'm going in for Eddie." He ran past me out to the end of the dock, jumped into the water, and started swimming.

Glad that someone was finally taking charge, I did as told and ran as fast as I could back behind the cabin to the old shed where I found a coil of heavy rope like we used on the anchor and then ran back onto the dock. By this time Grandpa had made it to Eddie and was struggling with my brother, trying to hold him up above the waves. The motor was still running and the runaway boat was circling around and around Grandpa, who was having trouble trying to both rescue Eddie and dodge the boat at the same time.

Grandpa Q must have seen me come back on the dock because he yelled, "Arnold, get me the rope. Quick." His call was weak. I could see he was losing his strength and becoming tired. Eddie was kicking feebly in his arms. I think Grandpa wanted me to swing the rope out to him, but it was way too short to reach. I quickly looked round, trying to figure out what I should do. Then I heard a scream and looked back to where they were floundering in the water. The boat had finally hit Grandpa Q a glancing blow. He stayed floating with my brother but I knew I had to act fast - they were starting to bob up and down, occasionally sinking under the water. I tried to figure out what to do. I had an idea that I might swim the rope out to where they were struggling and then throw it to Grandpa and...and then what?

I frantically looked back on shore. A better idea came to me. Next to the dock, floating in the water on the shoreline, was one of the inner tubes we kids played with. Maybe I could use it. I ran and grabbed the black rubber tube, ran back to the end of the, and jumped in. Still holding the rope, I began to work my way out to Grandpa and Eddie. By this time they were really struggling, sinking below the surface of the water more often than they were above it. I still have to this day a vivid recollection of Eddie coughing up lake water and looking pale green. It's not a pleasant picture.

I hurried through the water, stretched on the inner-tube, kicking as hard as I could, battling the waves, holding the rope in my right hand, and swimming with my left arm. I was slowly making progress, but it seemed to be taking forever to reach them. Then the boat hit Grandpa again. I watched in horror, expecting the two of them to sink beneath the surface and never come up again, but fortunately, they didn't. Grandpa gave me a feeble wave and yelled, "I'm all right, Arnie, just hurry." I thought I saw something red (blood it turned out) appear on his forehead.

He didn't have to say anything more. I began kicking harder than I thought possible, my adrenalin pumping, and my heart racing.

Finally, I got close enough to toss the rope. Grandpa Q reached and grabbed it after the second try and then pulled me to him. In a few moments we were all holding on to the inner-tube, gasping for breath. Grandpa and Eddie were exhausted and winded, nearly drowned and I was only marginally better off. As we trod water and rested I realized that, except for the cut on Grandpa's forehead, we weren't in too bad of shape. By now the boat had circled out further into the lake away from us and as it did, it dawned on me that we weren't going to drown after all. We were safe.

We hung onto the inner tube bouncing in the waves until we caught our breath. Nobody said much. Finally, after what seemed like forever but was really only a few minutes, Grandpa Q starting kicking and Eddie and I joined him. We began to slowly work our way back to shore. Close to the dock, we could touch the bottom so we stood and made our way through the weeds and muck the rest of the way in before collapsing on the beach.

Then Grandma was suddenly beside us, comforting Eddie and me, making sure we were all right, which we were. She gave

Grandpa a handkerchief for the wound on his forehead. I found out later she'd been on the shore and the dock the entire time, I just must have blocked her out in my haste to do something to save Grandpa and my brother. My sisters were there too, huddled behind Grandma and crying. They were terrified over what had happened and when they got a chance they ran and hugged Eddie as tightly as Grandma had done, maybe more. Then they hugged me and Grandpa. It was quite an emotional scene, I'll tell you.

"I'm taking Eddie up to the cabin," Grandma finally said, helping my brother to his feet. "Q, you bring Arnold. And keep that wound covered," she told Grandpa, giving him a look that at the time I didn't understand, but later realized it was one of both anger and relief, if not a little thankfulness mixed in for good measure. She could have easily lost her husband and two grandsons that day.

Grandpa and I watched Grandma, Eddie, and my sisters walk slowly away from us back to the cabin. Then we turned to look at the lake. The engine had run out of gas and the boat was floating about a hundred yards from shore, bobbing in the waves. Grandpa turned to me, put his arm around my shoulder, smiled, and said, "That was quick thinking, Arnie, bringing that inner tube like you did. I think you might even have saved our lives."

I'm not kidding when I say that coming from this man I admired so much...well, his words made me feel good, I can tell you that, really good, like I was finally starting to grow up and on my way to becoming an adult. We sat on that beach together for a long time after that, watching the lake together and quietly talking. It was like a bond had formed between us that day, one that became stronger over the years. Many years later, on the day he died, I wept, something I rarely did, and had to be consoled by both my wife and my son and daughter. I've never met a man I admired more than him, good old Grandpa Q.

I was enjoying reliving the memory of that long-ago summer day and all the other good times I'd had up at Big Sandy when suddenly Tillie let out a friendly little yip. I blinked myself back to the present and curiously glanced around. Off to the left, the sun was lower in the sky, more toward mid-afternoon. I must have been thinking and reminiscing for at least an hour.

Then I saw what Tillie was all excited about. She had recognized the Patel's, the Pakistani family who had moved into the apartments down the street three years ago, just after Alice had passed away. Suny, Mrs. Patel, was a friendly lady who kept containers of plants on her deck during the summer where she grew prolific bunches of tomatoes, beans, herbs, and all kinds of other produce. She was with her two kids and their little Chihuahua whose name I forgot, but who Tillie certainly recognized. Her husband Sam was a pharmacist who worked long hours at the Walgreens in Wayzata, the next town east of us, closer to Minneapolis. The couple were in their late thirties and were nice people, good neighbors. I waved and Suny waved back.

She turned to her children and said something I couldn't hear. Then she walked over to me and Tillie, leaving her kids, a boy and girl, Rashid and Neha, around ten and seven on the beach, playing in the shallow water with their dog.

She walked up to the picnic table and greeted me with a smile. "Mr. Gans, how are you today?" She had the whitest, brightest teeth I'd ever seen and her smile seemed to light up her face. "Out for a walk with little Tillie I see," she added, bending down and petting the dog's back, "How's my little girl doing?"

Tillie promptly flipped over, feet in the air and tongue lolling out the side of her mouth, imploring Suny to rub her tummy which the good-natured woman gladly did.

"Tillie and I go way back," she said, enthusiastically rubbing some more, while I swear Tillie groaned in pleasure.

My first rather selfish thought was that if they went back so far and were such good friends, then why wasn't Suny doing the dog-watching while the Levendoskys vacationed on the East Coast? My second thought, while watching Tillie roll back and forth in a fit of ecstasy on the shady grass, clawing at nothing but thin air and eyes closed in pure joy, was that the little white dog had no pride. My third thought? Quit being such a grumpy old fart and be happy that I had gotten the chance to take care of the cute little rascal.

I looked over at the nearby beach and watched Rashid and Neha playing with...Rex. The name of their dog suddenly came to me. That was it: Rex, a tiny, black and tan, long hair Chihuahua - a ball of fur and fire that was racing in and out of the water, running along the sandy shoreline and back to the kids, yipping and yapping like little dogs do. I watched for a while. All three of them were having a great time, playing made-up games and cooling off in the water, the kid's laughter carried to me on the warm breeze. Then I turned and watched as Suny fooled around in the shade next to me with Tillie, now making a spectacle of herself rolling around in pure delight, losing herself in the adulation of Suny's attention.

Taking it all in it suddenly dawned on me what a wonderful day I was having. I hadn't minded talking to Jerry. Our conversation had gotten me thinking about things I didn't ordinarily think about (like that bike path project up on the highway), and even if I couldn't get a word in edgewise, the companionship was actually kind of nice. I knew Suny well enough to be neighborly and say "Hi" in passing, so after a few minutes of me watching her kids and Rex and Suny fooling around on the ground with Tillie, I asked her if she wanted to sit and join me. She said she did and took a seat at the picnic table across from me.

We started talking and she told me that the plants in her containers were doing exceptionally well this year; the tomatoes and cucumbers were especially healthy and productive.

"But I don't have as much time for them as I'd like, working at the school now," she said with a hint of regret, looking longingly at her children, now making a huge sandcastle on the edge of the shore. She had her head wrapped in a bright yellow scarf and was wearing long, loose-fitting dark pants and a brightly colored tunic the color of beets when they are cut open, her apparel a compromise, she told me once, between the traditional Hindi sari and full-blown, one-hundred percent western wear. Like her kids wore. Today Rashid and Neha were dressed for the beach in American-style swimming trunks and tee shirts, and I'd often seen them wearing jeans and other clothes, the kind easily purchased at any big box store.

Suny was in early childhood education and worked as an aide at the learning center at the elementary school where, ironically, Alice had taught. A year or two ago, when I found out that particular coincidence it occurred to me what a small world it really could be. The fact that Suny enjoyed plants and gardening as I did only added to the small word theme in my head.

I liked her and her family so we had a lot to chat about as we took advantage of the welcome shade of the picnic table while listening to the joyful laughter of her kids who had given up on the sand castle and were now playing tag in the water. I even decided to let Tillie off her leash which she seemed to appreciate because she turned and gave me an expression like, 'What took you so long?' I guess I'm a bit of a slow learner when it comes to the wishes and desires of little puppy dogs, but at least I was learning. Once free, she happily ran to join the two kids and Rex on the beach.

With Alice having been gone these past three years, I will admit to you right now that I have become probably not the most sociable person in the neighborhood. Maybe 'withdrawn' would be the better word. In the time since my wife's passing my world has seemed to shrink in on itself, even though my kids have made it a point to stay in touch by phone and the occasional visit. But, you know, John and Linda have their own lives to lead and can't be held responsible for me. That's my responsibility, one I probably haven't performed at optimum potential, preferring to be by myself and stay out of the social spotlight and close to home with my housework, outdoor projects, and, of course, my ever-growing collection of one thousand-piece jig-saw puzzles.

But on this warm August day, sitting down by the lake, having had a long conversation with Jerry and then a short little chat with Lonny, and now talking with Suny, I have to say that I was feeling better than I had in a long time about being out in public and around people - not to mention enjoying the park and the laugher of the children playing in the water, the dogs running around and romping on the beach, the sun shining on my face; well, now the shade, but you get my meaning: The simple pleasures of life in general.

Rashid ran up to us, interrupting a lively conversation concerning the pros and cons of heirloom tomatoes.

"Mom, can we go up to the Quik-Mart and get something to drink? Me and Neha are thirsty." He was a tall, thin kid with bright green, baggy swim trunks and a soggy black tee-shirt that had the name of a band on the front that I'd never heard of. He was a trumpet player, his mom told me once, which she didn't need to since I could hear him practice perfectly well if the wind was right and I was outside puttering around in the front garden. (He was quite good, in my estimation, if not overly loud.)

"Neha and I, dear," Suny said as she reached into her shoulder bag, took out two bottles of water, and gave them to her son. "Here's some water for you, and one for your sister."

Grinning good-naturedly at his mother's admonishment (and then repeating his question using the correct grammar), Rashid took the water and ran back to the beach, tossing both bottles in the air as he ran, juggling them for about five seconds before he dropped them both in the sand.

I laughed, remembering years ago back in the early sixties when John and Linda were young and I'd come down to this same beach and taken them swimming. The lake had fewer houses around it in those days and the water quality was certainly better. Back then the city had roped off a swimming area to the right of the public dock where the beach still is. Beyond the roped-off area was a wooden raft on big fifty-gallon drums out about one hundred and fifty feet from shore that adventurous kids could swim out to. I taught my children to swim right here at this very beach and remember well the first time each of them had made the solo trek out to the raft and back; a rite of passage some might say. They were so proud of themselves, and I was, too. John was nine and Linda was eight, if I remember correctly, around the same age as Rashid and Neha.

Now the raft is long gone. So is the guard station and snack stand that used to be set up during the summer months when school was out. Parents these days are responsible for watching their kids because the city hasn't been able to afford a lifeguard in probably thirty years. Which, now that I think about it, maybe wasn't such a bad thing. With the hectic pace of the world nowadays, it's nice to see families making time to be together down at the lake on a sunny summer afternoon. And, no, I'm not waxing all nostalgic for the quote-un-quote good old days and living in my little dream world wishing time could magically go back to the fifties or the sixties again. It just seemed like what I was seeing today at the lake with Suny's kids playing in the water and the dogs running up and down the beach was a pretty good world to be living in, that's all I'm saying, and it occurred to me how glad I was to be out of the house and down at the lake on this warm summer day to be a part of it.

Boisterous activity drew me away from my thoughts. I glanced over to where some friends had joined Rashid and Neha. There were now maybe ten young people playing in the water and sitting on the shore. Some of the older kids had taken out their phones and were snapping pictures of themselves and their friends goofing off and messing around, no doubt with the idea of posting the pictures on their Facebook or Myspace pages or other social media accounts. I shook my head in (mock) disapproval and glanced at Suny who smiled and said only, "Kids, what can you do?"

I smiled back and said nothing, preferring my own little world where there were no Selfies, only fun-loving good times, simpler times, better times. Hell, maybe earlier I truly had been longing for the good old days. Then I had a more pressing thought; maybe the world was simply passing me by, which, I have to say, isn't the first time such an idea has surfaced, especially since Alice's passing. Then I shook myself, refusing to sink into a well of despair on this fine day. To hell with philosophic musings. Today was today and it was a good day to be alive and I was going to continue to make the most of it.

I turned to Suny and asked her which variety of pole beans she was using this year, always an interesting discussion for gardeners to engage in. She grinned and told me that this year she favored Kentucky Wonder which, along with Monte Gusto, was one of my favorites, and soon we were deep into a discussion concerning the benefits of each.

After we'd talked for awhile Suny stood up and said, "I think I'll go get Rex. I can tell he's getting worn out. He's not as young as he used to be, you know." She looked at me, and I wondered if she was silently implying that I was in the same boat as the dog, a comparison I found a bit presumptuous, I have to say, but I was wrong. My kind neighbor was just being helpful. "Should I bring Tillie, too?" she asked.

"No thanks, Suny," I said, standing to join her, feeling suddenly energetic after my little rest in the shade and chatting with my amiable neighbor. "I think I'll get her myself and then head up to the store for some more water and something to eat." Tillie and I had finished off our bottled water and slim-jims from earlier and I was thirsty and figured my little doggy friend was as well.

We strolled out of the shade, into the sun, and over to the beach, where by now more families and children had showed up and were playing in the sand and wading in the water. Suny and I put our dogs on their leashes and I said a final goodbye to her and her kids, both of whom were polite enough to wave to me. Then Tillie and I walked across the beach through the parking lot and left the park.

Sitting down by the lake at the picnic table in the shade of the big cottonwood tree with a soft breeze blowing off the water, the day felt mild and pleasantly warm; in fact, the proverbial phrase *Perfect summer day* would come close to describing it. But now up on the highway with the August sun beating down unmercifully, cooking the concrete and asphalt to blast furnace intensity, well, the day was just plain hot. In fact, scorching hot would be more apt, judging from the way Tillie lifted her little paws as she pranced across the pavement. I hurried along with my little doggy, wanting to get her out of the heat as soon as possible.

It was a welcome change to walk into the air-conditioned Quik-Mart, and even though the cold air was a shock to my system it still felt refreshing. Tillie seemed to appreciate it too, and I had a momentary vision of her little feet soaking up the coolness of the floor like little furry sponges. We wandered around for a few minutes, cooling off while I browsed the aisles full of candy, junk food, and automotive supplies.

I picked up a can of WD-40, shook it, and, turning it over in my hand, toyed with the idea of buying it before wondering what I was thinking. I certainly didn't need a can right at that moment, especially considering that I had about five or six of them back home scattered in various places around the house. You know, just in case. I put the can down, and Tillie and I went to the back of the store where the water was kept. I selected two bottles this time, one for each of us, and on my way to the front to pay for them grabbed another, bigger handful of slim-jims packets, plus an apple and a small box of raisins, thinking to myself that I couldn't live on slim-jims alone, even if it appeared Tillie was more than happy to.

Steve, the manager's son, had taken over for Lonny and was now working the cash register. He was maybe twenty-five and went to college in Minneapolis at the University of Minnesota, the same school I had attended back in the late fifties. He's pretty friendly with me. He knows I studied engineering there like he's doing, so we usually have a lot to talk about and this time was no exception.

"Hey there, Arnie," he greeted me with a smile as I came up to pay. "I see you've got the Levendowski's little dog with you." He leaned over the counter and said, "Hi, there, little girl.". Tillie responded by jumping straight up into the air three times, landing gracefully on her four paws and giving out a cute little 'yip-yip' each time, to which Steve laughed and clapped, which encouraged her more and made me wonder at all the free time Janice Levendowsky must have to teach her little poodle to do the tricks she could perform. But then who was I to judge someone else, given the amount of time I put into laboring over my jigsaw puzzles? To each, their own, I guess. But I have to say, Tillie's tricks and the happiness they brought Steve (and me, by the way) made the hours spent at my card table seem like a complete waste of time, if not just a little bit lonely and sad.

Tillie finally calmed down and I paid for my purchases. Steve put them in a plastic bag so it'd be easy for me to carry and I gave Tillie a slim jim to gnaw on.

Then Steve took the opportunity to tell me about something they were studying in class. I like the fact that he keeps me informed on new advances in engineering.

I stood quietly paying attention and listened to him explain what was now being done in the field of optical resonating and fluid dynamics - topics that were far beyond my current range of understanding. But that didn't mean I wasn't interested - I was, and I liked hearing what he had to say even though I didn't have much to add to the conversation. However, while he talked I accomplished something unknown to Steve and probably to his immense benefit; I made the decision to not bore him by telling him stories about life before the electronic age - before computers became a way of life and using computer-aided design, so often used these days, was just in its infancy when I was first starting. Part of getting old, I had found, was trying to be sensitive as to when to talk about my life and the things I'd done, and when to leave well enough alone. (Watching the lights dim in the eyes of the party you are talking to was usually a pretty good indication.) Plus, it was too nice a day out right now to rehash things that happened so long ago, even if I did remember them like it was only yesterday.

A woman and her two toddlers came in to pay for gas interrupting Steve's explanation of lead-free transparent ceramics, an area I actually knew something about, having worked with ceramics in my final years at Heartland. I glanced at a clock on the wall. It was after five in the afternoon. I glanced at Tillie. She seemed to be getting antsy to be moving on, probably tired of all the engineering jargon. Steve and I could talk another time, right now it was time to get on with the day.

I bid my young friend goodbye, took a firm grip on Tillie's leash, and went outside. The sun was moving further down in the west and it was shining brightly in my eyes. We found a place in the shade on the side of the building so Tillie's feet wouldn't burn. I wished I had my sunglasses and pictured them laying on the kitchen counter back home. I'd no idea when leaving this morning that I would be spending the entire day out and about, down at the lake with Tillie, chatting with acquaintances and reliving old memories. I have to say that it wasn't a bad way to spend my time.

I pulled the brim of my Twins cap further down to shield my eyes and knelt on the sidewalk. I put a hand gently on either side of Tillie's head and looked at her carefully, judging how she was holding up. She looked up at me, squinted her eyes, and let out an excited little yip before licking my face which I took to be a sign that she was happy and content to be with me. I patted her on the head and stood up. Then she turned in a circle and yipped again, seeming to be ready to move on. I was in no rush to go home, and I had a feeling Tillie wasn't either, so we didn't.

There was lots more traffic driving through town at this time of day with rush hour now in full force. Instead of taking a left at the stop light and returning to our neighborhood, I took a right and headed back down to the park. The kids who had been fishing were long gone so we went out onto the public dock and sat down, taking in the scene dominated by motor boats and sailboats on the water and raucous seagulls flying by overhead. I opened my bag and fed some slim-jims to Tillie while I ate my apple and some raisins. We shared some more water, too. A lot more. It was pretty hot out, and I was glad the dock was now completely shaded by the big aspen and cottonwood trees behind us on the shore.

All the young kids and families had left the beach, too, probably having gone home for dinner. The breeze had shifted, blowing the traffic noise on the highway away from the lake, but it was pretty much drowned out anyway by the constant calling of seagulls soaring overhead begging for snacks. I probably shouldn't have fed them, but I did. It was fun. They seemed to like little pieces slim-jims as much as the raisins. Tillie sat and watched, occasionally looking at me like I was a little crazy. Maybe I was, but it was pure joy watching the birds dip and dive all around us, catching the pieces I threw to them. And entertaining, too, lots more so than watching some stupid television show, which is what I'd be doing if I were home right now, sitting by myself on the couch. That's for sure.

I was hardly conscious of time slipping by. The early evening was so peaceful and relaxing that I almost fell asleep. But didn't. I was suddenly moved to reach down and untie my work boots. I took them off along with my socks. The breeze felt cool on my toes and I had a sudden urge to put my feet in the water, something I hadn't done in maybe fifty years. But, what the heck, I thought to myself, I was having a good day, so why not be adventurous? I rolled up my trousers to my knees and, with only the briefest hesitation, plunged my feet into the lake, expecting a cold shock. I think I might have even gritted my teeth a little. However, as I watched my pale skin sink beneath the surface, I was pleasantly surprised by how warm the water was. It was more than refreshing. It was a soothing balm, like a present from Mother Nature. An unexpected gift of utter bliss. I sat back with a contented sigh, bracing myself with my hands on the warm wood of the dock, and looked out over the lake, idly watching a sailboat tacking back and forth in the soft breeze. Little minnows came and nibbled at my white toes and they didn't bother me at all, only tickled my skin and made me smile. Why didn't I come down here and do this more often?

I don't know how long I had been sitting on the dock, Tillie resting by my side, both of us watching the lake and the sailboat and then a fishing boat which appeared out of nowhere, when all of a sudden I heard a commotion behind me. I turned and saw that some high school kids had came down to the beach and were starting to throw a Frisbee back and forth. I took my feet out of the lake and turned around, watching them from the dock. There were three guys and three girls, just goofing around and having a good time. The guys reminded me of when I was in high school. My friends and I all worked after classes were done for the day, so we didn't have a lot of free time. I do remember that we used to make it to Friday night football games where we'd cheer for our team the Spartans. Our school colors of deep red and gold are still vivid in my mind. Such memories...

Suddenly, a gull looking for a handout had swooped low near the dock causing Tillie to let out a yelp. Startled, I looked around, surprised to see that not only had the kids with Frisbee left the beach, but the sun had now dropped below the western tree line leaving Tillie and me in deep shadow. How long had I been on the dock? An hour or so? I must have trailed off down some long-forgotten path of memories. Maybe I had spent time reminiscing about working on my old '47 pale green Chevy Coup, getting my pride and joy cleaned up and waxed, all ready to go driving with my girl friend Kathy to Lake Harriet in Minneapolis to go for a night time walk and maybe do a little necking if we were in the mood, which we usually were. Maybe I was thinking about Saturday morning pick-up basketball games with my friends, Steve, Dale, and Dave, down at the local park, laughing and cutting up and blowing off steam. They were such good guys. I never had friends like them again. Ever. No wonder I had gone back for a visit.

But now was now and I was feeling stiff from sitting on the hard wooden boards for so long. I put my socks and boots on and Tillie and I got up and walked off the dock and jumped down to the sand. The park was virtually deserted, long shadows of the trees were stretching out along the ground. I saw only a few people wandering around in the dog area. It appeared Jerry had finally gone home with Edgar only to (no doubt) get ready to turn around tomorrow and come back to spend more time by the lake chatting with people. At one point in my life, I might have thought he was wasting his time, killing day after day in a dog park with his pooch, but hell, now that I thought about it, there were probably lots worse ways to spend the summer and get recharged for starting the fall season of teaching and coaching. Being with his dog in the summertime was certainly an innocent enough pastime. I knew how challenging and exhausting it could be dealing with kids all day long since Alice had been a teacher for nearly thirty-five years. So, more power to him.

There were a couple of boats fishing over along the far shore, nearly half a mile away. The afterglow of the setting sun was brushing a few low, wispy clouds on the horizon, coloring them soft pink, the color of Alice's favorite peony. I suddenly felt the weight of the day's end closing in, a feeling I didn't like. I wasn't ready for this remarkable time Tillie and I had been having to be over. Besides, there was still plenty of daylight left. I remembered what Jerry had said about the city maybe putting in a new walking trail over by the highway a quarter of a mile away, so I decided to go and check out the location. There hadn't been much rain this summer and the lake level was down so we started walking along the shore toward the highway instead of going back to the Quik-Mart, taking a left and walking along the highway itself. Tillie enjoyed playing in the water as we made our way, and I made sure to keep her on the leash so she wouldn't decide to go for a swim into deeper water or chase the ducks that were paddling nearby keeping us company.

As we walked, we left our footprints in the sand and when I turned around and saw them, they made me think of *Robinson Crusoe*, one of my favorite books to read when I was a kid. Just for the fun of it, I started pretending Tillie and I were actually on a desert island, searching for signs of civilization or turtle eggs to eat, and before too long I realized we had walked far enough to get past where the highway ran near the shore where the trail would be built. We had walked the shoreline far to the east to where a steep hill rose a hundred feet to my right. Time, once again, had somehow slipped away from me.

Next to me, Tillie seemed to have gotten a new burst of energy and was straining to go after a young raccoon running along the sand just ahead. I tugged on the leash to hold her back. We stopped and watched for a while until the young rascal scurried into the underbrush. Then I looked around. I was near the far end of the lake in a secluded wooded cove, about one mile outside of town.

Well, that's OK, I thought to myself and bent down and petted Tillie who was sitting patiently at my feet. Then I looked out over the lake and up at the sky. Twilight was fading fast and soon it would be dark. I had a decision to make. I should turn around and go home by walking back the way we'd come. But that was too easy. Why not do something different? I looked at the steep hill so thick with undergrowth that I could barely see the ground. I looked at Tillie. I swear she grinned at me and then wagged her tail. Alright, then, why not? I made my decision.

"I think we can make that climb, girl, don't you?" I asked her. I hadn't climbed a hill, let alone a forested one, in I couldn't remember how long. But I was up for anything new on this day of new experiences.

Tillie looked at me expectantly and then yipped, letting me know that she was as game to try a new adventure as I was. I got a firm grip on her leash and we started, fighting our way through tangled underbrush of chokecherry, blackberry, saplings, and low-growing shrubs. It was thick stuff and all of it under a forest of birch, elm, and oak. I was sweating by the time we made it to the top. And when we did and when we popped out into the open, guess what I found? Gravestones. Tombstones. I looked around and realized I'd come all the way along the shoreline to the lake side of the small local cemetery. The same cemetery where Alice's ashes were buried.

I immediately collapsed in the long grass under a canopy of trees to catch my breath. Tillie plopped down next to me, panting. After a few moments, we both recovered and I sat up. I scratched Tillie behind the ears and told her, "Good dog." She looked at me momentarily, thinking god only knew what, and then suddenly licked my face. I have to say, it felt pretty nice, though certainly much wetter than I imagined it to be.

I scooted around so I was facing the lake, pulled Tillie close to me, and opened my bag from the Quik-Mart. "Here you go, girl," I said, giving her one handful of water after another which she thirstily lapped up. Then we proceeded to have ourselves a little picnic of more shared water and slim-jims. They tasted better than they had all day, and believe me, they had certainly hit the spot earlier. *The best picnic in a long time* was my way of thinking.

The clouds to the west had changed from soft pink to deep red and orange. There was very little light left. As I sat and watched, the colors faded and the sky turned deep purple and then dark indigo. There was a peaceful quiet all around and the scent of freshly mown grass wafting in from somewhere. The thought that jumped to the forefront of my mind was this: *What a perfect ending to a perfect day*. And then, as we gazed out over the calm waters of the lake, watching the darkness deepen and listening to the final song of a nearby robin, just like that, the last light of day left the sky completely, and the first stars began to appear.

Now, I know that I should have gotten to my feet right then and there and made my way through the cemetery out to the county road, taken a right, and hiked back into town. It would have been the right thing to do, the expected thing to do, the prudent thing to do. Heck, I could have been to my house in less than an hour. But my day had given me a new lease on life and I felt that Tillie and I were now far removed from doing something so...well, something so normal and expected. I wasn't going to let a little darkness, let alone some misplaced nod to conventionality, hold us back. No sir. Besides, an idea had suddenly occurred to me.

I stood up and gave the leash a little tug. "Come on, girl," I said to Tillie. She immediately jumped to her feet. Off we went. Despite being difficult to see clearly, I was able to make my way carefully through the cemetery until a few minutes later I found what I was looking for - Alice's gravestone marking where her ashes were buried. I squatted down and caressed the marble marker, thinking of my dear wife and how much I missed her and how much she would have enjoyed being with me on this rare day, the first good day I'd had in I didn't know how long. I took more than a few minutes talking with her and telling her what the day had been like, and how nice it had been to be at the lake, talking with people, and reliving old memories.

Then I changed subjects and told her how our kids and the grandchildren were doing, telling my sweet Alice about this life that was now so much more empty with her not in it anymore. I suddenly found myself overwhelmed and a little teary-eyed, remembering the wonderful times we'd had together and the very full life we had led: raising our children, working at our jobs, working in our garden, going on family vacations (like the one to the Upper Penninsula in Michigan), all the ups and downs we'd experienced in our long and fulfilling marriage, the good times and the bad. In short, the shared life of two people immensely in love with each other.

Then I surprised myself by breaking down completely. I sank to my knees in the dewy grass, tears streaming down my cheeks. Oh, the intensity of those memories! Sometimes they can be emotionally dangerous and this was obviously one of those times. I was overcome. I finally stretched out prostrate in the grass, sobbing uncontrollably like a child or, more to the point, like a lonely old man.

After who knows how long, Tillie's soft tongue on the side of my face startled me back to reality.

"Hey there, girl," I said to her, rolling over and sitting up. I looked at the little white dog who had been my faithful company on this day of simple yet extraordinary events and scratched her ears, feeling a sense of security in her comforting presence. She stood and quivered in excitement, enjoying the attention. "Good girl," I said, sniffling a little. "You're a really good girl."

I took a minute to collect myself, petting Tillie and appreciating the soft feel of her fur, the closeness of this little living creature. Then I wiped my nose with the back of my hand, finally getting myself back together. I stood up, "You're such a good, doggy," I told her.

Was it me, or did Tillie give me a little poodle grin in response? It was so dark, I probably just imagined it.

Probably.

I stood in the darkness, the air still warm from the heat of the day, and listened to a chorus of frogs coming from nearby. They mingled with the low, sustained hum of toads calling and crickets chirping. There were other night sounds, too, that were somehow comforting to hear even though I had no idea what they were. My enjoyment was overwhelming and I think I lost track of time for a while.

A big splash near the shore startled me back to reality. A fish must have jumped, leaping out of the calm water before falling back into it again. Next to me Tillie stood up and put her front paws on my leg. I reached down and scratched her ears and she moved up next to me and licked my hand. I could have stayed in this peaceful place forever, but I knew I couldn't. Hadn't I procrastinated long enough? Probably. I really should be getting home, and I told myself, *Get off your butt and walk yourself and Tillie back to town, drop her off and go home to your nice soft bed, climb in and pull up the covers and go to sleep.*

But I knew I was only kidding myself. My little pep talk fell on deaf ears. I wasn't ready just yet to leave, and when I thought about it, why should I? Tillie and I weren't hurting anyone. The night was warm and mild. What was the rush? Plus, all I had to look forward to back home was an empty house and a half-finished jigsaw puzzle. They'd be there when I got back, but I wasn't ready to go back to them just yet. Maybe in a little while.

We made our way through the grave markers back to the far edge of the cemetery where we'd come up from our climb and sat down in the grass so we could look out over the lake. Even though it was now completely dark, I could see a few boats on the mirror-calm water with their running lights on, trolling quietly back and forth, probably fishing for walleyes.

About a hundred yards behind us was the highway. I listened past the swish, swish of the traffic and was rewarded with night sounds of crickets, toads, and frogs, plus the haunting hooting of an owl and the occasional quacking of a duck out on the water. It was all so peaceful and relaxing that I sat for a long time, enjoying the languid reverie of thinking about nothing at all, just enjoying the nighttime and the comforting companionship of Tillie. I hadn't felt so at ease in many months, certainly not since I'd lost Alice. It was a good feeling to have, like something sacred was taking over my spirit, revitalizing my soul with hope and happiness. But then I laughed, chiding myself, realizing that I didn't normally think those kinds of thoughts. Maybe I was just being a foolish old man, slowly losing touch with reality, quietly going crazy.

But, be that as it may, and putting thoughts of senility aside, after a while I started to get a chill. I guess I'd been out long enough on this wonderfully different, yet increasingly memorable day. It was finally time to go home. I looked up through the overhanging tree branches. Numerous stars had come out and were filling the sky with a fairyland of twinkling light. Looking to the east a bright, clear, yellow moon was starting to rise over the tree line on the far end of the lake. I looked at my wrist, thinking to check the time, but remembered that I didn't wear a watch anymore; hadn't, in fact, for thirteen years, ever since I'd retired from Heartland back in 2004. My goodness, how the time had flown.

I stood up to stretch and get ready for the walk back to town, but as soon as I did I got a little dizzy. I stumbled a bit and took a few steps to the trunk of a tree to catch my balance. I suddenly felt very tired. Maybe I'd rest a bit before leaving the cemetery. I walked a few yards along the edge of the overlook until I found some soft, long grass. When I sat down a sense of relief flowed in my legs. My long day was catching up to me.

"Just for a moment," I said to Tillie, who moved right up to my side, patiently watching me. "We'll rest just for a minute and then we'll head home, okay girl?"

Tillie seemed to understand because she put her paws in from of her and arched her backside into the air, stretching. Then she shook herself, gave up a big yawn, and shook herself again. I lay down in the grass facing the lake using my arm for a pillow and she lay down beside me. I pulled her close to my chest. Next to me, her little body felt warm and comforting. I began to relax. "We'll just rest a minute," I told her. "Then we'll go home." Tillie sighed a heavy sigh and snuggled closer. I closed my eyes and gave myself up to images of the day, the people I'd seen and talked with, and the memories I'd relived, all floating through my brain like big, white, fluffy clouds on a bright, blue sky summer day. It was as good a way as any to fall asleep and I did.

I awoke to the song of a robin and the sun peeking over the tree line to the east. What the hell? I couldn't believe I had slept all night long. Tillie lay peacefully right next to me and when I scratched her behind her ears she quickly came awake. Then I stood up; well, struggled to my feet was more like it. Man, I was stiff, but when I finally got myself upright and was able to look around I stood transfixed. Diffuse sunlight filtered through the trees filling the woodland with a golden glow. Where light found its way to the ground wisps of steam were rising only to then drift ethereally away in the softest of breezes. In addition to the chorus of more and more robins joining their solitary friend in song, there was a freshness in the air that bespoke of the promise of the coming of a brand new day. Nearby on the grass sunlight glistened jewel-like off the strands of a spider web. A woodpecker's drumming echoed through the trees. And then, like magic, a mother turkey with about ten young ones silently appeared off to my left and ran across the grass in front of me before disappearing into the edge of the forest fifty feet away.

I was damp with morning dew but no matter. Once on my feet, I discovered that I was perfectly fine standing in this cemetery that was suddenly transformed from a plot of land for the dead and departed into a forest glade of the alive and living. A sense of peace filled my soul and renewed my spirit like I was in Nature's own sanctuary. If this was what religion was all about, I was all on board.

Tillie was up now, too, standing beside me with her little head tilted to one side, looking at me curiously, less excited about the wonders of the natural world and more concerned with food. I liked how she was keeping me grounded in reality. After a moment's contemplation, I realized that I, too, was hungry.

"Let's get ourselves something to eat," I told her, and she wagged her tail and quivered with excitement. I smiled, happy that my new little friend was with me to join in this brand new day.

I was reaching in my Quik-Mart bag to check on the slim-jims supply when Tillie's ears perked up. She turned in the direction of the highway and started barking. I grabbed her leash so she wouldn't run off and a moment later heard what was upsetting her - the high-pitched scream of a siren. Then another one, both of them screeching through the stillness of the early morning like a classroom of kindergartener's fingernails on a chalk board.

Curious as to what was happening, I hurried through the wet grass and tombstones toward the parking lot and saw one, then another, squad car speed by on the highway. I quickened my pace and by the time I made it to the road, I was just in time to see their red brake lights come on. The squads each slammed to a stop, made quick U-turns and sped back to me. They turned into the packing area, tires skidding on the gravel, and pulled up right in front of where I stood (rather aggressively, I thought), sirens winding down but those red and yellow lights still flashing. I have to say that they completely destroyed the mellow mood of the tranquil morning.

I reached down and picked up Tillie who by now was barking non-stop. I petted her and talked softly to her, comforting her and telling her to calm down. "Everything's going to be alright," I told her, even though I had no idea if that statement was true or not. One thing was certain, I had no idea what was going on.

Tillie finally relaxed, quit barking, and nestled in my arms. I could feel her little body shaking. I watched as a cop got out of each car. One was a guy about fifty years old who was short, thin, and had a bushy, black mustache. The other was a young woman about thirty who had a couple of inches and maybe twenty pounds on the guy. Neither of them were looking too happy.

"Hi, there officers," I said, trying to be friendly as they approached. "Nice day, isn't it?"

"Are you Arnold Gans, "Mr. Moustache asked without preamble, stalking right up to me and not acting friendly at all, I might add.

"Why, yes I am," I said, courteously, wondering what the sudden interest in me was. Then it dawned on me. Of course. I'd spent the night in the cemetery. Maybe someone had seen me and reported me as a vagrant or something.

"Mr. Gans," the lady cop said, "we had a call come in this morning that you were missing. You haven't been heard from in a day." She stopped and gave me a pointed look, the kind of look my mother used to give me when I was a kid and misbehaved. A look that to this day the memory of still makes me shutter. I felt myself cowing under her gaze. "You're not being very responsible, Mr. Gans. Are you aware that people are concerned for you and are very worried about you? We're here to take you home."

Ops. So, not a vagrant, then. Plus I'd made the lady cop mad. Not a good way to kick off what a few minutes ago looked like it'd be a really good day.

Much later, when I thought back to how I handled the next minute or so, I probably could have done things differently. For sure, I would have kept my mouth shut. But I had been having a really good day the day before, and frankly, last night in the cemetery hadn't been so bad either. In fact, right up until the point when the police had made their noisy and assertive appearance, the morning was looking awfully darn promising as well.

"I'm not missing," I said to the lady cop, making a little joke. "I'm right here."

Well, I thought it was funny, even if she didn't. Not one little bit.

What happened was that Mrs. Levendosky had tried to call several times yesterday to check on how things were going with me and the dog-sitting job. Of course, I wasn't home, out as I had been with Tillie on our little escapade. Her final call came last night, and when I didn't answer her worry level went from slight to extreme. When she called early this morning and I still didn't answer she called my son John who drove to my home from where he lived in Apple Valley - a forty-five-minute drive in morning rush hour. After a quick search and finding I wasn't anywhere in the house he called the police to report me missing. The two police officers who found me in the cemetery were responding to the call and on the way to meet with John and organize a search party.

In retrospect, they should have been happy that I saved them the time and effort it would have taken to look for me, having me stumble out of the cemetery almost into their laps like I did. But they were more annoyed than anything else at wasting time over a false alarm and the inconvenience of having to babysit an old man. I was pretty much told to keep my mouth shut after my little joke about not being lost (even though to this day I will still insist I wasn't.) In the end, I should have been grateful the police took their jobs as seriously as they did. And I was but, man, everybody sure made a big deal out of me being "Missing," as they put it.

I was brought home and placed in the custody of John who insisted on taking me to the local clinic for a checkup. Of course, I was fine. Tillie was, too, I might add. When we got back to my place John spent the day with me, which was quite nice. He called Linda and she came over in the middle of the afternoon after she got off work with her twin girls Kala and Marie and take-out from Subway.

"Well, Dad," John finally said after we had eaten and were sitting at the kitchen table drinking iced tea that Linda had made,

"I hope you've learned your lesson and that you won't go traipsing off again."

He and Linda suggested that if my wandering away from home started to become a habit, "Next steps," as they called it, would have to be taken. And those next steps were clearly spelled out.

"I'm afraid we'll have to consider some sort of Memory Care facility or nursing home," Linda said, shaking her head and looking less regretful than I hoped she would.

"Or something along those lines," John added. He, too, didn't look very happy with the whole situation.

I didn't have to think but a microsecond to agree with them. I liked my freedom too much to make a bit deal and argue and try to prove some ridiculous point. Plus, between you and me, I didn't do anything all that awful, did I? Just went out for a little walk and stayed out longer than I'd planned. I hadn't hurt anybody.

"I really do appreciate your concern," I told them both, making sure I came across as both contrite and sincere. "I promise I won't wander off again. I'll be good."

After talking back and forth some more, and me continuing to assure them I would be conscientious and change my behavior, more just to keep my kids from worrying about me than anything else, I was able to finally convince them that didn't have to worry. Whew. Then with my immediate future out of the way, we moved on and chatted about John and Linda's lives, how things were going with them and their jobs, and how the grandkids were doing. You know, just catching up. It was nice.

Finally, John looked at his watch. "Ok, Dad, I should get going. It's been a long day. I'm sure you're tired. I know I am."

"Thanks for everything, son," I said. "I appreciate your concern." I looked at Linda, "You, too, sweetheart."

She came to me and hugged me, saying, "I love you, Dad, and just want the best for you, you know that, right?" I nodded and told her that I did.

"I do too, Dad," John said. He joined us and hugged us both and it was all a very nice, very family kind of feeling. I even got teary-eyed again, like back at Alice's grave last night, what with all the concern and affection.

After a minute, John said, "OK, Dad." He patted me on the back. "We should get going."

I walked him and Linda and Kala and Marie, out to their respective cars.

After another round of hugs, I said, "OK, goodbye, now."

I stood back and waved as they pulled out of the driveway, honking their horns and making more of a racket than necessary. "Sorry to have caused so much trouble," I added under my breath, as I looked down at Tillie, who, except for playing with my granddaughters, had stayed near me the entire day. "But it was sure fun, wasn't it, girl?"

She perked up her little ears and barked her assent. Yes, there was no doubt in either of our minds. It had been fun.

Earlier that day, after I got back from the doctor, I called Mrs. Levendosky to let her know that Tillie was just fine. She was relieved, but I could tell she was concerned that maybe I was losing my marbles even though I tried to assure her I wasn't. Let me tell you, that's one interesting conversation to have. At one point John finally got on the line and helped convince her I was mentally fit enough to care for her family's pet. His words seemed to help convince her because when she came back on the line she seemed calmer. She even told me about how well their East Coast trip had been going.

"Seeing Gettysburg was fantastic, Arnie," she told me enthusiastically, putting thoughts of my ability to care for Tillie aside. "It's been an amazing learning experience."

"That's great, Janice," I told her, trying to sound just as enthusiastic. "I'm glad you're having a wonderful time." We talked some more before I asked what was really on my mind. "Are you still planning to be home in nine or ten days?"

"Yes, nine days. Are you and Tillie going to be alright until then?"

Tillie was right next to me. I reached down and picked her up and held her under my arm. She licked the side of my face and gave a contented little sigh. In my mind, I said, *Good doggy*. To Janice, I said, "Yes, Janice, we'll be just fine."

After I hung up and hours later, after my family had driven home, Tillie and finally I had the house to ourselves. The sun had started its descent to the west and in an hour or so twilight would be settling in. I poured myself some ice tea and we went outside and sat on a comfortable old Adirondack chair in the front yard to watch the world go by. Tillie climbed up in my lap and I gave her a slim-jim from my shirt pocket for her to chew on. I looked out over my small but tidy yard, most of which Alice and I had turned into flower gardens over the last twenty years or so. What a sight they were. The annuals and perennials were in full bloom, the terra-cotta-colored Echinacea was looking especially pretty against the purple of the heliotrope. My hanging baskets were overflowing with healthy geraniums loaded with lush red and pink flowers and entwining vines of variegated ivy. Everywhere I looked there was color and life and exuberance; the yard looked as lush and vibrant as I'd ever seen it. It made me feel happy. It was as good a legacy for Alice to have left behind as were the thousands of children whose lives she impacted as their teacher. In some ways even better.

I thought back to the discussions I'd had that day with John and Linda and Mr. Moustache and the Lady Cop. The police suggested (in fact, strongly encouraged) that I get a cell phone of some sort to carry with me at all times, so I could stay "In touch" with my kids, as they called it. I pictured hourly phone calls from John and Linda checking up on me, making sure I was safe and sound and, especially, that I hadn't wandered off again. I had agreed to their wishes mainly so my kids wouldn't have to worry.

Plus, who needed the local police driving by every now and then to check on me? I certainly didn't. I was also banking on the fact that for John and Linda the newness of checking up with their dad by phone would wear off after a while and things would go back to normal. I hoped so anyway and was keeping my fingers crossed, figuring I could easily prove to everyone I was responsible for my own life and that no one had to worry. But whatever the case, agreeing to their wishes was a small price to pay for having the freedom to live in my own home. I'd get a cell phone first thing in the morning.

Tillie made a move next to me and jumped down into the grass. I blinked my eyes and came back from pondering my future. Out on the street Suny and her husband were walking by, Rex leading them on his leash. They each waved and I waved back. Rex gave a friendly little yip which Tillie returned.

"We heard about your big adventure," Suny called out. I immediately thought about how quickly news travels in a small town - blazingly fast, would be an apt description. I just smiled and waved, not really in the mood to elaborate, just now, on the adventure Tillie and I had been on. "How's little Tillie doing?" Suny asked. Was it me or was that a knowing grin I saw on my neighbor's face?

The dog in question was sitting obediently next to my chair. I reached over and scratched her ears and petted her along her back. Tillie quivered in excitement.

"She's just fine," I called back. "How's Rex?"

"He's good," she smiled, continuing to walk by, dutifully following the fireball of a Chihuahua straining at his leash. "Maybe the children and I will see you at the beach tomorrow."

I patted Tillie on the head and she licked my hand. "Sounds like a plan," I called back to Suny. "Sounds like a really good plan," I added to myself under my breath, smiling.

Suny waved once more and I waved back. I watched as they continued down the street and took a right at the corner. Twilight was beginning and the air was warm and moist, still holding on to the heat of the day. Most of the yard was in shadow. The sky was washed in soft reds and oranges behind me to the west. Down the street some kids were playing on skate boards, enjoying the evening's calm and the last light of day. The street lights were just coming on.

I probably should have mentioned to Mrs. Levendowsky when I was talking to her that I had decided keeping Tillie with me at my home instead of at her place for the duration of the vacation would be the easiest way of caring for the little poodle. I personally thought it was a brilliant idea but was aware there might still be some lingering concerns about my mental stability floating around in Janice's mind so why do anything to rock the boat and tell her? I'd just wait a few days to do that or maybe even until they returned home. Hell, when you thought about it, did it really matter when I told her? No, probably not. I reached down and scratched Tillie's head again and she spun around in a circle and gave out an excited yip. Then she started rolling around on her back, feet kicking in the air like she was running a race. I had to laugh. She was a fun companion to have around. More than fun. She was making my loneliness go away.

Suddenly I had an idea. I stood up and took hold of Tillie's leash.

"Come on, girl," I said, looking at her. She responded by jumping to her feet and happily wagging her tail - exactly as if she knew what was going to happen next. She was right. "Let's go for a little stroll and check out the neighborhood," I told her. "How's that sound?" She gave a short bark in agreement and off we went.

It was a nice evening for a walk so we went for a long one. We spent time looking at the variety yards and flower gardens in the area, some more cared for and pampered than others, but all unique and interesting in their own ways. We waved at friendly neighbors out enjoying the evening. We listened to the final chorus of the robins singing the day to a close, and, especially, we enjoyed each other's company - this old man and this little white dog.

A little while later we turned onto my block just as the first stars were starting to appear, dotting the nighttime sky, twinkling in own magical way. And we made it home just fine, too, my little companion and I. This time we didn't get lost.

"Come on inside," I told Tillie, leading her around to the back. "I've got something to show you."

I took her off her leash and let her in the back door which opened into my little kitchen. She immediately started sniffing around the edges of the cupboards, the stove, and the refrigerator. I followed along as she went into the living room where my jigsaw puzzle was set up. I took a look at it, half-finished, just the water lilies below the bridge were what I had to complete. I figured it'd take me at least two days.

Tillie jumped up onto my easy chair and circled around and around, making herself comfortable. Then she lay down with her head on her paws and looked at me as if to ask, "Well, are you going to join me or not?"

I know it sounds crazy, but I have to tell you that I answered her. "Just a minute," I said. "I've got something to do, first."

Then I did what I'd been thinking about doing ever since John had brought me home that morning. I went to the card table, took apart Monet's water lilies, scraped the pieces into their box and put it away in the closet along with all the other jig-saw puzzles I'd worked on over the last three years. I'd done enough thousand-piece puzzles to last a lifetime and certainly didn't need to finish this one. Monet's water lilies would just have to wait. Maybe forever. I put the card table away, too.

Then I went to my chair and picked up Tillie. I sat down and held her in my lap. "What do you think, girl?" I asked, scratching her ears. "Shall we go down to the lake tomorrow?

She yipped once and licked my face and I laughed. "Good doggy," I said and she licked my face again.

In the back of my mind, I knew Mrs. Levendosky and her family would be home in nine days. Tillie and I would have to make the most of our time together until they returned and I'd have to give her back. Going down to the lake like we'd done the day before sounded like the best plan I'd had in a long time. Who knew, maybe we'd even have another remarkable day. As far as I was concerned the chances were pretty good.

"All right," I said, gently petting her little head," Let's do it."

And the next day, we did.

On Rainy Lake

"I can't believe you forgot the marshmallows," my wife scolded me.

"And I can't believe you forgot the friggin' gram crackers," I spat back at her. "How do you except us to make smores with only these stupid chocolate bars?"

"Well, you're the friggin' genus, Mr. Hot Shot, you figure it out."

"Well...Well..." I couldn't think of anything else to say, except this. "Screw you, Shelia, I'm going for a walk."

I left our campfire and headed off into the woods. This was our first night camping with our rented houseboat on Scalawag Bay on the south shore of Rainy Lake. We were on the Minnesota side of the Minnesota, Canadian border and were supposed to stay three nights, but the way it was going we'd be lucky to last until morning.

I was steaming mad and pissed off to boot. I pushed through the jack pine and underbrush and tripped over a rock, half submerged in the mossy forest floor. I fell, smashing my knee on another rock when I hit the ground. Shit. I got up, brushed myself off and kicked at the granite outcropping, stubbing my toe in the process. Not a good idea. Damn, it hurt. I made the wise decision to quit doing battle with an inanimate object and continued on. A few yards further, I pushed through more underbrush and a branch wiped back and smacked my face. It stung like hell. I put my hand to my cheek and came away with a little blood. Shit and damn.

I slowed down to get control of myself and hiked on, silently cursing my fate, my life, my wife and this idiotic trip to Rainy Lake, not necessarily in that order. In a few minutes I came out of the woods and onto the backside of the little bay where we'd landed the houseboat. Hoping to calm down, I sat on a flat bolder near the shoreline and looked across a much bigger bay. On the horizon to the west was a sunset turning the sky a soft orange and crimson brushed with gentle traces of magenta and plum. It was probably beautiful. To someone else, it might even have been a glorious and awe-inspiring sight setting the stage for a lovely poem extolling the wonders of Nature. But I hardly noticed. I was still fuming. The only color I saw was the angry red behind my eyes. I took out my phone and checked that I had a signal. Good, I did, so I called my girlfriend, Leslie.

"Hi there Big Fella, how's the trip going?" she asked, picking up on the first ring, almost like she was waiting for me. She probably was.

"Like shit," I told her. "We're already fighting."

"Over what?"

"Smores, if you can believe it."

Leslie snorted out a laugh so loud I had to hold the phone away from my ear.

"God, Ben. That sounds so...so..."

I waited to hear what it sounded like to her. Now that I'd had a few minutes to think about it, our argument sounded ridiculous. And pathetic. I guess I was on Leslie's wavelength because what she said was, "Well, that just sounds sad."

Which, all things considered, I guess it was.

Shelia and I were both forty-five years old and had been married twenty-three years. Our marriage had definitely seen better days.

I shifted my butt on the rock, trying unsuccessfully to find a comfortable spot. I was tall and thin and I didn't have a lot extra body fat. Some people might think that was a good thing, being skinny. Right. Try sitting on a hunk of granite in the boundary waters for a few minutes and get back to me on that.

"So how are things going at work?" I asked, just to change the subject. Leslie worked with me in Human Resources for Heartland International, a worldwide electronic temperature control manufacturing company. She as a training instructor and I was in software design.

In answer to my question, she began rambling on and on until finally I began to listen with only half an ear. I mean, really, who cared anyway? Honestly, not me. I was on vacation, a time to forget about workplace dramas and office politics. But it was on me. I'd asked her about work, so I didn't interrupt and let her talk while I tried to make sense of how I ended up like this.

Shelia and I usually vacationed on Rainy Lake with our longtime friends, Bob and Iris Lansbury. This year, however, Bob was recovering from hip pointer surgery, brought on by years of playing catcher in a recreational softball league. Earlier in the summer he'd told me, "Sorry, buddy, I'm under doctor's orders to keep this bad boy rested." He pointed to his right hip and laughed. I did, too, but only to humor him. I had no idea what he was talking about. I did, however, decide to take him at his word (why not?) But, every now and then I wondered, maybe the real reason they were avoiding us was that he and Iris just didn't want to be around me and Shelia and our falling apart marriage anymore.

Honestly, who could blame them? My wife and I had been drifting apart for the last ten years or so, but things had really started coming unraveled a few years back after our kids began moving out of the house, Josh to live in Montana two years ago, and Julie to live over by the University of Minnesota last year. Our fighting, which had been subversively passive-aggressive while they lived at home, had become more out in the open, with yelling and verbal taunts becoming the norm. The more I thought about it, who would want to spend time with us?

"...and then good old Manager Randy, told me that I had to..."

I turned my attention to Leslie for a moment but had nothing to say except for the occasional, "Huh, huh," to let her know I was still there.

Leslie was a talker. When it came to her job, she could go on and on and I had to give her credit for that. She'd worked for Heartland for three years and still cared. I'd worked there for nineteen years and did not.

With Bob and his hip debilitated, Shelia and I had gone ahead on our own and rented a twenty-four-foot houseboat from Northern Lights Houseboat Adventures, the company we'd used on the three previous trips to Rainy Lake with Bob and Iris. The first time was twelve years ago, one of those bucket list things that was Iris' idea. None of us had any idea what we were getting into. Surprisingly, we'd all had a really good time, staying out in the middle of August for four nights and five days on the biggest houseboat the company owned, 'King of the Lake,' a forty-four-foot giant that I drove and inconveniently got hung up on rocks six times. I counted. So did everyone else. We went back three years later and rented a smaller, more manageable thirty-five-foot boat, 'The Queen of Rainy' which worked out well. But the smaller living space made it awkward on occasion, especially at night if you know what I mean.

Four years ago we decided to each rent a small twenty-five-foot houseboat so we could have some privacy if we wanted. The smaller boats were easy to drive and the living space was fine. In short, it worked out so well that Shelia and I rented one for three nights and four days in August this year.

But this time was different. Without our friends with us, the idea was to use our vacation to spend one-on-one time together and try to patch up the rifts in our marriage. Yeah, right. Easier said than done. You know that old adage, *Pissing into the wind?* Well, that's exactly what is was like from the moment we pointed our houseboat (called 'Looney Tunes,' ironically enough) away from Northern Lights base of operations and rode the calm waters of Rainy Lake eighteen miles east to Scalawag Bay. Along the way I came up with my own adage, *You can't put a bandage on a hurricane.* In my mind, it was more than appropriate.

When a marriage implodes who's to say where the fault lies? I'd like to say it was with Shelia, but, to be honest, probably not. She was a devoted mother to Josh and Julie. She carved out a career as an independent accountant, working from a home office she'd set up in a converted bedroom on the second floor of our 1920s bungalow in Orchard Lake, a small town located twenty miles west of downtown Minneapolis. In addition to her job, she found time to work out and run marathons. She'd even competed in the City of Lakes Triathlon in Minneapolis a few times. Me? I just tried to do a good job at work, keep our gardens weeded at home, the lawn cut and the driveway shoveled.

So, on paper I guess I didn't come out looking too good. Kind of boring, to be frank. Well, fine. I'm not going to defend myself. Sometimes these things just happen. Sometimes a husband and wife drift apart and can't figure out how to get themselves back together again. Sometimes they don't want to get back together. I didn't know about Shelia, but the question was, did I want to keep our marriage together?

I didn't have an answer. The more I thought about it, the more I came up empty. I just didn't know.

Most people would argue that having a girlfriend in the mix certainly didn't help things and at this stage, I'd have to agree. Leslie and I began our affair last winter with discrete, innocent flirtations in the break room and the occasional "working" lunch at the Black Forest Inn, a restaurant a few blocks from our office. She was twenty-seven years old. I found her attractive, intelligent, and baggage-free. I enjoyed her company. Do the math. She's eighteen years younger than me. I'm not sure what my expectations were, but I'll tell you this: I never planned on things going as far as they did. But, I guess, these things happen. In my case, they sure did.

Looking back, naive and stupid would be the first two words out of many that come to mind to describe what I had done.

It all escalated last spring on an office team-building trip to the Riverside Conference Center outside of Monticello on the shore of the Mississippi River, an hour's drive northwest of Minneapolis. After a day of activities like playing *Blind Person Bluff, Designing the Perfect Work Place*, and competing in a two-legged race, most everyone was ready for a night of blowing off steam. Me? I was looking forward to having a few drinks, dialing it back, hitting the hay, and reading the newest Cork O'Conner novel.

I was in the Riverside Bar, well on the way to becoming very relaxed when I bumped into Leslie. We started talking. One thing led to another and we ended up spending the night together in my room. It was the first time I'd ever cheated on my wife. I felt a little guilty, but not all that much. Leslie was a nice diversion then, and still is now. We have continued to see each other and have grown as close as two people can be, given the circumstances. But did I care enough for Leslie to leave Shelia for her? I wasn't sure.

I brought the phone closer to my ear and listened. "That class I'm teaching is just crazy. Most of them are from out east..."

She was telling me about the sales training seminar she was currently instructing. I listened, trying to drum up some enthusiasm to say something.. It was her job, after all, a job she was committed to; a job she loved and was good at. The more I listened, though, the more I realized that I honestly didn't care about what she was talking about. She was happy, young and single. She had her whole life ahead of her. She was excited about life. Me? I had my own problems to deal with.

Here's the thing. I suppose you could say I got involved with Leslie to take a break from Shelia. My home life wasn't fulfilling. Shelia and I rarely talked, we just went our separate ways. She had her friends and activities and I had mine. In addition to gardening and yard work, my hobby is collecting vintage tin toys made by Marx, mainly purchased in antique stores or off the internet. Not the most exciting life, I'll grant you, but I enjoyed it for what it was: simple, stable and uncomplicated. I really had nothing to complain about. But when I got involved with Leslie she gave me something to look forward to. She was fun to be with. She seemed to enjoy being around me. What was there to not to like about the situation?

With Leslie's voice droning on and on, I set the phone down and got up and stretched. The shoreline was made up of round, walnut sized pebbles that shifted under my hiking boots as I walked a few steps to the water's edge. I was on a tiny point of land. Behind me a hundred yards away was Scalawag bay along with Shelia and the houseboat. In front of me was one of the bigger bays on Rainy Lake, Beaver Dam Bay, stretching west to the far horizon, a least two miles away. Sixteen miles from there was Northern Lights base camp. Twenty miles from there was the biggest town around, International Falls. Right here, right where I sat, as far as the eye could see, there was no one around except for me and Shelia. We had the entire huge lake to our selves.

To my left was a high ridge that sloped down to the water and formed the shoreline of the bay. It was marked by granite outcroppings and pine and aspen trees, commonly found in the boundary waters. To the right, across the lake at least a mile, was the distant shore of Canada, now nearly lost to sight. Darkness was falling. The sun had set, and its orange afterglow of was fading. The air was still. The peace and quiet surrounding me was stunning.

I looked down and searched for a minute until I found a thin, smooth stone. I reared back threw it out over the calm water. It skipped a couple of times and then sank. Dang. I used to be better than that. I picked up another one and threw it. Harder. This time it went out five skips. Better. I smiled.

Then I looked up. Above me the sky was quickly turning to a deep purple ink well of darkness, the kind only found far away from the bright lights of civilization. Up here on the lake, we hardly ever saw anyone other than the occasional houseboat, fishing boat, canoe or kayaker out during the day. At night, there was no one around. I liked the peace and quiet. It helped me re-charge my batteries from work. From life, too, for that matter. It was one of the main reasons I liked coming to the boundary waters in general and Rainy Lake in particular.

A sudden splash to my right caught my attention. I looked, peering into the fast approaching darkness. More splashing. Then a sound, like a kitten purring. Something was in the water and it was coming right at me. Unsure what it was, I took a cautious step backward, tripped a little, but caught myself. Then I looked more closely and was able to see what was making the noise. It was the long, sleek body of an otter. I watched, mesmerized as it moved along the shoreline, diving and surfacing, diving and surfacing. It was coming right towards me, unafraid, only a few feet away.

I quickly squatted down so I wouldn't scare it. I'd heard otters were in the area, but had never seen one before. Now, here one was, swimming and playing not ten feet away, so close I had to fight the urge to reach out and touch it. Pet it. I was speechless. The otter rolled in a complete circle, came up on its back and slowly moved its tail back and forth, propelling itself confidently along, making a little wake in the water's smooth surface. I looked closer and could just barely make out something in its paws. Maybe a fish? Crawfish? I looked harder, but couldn't see it clearly. Probably a fish.

Transfixed, I watched as the beautiful, sleek, creature swam past right in front of me and then continued to my left, taking it's time moving down the shoreline. Finally it disappeared into the darkness. I blinked once or twice to clear my vision, hoping to see it again, but I didn't. It was gone. What a thrill! Seeing that otter was one of the coolest things I'd had the experience of seeing in quite a long time.

I stood up and stepped as close to the water line as I could, squatted down and put my hand in the lake. It was pleasantly warm, having soaked up heat of the day from the sun. I raised my gaze and looked out over the bay. There wasn't a puff of a breeze and the surface was mirror glass smooth. Above me stars were beginning to appear and, with them, some constellations I was somewhat familiar with. I could just make out Cassiopeia, the lazy W, low above the trees over the ridge to my left. Straight overhead was Ursa Major, The Big Dipper.

I took a deep breath, savoring the pine scented aroma of nearby evergreen trees. The air was still, not a leaf or pine needle moved. Once my ears adapted to the silence I began to hear the sounds of the night: The calling of a loon out on the lake over toward the Canadian side, the hooting of an owl somewhere behind me, the splashing of the otter as it moved further way down the shore. The sounds of the north country.

"...and then this one guy, I think he's from New Jersey, started in about..."

Geez. Leslie. The night was so still, I could suddenly hear her voice coming clearly from my phone. I reached for it and checked the time. She'd been talking non-stop for almost twelve minutes, and I hadn't paid attention to a thing she said. In fact, the longer I was on the shore, supposedly listening to my girlfriend, it was becoming apparent I really didn't care all that much about what she was saying or what she was talking about. She cared about her job, and I didn't. It was a simple as that. Did that feeling extend to her as a person as well? Did I really not care all that much about her, even though I'd told myself (and her) time and time again that I did? Had I, in fact, being lying to myself, and to her, all along? Very good questions. I wondered what that meant for the future of our relationship. Probably very not much. In fact, was it even fair that I continued to see her as a boyfriend girlfriend kind of thing and lead her on given the realization of how I truly felt? Was I really that kind of a shitty person? Hmm. I'd like to think not. Damn, I had figure this out.

On top of it all, I had Shelia back at the campfire to deal with.

I suddenly made a snap decision. "Hey, Leslie," I said, interrupting her telling me another anecdote about her class, "sorry, but I've got to go. Text me if you want."

I disconnected the call without even waiting for her reply. Then I turned my phone off.

Did I feel bad about how I had just treated her? No. Not really. I mean, we really weren't all that committed to each other, were we? We were just having a good time. Right? Damn, maybe I really was a shitty person.

I put aside my guilty thoughts of Leslie and looked out over the water. By now, night had completely fallen and it was nearly pitch black out. Above me the stars were beginning to blanket the sky with a wash of white that was stunning to behold, a million pin-pricks of light. I took a deep breath and exhaled, hoping to rid myself of work and Leslie. I'm not sure I was one-hundred percent successful, but I will say this: I was glad to have been on the shore of Beaver Bay in the middle of nowhere right then. The peace and quiet were a welcome balm. Even though it was hard to see, I could see well enough to know that there was no place in the world I'd rather be at that moment than right where I was.

With the sun down, the air was starting to turn cool. I was dressed in loose fitting hiking shorts, waffle soled hiking boots, a tee shirt, flannel shirt, and a Minnesota Wild baseball cap, but I still felt an involuntary shiver run through me. I needed to get back to the campfire and Shelia and face whatever wrath she'd cooked up to dish out. *What a great trip*, I thought factiously, starting to feel a little sorry for myself for having to face the music. Well, my problems were my own making, and I had no one to blame but myself. I sighed again and tried to mentally prepare myself, but with little success. Anyway, there was one good thing. At least I'd been able to see the otter.

I stood up and started through the woods, happy I'd thought to put a flashlight app on my iphone. It took me about ten minutes to get within range of our campsite. When I could see the campfire flickering through the trees, I turned the flashlight off, thinking for some reason it would be interesting to sneak up on Shelia and see what she was up to. I was cautiously making my way toward the light from the fire when I realized she wasn't there. Perplexed, I snuck closer, stepping carefully through the pine needle duff on the forest floor while keeping myself shielded by hiding behind tree trunks. At the edge of the tree line I stopped and looked up and down the shore. I didn't see her anywhere.

I was just about to step into the open when I heard a voice. It was Shelia. I could tell she was somewhere in front of me, but where? I looked more closely but it was so dark the only thing I could see was the glow of the campfire and the chairs we'd been sitting on, and she certainly wasn't there. I couldn't see her anywhere. I listened carefully before figuring it out. She wasn't on land or near the campfire, where I'd expected her to be. She had used the ladder attached to the side of the cabin to climb up on top of the houseboat. She was standing with her back to me, her hand pressed to the side of her head, and, surprise, surprise, she was talking on her iphone just like I'd been doing. Who could she possibly be speaking with? I wanted to run out in the open and yell something at her but had no idea what to say, so I stayed put and listened. By now my ears were adjusted to the quiet stillness of the woods. Even though I'm sure she was trying to speak softly, her voice was loud and clear in the calm night air. I could hear every word.

"Yeah, Logan, you can't believe the crap I put up with from him. He ran off into the woods somewhere. I hope he gets eaten by a bear. I mean...What? Oh, I know, not really, but my god, he's such a world class jerk, and that's putting it mildly. I don't know why I bother staying with him."

Well, by now I was more than curious. I was perplexed. What was she doing, standing up there talking to someone, this Logan character? Who the hell was he? What was going on?

I almost broke from my hiding place in the trees right then and there but didn't. I decided I wanted to find out more, maybe pick up a few clues, and see if I could get a handle on this secret life my wife appeared to be leading. So I kept quiet, stayed hidden and listened. After a minute it became clear she was talking to someone one who was more than just a friend. Much, much more.

"Yes, I miss you, too, honey. So much. I miss being with you. I miss your arms around me. Right now I'm picturing us..."

Honey? Well, I didn't need to hear that. And listen to her tell him what she was picturing? I certainly didn't need to hear that either. But I made the unfortunate decision to keep listening. I shouldn't have. Even though I couldn't see them, my ears, I'm sure, were burning red when she was done describing what she was picturing.

It didn't take long to figure out that my wife of twenty-three years was having an affair, sneaking around behind my back and spending time with this Logan bozo. Unbelievable. And, believe you me, the irony that I was doing basically the same thing with Leslie wasn't escaping me. Not one little bit. What a mess our marriage had become.

After listening for maybe five minutes, I'd had enough. I stepped out of the shadows of the forest and yelled up at her. "Hey, up there! What's going on? Who the hell are you talking to?"

Shelia quickly ended the call. The roof was flat and she walked toward the edge and called down, "Where'd you go? What were you doing?" I couldn't help but notice that she was avoiding my question.

"I went for a walk," I said, pointing behind me, as if it wasn't obvious enough, "Back to the bay behind us. I was watching the sunset. I even saw an..." Wait a minute. Who cared where I went and what I saw? There was something more important that needed discussing; this Logan guy and what Shelia was doing with him. I needed to get the conversation back on track. "Never mind where I went. I heard you on the phone just now. Who were you talking to?" I demanded.

Shelia started down the ladder and said, "Who, me? I was just talking to a friend."

"Ha!" I barked out a laugh. "Sounded like more than a just friend to me," I said, mimicking friend and using my fingers to make quotes in the air. I can be pretty dramatic if I need to be.

Shelia jumped off the ladder and laughed right back at me. She was on the deck and I was on shore. Maybe twenty feet separated us. In the faint glow of the campfire, I could see daggers in her eyes, and they were directed right at me. I don't think I'd ever seen her so mad. "Yeah, a friend. Probably like your little friend at work. What's her name again? Leslie?"

There was a wooden gangplank leading from the front deck to the sandy beach the houseboat was parked on. She hurried down it, pushed past me, and covered the twenty-five feet to the campfire in about a second. She was steaming. With her back to me, she stood watching the flames for a moment, her arms folded tight across her chest, quivering in anger. I thought maybe she was taking a few moments to try and calm down, but I was wrong. Way wrong.

I stomped through the sand, wanting to get an explanation about who this Logan guy was, conveniently forgetting I had been doing essentially the same thing with Leslie less than fifteen minutes earlier.

When I got behind Sheila, she turned and got right in my face, spitting out, "Don't deny it, Ben. I've known about her ever since that stupid team building thing you went to last spring."

No way, I thought to myself. *No friggin' way could she have known about that.* And right then and there I should have kept my mouth shut. But I didn't. Instead, I asked, "Leslie? Her? How'd you know about...?"

Oops. Oh, shit.

Shelia laughed, "See? Got you." She shook her head sadly at my incompetence and said, "God, you are such an idiot."

I'd admitted to my affair with Leslie without Shelia having to do anything other than accuse me of it. She was right, I was an idiot.

Shelia turned away and walked to the other side of the fire where her folding lawn chair was. She sat down, reached into the front pocket of her jeans, and took out a pack of cigarettes. She shook one out and lit up, inhaling deep and holding it before blowing a stream of smoke into the night. I watched it separate and fall apart as it drifted away. I felt kind of like the smoke, drifting and scattered. I wasn't prepared to have to face telling Shelia about Leslie. For some reason I thought I'd be able to keep my affair hidden. Who was I kidding? Shelia was a smart woman. Astute, as well. I should have known I was only living on borrowed time and she'd eventually figure it out, which she'd obviously done at some point. What was I going to do now? What was my next step going to be?

Shelia is five-five and very tan and fit from her work out regime. She was dressed in cutoff jeans, a yellow tank top and hiking boots. At some point since I'd stormed off earlier she'd put on a blue flannel shirt to ward off the chill. She wore it unbuttoned. She was wearing a red bandana as a head band to keep her long auburn hair pulling back. She had an oval face, gray-green eyes, and high, prominent cheekbones. To me, she'd always been pretty, and she still was. But right now she was angry and boiling mad. She stared at me, daring me to say something, anything. I knew a huge fight was brewing, but I wasn't in the frame of mind just then to argue. I still had a little bit of a leftover tranquil feeling from seeing the otter. Besides, I had to collect my thoughts.

I went over to the edge of the woods to the pile of logs I'd cut up earlier and picked up a few. I went back to the campfire and tossed them in, watching the red and orange sparks fly up into the night, marveling for a moment at their beauty. I walked to the shore, looked out over the still waters of the bay into the darkness, and breathed the scented air emanating from the pine forest. Behind me, the fire crackled as the new logs caught. It was a calm night and a peaceful setting. I should have been captivated by the magical spell of the north woods and been in a relaxed and mellow mood, but I wasn't. Far from it. Deep down my heart was doing summersaults; my mind racing.

I was mad at Shelia about Logan, that was for sure, but I was also mad at myself. Shelia now knew about Leslie. It had been much easier to accept my affair with her when I felt like I was pulling the wool over Shelia's eyes. But my wife was smart and I should have known better. Most people would agree that Shelia was the brains of the operation when it came to our marriage, and I'd have to begrudgingly agree. Plus, honestly, now that the truth was out about Leslie and me, I had to consider what my true feelings for her really were.

I liked Leslie, yes. A lot. But, as I said earlier, a pleasant diversion would be as apt a description as I could give. Could I picture being with her long term, her being eighteen years younger than me and in the prime of her life, only eight years older than my daughter? Leslie with me, a middle-aged guy who puttered around in his garden, collected tin toys, and hated his job? I was already going gray, for Pete's sake. Well, when I looked at it that way, the answer honestly was no. There was no realistic long-term relationship possibility there.

I walked back to the fire and sat down in my own lawn chair. Shelia and I had a lot to talk about. I glanced over to gauge her mood. We had both quit smoking years ago and it surprised me that she was smoking now, but, I guess given the circumstances, it was to be expected. She lit another cigarette and sat taping a foot in the sand, waiting, I was sure, for me to make the first move and to begin the conversation. Or, at least defend my actions with Leslie. Well, that made sense and I was all for it, but I was unsure where to begin. And, truthfully, I wasn't ready to feel the wrath of her anger.

So guess what I did? I took a safe route. Of all the things we had to talk about (Shelia and Logan topping the list, with me and Leslie coming in a close second), and all of the things I could have brought up, the first words that came out of my mouth were, "I didn't know you'd started smoking again."

If looks could kill, hers would have done it. Ten times over. Shelia calmly put the cigarette to her mouth, took a long drag and blew the smoke right at me. Then she said, "What the hell do you care, anyway?"

I thought back to my one-sided conversation earlier with Leslie. It had centered on the only thing we had in common, work, something I really had no interest in. I'd much preferred standing on the shore of Beaver Bay at sunset, watching the otter swim by as the day drew to a close and the stars were beginning to appear, instead of listening as she droned on and on about her job and the class she was teaching. The dichotomy was too apparent. My job was a means to an end, income for me and my family. Any passion for my work I'd had at the beginning of my career was long gone. Leslie's career was just beginning. She loved her job and that was good for her. I didn't care about mine and really didn't care all that much about the things she was interested in. Was it fair to stay with her given those kinds of feelings? When I got right down to it and was totally honest with myself, the answer, like before, was no. Not fair at all.

Take Leslie and our three or four-month affair out of the picture and look at Shelia and me. We had a history. We'd been married for twenty-three years and had been together for two years prior to that. We had kids. We had a home. We had a life we'd built together. And...and here's the crux of the matter...we had found a way to stay together in spite of the fact that we'd drifted apart. We were still married. We were still with each other. Maybe I still did care about Shelia more than I thought I did. Maybe we could begin to do what we said we were going to do on this trip, start to patch our marriage together. It had definite possibilities.

But did I tell my wife any of that, any of the personal things I was thinking about? No, not at all. Instead, I turned in my chair toward her and asked, "Say, can I have one of your smokes?"

Silently she tossed me the pack. Then she tossed me her lighter and gave me a resigned sigh. "Go for it."

Looking back, I think she would have liked me to have asked a different question. But you know guys and our ability to express deep emotional feelings. Not our strong suit. So I didn't.

Instead, I lit up and we sat quietly smoking, each lost in our own thoughts. I knew I should have asked about Logan. How long had they been together? How often did they see each other? Did she have strong feelings for him? Stuff like that. The more I thought about it, though, the more I wondered, did I really want to know about the two of them and them being together? Frankly, the answer was no, not really. It'd be a painful discussion and hard to hear the details of, if not more than a little embarrassing. It was enough to come face to face with the fact that Shelia, in her own way, was as dissatisfied with our marriage as I was. She'd rebelled with Logan, me with Leslie. Point taken. What more was there to say?

As I smoked, I glanced over at Shelia. She was gazing into the fire, lost in her own world. I figured she'd want to know about me and Leslie. In fact, I was preparing myself to tell her everything she wanted to know and take my medicine, but she surprised me. She didn't ask about her at all. Instead, she was quiet and contemplative. Maybe I should have asked about Logan, but I didn't. I tried to tell myself that what was done was done, but that would have been too simple of a statement. I mean, Shelia and Logan were obviously a couple. They had been sleeping together, just like Leslie and me. It was clear there was a lot to discuss, but we didn't open up and start talking. We just sat and watched the fire while the north woods night deepened and closed in around us. In a way, the darkness was like a comforting blanket, which was strange because we were so far apart emotionally.

The longer we remained silent, though, the more it became clear that each of us was taking the safe route by avoiding the inevitable fight with all its attendant yelling and screaming. Maybe being by the campfire, in the quiet of a Rainy Lake summer's evening, with the occasional owl hooting nearby and loon calling over the open water, sounds we never heard back home, maybe that helped to set a different tone between us. Maybe it mellowed us. Whatever the case, what we ended up doing was this: We avoided all of our issues and, instead, sat and smoked the occasional cigarette, looked at the fire, looked at the night, and looked at the stars.

After a while, Leslie said, "Pretty night out, isn't it?"

Her words broke the angry spell that had settled over us. I made it a point of looking straight up into the sky. It looked like it had been spray painted with stars. There was no moon. I could see so clearly it almost hurt my eyes. I picked out a few more constellations and a couple of stars I knew the names of and pointed them out to Shelia. She cracked the barest of smiles and nodded. Behind me the owl hooted again. The pine scented air mingled with the aroma of the fire. The night was so still and peaceful, it almost brought a tear to my eye. It occurred to me that this might be the last time I would ever be on Rainy Lake, and it made me sad. My marriage was over. That much was clear. My wife was with some other guy. My girlfriend was soon to be a distant memory. I hated my job. My life was a mess.

After a few moments of silence, I answered, "Yeah, it really is a pretty night out." In retrospect, my inability to express my feelings to my wife was so painfully evident that it was no wonder she'd become interested in someone else. I sounded like a fool. Or, as Shelia had put so succinctly, a little while earlier, an idiot. That's what I had become in her eyes. Man, let me tell you this, it was certainly nothing to be proud of.

Interestingly, though, in the end, we never did fight. We hesitantly started speaking to each other, mostly about inane things like the stars and the sky. Safe things. In fact, we ended up staying up late talking about everything other than the two elephants on the shore: Leslie and Logan. Maybe we were too exhausted to get into anything that heavy. Maybe we had given up on salvaging our relationship. Maybe we'd each silently accepted that our marriage was over. Whatever the case, it appeared we had reached a sort mutually agreed upon truce where we knew arguing and fighting wasn't going to solve any of the myriad of problems that had spread like a cancer during all the years we'd been together. Why bother talking about something that was dead, over, and done for? Why, indeed? Besides, how could I give Shelia shit about Logan when I'd been with Leslie. What a mess.

Anyway, it wasn't as bad sitting on the lakeshore with Shelia as it could have been. Not by a long shot. At one point, I even went inside the cabin of the houseboat, got out some Hersey's bars, and brought them back to where sat. We each had a couple, our nod to a smores-less campfire experience. We smoked a few more cigarettes, too. I checked my phone once when Shelia went onto the boat for a jacket. There was a text from Leslie. "Miss U!!" Geez. I deleted it and didn't text her back. I had nothing to say.

We turned in around midnight after the fire burned down to red-hot coals. Shelia took the bed. I took the floor. We had decided to take the boat back to Northern Lights base camp the next morning and return it. Neither us were in the mood to work on a plan to patch up our marriage. We were both silently accepting the fact that the rifts were too many and too big and our marriage was finished. The next morning we'd start the eighteen-mile trip back to base. If the weather held, it'd only take about four hours. We'd be at Northern Lights by noon if we were slow. We didn't intend to be. There was no reason to take our time. Our vacation on Rainy Lake, like our marriage, was over for good.

***

It was a loud 'THUD' that woke me. Shelia, too. "What the hell was that?" she muttered.

She sounded sleepy but was coming awake fast. I was, too. It sounded like something heavy had landed on the roof. The inside of the cabin was gray with early dawn, but it was light enough for me to see her eyes were wide open, the whites showing. The sound startled her. Me, too.

"I don't know," I told her. I was rattled and hadn't a clue as to what was going on. Then I became aware of the houseboat groaning; shaking and bashing itself up on the shore. Something wasn't right.

I scrambled to my feet and looked out the sliding glass door leading to the front deck. Oh, no! I couldn't believe my eyes. A storm had come up overnight, and the wind was blowing like hell. In our emotionally exhausted state, we'd slept right through it. Now, though, our exhaustion was immediately replaced by adrenaline. In a moment we were both wide awake and alert. The wind was a gale like I'd never seen before. Three-foot waves were crashing on the beach. Rain was pouring down and the shoreline had been eaten away by gullies of rainwater flowing out of the forest. Twigs, branches, and tree debris were falling on us, and I made a guess (later proven correct) that a big branch must have landed on the roof and awakened us.

The houseboat had been blown sideways on the shore and the waves were smashing up against it, banging it hard and threatening to damage it beyond repair. I'd heard about these sudden storms and how they could blow up without a moment's notice and apparently that's what had happened. All had been calm when we'd gone to bed, but that wasn't the case now. I silently cursed myself for not having checked the weather forecast on either my phone or the boat's short-wave radio before we'd gone to bed. Too much on my mind, I guess.

I pulled on my boots and ran onto the deck to take a look around. I couldn't believe what I was seeing. Everywhere I looked, the storm was wreaking havoc. I saw a number of pine trees that had been blown over, one leaning precariously on another which was all that was keeping it from falling onto the houseboat. If it did, we'd be trapped for who knew how long. The waves had destroyed the shoreline completely, leaving hardly any beach. The sideways houseboat was jammed up on what little beach and was stuck solid. The wind was howling and the rain was pelting down so hard it hurt. I rushed back inside for protection.

"My god," I told Shelia, "it's like a monsoon and hurricane combined out there." Then I filled her in on what I'd seen.

"What are we going to do?" she asked when I'd finished.

"Let's call base."

"I already tried. There's no signal."

"Shit." I went to the sliding glass door and looked out again. Shelia joined me. The rain, which had been buffeting the boat in sheets, seemed to be letting up. The gray pre-dawn was turning a little lighter. I turned to her. "Any ideas?"

One thing I've always admired about Shelia was her ability to not let things get to her. She was a solutions-orientated woman, a good person to have in a crisis, and that's what this was. I'd never in my life seen a storm like I was seeing right now.

She took one more look outside as a branch fell hard on the deck. Then she turned to me and said, "We need a plan. Do you think you can get us off the shore? You could use the dingy to pull us. I'll drive the houseboat. If we can get unstuck and get out on the lake, maybe we can get back to base."

It was as good a plan as any, even though base camp at Northern Lights was eighteen miles away. First things first. We needed to get free of the beach. Besides, her idea was way better than what I'd come up with, which was nothing.

"Let's do it," I said. I put on my jean jacket and baseball hat and went out into the storm. My hat blew off in an instant. I never saw it again.

Northern Lights had a rule that every houseboat had to have a rowboat for emergencies. Since we didn't own such a boat, we rented one from them, a twelve-foot aluminum Grumman with a ten horsepower motor, and towed it behind us from base to where we were on Scalawag Bay. Yesterday, when we made camp, I'd untied the dinghy and dragged it through the water down the shore about fifty feet from us. Then I pulled it up on the sand and secured it with a long rope to a pine tree. That's where I headed. I was wearing my hiking shorts and hiking boots. I had on a tee shirt and a long-sleeved cotton shirt under my jean jacket. It took about ten seconds before I was soaked to the skin.

Once I got to the dinghy my spirits immediately faltered. The little boat was jammed up on the sand and filled to the gunnels with rainwater. Fortunately, the plastic scoop bucket used for bailing was still tied to the engine and hadn't blown away. I untied it and started franticly scooping and dumping rainwater. It seemed to take forever before the boat was finally empty enough to attempt to drive. Shelia told me later it'd really only taken about five minutes. She also told me she was impressed by how fast I worked. It was a little thing, maybe, but I took it for what it was, a compliment, not something either of us was freely giving out at that stage of our marriage.

With the boat empty, I made my way through the branches and twigs and other debris on what was left of the shore to the edge of the forest to untie the rope. On the way I got hit in the head with a branch about an inch in diameter and maybe six feet long. My adrenaline must have been really pumping because I didn't feel a thing. In a moment, though, blood started trickling into my eyes. I wiped it away with a quick swipe and took a look at my hand. It wasn't too bad; not much blood. I figured the rain running down my face would clean the wound out and didn't think about it again.

I untied the knot and hurried back to the dinghy, coiling the rope with me as I ran. I threw it under the front seat when I got there. In just that short period of time, the little boat had been blown sideways onto the beach, but it was easy enough to drag the back end out into the water. The problem was that the waves were working against me and kept beating the boat back toward shore. I was finally able to get the back end steady by staying in the water and holding on. I waited for a break in the waves. When one came, I jumped in, primed the gas tank, tilted the motor's propeller into the water, and pulled on the starter cord. It sputtered and died. It took three frantic tries to get the little motor going, but I finally did, just before a big wave hit and tried to throw the boat back on the beach. I jammed the motor into reverse and backed quickly away from the shore.

With the waves pounding the shoreline controlling the boat was hard, but when I was able to get it away from the beach, maneuvering was somewhat easier. When I felt I was under as control as I could be, I looked toward the houseboat. Shelia was outside on the deck under the overhang in front watching. I could tell she'd cleared the roof and the deck of all the branches that had fallen on it. Like I said, she was a great person to have in a crisis. When she saw I was free of the shore, she waved excitedly and gave me the thumbs-up sign. I signaled back to her. I also took a deep breath and let it out. So far so good.

Next, I had to drive to the houseboat, tie on the rope, and somehow drag it off the beach. In my mind I calculated my chances, figuring that maybe a ten percent probability of success was realistic. Better than nothing, I grimly told myself.

I gritted my teeth and worked my way through the waves away from shore. The dinghy took in water but not enough to worry about. At least not for right now, just a few inches sloshing in the bottom. As I got close to the houseboat, I set the throttle on idle and carefully climbed to the front of my boat, got the rope, made my way back, and tied it to one of the gunnels next to the motor.

Then, as I tried to position the little dinghy, Shelia stationed herself on the back corner of the houseboat, ready for the next step.

"Try to get as close as you can," she yelled. "Then toss me the rope."

Trying to maneuver a twelve-foot aluminum boat rocking all over the place in two to three-foot waves was not easy. The little dinghy was bobbing like a cork in a hurricane, which in retrospect, it pretty much was. Doing all that maneuvering while driving backward was even harder.

It took some getting used to, but I was eventually able to get close enough to Shelia to throw the rope. The first time I tossed it, the wind caught it like it was a piece of string and blew it way off course. I only missed by about ten feet. (I'm being facetious. I wasn't even that close. The wind was really strong.) I pulled the rope in through the water, coiled it up, and tried again. This time Shelia was able to grab it. Yea. Success! We both gave out weak cheers. It wasn't much, but at least it was something. We were making headway and that's all that mattered.

Shelia tied the rope to the back corner railing and yelled. "Okay! We're all set. You try to pull us off the beach. Once we get into deeper water I'll try and get this baby started."

"Okay! Good luck!"

She gave me a determined smile and another thumbs-up. I have to say, it felt good to be working as a team right then. It was something we used to do really well together, way back before the shit that became our marriage hit the fan.

I returned Shelia's thumbs-up with my own and also gave her my own version of a determined smile, which probably turned out to be more of a grimace than anything else. But I was committed to doing the best I could. In my head, I prayed a silent prayer, and I'm not at all a religious person. Right now, though, any port in the storm, so to speak.

With the rope securely tied to the houseboat, I positioned the dinghy to pull straight back. Then I jammed the throttle forward to high and held on. The little motor whined and whined as it dug into the water, kicking up a deep wake. I watched the rope. It was a one-inch thick, braided utility rope, the kind you'd find on any serious water vessel (which our houseboat was.) If I thought it might break, I was soon proven wrong. It held fast.

Unfortunately, the heavy houseboat didn't budge.

Shelia came out of the cabin to encourage me. "Run the dingy back and forth. Work it at different angles."

I was out about twenty feet. The big waves were throwing me all over the place, threatening to smash me into the back end of the houseboat. Not only that, there was the very real threat that I might start taking in more water and get swamped. But I was learning on the fly so to speak, and was able to keep the dinghy from capsizing by judging when the waves would break and then riding the troughs between the crests up and down. I was also able to keep myself away from smashing into the houseboat. So that was good. Now, all I had to do was figure out a way to move it. Shelia's advice made sense.

I waved back, and yelled, "I'll try!" I gunned the motor and drove to the left. Then to the right. Back and forth, back and forth, the rope straining. Nothing happened. The houseboat didn't budge.

After a few minutes of getting nowhere, I took a break to let the little motor rest and idle while I rocked on the waves. A couple of things happened while I was struggling to free the houseboat. One, the rain had completely stopped. Two, the day was now less grey. I figured it must be around seven in the morning.

Shelia had been watching my progress or lack of it the entire time. She called out, encouraging me, "I think I feel it starting to give. Keep at it. I'm pretty sure this is going to work."

I yelled back."Okay. I'll get to it."

I positioned myself so the rope was taut and turned the throttle to full once again. The little motor responded and the dinghy jumped forward. Back and forth, left and right, and back and forth, right and left, I went, fighting the waves, the rope straining. I was making no progress at all and starting to get discouraged. Were we going to stay stranded here in Scalawag Bay for who knew how long, getting beaten by the wind and waves and battered by the storm forever? It was not a pleasant thought.

I'd been driving back and forth for maybe ten minutes and beginning to give up hope that our plan was never going to succeed. Then, all of a sudden I felt the houseboat shift a little. A glimmer rose in my chest. Could we do this? Maybe? I positioned myself so I was right off the corner where the rope was tied and pulled straight back, gunning the motor and saying another silent prayer. I felt the houseboat gave some more. Could it be? I leaned into the throttle and held my breath.

On the houseboat, Shelia was elatedly jumping up and down. "I can feel it move, Ben! Gun it some more!"

I already was, but, what the hell. I yelled back. "Here goes!" I leaned into the throttle one more time.

The rope strained. And strained some more. And the corner of the houseboat moved a little bit. And then some more, little by little, until, all in an instant, the big houseboat broke free of the sand and the back end swung out away from shore. When it did, we both cheered, "Yea!" We'd done it.

Shelia yelled. "Hold it steady, if you can. I'll try to get the motor started."

She ran inside to the cabin where the controls were. I tried to hold the heavy houseboat steady, but it was hard. The wind and waves wanted to blow it right back on shore. I had all I could do to keep the back end just far enough out off the beach so that when

Shelia got the engine running, it would be in deep enough water so the propeller wouldn't smash on an underwater bolder and break. If that happened, we'd really be up shit creek.

After a minute, I heard the engine turn over. I held my breath as it ground away. The power came from a battery and I hoped it would hold its charge long enough to get us started. After maybe half a minute of grinding, instead of the battery dying, we lucked out; the engine coughed and then started. Shelia revved it once for good luck.

I yelled, into the wind, "Yea! Way to go, Shelia! Way to go!"

I knew she couldn't hear me, but I didn't care. It was a big moment. We might make it out of this yet. From inside the cabin, the horn tooted. Shelia was ready to go. I drove the dinghy close enough to untie the rope, freeing it from the houseboat. Then I backed up out of the way. Slowly but steadily Sheila backed the big boat away from shore out a hundred feet or so into the bay. Then she turned the boat around and held it steady into the wind while I drove the dinghy up next to it. I grabbed the side, killed the motor, and scrambled onto the deck. Then I tied the dinghy to the back railing and left twenty feet of slack in the rope so we could tow it behind us. When I was all set, I went inside through the back door and made my way to the cabin where Shelia sat at the captain's chair, looking out the front window.

I was fired up with our newly won success and ready to congratulate her (and us) on our hard-won victory. I took one look at Shelia, though, and stopped. Her expression was grim. She wasn't happy at all.

She pointed out the window. "My god, Ben, look..." Words failed her.

I'd been so focused on getting the houseboat free from the shore that I hadn't been paying any attention to what was going on out past the bay we were in; out on the big lake. Rainy. I followed her line of vision and I'm not sure, but I probably turned green or at least pale, when I saw what was waiting for us out there. I know one thing: If I thought the waves in our bay were big, I had another think coming. Out on Rainy Lake, they were enormous, five feet high at least.

Scalawag Bay was small, as bays went, maybe twenty or thirty acres total, shaped like a horseshoe. Where the ends of the horseshoe came together was the entrance. It was guarded by a small island maybe fifty feet across comprised of jagged granite boulders and wind-bent jack pine trees. Once we navigated past the island we'd be on the main part of Rainy Lake, a big, narrow lake that ran east and west. The wind was blowing out of the west. Our bay was at the far east end. Northern Lights was at the far west end. We'd have to travel from where we were eighteen miles into the wind to get to base. The distance and the wind were two things. The huge waves we had to contend with were another. I grabbed a pair of binoculars to get a better look. It was foreboding. The waves were gigantic, the biggest I'd ever seen, at least four or five feet high. The wind was pushing them in swells that left dangerous, deep troughs between the crests. I pictured our little twenty-five-foot houseboat out there and the image of a child's toy boat being tossed around like a leaf on the ocean came to mind. It was not a comforting vision. Our boat was made of heavy-duty aluminum, but was it strong enough to withstand the pounding of the waves out there? God, I didn't know. I sure hoped so.

I handed the binoculars to Shelia. "Have a look," I told her. "What do you think?"

After a minute, she handed them back to me. "Let's call base one more time. See what they want us to do."

The shortwave radio was on the wall next to the steering wheel. I turned it on. There was power and that was a good thing. Unfortunately, there was nothing but static on the airwaves. I tried to call out to base a few times, but nothing went through. Like our phones, communication was impossible. We'd have to decide what to do on our own.

Shelia had set the boat idling in neutral while we deliberated our next move, and the waves were beginning to push us back toward shore. She put the engine in gear and we motored into the middle of our little bay where she cut the throttle and kept us pointed both toward the island and away from shore. Compared to the big lake, the waves in Scalawag, at two or three feet, were relatively small. But still, to inexperienced drivers like us, they were challenging. On second thought, even to experienced operators, manipulating the houseboat in these kinds waves would be hard. Then there was the big lake. I didn't want to think about what it'd be like out on Rainy. If it was hard going on Scalawag Bay, it would be ten times worse out on Rainy. At least. Daunting was the word that came to mind and stuck. I started to lose what little confidence I'd had. How would we ever be able to make it back to base?

Shelia broke into my thoughts. "We've got to get across Rainy." She pointed behind us. "We can't go back on shore. The waves will just beat the boat to hell. We've got to figure out a plan."

I looked back to where we'd set up camp the day before. The smooth sand beach was now littered with branches and tree debris. Rain water running out of the forest had carved out deep canyons while waves relentlessly pounded what little shoreline was left. There was no place to beach the boat even if we wanted to. We both turned and looked out toward the big lake. Like Shelia had said, we'd have to come up with a plan to get us across it. Good idea. I glanced at her and could see the wheels already turning as her mind worked through various scenarios. She was good with those kinds of things, figuring out plans and implementing them.

But, me? Maybe it was shock at our situation, but I'm afraid at that moment I started to cop out on figuring out what to do.

Instead, I started envisioning us safely back home in Orchard Lake, the warm sun shining brightly on my face as I worked peacefully in the garden, planting marigolds and stopping occasionally to sip on a refreshing glass of iced tea. Not a very useful thought, given the situation we were in. Fortunately, Shelia was not like me. She had put her brain to good use. She grabbed me by the shoulder and shook me back to reality.

"We'd better make a run for it," she said.,"Let's try to get out on the big lake, get this bad boy pointed into the wind, and see if we can make it to base." She took my face in both her hands and turned my head so I was looking directly at her. There was a hint of fear in her eyes, but that wasn't the only thing I saw. There was determination present, as well. A lot of it. And courage. Her fearlessness helped get me focused and back on track.

"Do you think we can do it?" I asked.

"I don't think we have a choice, do you?"

I picked up the binoculars and took another look at the waves raging on Rainy. I made myself choke down my fear. Her confidence was contagious. I turned and looked at my wife. She had more will and strength of character in her on a normal day than I had on my best day. Or a year of my best days, when it came right down to it. If she was willing to make the drive, so was I.

"Let's do it," I said, hoping I sounded more confident than I felt.

"Good man!" She clapped me on the shoulder in a show of solidarity. Then she took another long look at Rainy through the binoculars before turning to me. "Flip to see who drives?"

"Sure," I said, gamely. "You're on."

She dug in her jeans and pulled out a quarter. "You flip or me?"

"Go ahead."

She flipped, caught the quarter and smacked it on her hand. "Call."

"Heads," I said.

She removed her hand. It was heads. "You drive," she said. "Then she grinned, the first time all morning. "At least for a little while."

I rubbed my hands together to get them warm and to keep them from shaking. Then I nervously took the wheel, sucked in a breath, and exhaled, getting myself mentally prepared. Who was I kidding? I'd never be ready. But I had to give it my best shot.

Shelia was standing next to me. Her presence calmed me. She said, "You can do it, Ben. Just take it slow and easy."

I appreciated her vote of confidence, something I wouldn't have cast a ballot on. But, we were a team, right? I turned to her and said, "I'll do my best."

She smiled at me, "I know you will."

It was a pretty serious moment.

I made myself ease the throttle forward. The houseboat moved slowly ahead, waves pounding against it and occasionally breaking over the bow, causing water to splash up on the sliding glass front door and the windshield. I could see well enough to drive, though, and motored on. We carefully made our way across the rest of the bay, the houseboat rocking more and more on the swells as we came up to and then passed the little island. Shelia stood next to me, holding tightly to the side of my captains chair, a term I use only in the most basic sense of the word. A skilled houseboat driver I wasn't. A captain, never, but I was willing to do my best.

After a few minutes of driving, I was starting to get used to the rolling motion of the boat and learning to read the water and ride the waves. In fact, I was even beginning to feel somewhat confident about my ability to navigate. That was a feeling that wasn't going to last long.

While in Scalawag Bay, the trees and rocks on the island offered minimal protection, but at least it was something. Once I guided us past the island, however, the full force of the west wind caught us and threw the front end of the houseboat hard to the right. At that moment a huge wave hit the side with a booming crash, causing us to rock dangerously and the engine to lift out of the water, screaming in protest. For one terrifying moment I thought we were going to capsize.

I grabbed the wheel tightly and pulled us back so we were pointed into the wind and the oncoming swells. I fought to hold us steady as each incoming wave raised the bow up in the air where we hung suspended for a moment before slamming down, shaking us to our bones and the boat to the rivets that held it together. Every single wave that hit the front of the boat broke over the bow and deck and flooded into the cabin before streaming back out again. In a minute the indoor outdoor carpeting was saturated and squishing under our boots.

I looked at Shelia as I tried to hold the rocking boat steady. "Christ, do you think we can do this?"

She squeezed my shoulder and said, "We'd better. I don't think we have any other choice."

Talk about an understatement. But she was right. We had no alternative but to do our best to fight through the wind and the waves and navigate the eighteen miles across the lake to Northern Lights base camp.

"Okay, then," I said. "Hold on."

I pushed the throttle forward and we moved ahead out onto the big lake. Oh, man, let me tell you, it was a trip I'll never forget.

Rainy Lake is fed from the Kettle River to the east. It's part of the Hudson Bay water shed which includes the Boundary Waters Canoe Area Wildness, Superior National Forest in Minnesota and the Quetico Provencal Park in Canadian. To the west, the lake drains into the Rainy River near International Falls, Minnesota, a river which forms part of the border between the United States and Canada. From the Kettle Falls to International Falls is roughly forty miles, roughly half of that distance taken up by Rainy Lake. In other words, it's a big friggin' body of water.

In fact, it's actually two lakes in one, the upper and the lower. We were toward the east end in the upper lake and had to fight our way across it to a narrow channel called the Brule Narrows that led to the lower lake. Normally the trip would take around thirty minutes. Today, getting to the channel took us until one in the afternoon, about six hours. It was a bitch the whole way. We could have walked that distance faster in different circumstances.

I kept the throttle about half speed. We just couldn't go any fast for fear that we'd do damage to the boat. Even though it was heavy gage aluminum, I could just picture what would happen if one of the big floats that supported the cabin suddenly gave way and broke free. I shuddered at the thought. I kept a firm grip on the wheel and fought every single wave that hit the boat as it tried to throw us off course. Or capsize us. It was exhausting.

Shelia stood by me the entire way to the Brule Narrows, offering encouragement. The cabin was enclosed and protected from the wind. That helped. We got used to the water from the waves crashing over the bow rushing into and out of the cabin. We more than once told each other that we were glad we were wearing our water proof hiking boots. Sheila was also able to fix us a small pot of coffee which we shared along with one or two cigarettes. She even cleaned the cut on my forehead.

We were so focused on the task at hand, though, we didn't talk much. What was there to say? But we were working together, that was the important thing. Plus, we weren't fighting about Leslie and Logan. We seemed to have reached a détente of sorts, and were more focused on battling the waves and keeping the houseboat afloat than anything else. I was fine with that. I'd pretty much decided to end things with Leslie anyway. The more I thought about it, the more the different in our ages and life experiences seemed more than enough reason for me to grow up, get my head out of my ass and call it quits.

By the time we'd crossed the upper lake my arms were so tired I could barely hold onto the steering wheel, but I had done my best. At least we'd made it. The entrance to the Brule Narrows was marked by large buoys. I worked the boat past them into the relatively calm waters of the channel and throttled back, letting the boat idle and bob on swells that were still prevalent, but were gentler than out on the big lake. We were also protected from the wind and that helped somewhat.

"Whew," I said, standing up from the chair and straightening my back, "we made it." I made a motion to wipe my brow, trying to add a little levity to our situation. Was it dire? Maybe. But we'd made it almost halfway to base camp. All we had to do was steer our way through the Narrows out onto the lower lake, and then cross another eight miles of open water on the way to Northern Lights base. Easy, right?

Ever the pragmatist, Shelia asked, "How are you holding up?"

"Fine. My arms are tired. My legs are kind of stiff." In fact, my whole body felt like I'd tumbled down a long flight of stairs. Every bone ached.

"You did good, but I'm going to take over."

"No. I won the bet. It's my responsibility," I said, making a vain attempt to argue, hoping my voice didn't sound as feeble as I felt. Truth be told, my arms were nearly numb from fighting the wheel, the wind and the waves. My strength was pretty much gone.

Shelia held up her arm in my face, smiled, and flexed a muscle. "I'll take over," she said. You rest a bit." I felt her arm. Her muscle was like a rock. God, all that working out she'd done while I fooled around planting flowers in the garden. I guess it was about to pay off.

"If you insist," I said, joking, trying to sound magnanimous.

She just laughed. "No sweat."

We switched places. When she was settled in the captain's chair, I squeezed her shoulder like she'd done to mine earlier. She smiled at me and squeezed my hand in return. It felt good to have that contact with her. I wondered if she felt the same way.

But before I had a chance to ponder that thought any further, she jammed the throttle to high and yelled, "Off we go!" The boat lurched ahead. I stumbled and then caught myself on her chair and hung on. I glanced at my wife. Shelia's eyes were glued on the surface of the lake out the windshield, watching the water for whatever lay before us, intent on guiding us safely to base camp, our final destination.

The Brule Narrows wove serpentine through reeds, cattails and other water grasses that formed a barrier between the channel itself and the pine forests and granite rocks along the shore. Our houseboat was twelve feet wide. In most cases the channel was four times that width. It was tricky going, but Shelia confidently took us along the mile journey from the upper lake to the lower lake without a hitch. While she drove we both breathed a sigh of relief. Other times coming through the Narrows we'd had to deal with boats coming at us or coming up from behind, which made for some tricky navigating. Today, we'd been on the water for over six hours and seen no water craft whatsoever. No pleasure craft, no houseboats, no nothing. Everyone was taking their cue from Mother Nature and doing the smart thing, which was to stay put.

But, of course, not us. We had a job to do and Shelia guided us with the skill of a seasoned mariner. I was really proud of her, glad for her confidence and her level-headedness. If she was nervous, she didn't show it, just kept the throttle at half speed and motored on. Her firm conviction that we were going to not only survive our journey, but also make it unscathed back to Northern Lights base helped me settle down. While she drove I fixed her a cheese sandwich and gave her some mixed nuts and raisins. That's all she wanted. She was focused and intent on the task ahead, but at least she ate everything.

Once we cleared the channel she took us out onto the big lake and pointed us once again into the wind and the waves. We had hoped as the day wore on the storm might abate somewhat but it hadn't. It was two in the afternoon and the wind was blowing just as hard as before and the waves were as big as they had been on the upper lake, if not bigger. We had another bitch of a ride ahead of us. We heard later that the winds were sustained at thirty miles an hour with gusts up to fifty. Even seasoned veterans of the lake stayed put and off the water that day. But not us. We were neophytes and didn't know any better. In spite of the challenging conditions, though, there was one good thing: at least the rain stayed away.

Before we left the relative sanctity of the Brule Narrows, I tried calling base once more but only heard static on the line. Our phones had no signals either, so we were on our own. We steeled ourselves for the crossing and started out. The sky was dull gray and thick with clouds. The temperature was maybe fifty degrees, and we were both wet and chilled from getting our boat unstuck back in Scalawag bay hours earlier. I longed for sun, something to warm us up, lift our spirits and give us hope. Even seeing a loon would have been nice. But, no. The day stayed cloudy, the loons stayed hidden and we were the only living creatures out on the lake. We didn't even see any gulls. Every bird, animal and human being was hunkered down, riding out the storm. But not us.

Shelia not only was a was a trooper, she was also a really good driver. She gamely took us across the lower lake, holding the boat steady into the wind, fighting the waves as they smashed into the front, broke over the bow, and flooded into the cabin. She wrestled us out of the deep troughs that rolled us back and forth, side to side, and threatened to capsize us at any moment. She did it all with no complaint, just steely determination and strength of will. If I graded myself as a C+ on my navigational skills, getting us across the upper lake, I'd give Shelia an A+ on the channel and the lower lake. She was great. Me? I kept her company, fixed us coffee, gave her bites of chocolate and lit the occasional cigarette for her. It was good teamwork on both of our parts, if I do say so myself.

I also watched the shoreline. We kept to the middle of the lake, aiming ourselves between the red and green buoys put out by the park service to keep boats not only in the safe part of the middle of the lake, but also away from dangerous rocks hidden below the surface. There was maybe a half mile between us and the shoreline on both our right and left. In watching our progress as Shelia drove my main thought was this: I'd seen cold honey move faster. Talk about a slow moving boat. God, most of the time it seemed like weren't progressing forward at all, and sometimes even going backwards.

When I mentioned this to Shelia she grinned and pointed out the window. "I know, but it's just an illusion. Pick out something ahead of us on the shore. Watch that. Eventually we'll get to it. When we do, look ahead and pick out something else and watch that." She turned to me, hair falling out of the sides of her bandana, and smiled. "We are moving, you know, Ben. Foreword. I guarantee it." Just then the millionth wave of the day smashed into us, shaking the houseboat to its core, and she calmly went back to driving, keeping us on track.

I did as she suggested, picked out a tall pine tree up ahead and watched as we inched our toward it. We eventually got there. Like so many things in the course of our life and marriage together, she was right. We were moving.

I have to say that as the day wore on, we settled into a rather companionable routine. Our fighting and arguing the night before was replaced by the effort of working together to get us from

Scalawag Bay to Northern Lights base. Shelia was by far a better driver, so she kept at the wheel. I used a push broom to keep as much water out of the cabin as I could. I think I did a pretty good job. We never flooded. I fixed us peanut butter and crackers to munch on and made more cheese sandwiches for us whenever we got hungry. I didn't want to start the gas stove, but risked it a couple of times to make us both much needed cups of coffee. And I also kept the cigarettes coming.

By seven in the evening, we'd cleared the big part of the lower lake. The wind had abated somewhat, but it was obvious we weren't going to make it back to the Northern Lights base. Daylight was fading rapidly and we still had two or three miles to go.

Shelia throttled back and we bobbed on the waves out of the wind behind a nearby island. She turned to me. "What do you want to do?"

"It'll be dark pretty soon. I'm not confident driving the houseboat at night, are you?"

"No. Not at all."

We both looked around. Since we were off the main part of the big lake the shoreline was closer to us, maybe a hundred yards away. There were lots of small islands, too.

I suddenly had an idea. I went to a storage cupboard and took out a three-ring binder provided by Northern Lights that showed shoreline camping sites. I brought it to Shelia, opened it up and balanced it on the steering wheel. "Maybe we can find someplace out of the wind and put up for the night."

We paged through it until we found a map that included our location. We were in luck. A quarter mile ahead and to our left was a site on the lee-side of a small island. It'd be perfect for us.

"Let's do it," Shelia said.

"Want me to drive? You must be exhausted."

"No. I'm good." She pointed to the map. "You navigate and watch for buoy markers. Make sure we don't miss it. Keep an eye out for submerged rocks, too."

I gave her a mock salute, "Aye-aye, captain."

She laughed. We hadn't done much of that today, if at all. It was good to hear. It was also a ringing endorsement that we had survived a twelve hour journey covering nearly eighteen miles and that were going to make it safely back to base camp after all, even if it would be the next day. Better late than never was our way of thinking.

Shelia eased the throttle forward and half an hour later had gently brought us in over some underwater rocks onto a sandy spit of a beach on tiny, rocky, jack pine covered island the map called Pelican Rock. I jumped off the deck in front with the rope and waded through shallow water to the shore. I had my eye on a strong looking aspen tree and soon had us tied to it, tight and secure. I came back to the front of our boat where Shelia handed me the wooden gangplank. I set it firmly in the sand and walked back up it to the deck, dripping water from my boots and shorts.

Shelia had gone into the cabin and was trying the radio.

"Anything?" I asked.

She shook her head, "No. Nothing."

What little light left in the day was rapidly fading, and it would soon be dark. I looked back on the shore. Someone had at one time used rocks to build a fire ring. I pictured how nice it'd be to get a blazing campfire going, sit next to it, relax and warm our tired bones. Trouble was, with all the rain we'd had, I doubted I could find any dry wood. On the other hand, maybe it'd be nice to get off the boat for a while anyway, fire or no fire. My leg muscles were still tense from trying to keep my balance while riding four and five-foot waves all day. I was sure Shelia's were, too. In fact, I still could feel the rocking and rolling motion of the houseboat even just standing still. Yeah, getting on dry land would be good.

While I was staring at the fire ring, Shelia stepped next to me. "Thinking about building a fire?"

"Yeah. But the wood will be pretty wet, though. Hard to start."

"Hold on."

She went back into the cabin, rummaged around for a minute, and then returned, carrying a bundle of dry firewood.

I laughed. "What have you got there?"

"I remembered that Northern Lights always supplies these boats with some firewood. You know, just to help out us rookies." She laughed. "How about we use this to get a fire started? Then maybe you can find some more wood on shore and dry it out by the fire. Once we get it going, that is."

"Great idea. You're on."

In the day's last light, I got a fire going. Shelia brought out our lawn chairs. I was able to search for and find some wood that wasn't too wet and use my little portable hand saw to cut it up. We sat by the fire late into the night, long enough to see the sky clear and the stars come out. We even saw the constellation Orion and a shooting star.

We ate cheese sandwiches, peanut butter, and crackers, and shared an apple. We had coffee and Sheila even found a couple of packets of Swiss Miss, which, of course, we made into big mugs of hot chocolate. We found some Hershey's bars for us to munch on. It all tasted wonderful.

The wind abated, a sure sign the storm was over. We didn't argue, just talked, at first about the harrowing trip from Scalawag Bay to our little campsite on Pelican Rock. Then we got down to brass tacks and talked about Leslie and Logan. All in all it was a pretty good way to end the day.

The next day we broke camp early and flipped a coin to see who drove. I won (again) and was able to make an uneventful trip to base. In other words, I didn't get hung up on any rocks. We arrived by ten in the morning. We unloaded our gear and were in Orchard Lake late that afternoon, exhausted but happy we'd made it home safely. I was back to work the next day, Monday. One of the first things I did was text Leslie, "Wed. Me & U, lunch BFI?" She texted back with a smiley face.

I won't go into the details about that Wednesday lunch at Black Forest Inn except to say that she was less broken up about me ending things with her than I thought she'd be. After I told her that I just didn't think things were going to work out, she'd responded with a shrug and, "Yeah, I can see that. I kind of feel the same way."

There wasn't much to be said after that. I drove home that afternoon, though, feeling strangely relieved. Happy, almost. After working together while fighting the storm on Rainy Lake, I realized I wasn't ready to give up on Shelia and me and our marriage. Not by a long shot. I felt we still had something going for us. A lot, actually. Shelia, on the other hand, saw things differently.

After we'd built the campfire on Pelican Rock that last night, eaten our make-shift meal, and relived our harrowing journey across Rainy Lake, we'd finally talked about our relationship. Neither Leslie's name nor Logan's had been mentioned all day; we'd had too much to do, getting our boat to safety and all. Finally, now, safely relaxing by the campfire and the talk of the day's adventure having run its course, both elephants in the forest couldn't be ignored.

Shelia took a sip of coffee and lit a cigarette, then asked, "So what about this Leslie, this girlfriend of yours? What's the deal with her?"

I wanted to tell her. I had thought off and on during the day of how to put it; there were such a variety of different ways. Finally,

I settled on the most direct ."I'm going to end it when I get back home."

I looked at her to judge her reaction. She blinked once, took a drag and said, "I didn't expect that."

"I know," I said. "But it's for the best." Even though she didn't ask, I told her why. "It has to do with us getting across the lake today. Me and you. I liked that we worked as a team, and I'd forgotten how much I appreciated that we could do that. Not everyone would be able to. Look at Bob and Iris; they can't even cook dinner together without getting into a fight. We've never been like that. We could always start a project and each of us would naturally gravitate to one set of tasks while the other found their own niche. We worked great together, always did." I paused, then said, "Even with the kids. Remember? We always talked over any issues we had with them and never let them drive us apart." I stopped and looked at my wife. She was nodding her head, agreeing, I think with my assessment. I went on, "I think we drifted apart for other reasons." I sighed. "And I'm sorry for that. Sorry that I hurt you. Sorry that I made you feel alone." Then I added the name I wasn't sure I wanted to add, but figured, what the hell, why not? "Sorry I drove you to Logan."

After my little speech, I was silent. I couldn't remember the last time I'd spoken so freely, so from my heart. Or for so long. It felt good to unburden myself and come clean with my feelings.

Shelia tossed her cigarette in the fire and opened up a Hersey bar, broke off a piece and put it in her mouth. She sucked on it for a minute before saying, "I was so mad at you. After Josh and Julie left home and the house was empty I felt empty, too. When we got married I pictured our life together. We would raise our kids, go on vacations, celebrate birthdays and holidays, you know, just be a family. I figured any problems we had, we could work through them." She shook her head and broke off another piece of chocolate. "I don't know what went wrong." She put the chocolate in her mouth and contemplated the fire.

I got up and threw another log on, hoping to break the mood. Out on the lake a loon started calling. When it stopped, another one started up. Soon they were calling back and forth. Perhaps they were a couple. Whatever the case, they were doing a lot better job breaking the mood than my pretending to fool around with the fire was doing. I sat down and said, "I think I do. Know what went wrong, I mean. At least from my standpoint." Shelia looked at me, waiting for my answer. "I think I just got lazy," I said. "I think I started taking our relationship and marriage for granted. I think I just forget to let you know how much you meant to me."

I pulled a cigarette from the pack lying on the sand between us and rolled it back and forth in my figures, but didn't light it. After a minute, I put it back in the pack.

"I guess I forgot how much I really loved you," I said. "Until today."

I looked at her. She had a tear in her eye. Suddenly, so did I. It was an emotional moment, let me tell you. I was glad, though, that I had said what I had to say. In fact, I was naive enough to think that maybe this little talk, and me opening up my feelings, would be all we'd need to get back together. Maybe our marriage would survive. Maybe all the shit over the last few years would be forgotten.

Shows you what a fool I really was.

Shelia picked up the pack, shook out a cigarette, and lit up. "Too bad you didn't tell me all of this years ago," she said, blowing out a plume of smoke. "Or even earlier this year, for that matter." She looked straight at me to make her point. "Before I met Logan."

Well, that was a good point, a very good point.

We stayed up late. We didn't argue or raise our voices. Instead, we kept talking reasonably, getting our feelings out in the open, and that was a good thing. However, the long and the short of it was this: Shelia cared deeply for this Logan guy. She'd met him while running Grandma's Marathon in Duluth the past spring, just after she'd figured out about Leslie and me. He was a thirty-eight years old, an investment banker, single and, apparently, carrying no baggage, emotional or otherwise. She wasn't ready to give him up.

Later that night, I gathered up my courage and asked the question I most wanted an answer to yet was most afraid to hear the answer of. "Are you going to leave me for him?"

Shelia told me she wasn't sure. In fact, her very words were, "I don't know. I'll have to think about it. I'll keep you posted."

What a mess I'd made of things. I told myself I'd have to accept the situation for what it was and learn to live with where Shelia was at, but I knew it'd be hard. Here I was ready to dedicate myself to doing whatever I could to salvage our marriage, but she wasn't ready to do that. It was clear that Logan was very much in the picture. We didn't talk much after that.

I spent the night on the floor again, next to Shelia's bed. In spite of our exhaustion, I know neither of us slept very well.

Once we were back home in Orchard Lake, though, things didn't go too badly between us. Our détente' continued, and I was happy for that. At least I hadn't been kicked out of the house, which, in my mind had been a very real possibility. On Wednesday evening, when I told Shelia that I'd broken off my relationship with Leslie, she'd said, "If that's what you want, good. I'm glad for you." Not the most enthusiastic response in the world, but then again, what did I expect. I'd been the one to screw up in the first place. I had a lot of dues to pay.

When I asked Shelia later that week about her and Logan all I got was a non-committal, "I'll get back to you on that."

When I tried to clarify, "What does that mean?" what I got back was, "Exactly what I said, I'll get back to you."

"Are you still going to see him?" I persisted.

The response? A long stare and, "I'll. Get. Back. To. You."

Okay. Message received. I finally was getting the point. Shelia had some thinking to do, and when she was done, she'd...Get back to me.

Our first weekend back home, we had Bob and Iris out to our place for a Saturday night backyard picnic. Iris had called Shelia earlier in the week to catch up and when Shelia told her the tale of our crazy journey across Rainy Lake, Iris told Bob. They both were excited to hear more, so we invited them over to fill them in and show them pictures we'd each taken with our phones. That Saturday evening I fired up the grill and did corn on the cob and black bean burgers. Shelia put together a fresh salad with greens and veggies from our garden and we ate outside at our picnic table on the back patio.

When we were finished, Bob and I were inside doing the dishes when he turned to me and said, "So what's up with you and Shelia?"

I handed him a plate. I was washing, he was drying. "What do you mean?"

"Well, you both seem..." he paused, trying to frame his thought before saying, "You both seem different."

"Okay," I said. "Different like how?" I handed him another plate.

"I don't know. Better? Less argumentative, maybe?" He took the plate and dried it before setting it aside. He wiped his hands on the towel, set it on the counter, and turned to me. "Did something happen between you guys up there?"

"You mean like the wind storm and almost capsizing the houseboat a hundred times on Rainy?" I grinned at him.

Bob, laughed, "No. I mean with you and Shelia. You seem more comfortable together. Less tense, that's for sure. Better with each other." He paused again and then asked. "Are you?"

Bob was a good friend of mine, we'd known each other for over fifteen years, but I'd never told him about Leslie and I wasn't going to now. Instead, I said, "Yeah, I think we are. Better with each other, I mean. We had a pretty good time up on Rainy." I knew I was sounding vague, but too bad. If Shelia and I seemed good to Bob, fine. In a way we were. Deep down, though, I knew things between us were still tenuous, and they would stay that way until Shelia resolved her feelings about Logan.

I started washing a salad bowl and looked out the window into the backyard. Shelia and Iris were deep in conversation. About what, I had no idea. I turned to Bob and said, "So, yeah, I think we're pretty good. I think we're more than pretty good." Even though Shelia's jury was still out on Logan, between Shelia and me it sure seemed like things were better than they had been in a long time, years even. I sure hoped they were, anyway.

Bob slapped me on the back and said, "Well, that's good news, buddy. I'm happy for you."

If it was true, I was happy, too. Very happy. But, honestly, there was still the issue with Shelia and Logan. Until that was resolved, moving ahead with repairing our marriage was going to be difficult, if not impossible.

The next weekend was sunny and warm, the temperature in the low eighties. I was out in the garden on Saturday, weeding and deadheading in one of our five front yard flower beds, and trying to make sense of it all regarding my marriage. I was happy I broke things off with Leslie. The age difference was too great, and our interests...well, honestly, there wasn't much there. I'm glad I had done what I did, and, truth be told, I'm sure Leslie was, too. She texted me the next day, "Thx Ben. U were fun! :)" Fun? Well, what can you say to that?

Did I want to stay with Shelia? Yes, absolutely I did. But, I was preparing myself for her to kick me out and move on to a life without me. I had let her down so many times over the years that I was surprised she hadn't already told me to pack up and leave. Especially now that she had Logan in her life. How could I expect otherwise?

For my part? Well, over time, I had become vaguely unhappy with my marriage. I'd ended up using Leslie as a pleasant little diversion, an ill-advised decision that I realized on Rainy Lake was something I didn't need or want. But, of course, I had, and, in so doing, I may have damaged my relationship with my wife irrevocably.

Honestly? I still loved Shelia. I would give anything to have her back and to spend the rest of our life together, trying to make our marriage as good as it could possibly be. After all, when it came right down to it, not every couple could work together to fight their way across a huge, storm ravaged lake in a little houseboat, and live to tell the tail. Did that sound overly dramatic? Maybe, but from where I was coming from, it made perfect sense. There was something there between us worth fighting for.

My thoughts were interrupted by a sudden unexpected scent of spearmint in the air. I smiled. Shelia had taken up chewing gum ever since we'd gotten off the lake and she was favoring Wrigley's Spearmint. She told me it was to help her quit smoking and apparently it was going well. She's essentially stopped. I'm happy for her. Me? I was just smoking with her to share the moment. I hadn't had one since we got in the car at Northern Lights base camp and drove home.

I stood up, straightened my back, and turned to greet her. Two weeks after the fact, I was still stiff from fighting the huge waves on Rainy. Shelia, in much better shape all the way around, recovered right away. In fact, she'd been running regularly, training for the Twin City Marathon coming up in October. I tried not to think about if Logan was going to be running it, too.

"Hi," I said, as she walked up. "How's it going?"

We'd been getting along fine ever since we'd returned home. She knew I'd broken things off with Leslie. A few days ago when I asked her about Logan, she'd told me, "I've only texted him that I've got a lot on my mind. I haven't seen him or talked to him since we've been back. I don't really have anything to say to him."

That was the last we'd talked about either of them. Other than having Bob and Iris over, mainly we'd just worked at our jobs, cooked our evening meal together, watched television, and gone on a few walks in the neighborhood, stuff we'd pretty much always done. But...and I'm pretty sure this wasn't just my imagination...I'm pretty sure we were more comfortable with each other than we'd been in years. As Bob had pointed out. We'd even laughed together a few times. It'd been nice.

"It's going pretty good," Shelia said, in response to my question. She moved in so she was standing close to me and asked, "How about with you?"

"Good. I'm almost done with the zinnias." I looked around. The sun was low in the west over the roof of our home, shadows lengthening. Late afternoon. The sky was blue and cloudless and it was still warm out but not too hot, a perfect ending to a perfect summer day. "I'm going to start deadheading these babies next. I pointed to some nearby bachelor buttons, waist-high, blue and white annual flowers that self-seeded themselves every year. Butterflies loved them. I had a big clump in the middle of the garden and they needed some attention.

Just then a movement caught my eye. I turned and watched an early Painted Lady land on one and start feeding. I smiled and looked at Leslie. She was smiling, too, but it wasn't at the butterfly. She was smiling directly at me. Something was up.

"What?" I asked, curious.

"I've got something here. Thought you might like to see it." She handed me an envelope.

The mail must have been dropped off earlier, and I'd been so lost in thought I hadn't even noticed. I looked at the return address. It was from Northern Lights Houseboat Adventures. My first thought was that it was a bill. We'd paid for our houseboat before we'd taken it out that first day, but we'd lost the dingy on the way across the upper lake after we'd left Scalawag Bay. At some point that one-inch boat rope had snapped in the storm like a rubber band. We'd been so focused on looking ahead, watching the waves, and judging the position of our boat, we never noticed it was gone until we were getting ready to enter the Brule Narrows. I opened the envelope expecting the bill for the dingy. It wasn't a bill at all.

I looked over the one-page letter. Then I read it more closely before turning to Shelia, "What's this all about?" I asked, "What have you done?"

She broke into a big smile, "You like my surprise? I booked us in for next year. What do you think? Want to do it? Want to go back?"

What I held in my hand was a reservation. Guaranteed, for a week in the middle of August on our boat, Looney Tunes. Next year!

I was stunned and at a loss for words. Finally, I was able to ask, "You want to go back? With me?" It was the last thing I expected, and I was quick to answer, "Of course I do!"

Absolutely, I wanted to go back with her. I began to envision us crossing Rainy Lake, in much calmer waters, of course, letting my imagination run away with me. Moonlit nights. Loons calling. A warm, crackling campfire. Smores. Then I put the brakes on. "Wait a minute. What about...?"

I was going to say Logan's name, but Shelia stopped me and put her finger on my lips. "Don't worry about him. That's over," she said, leaning closer. "I ended it. No more fooling around for me. And no more fooling around for you, either, okay? From now on, it's you and me, Ben, for better or worse, just like in the movies."

I couldn't believe I'd get another chance, but I was. Overjoyed, I said, "I promise. I swear to you, I'll do everything I can to keep us together."

"I'm counting on you. You know that, don't you?"

"I do," I said, looking into her eyes and holding her gaze, "But, you know, this isn't a movie," I added, stating the obvious.

"I know," she said. "It's better. It's our life.

To say I was overjoyed was putting it mildly. In fact, I think words will always and all time be unable to do justice to the happiness I felt at that particular moment. But I will say this, I saw a vision of our future right then. Shelia and I, living our life together, growing old together, and that's all I needed to see. It made me the happiest man on earth. I had ended things with Leslie and she had with Logan. Now, it was the two of us, as husband and wife, and we had another chance. Another opportunity to work on our marriage and forge ahead together into our future. It was something that didn't always happen; the chance to start over. I was all for it.

They say a wound heals stronger when it mends and I have no reason to doubt that statement. Hopefully, it will be the same with our marriage. I believe it will. But, over the years there were a lot of wounds inflicted, all caused by me, and there's a lot of healing to be done. Will we be successful? We'll find out. I will say this: I'm committed to saving our relationship and moving ahead together. So is Shelia. What I know for sure is that something happened to both of us up on Rainy Lake. It's like we each caught a glimpse into the depths of what we had built together over our twenty- three years of marriage, and we didn't want to let it go. Somehow our love for each other had not only survived but had also been rejuvenated.

I have no answer for exactly how it happened. I only knew that it did.

Shelia stepped into my arms and I held her. It had been years. Her closeness felt wonderful, just like I remembered, the best feeling in the whole wide world.

"Yes, I want to go with you," I reiterated. "Rainy Lake, here we come." Then I whispered in her ear. "I can't wait."

"Me either, "Shelia said, and we held each other tight. It was all she had to say. In fact, it was more than enough.

Acknowledgments

First of all, many thanks go out to my friend, mentor, and author of *The Magic Circle* series (and much more) PC Darkcliff who has encouraged my writing from the very beginning. He has also recently led me into the self-publishing world for which I am exceedingly grateful. PC, thank you so much.

I've made many friends along the way on this writing journey. I want to call out Justin Wiggins, not only a terrific writer but a wonderful human being. Justin, the world needs more people like you. Keep up the great work.

I spend a lot of time walking around outdoors working on story ideas. Most of that time is alone, but now and then my brother Tom accompanies me. It's always fun. Tom thanks for being there and for all of your support. It means everything to me.

Andjela Vujuc is a tremendously talented designer. The cover of this collection is her creation. Thank you so much, Andjela!

And, as always, many thanks go out to Debra for being in my life.

Here's what some readers say about Jim's most recent book, The Stargazer and Other Stories, published in August 2024

"The Stargazer is another great collection by one of my favorite storytellers. As is the norm in Jim Bates' work, some stories are humorous and brimming with energy, while others are a little sad and filled with nostalgia, and together they make for an exciting read.

I loved the way the characters had diverse voices and personalities. Even in a collection of short stories - although they aren't that short! - the author managed to bring each of the numerous characters to life, giving them inner thoughts and unique personalities, which demonstrates what a talented and versatile writer he is.

As usual, I really enjoyed the wonderful descriptions of the wilderness. The author's passion for nature breaths at you from those passages, which helps you plunge right into the story.

I think the tale I enjoyed the most was The Kid from Arizona. The author seemed to put the most feelings in that piece, and I guess it was a story that was most influenced by his experiences.

It is hard to pick just one favorite, though as all the stories are exciting and top-notch. Highly recommended" By PC Darkcliff author of the Magic Circle series among other works..

"Once again Jim Bates brings us intriguing and interesting stories with characters that are both relatable and believable. This is a great read. I recommend it to anyone who appreciates quality writing." *By Author Lynn Phillips*

Biography

Jim lives in a small town in Minnesota. He loves to write! His stories and poems have appeared in over five hundred online and print publications. His collection of short stories *Resilience* is published by Bridge House Publishing. *Short Stuff* a collection of flash fiction and drabbles is published by Chapeltown Books. *Periodic Stories, Periodic Stories Volume Two, Periodic Stories Volume Three – A Novel,* and *Periodic Stories Volume Four* are published by Impspired. *Dreamers,* a collection of short stories, is published by Clarendon House Publishing. *Something Better,* a dystopian adventure novella, and the novel, *The Alien of Orchard Lake,* are published by Dark Myth Publications. In the fall of 2022, his collection entitled *Holiday Stories* was published by Impspired as was his collection of poetry, *Haiku Seasons.* In February 2023, a collection of flash fiction *Dancing With Butterflies* was published by Impspired. In July 2023 his YA novella *The Battle of Marvel Wood* was published by Impspired. In July 2023 his collection of poems *The Alchemy of Then* was published by Impspired. In August 2023 his novel *Conversations With the Dead* was published by Impspired. In September 2023 his collection of poems *The Metaphysics of Now* was published by Impspired. In October 2023 his collection of short *stories Old Man Jasperson and Other Stories* was published by Bridge House Publishing. In January 2024 his collection of poems *The Evolution of Tomorrow* was published by Impspired. In January 2024 his novella *Eye of the Beholder* was published by Dark Myth Publications. In March 2024 his collection of poems *The Science of Forever* was published by Impspired. In August 2024 his collection of long short stories *The Stargazer and Other Stories* was published by Jim. His short story "Aliens" was nominated by The Zodiac Press for the 2020 Pushcart Prize. His story "The Maple Leaf" was voted 2021 Story of the Year for Spillwords. He was voted December 2022 Author of the Month for Spillwords. He also reads his stories for *Talking Stories Radio* and *Jim's Storytime* on his website. He lives in a small town west of Minneapolis, Minnesota. All of his work can be found on his blog at www.theviewfromlonglake.wordpress.com[1].

---

1. http://www.theviewfromlonglake.wordpress.com